A THOUSAND
YEARS OF RAIN

MICHAEL LIPINSKI

Dollarbird

Dollarbird

First published in 2020
by Dollarbird, an imprint of Monsoon Books Ltd
www.dollarbird.co.uk
www.monsoonbooks.co.uk

No.1 The Lodge, Burrough Court,
Burrough on the Hill, LE14 2QS, UK.

ISBN (paperback): 978-1-912049-66-0
ISBN (ebook): 978-1-912049-67-7

Cover design by Cover Kitchen.

A Cataloguing-in-Publication data record is available from the British
Library.

Printed and bound in Great Britain by Clays Ltd, Elcograf S.p.A.
22 21 20   1 2 3

One

He hadn't slept at all, though he had been lying in bed since eleven. It was now 3:50 a.m. and his Timex Indiglo was beeping. John Hunter slipped into his black jeans, put on his black long-sleeved turtleneck sweater, and tucked the gloves and the army green balaclava into his back pocket.

Hell of an outfit for the tropics.

The knife was in his belt, hidden by the long sweater, and the bolt cutter was in his backpack, which he now shrugged onto his shoulders as he quietly opened the door.

The noxious odor of fishmeal rose from the canneries along the inland sea. The night air was humid and thick against his skin like a layer of gauze, and the moon bathed the town in pale light.

He stole down the outside stairway of the guesthouse and around to the front. Anek, the owner, always locked the front gate at midnight, but Hunter had long ago asked for a spare key on the excuse he could let himself in after a late night of drinking. Once through the gate, he wrapped the chain around it and snapped the padlock shut. Then he walked quickly down the soi to the road

7

that crossed to the museum.

The street was silent except for the chirp of cicadas and the distant buzz of a two-stroke motorcycle. The main road was awash in the harsh fluorescent glare of the street lamps, but there was there was no movement anywhere, except for a few dogs nosing at the piles of trash in the empty market. Faint music drifted from a karaoke club up the street.

He crossed the road to the museum and was surprised by a pair of headlights coming from a side street. He staggered deliberately as he reached the curb – just another drunken farang oil worker stumbling home much too late at night. He walked past a tricycle driver slumped asleep on the passenger seat of his vehicle and followed the museum wall to the small soi that ran parallel to the main street. This soi was not as garishly lit as the main street, and he briskly moved to the shadowy pocket between the light of two street lamps.

He quickly found the spot he was looking for – a chink in the wall about 18 inches from the ground which he could use as a step to shinny over. He fell softly to the grass on the other side.

The ancient museum building, built two hundred years ago for a rich Chinese merchant, was lit by floodlights, but here at the edge of the garden it was as dark as a forest. A cluster of towering, thick trees and some trimmed bushes provided concealment. Hunter moved stealthily along the wall until he was behind a shrub nearly parallel with the main entrance to the museum. He pulled the ski mask over his head and put on the gloves. The luminescent face of his watch showed two minutes to the hour. He switched it to stopwatch mode and with his finger on the button waited for the door to open.

His sweat soaked through the woolen mask. Just as his right knee was beginning to ache from crouching, the door opened and the guard emerged. It was the one with the thin mustache, the one he called Poncho. That was a good sign. Poncho always stopped for a smoke, and on average it took him two minutes longer to complete his rounds than his alternate, the one Hunter called Bean Pole. Hunter started the stopwatch and let Poncho walk twenty feet into the garden, shining his flashlight onto the wall and into the trees opposite him. Hunter jogged along the perimeter in the opposite direction to the guard, then cut diagonally toward the back door of the museum.

He knew the guards' routine, having watched both of them dozens of times from his guesthouse window, following their movements with binoculars and a stopwatch. There was only one guard on duty from 6 p.m. to 6 a.m. Every hour on the hour he, whether it was Poncho or Bean Pole, made exactly the same circuit around the perimeter of the museum, punching his time card at the four clocks located in the corners of the compound. He'd go out of the front door and to the far corner of the garden where the old iron cannons stood, then cross to the spot where Hunter had climbed over the wall, then walk along the boundary to the back door, and finally head around to the street side of the building. From there, the guard would walk along the side of the building, checking the shuttered windows, until he made it back to his comfortable chair just inside the main entrance. With Poncho, Hunter had at least twelve minutes; and he would be staying one step ahead of him all the time.

As Poncho walked past the cannons to the first clock, Hunter slipped through the shadows to the back door. He took the bolt cutter out of his back pocket and held his breath as he snipped the flimsy padlock. He pocketed the pieces and silently eased open the heavy wooden door. Once inside he closed the door behind him.

He was in an enclosed courtyard, his moonlit shadow falling across the red tiles. Surrounding him were earthenware vessels of various shapes and sizes, salvaged from the many Chinese ships that had met their end in the Gulf of Thailand. He quickly walked to the dark inner corridor and then counted off the seven steps to the Srijaya room. It was to the right of the corridor, just before the reception desk near the front entrance. The rooms were all unlit, but Hunter didn't need his penlight yet. He had paced off this distance countless times during the museum's open hours, pretending to admire the prehistoric pottery and beads in the cabinets lining the main corridor. He reckoned that Poncho was at this moment having a quiet smoke at the side gate. He would smoke the cigarette halfway down, then flick it over the wall onto the soi and make his way to the back door, taking his sweet time. Since all the windows were shuttered, there was no chance of Poncho hearing Hunter as he moved through the rooms, much less seeing him.

He went to the case in the middle of the room, the one that held the Ranod Bodhisattva. He turned on his penlight and held it in his mouth. He took the knife from his belt and slipped it into the crack between the cabinet frame and the glass door. With a quick upward stroke, he sliced the alarm wires. With the bolt cutters he snipped the small fifty-baht padlock that secured the door of the cabinet.

They're begging someone to steal it.

Then the flashlight slipped from his mouth and clattered on the cement floor. The clash of metal on cement echoed through the dead air of the ancient building.

His heart was racing like a sprinter's. He raised the door of the cabinet and lifted the statue from its dusty case. Its bronze surface was rough, and it was heavier than he'd thought it would be. He slid it between the foam pads in his rucksack, picked up the flashlight and put it in his pocket, then zipped up the bag and cinched the belts tight along his shoulders and abdomen. His balaclava was soaked with sweat making it hard for him to draw in air. His heart was pounding in his throat.

He was beginning to think Poncho hadn't heard the flashlight fall. But just as he reached the main corridor, a swath of light fell across it.

"Aray wah," he heard Poncho say in a surprisingly aggressive voice. The guard had heard Hunter's footsteps and was pointing the flashlight at the entrance of the room. Hunter stepped back out of the corridor but there was no place to hide. Poncho would find him in minutes and there was no chance of running for the back door. Now there was only one way out. Through the front door. Through Poncho.

Sweat was running down his back, and his face was hot and itchy from the balaclava, but his breathing was steady. The only option left to him was violence, and accepting that fact cleared his head. It was like a white heat that grew from behind his sternum and burned all thoughts out of his mind except those necessary for survival. It was the difference between the winners and chumps in this world, of that Hunter was certain; and he was dead sure the likes of Poncho had never felt it.

He lifted the penlight from his pocket and tossed it down the corridor towards the courtyard. It clanged on the hard tiles, and as Poncho's light searched out the noise, Hunter pounced. He sprang out of the shadows and sprinted full speed toward Poncho. Before the guard knew what had hit him, Hunter brought his right knee into his groin and his forearm hard into his windpipe. Hunter could smell cigarettes and garlic and the guard's freshly laundered khakis. Poncho fell hard, sputtering, his head hitting the floor. His flashlight crashed against the tiles and went black. Hunter raced for the edge of the garden, laughing at how soft Poncho's body was and how easily he'd gone down. His head hitting the terrace reminded him of Halloween – the *thump* of the baseball bat whacking the pumpkin. Sheer adrenaline carried him over the shoulder-high wall and onto the dark back soi. Once he turned the corner, he forced himself to walk, not run, following the darkest streets and back lanes, always conscious of the dull weight on his back.

When he felt he was safely away from the museum he stopped to catch his breath. He was in a dark soi that ran along a warehouse near the jetty. He could hear a crane lifting a container onto a supply ship. Rats skittered out of sight. He was drenched in sweat and his hands were shaking, but with excitement, not fear.

He took the statue out of the bag and ran his hands across it. He felt nothing when he looked at it: no awe or wonder at this supposed masterpiece created over a thousand years ago; no amazement or curiosity about the religion that inspired it or the lives of the people that had created and worshipped it. It was nothing more than a bronze statue – and not of very good workmanship at that, considering the rough spots along the arms and torso. The only meaning it had to Hunter was the price it would fetch in New York or London, or wherever it finally ended up. It was a commodity, nothing more or less, and he put it back into the rucksack with the triumphant feeling that this was the first step in putting his days as an offshore oil flunky behind him forever.

Two

Alex Marek walked up the wooden steps to the door of the one-story frame bungalow, holding in one hand the guitar case that protected his sunburst Guild acoustic. He paused and turned at the top and looked back across the yard to the sea. The station's black Toyota pickup truck sat in the gravel driveway, behind it the BMW they'd arrived in. In the front yard, pitched in the weeds and scrub grass, were the two six-meter transmission antennae held in place by thick guy wires secured to bolts set in concrete. A torn chain link fence fronted the station property. Beyond that was a potholed, asphalt road, a slim strip of sand, and the calm blue of the Gulf of Thailand.

Up the beach toward town, the Serene Bay Hotel towered above the casuarina pines, a ten-minute walk from the front door of the station. Despite the brand spanking new first-class hotel, the beach was desolate; the whole area as far as he could see looked deserted and bleached out by the horrible midday sun that seared his bare arms and face.

Marek was exhausted from the flight and, he decided, it was too hot to think.

Mr Niwat, the company rep, put Marek's suitcases down on the porch and held the door open for him, bowing slightly as

Marek entered. Inside the house it was cool and dark. He eased the guitar to the floor and plopped down on the couch in front of a window unit air conditioner that was blasting cold air into the room. He leaned forward and opened the collar of his shirt to let the chilly air cool the sweat on his chest. Mr Niwat brought him a glass of ice water from the kitchen.

"Very hot," he said, giggling. He sat on the sofa and fanned his face with his hand. "Where you from in America, Mr Alek?"

"Wisconsin," answered Marek. "Madison."

"Ooh! Very cold, I think." He hugged his arms and shivered. "I never go to Wisconsin. But I stay in Texas for six months. I stay with my sister. She was married to American army guy. I think I stay in Texas I can learn English pretty good, but know what happens? I speak Thai all the time. All my sister's friends Thai, so I never improve my English. Speak only broken English." He threw his head back and laughed, showing dazzling white teeth. "Yeah, very broken. I don't learn English in Texas, but you know what I learn? I learned about American football. Yeah. Dallas Cowboys. Cannot speak English but can tell you about Dallas Cowboys. Sure! Troy Aikman, Emmett Smith, Michael Irvin... Ha!" His eyes disappeared in his smile.

"Your English is good, Niwat."

"No, no. Not so good. Too much broken."

It had been a twenty-six hour flight from Chicago with stopovers in San Francisco and Taipei before finally reaching Bangkok early that morning. Marek had dozed for no longer than twenty minutes during the whole flight. He had been pinned into a middle seat near the bank of toilets, and every time the door banged open and the lavatory light beamed a wedge of yellow into the cabin, he was wrenched awake. He gave up trying to sleep and watched the three movies and read *Time* magazine cover-to-cover. In Bangkok airport it was morning but felt like it should be night, so he quickly downed three beers and then had to woozily sprint to the domestic terminal to catch his flight to Had Yai. Mr Niwat met him there, looking suave and gentlemanly and holding a cardboard sign with his misspelled name and new employer hand-printed in large block letters: MR ALEK MAREK, SOUTHERN CROSS NAVIGATION SYSTEMS. They rode the final thirty kilometers from the airport to the city of Songkhla in Niwat's BMW.

Now Marek had been without sleep for so long his body was humming louder than the a/c. He felt as if his eyes were sliding off the side of his head. Niwat kept refilling his water glass as he chattered amicably about the attractions of Songkhla. Marek asked if there was any coffee and within minutes Niwat brought him a mug of scalding Nescafe. When Marek had finished half of it, he decided it was time to take a look at the rest of the house.

There wasn't very much to it. Besides the living room there was one bedroom with a toilet and shower, a kitchen, and the office. A hall closet served as storage space for empty cardboard boxes, an old pair of work boots and an ironing board. The house had the shabby furnishings and slightly run-down feel of itinerant male lodging. There was something in the air of the place - lonely men working far away from home – that made him depressed. Despite Niwat's cheerful attentiveness as he guided him through the rooms, he was beginning to wonder if he had made a mistake in coming here, if maybe his snap decision would backfire. He tried to shake off his melancholy by staying firmly in the here and now. He thought: *this is a work station, and no one ever put much time or effort into making it more than just barely livable, because no one ever planned on staying here very long.* It wouldn't take much to make this place more comfortable, and he'd probably have the free time to do it. Anyway, it wouldn't cost him a cent. That in itself made the place a palace.

He would be making good money, he reminded himself, and this would be an adventure. It was what you had to do sometimes – close your eyes and take a step off the ledge. No parachute or safety net. Just for the hell of it. Just to see what was there when you landed. Otherwise you'd wake up one day and find yourself old in your Lay-Z-Boy, with the biggest thrill you'd had for months the latest rerun of Cheers.

Niwat led him into the office, the station operations room. It was furnished with a desk, PC and monitor, printer, fax machine, telephone, and the DGPS satellite positioning transmitters. The heart of operations was an impressive SunSPARC workstation with three 21-inch monitors. The room was clean and cool and tidy and had a large window with a view of the forested hill behind the beach. The equipment looked reassuringly up to date. Technical manuals crammed the shelves and maps were Scotch taped to the walls. There was a map of Thailand, another of the city of Songkhla, and a third of the Gulf with the oil and gas concessions outlined in blue pencil. Colored plastic pushpins marked the locations of wellhead and production platforms and drilling rigs.

This is where I'll be spending the next year, thought Marek, as he studied the map and the names of the concessionaires. *Maybe by the end of it, I'll have some idea of what the fuck I'm supposed to be doing.*

It was almost as if Niwat didn't want to leave Marek alone, as if he thought he had to stay with him, keep him company, cheer him up. He lingered in the house for nearly two hours, chatting away, telling anecdotes about his stay in Texas. Maybe he thought Marek would be lonely or homesick. Finally, Marek shooed him out of the house by telling him that, even though it was the middle of the afternoon, he was too tired to do anything but sleep.

"OK, I go now. You sure you gonna be OK, Mr Alek?"

"Yeah, Niwat, I'm gonna sleep for two days."

"OK, the guard will come at six. He a good man. You can trust him. Actually, he's my cousin, ha ha. He stay here all night, every night. Make sure there no khamoys, you know, thieves. And the maid, his sister, will come in the morning. She clean house, do laundry. We take care you good, Mr Alek."

"Right, Niwat."

"Tomorrow we go into town and take care of business. Get work permit, visa. Get you driver's license, open bank account. We should start early, maybe eight. That OK with you?"

"Sure, eight o'clock is fine."

"OK, see you tomorrow."

Niwat was down the stairs and heading toward his car when Marek called out to him.

"Oh, and Niwat?"

"Yes, boss?"

"It's the Green Bay Packers now."

"What say, boss?"

"No more Dallas Cowboys. Now your team is the Green Bay Packers."

"Right, boss," answered Niwat. He laughed and saluted sharply before ducking into the car.

Marek closed the bedroom curtains as tightly as possible and turned the a/c up full. Since it was the middle of the afternoon, it didn't help much to make the room either dark or cold, but he was too tired to care. The bed sheets and thin cover had a freshly laundered, pleasantly homey scent. He would have to remember to thank Niwat for that.

He lay on the bed and thought about the last phone call he'd had with his sister, after he'd flown back to Milwaukee from Singapore to tie up some loose ends before taking this job in Songkhla.

"I got a job, Elly," he'd told her. "It's in Thailand. Running a satellite navigation station."

"What the heck is that?"

"They use GPS, you know Global Positioning Satellites, to help ships navigate. It's for the oil industry. There's offshore oil fields there."

"How in the world did you get that job?"

"I met a guy in a bar," he laughed. "Honest. In Singapore. An English guy who turned out to be the area manager for the company that owns the station. It's called Southern Cross Navigation. We got to talking over a few beers and one thing led to another. I told him I had some experience in computer hardware and had once taken a course in UNIX, and he asked me if I wanted a job. It pays one hundred dollars plus thirty dollars expenses, every day. That's forty-seven thousand four hundred and fifty dollars in most years; and forty-seven, five hundred eighty in leap years." He paused to give her a chance to laugh, but she didn't. "Housing is provided free by the company, including all utilities, I pay no taxes either in Thailand or the US, and if you eat Thai food you can live on about half of what you do in the States. Congratulate me. I'm now officially well off."

"Alex, you sure you know what you're doing? I mean, my gosh, you meet a guy in a bar, and he gives you a job just like that? You sure he's not involved in drugs or something?"

Elly was the only family Marek had, and though she was younger than him, she always acted like his parent: more reasonable, more mature than he was. She lived a comfortable life with her surgeon husband and two young girls in Detroit. She liked to watch foreign movies on cable and read about the international art world but, Marek knew, she was really quite wary of anything alien to her suburban, middle class life.

"I checked them out, Elly. I asked questions at the US and British Embassies in Singapore. I called their home office in Australia. I even checked with the Better Business Bureau in Singapore. They're a legitimate company. They were in a bind because the last guy left unexpectedly. He had family problems or something. Hey, if it gets bad, I'll do the same. I'll just quit."

"But Alex, you were making nearly as much money with Lake Consultants. And also – and excuse me if this is a dirty word with you – you had a career, a future."

"No, Elly, I had nothing there. I was just a gofer. It was a dead end job. Without the right degree you get nowhere in that company, and I didn't have it. Remember Elly, mine is in history, not computer science. They have a special word for people like me, people who learn this stuff on their own. They call us hobbyists. Oh sure, they let me go around and change hard discs and unjam printers for their clients, and play around in DOS, but that was about it." He heard the edge creeping into his voice and felt the back of his neck get hot. "Elly, I was suffocating in that office."

Thirty years old, he thought, and there'd been nothing in front of him but two decades of being a slug and working with guys whose conversational limits were football, the kids and snowblowers. So after two years of servicing computer hardware for his company's business clients, he'd quit. It had been a Wednesday morning, and he was kneeling on some plush maroon carpet in an insurance office, searching for a tiny screw from a hard drive connector. Somebody at a desk had said the word "actuarially", and he was seized by a panic. He felt the walls closing in on him. So this was it? The rest of his life would be spent on his hands and knees, getting about as much respect as the Mexican cleaning woman, listening to self-important idiots throw ridiculous words around. He had a letter of resignation on the boss's desk the next morning.

He fled Milwaukee for Asia. He was tramping the Hippie Trail – Nepal, India, Burma, Thailand, Malaysia and finally Singapore. He had more money than the other backpackers and traveled a little better, staying at tourist hotels rather than dirt cheap hostels and dormitories, taking the second-class sleeper train rather than all-night buses.

He was in Singapore, on his way to Jogjakarta and Bali, when one afternoon the skies opened, and he ducked into the Hard Rock Café. It was there that he met Mr Brian Sturges of Southern Cross Navigation who, before the third drink, had offered him the position of Base Manager for their Songkhla, Thailand station.

"You could have gotten another job. You know your stuff. Lots of companies are dying for people like you."

"Elly, I needed a change."

"So you have to move 10,000 miles away? Some change."

There was silence across the wires for a few minutes as both of them tried to find their composure, neither wanting this last telephone conversation to deteriorate into an argument.

"Alex, look. I know we've been through all this before. I know you think that middle class, suburban life is a living hell, but it's not. Not on most days anyway. And did you ever stop to think that some of us who live this life might actually be happy? And that you might be too?"

"Hey, El, there's nothing wrong with it if that's what you want. I just don't want it."

"So what do you want?"

"I'm working on that one. Let's put it this way. I know what I *don't* want. Number one is a lifetime of working for Lake Con. So let's say I'm narrowing it down."

A long sigh of exasperation came over the phone. "Honestly, Alex, you're too old to be rebellious, and too young to be having a mid-life crisis. I'm only giving you shit about it because I worry about you. I just really hope you know what you're doing. Christ, you're gonna be a long way from home. What are you going to do if you need help?"

"Don't worry. There's an embassy in Bangkok. I'll have a phone and a fax machine. An email address. It's a small world, Elly."

"Not small enough for me."

He gave his love to Kelly and Erin, and his best wishes to Elly's husband Joe.

"I sold the car," he concluded, "and left the apartment with an agent."

"It all sounds so final."

No safety net. No bungee cord to bounce you back home.

"Don't worry about me, Elly. I'll be fine."

"Just remember one thing, Alex. You deserve to be happy. Don't think for a moment you don't. Because you do."

I deserve to be happy, he thought. *If only it was that easy, little sister. If only people got what they deserved.* He closed his eyes and with his fresh sheets and his fresh new life ahead of him, tried not to think about Rachel.

That was the part he hadn't told his sister: how he had fled to the opposite side of the earth so that he would never have to see Rachel come on to another man again. But the shit of it was, he *could* still see her. He was 10,000 miles, twelve time zones and twenty-four hours on commercial flights away from her, but he was still watching her in McGuire's Pub, flirting with the guy from Great Lakes Naval Base, her eyes dancing, tossing her hair at him when she laughed, the little finger on her left hand reaching out to stroke his forearm, the very same way she had once stroked his.

He got out of bed and got his Walkman and a John Fahey tape out of his rucksack. It was sunset now, and under the pines the light was shadowy and cool, and the sky was streaked with magenta. He went back into the bedroom, lay down on the cool sheets and started the tape. He closed his eyes and let his head sink deep into the soft pillow and turned his thoughts to the new day that would be tomorrow. It was just a matter of time, that was all, and then she would be nothing but a cool, unemotional shard of memory. He tried to convince himself of this as he let Fahey's ringing twelve-string fill the hollow places in his heart.

Three

The house was full of light and sound by the time he emerged from his room the next morning. A woman was on the porch scrubbing his shirt out in an aluminum pan of soapy water and chatting with a middle-aged man: the brother and sister team of guard and housekeeper, Marek surmised. They both grinned at him and said "hello", and Marek quickly established this was about the full extent of their English.

He learned their names and wrote them down in a notebook, which amused them greatly. He transcribed them phonetically as best he could, yet when he tried to say them, they just laughed.

By the time he finished showering and dressing, Niwat was waiting for him on the couch. His thick black hair was freshly oiled and brushed to perfection, with a part that could have been made with a razor. He wore a pale blue dress shirt with knife-edge creases down the middle of the short sleeves, and a pair of tan slacks with identical creases from the cuffs to the belt.

"You sleep OK, Mr Aleck?" he asked.

Marek shrugged. "Like a rock."

The morning turned out to be a whirlwind tour of the Songkhla's government offices: immigration, labor, Department of Land Transport to get a driver's license, the bank to open an account, the post office to get another key for the station's postbox. At each place Marek found a place to sit until beckoned by Niwat to scratch his name onto some form. Most of the time he sat quietly and watched Niwat perform. He seemed to know everybody and was charming and animated with the staff, waiing the officious men in epaulettes and flirting with the female counter clerks. At immigration he passed over Marek's passport and a small stack of loose papers and then looked for someone to gab with until they returned. Sometimes he joked with one or two other citizens who, like Marek, sat on the well-worn benches or chairs, waiting for their name to be called. An old woman with a reed basket of mysterious yellow fruit cackled at his stories.

"You have many friends, Niwat," Marek said as they got back into his BMW.

"Well, you know, I do this for a long time," he answered, with an expression halfway between pride and humility. "Good to be friendly to people who can help you, you know? You see that guy in immigration, big chief with all the ribbons on his chest? Every New Year I bring him a bottle of Johnny Walker. Black Label."

"Like you say, it doesn't hurt to be friendly."

Their final stop was the market near the bank, where Niwat purchased large bottles of drinking water and other supplies. As they drove to the station, Niwat nodded toward a side street.

"Down that way, that's what the farang call the Dark Side. Many bars, many girls." Niwat giggled. "You can try it sometime, Mr Aleck."

At a stop light Niwat pointed to a large Chinese style mansion behind a low brick wall. "That's the National Museum," said

Niwat. The building appeared to be closed up and there was yellow crime tape around it, but no people were around. "Everybody talking about what happened couple nights ago. Some guy break in, middle of the night. Steal one statue and run away. Guard tried to stop him but the thief knock him out. He's in the hospital now, how you say, like sleeping."

"Coma?"

"Yeah, a coma. Cannot talk, cannot identify the thief."

"What did the guy steal?"

"Old statue. Religious statue like a Buddha."

"Is it very valuable?"

"Sure! Very old. I think the guy who stole it knows very well what he is doing. Many old things in this museum, but he takes only one thing."

"And they have no idea who the thief was?"

"No idea. Some people say it's the spirit of that Buddha coming back to get his own statue. Like a ghost." He laughed. "Thai people think like that sometimes. Me, I'm not sure about ghosts, but I think anybody who steals something like that gonna have a lot of bad luck. Bad luck gonna follow him around until that statue come back where it belong."

Marek spent the next few days poring over technical manuals and familiarizing himself with the equipment. When Sturges had offered him the job, he'd protested that he knew nothing about GPS outside of the basic principles, and even less about navigation and the oil industry.

"Bah, there's nothing to it, lad," said Sturges. They were in the Hard Rock in Singapore, sipping overpriced vodka and orange juice and dining on shelled peanuts. "All you need is the basics. You Yanks put up these satellites in the eighties, thirty-six of them all together, which give a continuous transmission of latitude and longitude. But that commercial signal is only accurate to a radius of about a hundred meters or so. Good enough for the weekend sailor and most commercial vessels, but not for your petroleum engineers. A distance of one hundred meters can mean the difference between pay dirt and a dry hole. That's where we come in."

He shoveled another handful of peanuts into his mouth and continued talking as he chewed. "Our station in Songkhla – all of our stations all over Asia – are built on a precisely surveyed point. So when we get a signal from the GPS, we know exactly how far it's off, automatically calculate the difference, and then send out the corrections to anyone who leases our receivers. Brilliant, isn't it?"

"Yes, genius. But still, I don't really know anything about running a navigation station, or about the oil and gas business."

"The station more or less runs itself. You've got the hardware and software background; you can learn about the equipment hands-on when you get there. Our local man there, Niwat, can help you with anything you need and take care of any maintenance at the station. He's a good man. Our biggest problem in Songkhla is the local power supply. It's pretty much crap, goes out all the time, so your most important job is to baby-sit the UPS when there's a signal going out to a ship. There has to be a constant, uninterrupted signal or else our customers get a little testy, which is understandable. When the city power goes out, the UPS will keep the transmitters and computers running until the generator kicks in. So that's your main responsibility: keep the UPS batteries topped up, make sure there's diesel for the generator. Oh maybe, every once in a while, a diode blows out but it's easy to replace. Two screws, two plugs, five-minute job. Anyway, Niwat knows all about it. He'll keep you on top of things.

"As far as knowing anything about the oil industry, hell, you'll pick up what you need. And I'll let you in on a little secret: there's lots of people in this business who don't know what they're doing. Believe me, the industry's full of them. I knew of an offshore maintenance manager who was hired only because he was the Vietnam War buddy of the area supervisor. He'd never seen an oil rig before in his life. And I once worked for a company that hired a training manager because he went to the same bloody church as the managing director. His only experience in anything close to training was as a Boy Scout troop leader. God's absolute truth."

Sturges wouldn't listen to any protests from Marek about his inability to run the station. He went on to explain that there were other, minor tasks Marek would have to perform from time to time. When there was a new customer, he'd have to install the receiver on the ship; he'd also have to remove it when the lease was up or when she was sailing to another location outside the area. Occasionally he might have to make minor repairs to the receivers. "But it's all black box engineering," said Sturges. "You don't have to know how any of it works. You just replace a power supply or a circuit board. Nothing to it. So what do you think? Will you take the job?"

Why not? On the road they always said living in Thailand was about as good as it got, and anyway, he had nothing to go back for. "Sure, Brian, I'll take it. When do I start?"

Sturges ordered another round of vodka and orange juices to celebrate.

Despite Niwat's daily assurances that there would be work soon, there was no rig move the next week or the week after that. The days fell one upon the other with nothing much to do, and Marek quickly realized he needed to establish a routine.

In the mornings he'd go for a long swim in the mirror smooth waters of the Gulf of Thailand. By mid-morning there was a comforting air of domesticity around the house. The housekeeper sometimes brought her young son who, whenever Marek was around, stared wide-eyed at him as if he were a creature from another world. Niwat dropped by a couple of times a day in order to check the generators and transmission lines – or so he said. Marek had the feeling his real purpose was to make sure he wasn't getting lonely. He always left with cheery assurances that work would be coming soon, "prob'ly next week".

Marek spent several hours in the office each morning. The first thing he did was customize the PC, cleaning up the configuration files and writing DOS commands to get the system to work as fast as the hardware would allow. It was a couple of years old, which meant it was sluggish and short of memory, but it would serve his purposes. He checked to see if his predecessor had left any interesting files or at least some games on the hard drive; but the only things he found were old monthly reports addressed to Sturges, and a program of one hundred varieties of Solitaire. At least for the previous tenant, the workload had not been overwhelming.

He spent a few days organizing paperwork the former station manager had left in a shambles. He gathered all the old faxes (which, when he'd found them, were bound together with paper clips and thick rubber bands) sequenced them by date, put them into three-ring binders, labeled the binders, and shelved them in order of the dates they covered. He organized the correspondence by sender and filed it alphabetically in the four-drawer metal file cabinet. He carefully read all the post-survey reports that he found in drawers or in loose piles around the office. Preparing these, Sturges had said, would be another one of his tasks. He browsed through the software on the PC - it was the standard stuff - and had no doubt he could turn out niftier documents than his predecessor. He knew he could churn out impressive pie charts and three-dimensional bar graphs of three different shadings. His readers would be mostly engineers and geologists, and even if he didn't know exactly what he was talking about, maybe he could at least seduce them with pretty visuals.

The housekeeper left at five, and the guard came about the same time to begin his night shift. The evenings were quiet, and Marek mostly stayed in the station reading or strumming on his guitar. Occasionally a car would pass on the beach road or he'd hear laughter cascading over the hotel wall. Sometimes, even though the guard knew only a smattering English, Marek would walk back to the shed and share a beer and small talk with him as they watched the insects buzz around the spotlight that illuminated the yard.

One night he almost called Rachel, but it was nine thirty in the morning, Central Daylight Savings Time, and by then she would have been at her downtown office for over an hour. It was just as well; a goodbye was a goodbye, no matter how many promises to write or call were attached to it. He had been the one who was reticent even to touch her when they parted.

"You are allowed to kiss me, you know," she'd said.

"That's right, we used to be lovers."

"I hate that word. It's so ... I don't know ... melodramatic."

"So what were we then?"

"Alex, c'mon. Let's not start again. It's like I keep telling you. You're a nice guy. You did more caring things for me than my husband ever did. You're fun to be with. You're terrific in bed."

"If I was that good, baby, I'd still have you."

"I got scared. I wasn't ready for what you wanted. I just couldn't handle it."

He had one night half-jokingly suggested they get married; and she, perhaps joking as well, had agreed.

But that was before some chemical imbalance in her brain triggered another four-day funk of depression, when she refused to see him – or anybody else for that matter – and did nothing but lie on the couch in front of the television, alternately weeping and filling the ashtray with cigarette butts, answering neither the telephone nor the door, until she found enough strength to lift herself out of the room and visit the friendly Dr Jordon for a refill of Prozac.

"I have two strikes against me already," she said that final night. "You should consider yourself lucky. You're gonna end up with somebody much better than a fucked-up divorced nutcase like me."

He called Sturges every day at 3:45, just before the end of the working day in Singapore, and reported everything he'd done, even if it was nothing more than organizing the telephone and electricity bills for the past six months.

"Yeah, well, Jimmy was not such a great one for organizing things now, was he?" Sturges said. "Didn't really have the head for it. Actually, didn't have the head for very much." There was a pause as Sturges took a long pull on his cigarette. Marek knew Sturges loathed sitting in an office in Singapore wearing a tie and chained to a telephone; he had confessed as much during one of their afternoon drinking sessions at the Hard Rock. He had started out as a surveyor, working with a team across a corner of Saudi Arabia's Empty Quarter in a four-wheel drive, and later tramping through the rain forest of Irian Jaya. "But that's a young man's work," he had said. "And they pay you more for sitting in an office all day."

"Niwat mentioned something about a rig move coming up. Any news about that?" asked Marek.

"Ah ... let me check." There was a rustling of papers and then Sturges cupped his hand over the mouthpiece and said something to someone in his office. "Let's see ... ah yes. The Ocean Drill-545, exploratory well for IndoAsian Oil. Due to move to block 13 sometime near the end of the month. Date unconfirmed. There should be a map on the wall showing the blocks and locations of the drill ships, platforms, and so forth. Can you see it from where you're sitting? The OD-545 would be a red push pin." Marek could see the map on the far wall and dots of red, green, yellow and blue, but that was all he could make out from his chair.

"At least that's the system we had, but Jimmy probably screwed it up. The Captain will fax you when he's ready to sail, saying exactly when and to where. I'll also call you to confirm. There's not a whole lot you have to do during a rig move, just make sure the generator is topped up, so you're guaranteed continuous power if the main power goes out. The company man tends to get a little excited if he's not getting a steady signal."

"Yeah, Niwat and I have taken care of that."

"Good. Then you've not got a bloody thing to worry about. So, how are you finding Songkhla? Have you found all the evil places yet?"

"Evil places? What Niwat called the Dark Side? No, I haven't done the tour yet. Still a bit jet-lagged."

"Best time to do it. You can drink all night. Anyway, when you get around to it, check out the Number One Bar. You can't go wrong there."

"Number One Bar?"

"Never miss the place when I do my station audit, couple of times a year. Ask for Nit. Ask her if she remembers Brian. She took quite a fancy to me last time."

"OK, I promise I'll do that.

"Right! So anything new in town? All the oil trash keeping their noses clean?"

"Like I said, Brian, I've not been out much. Big news in town is the museum theft. Seems somebody broke into the Songkhla museum and stole a statue, very old, very valuable. Niwat says the Thais think it was a ghost."

"Yes, well they would. No doubt it was an inside job."

"But he knocked out the guard on the way out. Still in a coma."

"All the more convincing, I suppose. Must be worth a lot of money to someone. Anyway, I'll let you know as soon as the rig move is confirmed."

"OK, Brian."

"And don't forget. Number One Bar. The name's Nit. Means small or tiny, something like that. Lovely girl, that Nit."

Four

In the days that followed, Alex Marek learned and adapted.

He learned to drive on the left, breaking years of habit of reaching for the shift with his right hand, and through sheer concentration never once turned into the wrong lane. He learned that most household wiring was haphazard and ungrounded; that the hot water heater and the stove were fueled by propane from bottles stored on the patio, potentially lethal bombs that were delivered by motorcycle carts every few months.

He learned to leave his shoes on the porch before entering the house, not to point with his feet, and not to touch anyone, even children, above the shoulder. He learned that Thailand was an overwhelmingly Buddhist country; and then he learned that the little shrine on the pedestal behind the bungalow, the one the maid put fresh fruit and garlands on every morning and the one the guard lit candles and jasmine sticks to every dusk, had nothing to do with Buddhism but was there to appease the spirits of the land.

He learned that schedules were loose; that things got done or not done according to some cosmic sense of time, rather than the rigid hours and minutes he had grown up with. He learned to live with the feeling that you never knew quite what was going on, that you were floating in a river, being pulled along by an unaccountable current, with no idea which shore you'd end up on. He learned to accept the free-flowing nature of life in the tropics, the sudden changes of direction, the "yes's" which didn't necessarily mean "yes" but were the only alternative to a rude and barbaric "no".

He learned to smile and let go.

But he had spent three weeks in the bungalow and still there was no work.

"Well," said Sturges, "it's just the nature of the beast. Things keep changing all the time in this business. Just be patient, it *will* happen soon. Guaranteed."

One afternoon he was studying Thai in his office, forcing his lips and tongue to imitate the strangely comic sounds of Thai conversation on his tape, when there was a timid knock on the door. Standing behind the housekeeper was a tall thin man around Marek's age, with an ear pin and wire rim glasses, grinning and holding a line of plastic twine with two large fish at the end of it.

"G'day, mate! Er ... I'm looking for Jimmy." He raised the fish higher as if to provide an explanation.

"Jimmy ...? Oh, Jimmy. No, he's not here anymore. He left. I took his place."

"Left, eh? That was right quick. What did old Jimmy do then? Ravish the boss's daughter?" Sunlight from the office window glinted off the man's glasses and lit the jeweled pin in his left ear. He wore a pair of baggy, plaid shorts and a T-shirt that looked as if it had been borrowed from someone much larger. "Been on holiday, y'see. Just got in from Perth last night."

"He just left," Marek said. "I really don't know why. I met a guy in Singapore, and he offered me the job before the third drink."

The man laughed, a generous laugh full of goodwill. "Right place, right time, eh? Good on ya, mate. The name's Drew, Andrew Philips. Pleased to make your acquaintance."

Marek introduced himself and Philips shifted the fish to his left hand to shake hands. "Let's sit in the other room. Bit more comfortable."

"You sure I'm not interrupting?"

"Not at all. Anyway, my mouth needs a rest from trying to speak Thai."

Philips looked at the Thai book on the desk and, still holding the dripping fish, picked up one of the cassettes. "Right, our famous Dr Choonthan's course of conversational Thai. How're you finding it?"

"Rough going."

"Yeah, well, old Dr Choo could improve his product if he maybe used some instructional methods that didn't date from the stone age."

The housekeeper hovered, moving her eyes from Marek to Philips as if waiting for instructions. Marek eyed the two fish, still dripping onto the floor.

"Oh, these, right!" said Philips as if he'd forgotten all about them. "Plaa kapong. Sea bass. Picked 'em up in the market on the way over. Raised in bamboo cages off Koh Yor. To get them any fresher you'd have to raise them yourself." He said a few words in Thai to the housekeeper and then handed her the line. Marek gestured toward the large rattan chair with the thick cushions, but Philips ignored him and sat cross-legged on the floor. Marek sat on the couch.

"Well good on ya, mate. I mean about studying Thai. There's lots who spend years here and never even bother to learn 'hello' or 'thank you'. Pretty lame, I think. Jimmy's a perfect example. Don't think he ever learned much more than 'One black and soda on the rocks,' and 'How much for a short time, luv?'" He reached across to a small pile of books near the chair. "Real live books, eh?"

"Pulp fiction, mainly. Help yourself if you want. I found them in the closet. I guess they were Jimmy's."

"Not bloody likely. Never saw him read anything except the price list at the Pink Lady massage parlor. Much like the rest of the oil trash crowd in this town. And I say that with all due respect. They're my mates. Good guys, actually, and fun to have a piss-up with, but not exactly at the forefront of the intellectual movement in Songkhla. Not that there is such a thing."

"So I take it you're not working in oil?" Marek asked.

"Me?" he laughed. "Not exactly at that pay grade. I'm a teacher at the Fisheries College. Three years now. Came over originally with AVID, Australian Volunteers for International Development, something like your Peace Corps. When that contract finished, I signed on as a locally hired ajarn. University instructor. Doesn't pay much but the title just reeks of respectability." He smiled an off-center grin and leaned back against the chair, locking his hands behind his head.

"Aquaculture. Big important-sounding word, ain't it? It's prawn farming actually, and it's big business here. The college gives me a bungalow in Khao Seng village, just outside the school. You oughta come there sometime. I warn you though, it gets a bit chaotic at times. There's my roomy, for one. He plays drums. And I tend to pick up strays. Let's see, there were some French travelers I met in Had Yai, the research team from the Netherlands, a few dogs and cats, several girls from the Sea Side Bar who needed a place to stay for a couple of nights. I have one house rule that keeps everybody in line: 'Clean up your own shit.' Anyway, fancy a beer?"

"Yeah, sure, help yourself. There's some in the fridge."

"Yeah, I know, I put them there." Philips came back with two frigid cans of Victoria Bitter. "Brought a few back from home. Enjoy them while they last. Ah, here's our dinner, then."

The maid quickly set the table and brought in steamed rice, tomatoes, baby corn, a stuffed omelet and the fish. Philips chatted with her, his Thai as effortless and natural as his English, and Marek couldn't help but feel a stab of jealousy.

The white meat of the sea bass was so moist and fresh it flaked off the bone and melted in Marek's mouth like butter. They ate heartily, and even Philips was quiet until the fish was nothing more than a skeleton and a tail.

"About the most fun you can have and still keep all your clothes on," said Philips as he handed Marek another VB. "And by the way, I told the maid the other fish was for her and her brother, if that's OK with you?"

"Of course."

As the maid cleared the table, the two men took their beers and sat on the rattan chairs outside. They drank and talked and watched the day meld into dusk. The joggers and strollers came out to the beach to enjoy the evening breeze and the sea turned violet with the sunset. The guard arrived for his night shift and greeted Philips as a long lost friend.

"Man, your Thai is excellent, Drew."

"Not so great, really, but when I first came to Thailand I lived with a Thai family outside the city. Nobody around me spoke a word of English and I had no contact with any other foreigners. What they call total immersion; best way to learn a language."

Marek asked if Philips had heard about the museum theft.

"No, what happened?"

"Not a lot of details around. Niwat says the guy broke in, middle of the night, grabbed a statue, knocked out the guard and escaped. Guard is still in a coma."

"Really? What did he take?"

"Some statue. Buddha image, I guess, old and valuable. My boss in Singapore reckons it was an inside job."

"Often the case. I remember there was a temple in Bangkok, somebody walked off with several gold Buddhas. Turned out to be one of the monks. One of the senior monks, mind you."

"Think they'll catch the guy?"

"Here? Doubtful. These things usually blow over in a couple of weeks and everybody forgets about it. But I know the director at the museum because I did some pro bono work for him, translated some of the description labels from Thai to English. I may stop by there in the next couple of days and find out what happened."

"Went past the other day with Niwat and it was closed."

"Really? Maybe they'll open again in another day or two. Any other major news in town?"

"No, but I don't get out much. My major source of information is Niwat."

"You've not seen the Dark Side of Songkhla?"

"No, Drew, but everybody keeps telling me I should go there."

"You should! How does Friday sound?"

"Supposed to have some work coming up soon, a rig move, but nobody seems to know when."

"Yeah, Jimmy always said it was feast or famine. No worries. I'll give you a call on Friday. If you're free, say about seven, we can meet down there. I'll tell you where. We'll do a real pub crawl. Have a few beers, meet the guys, check out the girls. Should warn you, though, they're always looking for fresh meat."

"You mean me?'

"Who else? What I'm saying is, you'll have a great time with them."

They'd finished the last of the beer, and Philips said he had a class at eight the next morning. Before getting onto his motorbike, he picked a few books out of the cardboard box in the closet and slipped them into his backpack.

"Us readers have to stick together you know. I'll call you Friday. Happy hour starts at seven."

Philips turned the ignition and the motorbike coughed to a start. As he sped off the back end fishtailed, sending out a spray of dirt and stones. Then he was on the paved road heading down the beach, one hand waving above his head.

Five

Five

Marek had spent two weeks in Bangkok during his first swing through Thailand, visiting the temples and museums by day and the bars and red-light areas at night. He had been to the go-go bars in Nana Plaza, where there were sometimes twenty naked young girls on the stage at once. He had seen a live sex show in a Patpong bar, where a girl pulled a string of razor blades out of her vagina and a couple had intercourse on stage while girls cadged drinks with expressions of utter boredom. And he had climbed the narrow stairs to a dark room above, where staff offered oral sex as he sat on a barstool nursing a Heineken.

Compared to that, the bars of Songkhla were as tame as a neighborhood tavern back home; except there were a few more women, they were more attractive, and they were probably available for after-hours entertainment.

"If this is the Dark Side," said Marek when he arrived, "what's the sunny side look like?"

He and Philips were sitting on rattan stools at the end of a long bar. There were three customers, a couple of girls behind the bar serving drinks, and another pair sitting on a large ice cooler, one of them scrupulously filing her fingernails. Rod Stewart softly sang "*I am sailing*" from two speakers suspended halfway up the back wall.

"Just you wait," said Philips. "It's still early."

"This is Apple, by the way," he said, nodding to the barmaid bringing Marek's beer. "We were just discussing the museum theft. The guard's still in a coma. Nearly a month now."

"Did you go over there?"

"Yeah, but nobody around. All shuttered up, just as you said."

"According to Niwat a lot of Thais think a ghost did it."

"Yeah, well, why not? It's as good an explanation as any. No one saw him come in or out, except maybe the guard, and *he's* not talking. Makes perfect sense a ghost did it. Or possibly aliens. What do you think Lek? You think a ghost, phii, steal that statue from the museum?"

She shrugged. "Maybe, but if ghost I hope he stay away from this bar."

"You'd better put an extra bottle of Mekhong on the spirit house outside, just in case. As for me," said Philips, turning toward Marek, "I tend to agree with your boss. Inside job gone wrong. I think the guard just got caught in the middle, poor bastard."

The bar was called the Full Moon Pub, one of five in a strip of shophouses on Sri Saket Road. From the outside they were nearly identical, and the only reason Marek knew to come to this one was that Philips had told him, "It's the one with all the fairy lights".

Philips's nervous energy wouldn't allow him to sit too long at any one place; that and the fact that he felt compelled to show Marek everything Songkhla's nightlife had to offer. They bounced from one bar to another in the strip, never staying for more than two beers before moving on to the next.

Philips knew everybody. He greeted all the girls in the bars by name, and just the fact that he could recall every one of them was amazing to Marek. He knew most of the customers as well and made a point of introducing Marek to everyone within shouting range, usually with, "This is Alex. He's one of us."

For his part, Marek hardly had a chance to say more than a few polite words of introduction before Philips was pulling him over to meet someone else or whisking him off to the next bar. He had a few fleeting conversations with the bargirls, all of which followed a similar pattern.

"What your name?"

"Alex."

"Ah lick..?" (Philips was amused by that one, and before the night was over started introducing Marek as, 'That famous Chinese general, *Ah Lick*.')

"Where you come from?"

"Madison, Wisconsin."

"Mad as a...?"

"America."

"Ah..." An expression of recognition. Now they were communicating. "How long you stay Thailand?"

"*Have* I stayed or *will* I stay?"

"Sorry? No understand. I speak only little English."

"No problem. I've been in Thailand one month."

"You work offshore?"

"No, onshore. Southern Cross Navigation. GPS station. On

the beach, near the big hotel."

"Sorry. Cannot unner-suhtan. English not so good."

Now they were in a place called The Stable Bar, with framed pictures of racehorses on the walls. Philips was playing Connect Four with one of the girls behind the bar. She dropped her yellow chip into the slot, clapped her hands and squealed with delight. Philips pushed a ten-baht note across the bar to her.

"Not bloody fair," he complained. "It's all they do all day. C'mon, let's move."

They went to another place: different music, different girls, more beer and more introductions. They were standing at the bar now, drinking in the midst of an ever-moving flux of men that included a Scottish drilling engineer, a German boat captain, a Canadian helicopter pilot, an Indonesian roughneck and an English firefighter. Snatches of dialect and accents from every corner of the earth flew around them.

"You met the new girl in the Cat's Eye?" asked the captain to everyone in general. "Asked her where's she from and she said Piss Up A Rope. That was a bit rude, I thought. Really uncalled for."

"Phitsanalok," said Philips.

"Eh, what?"

"She's from Phitsanalok, central Thailand. Not piss up a rope, you thick bastard." Everyone laughed.

Before the captain could fire a retort, they were out the door.

"We'll take a couple of motos to the other side of town. This here is Warin, my trusty steed. He looks after me when I'm drunk. And your man there is Somchai. Right, let's roll 'em out."

"What about the truck?"

"Leave it. We'll be back."

The motorcycles dropped them off at another short strip of bars, which Philips called "the northern sector". They went through a glass door into a room that was darker, louder, and more crowded than any of the others they'd been to so far. Near the back they found an empty corner of the bar to lean against. They ordered their drinks and their attention was soon captured by a little barroom drama that was being played out in front of them. A girl was sitting on a stool with her back to the bar. She was surrounded by two or three others, and there were four shot glasses on the bar next to her. The girl leaned back on the stool until her head was lying on the bar. Then one of the girls who was standing picked up a shot glass and, as the others cheered in crescendo, poured it into the first girl's gaping mouth.

"That's number three," said the guy next to them. "She'll be dancing on the bar in no time."

"This place has the reputation of being a bit wild," said Philips, shouting above the din of the music. "Lots of freelancers."

"Freelancers?"

"They don't actually work in the bar. They just come here for a good time."

"So it's kinda like a pickup bar back home?"

"Nothing's like it is back home."

Behind them, in the crowded little space between the bar and the alcove that led to the toilets, some couples had begun to dance. Their movements created a chain reaction, and soon

Marek and Philips were being jostled and bumped by every person who went by.

"I'm getting crushed," said Philips. "Let's move next door for a time out. We can come back later."

In fact, Time Out was the name of the bar next door, and it turned out to be apt. In stark contrast to the place they'd just left, Time Out was brightly lit, sparsely populated and instead of music blaring from a sound system, the television was tuned to a soccer game, the sound just above the threshold for hearing.

There were checked tablecloths and the beer was served in Mason jars. One wall was covered with framed photographs of customers and the portly proprietor. There were two dartboards on the wall, and a couple of guys in orange coveralls were playing pool at a table in the back. The girl behind the bar handed them laminated menus.

"I'm feeling a bit peckish," said Philips. "The chili is not bad."

"Nothing for me, thanks," said Marek. He smiled at the girl as he handed her the menu, and she smiled back.

"Maew, darling," said Philips, "give me a bowl of your famous chili. And two Singhas."

"You want it hot spicy, Drew?"

"Yes! Hot and spicy like you! *Phet maak!* I want it to burn the skin off the roof of my mouth. I want it to rip my eyeballs out. I want it so hot it'll sober me up so I can drink all night."

"You crazy, Drew," said Maew as she went off to the kitchen.

Another girl shyly poured out their beers into the Mason jars and then retreated to lean against the wall. She looked at them with a wide-eyed expression, half-fearful, half-curious, as if waiting for them to do something outrageous or turn into ogres. When Maew came back, Philips made the introductions.

"This is Miss Maew," he began. "Maew means cat. Be careful of those claws. Maew, this is my mate, Alex."

"Nice to meet you, A-lick." She reached out her hand; her fingernails were painted purple. "Drew, why you not tell me you have handsome friend?"

"OK, Alex is a handsome bugger. There, I've told you. Anyway, what's wrong with me? I'm handsome, ain't I?"

"No, you very ugly. Red hair, big nose, too skinny."

"You're all charm, darling."

Maew noticed Marek looking at the gaper, the girl sitting in the shadows watching them.

"She new girl, country girl," she explained. "Very shy, first time in bar. Cannot speak English. Still virgin girl." She laughed as if saying something beyond belief.

"And what about you?"

"Me? Sure, I virgin too. I virgin like Madonna." She laughed.

"No, I mean how long have you been here."

"Oh, about six month."

"Like it?"

She shrugged. "It OK. Mostly quiet. Not like next door. Next door too crazy sometimes. Have fights. Girls no good. Have many thief, you know?"

When Philip's chili arrived he dug into it like a man deprived of food for weeks. He consumed the whole bowl without a word or, it seemed to Marek, a single breath, until his spoon was scraping the bottom of the plastic bowl. Then he polished off his beer and belched.

One of the guys at the pool table called out to Philips. "Right," he said. "I'll have a chat with my mates from Perth. You get to know Miss Cat here, and watch out for her claws."

Marek and the girl chatted about nothing for a while, and when his beer was finished, he ordered another one and asked her what she wanted.

"You buy me a drink?" She looked at him with a puzzled expression, as if she thought he was pulling her leg. "Margarita, OK?"

"Whatever you want."

He watched her walk back to the cooler. She wore a tight canary-yellow mini-skirt, showing off nicely shaped legs and a rounded backside, and a black mesh vest over a low-cut red top that revealed the tops of a pair of breasts much larger than those of the average Thai girl. He noticed she was barefoot, but she still managed to strut as if she were wearing a pair of heels. He watched her with a kind of fascination. She had a *presence*, a look-at-me, I'm-hot-shit attitude that belied this quiet bar in this quiet, up-country backwater. When she returned she poured Marek's beer, tapped her glass to his, took a hefty slug, then sat silently with her chin in her hand and her salt-rimmed Margarita in front of her.

Her skin was smooth and unblemished, and the whites of her eyes were the color of fresh milk, in contrast to the deep black of the irises. Her teeth too were dazzling white. Her nose was straight and fine, and it occurred to Marek that she might have had a nose job. Then he began to wonder if the breasts too had been augmented by modern day surgical techniques. She caught him looking, snapped her chewing gum and laughed at him.

"Where you come from, Alick?"

"Madison, Wisconsin."

"Mad as sin...?"

"America. I come from America."

"Aha, America good. Man not stingy."

"How do you know? Your boyfriend American?"

She smiled close-lipped and looked away. "Before, maybe. Now no boyfriend. I think maybe too old."

"How old are you?"

"Twenty-five."

"That's not old. That's very young."

She shrugged. "How old you?"

"You guess."

She pretended to look at him critically. "I think twenty-six."

"*Paak waan.*"

"No, I never sweet mouth. You look like young man to me."

"I'm thirty."

"No, I never believe that."

She said she was from Chiang Rai and had lived in Songkhla for two years. She came to visit a friend of hers, another girl from her village, who had been working at the Bamboo Bar next door. She had even worked there herself for a while.

"But I don't like. Too crazy there. After one month I come to working here. Better."

She liked this place, she said, because the owner was kind and the other girls were her friends.

"And what about your friend, the one from the village?"

"She get married to farang guy. Now she living in Houston. Very lucky."

The bass from the music next door was booming into the Time Out, overpowering the television and the click of the pool balls. The party seemed to be growing.

"What about you?" asked Marek. "You want to marry a farang guy?"

"Sure! Very soon, I hope!" And she smiled at him, a dazzling smile that seemed to transform the whole room. It overwhelmed him, and he found himself ordering another beer before the one in front of him was half-finished.

She laughed at him. "You drunk, *chai mai?*"

"*Nit noi*," he said. "Little bit."

Philips clapped him on the back. "Hey, Mr A-Lick, we're heading next door for round two," he said.

"OK, I'm right behind you."

She was right, he was a little drunk. But what did it matter? It seemed like the right state to be in at this time of night and in this place. He had a good friend in Philips, and he was now part of this club; this wild and slightly demented group of expat oil workers who really didn't give a shit about what society thought right and proper. And what a treat it was to be with this beautiful young girl who liked to smile and laugh. What did it matter if she worked in a bar, and went with customers, and couldn't speak much English? Wasn't it a million times better than trying to deal with someone's hang ups and excess baggage?

"You want to go next door, Maew?" he asked. "Have a few drinks? Get something to eat?"

She looked him in the eye and put her hand on his wrist. "Maybe you should go back now. Maybe you too drunk."

"Nonsense, I'm just getting started."

"OK, but have to pay the Mamasan three hundred baht."

They had to squeeze their way into the Bamboo, and then Marek had to fight his way to the bar to get their drinks. Bodies were bouncing under strobe lights to a reggae beat. The girl who had been taking the shooters was, as predicted, dancing on the bar, but now wearing only shorts and a bra. He and Maew were crushed together in a corner. He spotted Philips across the room, shirtless, waving a bottle of whiskey. Marek had fleeting, inane conversations at shouting volume with anyone who happened to be next to him or passing by. There was laughter and spilled drinks, and Maew and he were forced to hold tight to one another or else be split apart by the current of shifting bodies. After twenty minutes or so, she pulled him outside.

She had met some friends, she explained, and they wanted to go to a karaoke bar; have a few more drinks, maybe get something to eat. Maew had a scooter, so he and another girl got on with her, and the other two girls followed on another bike. The karaoke bar was dark and smoky, and they found a booth in the upstairs balcony section. Plates of food appeared on the table, a bottle of Regency. The other girls were continually disappearing and reappearing, and other friends of Maew stopped at the booth to have a drink or chat. Somebody handed the microphone to Marek and he looked through the songbook for something he thought he could sing, but there wasn't much. Finally, desperate and feeling he had to choose something in order to save face, he ordered John Denver's "Country Roads". They clapped when it was over and, relieved, he handed the microphone to Maew. She sang a Thai torch song in a squeaky voice, mournfully off-key, but the applause when she finished was much louder than he had gotten. She sat down next to him, smiled and kissed him. "Where you stay?" she asked.

* * *

He awoke the next morning in a strange bed with the sun on his face. He sat up quickly and took deep breaths to clear his head. Where was he? He felt as if all the fluid had been drained from his brainpan and his cortex was scraping against the inside of his skull. Ah yes, this was a hotel room. And that was Maew showering in the bathroom.

What time was it now? He found his watch on the bedside table: 11:30 a.m. What day was it? Ah yes, Saturday. He searched back through the fog in his head to try to recall how he'd gotten here. He vaguely remembered checking in, the dawn light coloring the sky to the east. Thank God that even in his legless condition he'd had the sense to agree with Maew when she'd suggested a hotel, and not tried to make it all the way back to his bungalow.

There was a mirror behind the headboard, and he caught sight of his reflection. He was heartened to see he didn't look as bad as he felt. Why in God's name had he drunk so much? And had he eaten anything at all last night? He remembered the food at the karaoke table, but he couldn't recall actually putting any of it in his mouth.

He heard the shower stop running. He went to the minibar and got out a bottle of water, snapped open the top and drank half of the bottle. Maew came out of the bathroom with a towel wrapped around her body. She began humming as she combed out her long hair in front of the mirror.

"You're up early this morning," he said, his voice sounding like the croak of some forest creature.

"Have to meet my friend in Hat Yai," she said, not taking her eyes from her image in the mirror.

He was suddenly aroused as she leaned over and ran a tube of lipstick across her lower lip, the towel tight against her rounded buttocks. He was stung with the memory of last night's fiasco; he being too drunk to even get a condom out of its wrapping. He sighed. Then he walked behind Maew and put his hands around her waist and met her eyes in the mirror. "Why don't you stay a little longer."

She turned around and pinched his cheeks and kissed him on the mouth. "I told you already. Have to go. Last night you very drunk, huh?" She laughed a throaty, good-natured laugh. Her hair was wet, and she smelled of talcum powder. She disappeared into the bathroom and in a few minutes came out wearing the canary skirt and black mesh top from the night before, an outfit that was going to look quite odd on the streets of Songkhla in the glare of the midday sun.

She spent a long time adjusting her skirt and top, smoothing out the wrinkles, tucking and twisting the cloth until she was satisfied. Then she turned away from the mirror.

"Last night you very sweet. You nice man, good man, not stingy man. You come again tonight to Time Out?"

Just then he felt like he would never step into another bar in his life unless forced to at gunpoint. "Sure, come again," he said. "I come again soon." He realized his English had degenerated to her level, and he didn't really care. She pinched him hard on the cheeks and grimaced at him in a mock threatening, motherly sort of way. She growled at him, then went to get her purse.

He went to his pants slung over a chair. He felt suddenly sick and held his breath until the feeling mercifully passed. She was going to need some money. How did one delicately do this sort of thing? And how much? He fished out his wallet. There was twenty baht in the billfold. He checked the pockets of his jeans. There was seventy baht in one, and his keys and a few coins in the other. This was bad.

"Honey, Maew, I ... I don't seem to have any money."

She was close to the mirror, brushing her face with something, and didn't bat an eyelid. She turned and hugged him. "I no want money from you. You good man. I sleep with you for free." She kissed him on the mouth and pulled his head down so she could whisper in his ear. "You come see me again at Time Out soon, OK?"

"OK," he mumbled.

"Good. Don't forget!" She gave him another of her dazzling smiles, looking as fresh and youthful as if she'd slept ten hours and hadn't had a drop of alcohol in her life. Then in a whirlwind she packed her accoutrements into her bag, kissed and squeezed him, and with a final, singing, "bye-bye" was out the door, leaving him with the scent of talcum powder and shampoo.

He chugged the last of the bottled water. *I sleep with you for free.* But at the beginning of the night he had had over 3,000 baht!

He looked in his wallet for Philips's number.

"It's Alex."

"Awright, mate. How the hell are you?"

"Barely alive. You?"

"No worries. Didn't mean to leave you on your own there but reckoned you were in good hands with our Miss Maew. Where'd you end up?"

"Some karaoke joint. And then the ..." he fished a matchbox out of the ashtray "... the Lake Inn hotel. That's where I am now."

"So what you're saying is basically you had a smashing time."

"Judging by how much money I spent, I must have."

Drew laughed. "Another notch on the old belt, mate. That's what it's all about."

"And you ... last time I saw you, you were dancing half naked and had a stranglehold on a bottle of Jack Daniels."

"Well, yeah ... but it was still early."

Marek used his credit card to pay for the hotel room, then waved down a moto and had the driver take him to his pickup, still parked across the street from the Full Moon. The bar was open so he went in, priced the cost of coffee and ordered two cups.

He was beginning to feel human again on the drive home but still had patchy areas in his memory of last night. Had Maew taken any money from him? He didn't think so. She had no reason to; he had been quite willing to give it to her. Anyway, if she were going to steal something she would have left in the dead of night when he was still asleep. But she wouldn't dare do it – she knew he'd know exactly where to find her.

No, he finally decided the only logical conclusion was that he had spent it all. He'd bought a bunch of beers – and of course her Margaritas – in the Time Out and the Bamboo. And he had to pay the mamasan. They'd gone to the karaoke bar; there was all that food and the bottle of Regency, and of course he picked up the tab for her friends' drinks as well. He was beginning to think he'd got off light at 3,000 baht.

Chalk it up to experience, he told himself. There was a feeling of self-reproach nagging him like the dull headache behind his eyes; the old Catholic upbringing, something always there, like a toothache, but he had learned to live with it. This is what happened when you took the leap. But next time he would be sure at least to stay sober enough to have sex.

When he pulled into the driveway of the station, he saw Mr Niwat's silver BMW and then the man himself standing sharp and erect on the shaded porch.

"Hey, Mr Alex." He was grinning from ear to ear. "You out early huh? Go for a drive maybe, hee, hee." He winked at Marek as he came up the steps and gave him a thumbs up sign. "Have good time?" he whispered conspiratorially.

"Must have, 'cause I don't remember much of it."

"Hee hee! Why not? Like me in Texas. Anyway, look at this. Good news." He handed a curling piece of fax paper to Marek.

```
TO:              NORTHERN CROSS DGPS
FROM:            OD-545
SUBJ:            RIG MOVE

WILL COMMENCE RIG MOVE 31 MAY FROM
BRAVO 7 TO BRAVO 9.

COORDINATES
LATITUDE:        O90 21' 29.735"(N)
LONGITUDE:       1010 22' 53.254"(E)

WATER DEPTH:     233 Ft.

DISTANCE AND BEARING FROM BRAVO 7 TO
BRAVO 9
DISTANCE:        23.6 Km/12.7 Nm
BEARING:         357.6 Deg.

ESTIMATED TIME OF ARRIVAL: 31 MAY

REGARDS
RADIO OPERATOR, OCEAN DRILL
```

"The thirty-first," said Marek. "What's that, Wednesday? Anything we need to do before then?"

"Nothing. Everything ready. UPS OK, diesel for the generator. We all set. Captain gonna call again when she ready to sail. We just wait for him to call."

"So there's nothing I need to do now."

"Nothing."

"OK, then I'm gonna get some sleep."

"Hee hee, OK, Alex, see you tomorrow."

The maid fixed him some scrambled eggs, and within minutes of finishing it he was undressed and under the covers. He thought he should call Sturges about the rig move, and just before he went under, he tried to remember if they had been in any place called the Number One. He had, until that moment, totally forgotten about Sturges' girl, Nit.

Six

The Sikorsky 61 shuddered off the helideck and Hunter felt the old terror belt him in the stomach like a cold fist. The big chopper paused as it always did, trying to stabilize, as if instead of rising it could just as easily slam back into the concrete surface and become a fiery tomb for the twenty-one men on board. The stench of jet fuel filled the cabin and made his eyes burn, and the choking heat made it hard to breathe. The roar of the engines drowned out every sound; he could scream, he thought, and no one would hear him. As the aircraft drifted toward the edge of the platform, just a few feet off the deck, he saw the safety officer in his silver hood and fire suit tracking the chopper with the water cannon they called the fire monitor.

A hell of a lot of good he'll do. If this baby goes down, we'll all be cinders by the time he gets his finger out of his ass and figures out how to turn on the water. Who the fuck ever decided the Thais could run the whole goddamn show offshore, even the safety part of it? Just wait till there's an emergency. These numb nuts could screw up a binge in a brewery.

The yellow lettering on the deck and then the safety netting bordering it slid past him, and then there was nothing but the frothing sea 120 feet below them. In one heart-stopping instant the helicopter's nose dipped toward the water. Hunter gripped the arms of his seat as his stomach churned, and he was sure, absolutely certain, that even the pilot didn't know at this point whether they were going up or down. Then they slowly accelerated, inching past the licking orange flame of the flare boom, before gracefully leveling out and beginning to climb. The living quarters and production platform, the wellhead platforms and the drilling rig, quickly became miniaturized by altitude and looked like sophisticated toys in some child's wading pool. Within minutes they were cruising at 1,000 feet. It was a perfectly routine take off, one Hunter had experienced hundreds of times. And it still scared the juice out of him every time.

Every seat in the helicopter was occupied, a full crew heading home after their work rotation offshore. It was an hour's flight to the shore base in Songkhla, and the men were settling in for the ride. The Thai in the seat next to him was already asleep. But Hunter wouldn't be sleeping. There was no way he could relax long enough on a helicopter to doze for even ten minutes, at least not without the aid of ten milligrams of Valium. He opened his paperback and looked at the words.

The weather was good just after departure, but now and then they'd fly through a puffy cumulus cloud and the aircraft would float upward then down, the rotor seemingly trying to slice through a vacuum. When that happened, Hunter would close the book on his finger and look into the dead whiteness of the cloud, as if looking at it would somehow make it less threatening. He tried not to look at his watch, thinking time would pass faster if he didn't. Only another fifty minutes, that's all he had to endure.

Once you saw the thin line of sandy beach, it was OK. It was like a lifeline reaching out to the chopper; nothing could happen to you then.

Soon the clouds began to pile up. They were dark and menacing now, and big drops of rain started to pelt the windows. The rotor groaned as the helicopter rocked through the gray-black masses. Drops of rain fell from the ceiling and hit his shoulder. What was it that one pilot had told him? *Spend ten thousand dollars on a car and it sure as hell better not leak, but pay ten million dollars for a helicopter and you can be darned sure it will.*

The big machine was rocking like a ship at sea. There was no reading now. Hunter looked through the cabin into the cockpit to watch the pilots. If anything was wrong, surely they would show it; but then again, these guys were so cool they wouldn't break a sweat if they were hitting the water, just push the life raft out the door and grab the beacon. Though Hunter could only see their backs and their hands as they reached for the instruments, they seemed totally nonchalant, chatting to each other through their headsets just as easily as if they were sitting in a bar discussing the stock market.

The aircraft surged up and swooped down. Hunter could see the radar screen between the two pilots. That splotch of green ... was that a storm they had to get through, or was it land?

He looked at his fellow passengers. They were all dozing, except for one young Thai engineer across the aisle who was chewing gum very loudly and staring straight ahead. Then they were slammed downward, as if against something hard. The other passengers were jolted awake. They had entered a full-blown storm now, and the chopper was bucking and yawing through the darkness. Metal groaned inside the cabin and the rotors whined, as if desperate to grab on to something.

He could see nothing out of the rain-streaked window except shades of gray and black. There was no telling how near they were to the water, or even if they were flying level. There was another tremendous surge and fall as the chopper was tossed around like a piece of driftwood at sea. Bodies were jolted side-to-side; the only things keeping them in their seats were their safety belts. No one was sleeping now. There was a buzz in the cabin; even the veteran fliers were nervous.

So this is how it ends? Ditched in the Gulf of Thailand in the midst of a tropical storm. You always think it can't happen to you, but the fact is it has to happen to somebody – and why not you? You end up a statistic, something people read about over their morning coffee, momentarily shudder if they've got half an ounce of humanity in them, before they turn the page to the sports section.

The young man next to him was gripping a Buddha medallion around his neck and mouthing a prayer. Even with his ear plugs in, Hunter could hear somebody vomiting violently behind him. But he wouldn't allow himself to show any fear. Instead he tapped into that blue-white core of rage and anger seething just behind his breastbone. It was all their fault: the ex-wives who'd bled him dry, the company men who thought of nothing except profit and made him work longer hours for less pay; and everyone else along the line who'd trapped him in this hellhole of a job.

There was a sudden peacefulness, as if the engine were cut off and they were drifting toward the final plunge into the sea. *This is it. We're going to hit water.*

He could imagine it all; both sequentially and instantaneously: the helicopter smashes into the sea like it's dropping onto concrete; the electrical system explodes; the fuselage breaks open and huge waves swamp them; panic and screams as all the men fight for air; and then, with a sickening groan, the aircraft capsizes and sinks. And all the helicopter evacuation training you'd done, all those hours in the pool, wouldn't do you a damn bit of good. He felt a dull pain behind in his chest as he held his breath, waiting.

Then suddenly, as if going instantly from midnight to noon, they broke through a gray mist and into a blue, cloudless world. There on the horizon was land: a shiny, narrow golden strip of beach, the lush green interior, the sparkling azure waters of the inland sea gleaming under the tropical sun. The sky was ridiculously blue, a color you saw only on postcards. Sunlight poured into the cabin. They banked over the Red Mountain, where Hunter could make out the ruins of the old Portuguese fort, then floated gently down to the airstrip as if on the back of some huge, mythical, graceful bird.

At the bottom of the metal stairs, Hunter could feel the heat of the tarmac through the soles of his work boots. Despite the queasiness in his stomach and the throbbing in his head, he felt like doing a pope – dropping to his hands and knees and kissing the tarmac. Was there any feeling in the world sweeter than this? Landing safely on solid ground again after twenty-eight days offshore, another twenty-eight days of freedom stretching in front of him like an endless summer. Four full weeks to do whatever he damn well pleased. Fuck until his dick was raw and his balls ached; drink whiskey and smoke ganja until every fear and worry were nothing more than laughable caricatures.

In the busy hangar he retrieved his bag and boarded the company van to go into town. He forced a yawn to pop his ears and then laid his head back on the headrest while he waited for the others to fill the seats. He had entered what he liked to call the dream world: reality for most people, but peaceful and bearable compared to the hyper-reality of life offshore. It was funny how, once away from it, even after only an hour, it was impossible to imagine what things were really like offshore. He felt a heavy weight lift from his shoulders. He could be calm, patiently wait for the others to fill the van; the usual irritation he felt toward his Thai coworkers had melted away.

He found his Walkman in his flight bag, put the felt covered phones in his ears and turned on Willie Nelson. Willie's voice always made him feel sappily sentimental but also dreamily hopeful.

It'll soon be over. I'll never have to get on one of these birds again. I won't need this job, no matter how much it pays. Two more tours offshore, three at the most, and I'll be free of all this. Just a couple more pieces to move and everything will fall into place. All I need is a little luck, and to be able to read the mind of a tenth century Buddhist monk.

It was just in front of him, and so real he could almost touch it: a future full of freedom and promise.

Hunter walked through the front doors of the Songkhla Regent

Hotel and past reception to the phone booths tucked away in a back corridor that led to the restrooms. They were old-fashioned booths with glass and wood doors and wooden paneling. Hunter liked their privacy and the fact they were wrapped in the anonymity of the big hotel. He tapped out the number he'd memorized. A woman answered on the third ring.

"Mr Jack, please."

"Who is calling, please?" Jack's secretary spoke English with an upper-crust British accent, and Hunter had often fantasized about the face and body behind the voice. But he knew he would never see her. Hunter had never been invited into Jack's office, and he was sure he never would be.

"John Hunter." He was made to listen to a synthesized version of *Moonlight Sonata* while he waited.

"Hello, John, it's good to hear from you. Have a good tour offshore? Produced lots of gas to keep our Thai economy running at full speed?" Jack's accent, unlike his secretary's, was unidentifiable, a mixture of British and American, and the first thing Hunter always thought of when he heard it was: *this guy is one sweet faggot.*

"It's good when it's over, Jack."

"Yes, I see. Somewhat like hitting your head against the wall. Do you plan to stay in Songkhla long?"

"Possibly. I have a few things to look into before I go to Singapore. How did everything work out from the last job?"

"Wonderfully. It is a beautiful piece. We found a buyer within a week. And by the way, Toi was so convincing as a monk he was offered food by several people. He was forced to take it to complete the ruse. Came back to the office with enough rice to feed a family of ten. And of course, your not-so-modest little offering as well."

It had all been part of Jack's deviously ingenious plan: transfer the stolen statue as a dawn offering to a fake monk. Hunter had to suppress a grin. The last time he'd seen Toi before their final meeting, he'd been bloodying the Lumpini boxing ring with his ferocious roundhouse kicks, while his pummeled opponent tried desperately to remain standing. But that morning a month ago, he had stood in the dawn light – shaved head, the scorpion tattoo on his hand peeking out from his yellow robes – waiting silently as Hunter passed over the ancient statue hidden in a burlap bag beneath a pile of oranges.

"Your share was deposited as agreed. Have you checked your bank statement?"

"It'll be waiting for me in my mailbox in Singapore. Don't worry, Jack. I trust you."

"How refreshing it is to do business with someone who trusts you. Not like these Mainland Chinese, John, let me tell you. There's nothing more ruthless than a communist turned capitalist."

"So everything went according to plan?"

Jack hesitated. "More or less."

"What do you mean?"

"You don't get much news out there, John, do you?"

"Offshore? Yes, of course we do. We've got satellites. CNN, BBC."

"I was thinking more of local news."

"We get the English language newspapers two or three days late. They're not high priority on the supply boats."

"The guard from our local museum, the man so valiantly protecting our Thai treasures. The one who's been in a coma for the past month. Do you know who I mean, John?"

Now he's toying with me.

"Unfortunate, really. Seems he passed away early this morning. Massive brain injuries. Quite a pity." Jack's voice was calm and even, as if they were talking about an event that had happened five thousand miles away, in some place he'd only read about, like Kenya or Antarctica.

Hunter felt the heat rise in his chest. *Why did the stupid motherfucker have to get in his way?*

"Anything else, Jack?" he asked, keeping his voice steady.

"No, John. Enjoy your vacation."

"Field break, Jack. It's not a vacation, it's a field break."

Hunter walked unhurriedly toward the front door of the hotel. He needed a drink very badly but didn't want to show it. As he passed the front desk, the pretty receptionist smiled at him and he smiled back. Mr John Hunter, with twenty-eight days of a dream world in front of him and not a care in the world.

Seven

Babysitting the hardware. That's what Sturges called it. But when you baby-sat, didn't you occasionally have to feed the baby, or change its diapers, or play with it, or at least make sure it was out of harm's way? But the sailing of the OD-545 took barely any effort on Marek's part, and he began to realize that as long as the power was turned on, there was hardly any need for him to be there at all.

For the first two hours, Marek, like a worried mother, watched his baby as if it would stop breathing at any moment. He stared at the blinking lights on the UPS every ten minutes and ran his fingers across the reassuringly steady digital readouts on the SunSPARC. Once or twice he went outside to look at the transmission towers to make sure they were standing tall and not about to topple over with the slightest breath of wind. Eventually he was satisfied that all the station's equipment wasn't going to betray him, and he started to relax and let the baby have the run of the place.

The afternoon lengthened; Niwat came, nodded confidently over the equipment, and left. The maid cooked chicken curry and rice. He played his guitar, running blues scales up and down the neck. He started a letter to Rachel in his head: "*You wouldn't believe this business. They pay you to sit on the beach and drink beer."* But he knew he couldn't maintain the phony cheeriness for more than a few lines, so he abandoned it.

He dozed in his chair, as through the open channel he listened to the mundane conversation between the rig and the tugs. Then he was suddenly yanked alert by a message directed to him.

"Calling Southern Cross DGPS at Songkhla. Rig move completed. OD-545 secure at Bravo 9. Your signal was continuous and faultless. Well done and cheers until next time. Radio transmission over."

It was after seven by the time Marek finished tapping out the report. He printed off three copies: one for the office file, one for Sturges in Singapore, and one to be sent to the Ocean Drill office in Bangkok. He stapled the reports and put them in the wire basket for tomorrow's trip to the post office. *At least I'm earning my keep,* he thought, even though it hardly took a lick of technical knowledge or skill. He stood and stretched, feeling tautness in his lower back.

He needed to get out of his house and thought about inviting Philips out for a beer, but then remembered Philips had said he'd be busy with some night tutoring this week. He got into the pickup and drove along the quiet beach road, then by-passed the Dark Side, deciding that he didn't want that expat scene tonight. He wanted something different, something more authentically Thai. He remembered that once, with Niwat, he had seen a couple of places along the waterfront, open shophouses where the locals went to drink. He parked on the side street parallel to the jetty and walked along the quiet, dark road. There was a tang of fishmeal and saltwater in the air, and between the warehouses and shops he caught glimpses of the black, oily water of Songkhla Lake.

He went past an old clapboard ice factory and found what he was looking for: a brightly lit shophouse with a jukebox twinkling in one corner and three girls half-dozing at a table. The shophouse was open to the street, and as he stepped into the room, the girls leapt up from the table. One of them grabbed his wrist and the others gently pushed him from behind, all the while giggling, "You! You!" and "OK! OK!" as if these expressions were some kind of greeting. As they led him to a table, a woman poked her head out from behind some faded blue curtains. She had a towel wrapped around her hair and was wearing a striped sarong. She offered him a brilliant smile and said, "Please sit down," before disappearing again.

Marek sat on a low stool at a table in the corner and ordered a Mekhong whiskey. An overhead fan began to whirr. The walls of the shop were painted a sickly bluish-green, and the only other furniture besides the tables and the jukebox was a baby's highchair. Each table had a small plastic vase that held a green and yellow vine. On the back wall was a sign made of cutout foam letters in silver and gold saying "Happy New Year"; a permanent fixture, he guessed, since it was the last day of May.

It took all three girls to bring and arrange his set: a small bottle of Mekhong, a small plastic bucket of ice with tongs, a glass and a bottle of soda water; and when they had finished they crushed in around him and stroked him as if he were a teddy bear.

"What you name?"

"Where you come from?"

"You working Thailand?"

"You holiday?"

At least it was a chance to practice his Thai. He answered their questions, then asked them their names and where they were from. All of them were from Chiang Rai, and this made him think of Maew and her compact body in the tight canary-yellow skirt. *You come see me again at Time Out soon, OK?*

One girl with bangs down her forehead was stroking his right arm while another intertwined her fingers with his left hand. A third was messaging his neck. He bought them all a drink and gave them some coins to play the jukebox.

"What's the name of this place?" he asked.

"Jinda's," they answered in unison.

"And Jinda is?"

"Mamasan," said the one cracking the fingers on his left hand and nodded toward the curtain: the woman with the towel around her head.

The jukebox hummed and crackled. A Thai pop song rattled out of speakers that sounded as if their cones had turned to dry leaves.

"What you name?"

"A-lick," he answered preemptively. They all nodded as if they met 'Alicks' every day.

"Where you come from?"

"America."

"Very good," said the one of them. She gave him the thumbs up sign. "America man good. Good heart." She tapped him on the sternum.

He held up his Mekhong and soda and they all tapped glasses. He decided he liked this place, with its friendly girls and ancient jukebox and five-month old holiday greeting. And the highchair. Especially the highchair. It gave the place a special appeal. Everyone's welcome in this bar, even families.

Suddenly from behind the wall there was a tremendous crash. Something heavy had smashed to the floor in a back room behind the blue curtain. Marek imagined a big piece of furniture crashing down and splintering to bits. There was shouting from the back - a woman's voice and then a man's - but Marek couldn't make out any words.

The girls at the table didn't flinch. They smiled at him without a hint of concern. There were a few more loud thumps against the wall. The wall itself didn't sound very solid and Marek was beginning to think he might see someone or something crashing through it. The girl next to him picked up his drink and held it to his lips. When he took it from her, she tapped her finger to her temple. "Never mind. He crazy farang," she said. "*Baa baa, baw baw.*"

There was another bang against the wall, and this time Marek was sure he heard a dull thud and the crunch of broken plaster. Then he heard a loud *smack* – fist against skin. There was silence and then a pitiful moan that turned his stomach sour.

A large man staggered through the curtains. He had to stoop to get through the doorway and paused for a moment while he untangled the flimsy cloth from around his neck. His head was shaved, and he had shoulders and arms like a bodybuilder. He was wearing an old gray T-shirt with the sleeves cut off at the shoulders, a pair of jeans and running shoes.

A loud wail came from the back room, and then a choking, angry barrage of Thai, broken by more wailing and crying. The man ignored it while he looked around, taking in the girls, Marek, and the jukebox with a dull, drunken gaze. An arrogant smirk flicked across his face. He sucked on a knuckle and looked directly at Marek.

"I told the bitch not to get in my face," he said.

Marek said nothing. The girls around him smiled flatly but wouldn't make eye contact. One forced a yawn.

The jukebox was playing a plaintive Thai love song. The songstress had a soft, ethereal voice but the speakers' buzzing complaints at every other bass note spoiled it. The drunk tilted his head to listen for a moment then took an unsteady step toward the machine. In a sodden, woebegone voice he began to sing along. Or tried to. He didn't know the Thai words but was substituting nonsense English words which, to his mind at least, rhymed with the Thai. He closed his eyes as he crooned along off-key, then stopped after a minute or so. The girls around Marek's table began laughing, humoring him. "Jinda darling," he called to the back room, "they're playing our song."

No sound came from the back. Then the mamasan reappeared. "Shut up," she said as she burst through the curtain. She no longer had the towel on her head and was wearing a denim skirt instead of the sarong. Her face was contorted and red, and there was an angry red welt under her left eye. She looked hard at him.

"You crazy, drunk farang. *Khii maow.* Someday somebody stick a knife in you. Cut off your dick. What you do then? Huh?"

"Aw baby, you'd never do that. You'd lose your good thing." He clutched her around the waist and tried to spin her in a boozy waltz. She yelped and pounded him on the shoulders, then twisted out of his grasp. He flinched, pretending her weak blows had hurt him. Then she shoved him towards a table.

"You gonna fall down. You better sit down first."

"Hey, don't you love me no more?"

"Ha! Nobody ever love you. You crazy drunk fucker." She went into a loud tirade, all of it in Thai. The drunk looked in Marek's direction, rolled his eyeballs into his head and dribbled his lips with his forefinger. The mamasan disappeared into the back room and two of the girls from the table followed her.

The music ended. The big man shrugged his shoulders and sighed. "Shit happens." He tottered to the table and thrust out a huge paw. "John Hunter. Pleased to make your acquaintance. Where you from, my friend?" Marek felt his hand being crushed and heard a knuckle pop. Hunter collapsed into the plastic chair opposite Marek. He stretched out his long legs and his shoes collided with Marek's.

"States."

"Well I'll be damned, another Yank. I get so godawful tired of talking to Brits and Aussies. Brits are the worst though, ain't they? Always lookin' down their snooty noses at you. What the hell. Damn good to meet you. Let me buy you a drink. Get my friend here a drink, would you *thii rak*?"

"That's OK," said Marek. "I've already got one."

"Waddaya got there? Mekhong?" He made a face. "Naw, you don't wanna be drinkin' that shit. Where's my bottle of Cat, for chrissakes?" Without a word the remaining girl jumped up and went behind the makeshift counter. She came back with a half-filled bottle of Golden Cat whiskey with a strip of masking tape on it and the name "John" scribbled on the tape.

He took the bottle and glass from her and poured a few inches, then quickly drank it down. "That's better," he said, wiping his mouth with the back of his hand.

He took Marek's glass and tossed the ice and whiskey on the concrete floor then refilled it from his bottle. "How can you drink that rot gut? You gotta switch to this Golden Cat. Doesn't give you those awful hangovers that make your teeth hurt. Only sell it in Yala province. Jinda smuggles it up especially for me. Go ahead, down the hatch."

Marek drank.

"Beats the shit outta that Mekhong, don't it? How long you been in The Land of Smiles?"

"About a month now."

"Shithole, ain't it?"

"What?"

"I said, it's a lousy fucking shithole of a country, ain't it? Garbage everywhere, stinks like cat piss, men are all lazy and dishonest ..." He raised his voice so he could be heard in the back room. "And the women cheat on you and steal you blind. Ain't that right?"

Marek noticed a fishhook scar across Hunter's nose and wondered what act of violence had caused it. The man's neck, his face, even the tight skin on his bony scalp, seemed to be all tensed muscle and tendon. An unfriendly grin spread across Hunter's face. "Or maybe you like it."

Marek shrugged. "What's not to like?"

The bars of the world were full of guys like this: resentful, drunk, daring some guy to say the wrong thing or look at him the wrong way.

Hunter snorted. "What's not to like?" he repeated with a nasal sneer. "Welcome to Toy Land, the ugly man's paradise. Even the guy who can't get a dog to piss on him anywhere else in the world can get laid every night in this country. That's probably why you like it."

"Probably," said Marek, forcing a laugh, feeling small and defenseless.

Hunter laughed too, sardonically, and then leaned forward and inspected Marek's pants leg. "I'm just looking for the dog piss, but I guess it's all dried up after a month."

"Ha ha!" said Marek weakly, wishing he hadn't felt so adventurous and had just stopped into one of the predictable bars in the southern sector.

"Hell, I won't hold it against you. It's all mind over matter. If you don't mind, it don't matter." Hunter drained his drink and fixed himself another one. "And you know what the best part is?" He leaned forward and with a huge hand gripped Marek behind the neck. He brought Marek's ear to his mouth so that their cheeks grazed. A large Buddhist ornament on a thick gold chain swung out from under his shirt. Even sitting in the chair, he was weaving unsteadily, but Marek could feel the strong, bony fingers digging into his neck and shoulder. His lips brushed Marek's ear and the stink of his breath assaulted Marek's nose as he whispered hoarsely. "There ain't no fucking feminists with hairy armpits to scream about how wrong it all is. No politically correct motherfuckers to say we can't do this, and we can't do that. *'It ain't right. A man can't have a good time and get away with it. Hell no, we won't allow it.'*"

Hunter guffawed and fell back in his chair. "Shit, those women back home, all they want to do is cut off your balls and make a purse out of them. And you know what beats the shit out of me? Even the ugly, fat ones think they can do it."

Hunter raised his glass and leaned back in his chair until the plastic creaked. He took another long drink and grinned hard at Marek. "So what part of the States you from?"

Marek could still feel wetness around his ear where Hunter's lips had touched his skin, but he was afraid wiping it off might provoke Hunter.

"Madison, Wisconsin."

Hunter slapped his head. "Nice to meet you, Madison. Shit, what time is it anyway?"

"Eight thirty."

"Christ, I've been here since three. Time flies when you're having fun. So tell me, what's a guy from the great Mid-West doing in this shithole?"

"Southern Cross Navigation. The DGPS station on the beach, near the big hotel?"

Hunter thought for a moment and then threw his head back and laughed. Marek could see the silver fillings in his molars.

"Oh, yeah, I know all about you mothers," said Hunter. "You guys got the best scam in the whole business. You make these chumps buy your receivers and then you make them buy the radio signal you send them, when, in fact, anybody could buy their own and cut you out completely. Hell, last time I was in Singapore I saw a hand-held GPS receiver for less than 500 Singapore. What do you sell yours for?"

"We don't. We lease them."

"Shit, it's better than I thought! Well come on, friend, how much do you lease it for?" Hunter leaned over the table and poured himself another drink. This time he splashed in some of Marek's soda water and then stirred it with his finger. "Can't tell you. Trade secret." said Marek, forcing a smile. Then he got bold. "Well, I could tell you, but then I'd have to kill you."

Hunter stopped smiling. There was a long dead silence that felt like an eternity. Marek was wondering how he should best brace himself to be hit. But then Hunter's malicious smile reappeared. "What a lot of horseshit."

Marek wanted this to end. He wanted to just stand up and walk out, but that would mean stepping over Hunter's outstretched legs and wedging himself past his big shoulders. He had a bad feeling Hunter wouldn't let him. *Better to just bide your time,* he told himself. Anyway, Hunter was drunk and Marek wasn't. That was an advantage he intended to use in his favor if things got out of hand. He poured more water into his glass to dilute the whiskey.

"Well see, that receiver you buy in Singapore isn't accurate enough. Cause it doesn't have the triangulation, y'know?" said Marek. "Or at least, that's what they tell me. But I don't really know. Like you say, a lot of horseshit. And the fact is, as long as they keep paying me, I don't really care. I'm just along for the ride."

Hunter looked at him with glazed eyes for a long moment, then suddenly threw his arm out for another handshake. "You're all right, Madison. Let's take these fucking oil companies for everything they got."

Marek, feeling like he was out of the woods, began to relax. "What about you?" he asked. "Work offshore?"

"Shit yes," he laughed. "I'm a fucking whore like all the rest of 'em. I sell my services to the highest bidder, in this case EastAsia Oil. Maintenance specialist at the Ratchada field. I just got onshore today. That's why I'm celebrating. Well, that and other stuff." He lifted his glass and gave Marek another razor thin smile. "Lemme tell you, I've got a very special job. My job is to watch over the Thai maintenance guys so they don't fuck up and blow us all to bits. That is, until the day the company decides for the sake of politics that they have to nationalize all offshore positions and replace me with a Thai. Then, of course, the platform will be blown to bits but hey, I guess it's worth it to EastAsia to say they had an all-Thai workforce."

"You on a rotation?"

"Ahuh. Twenty-eight, twenty-eight."

"Nice."

"Yeah, it's nice. Real great." He was shaking his head as if he'd heard something pathetically funny, amusing but in a sad, mistaken way. "Sounds wonderful to guys like you, don't it? Work only six months a year. Sit on your ass for six months. But what the fuck do you know about working offshore? Got any idea what it's like? Last month an oxygen canister exploded because some idiot put grease on the valve. Almost took somebody's leg off. Cranes haven't been inspected in six months, costs too much to fly the inspectors out. Do it later, when the price of oil swings back up. Compressor needs to be replaced because it's run its useful life. Too expensive, just replace a few parts and keep it running for another five hundred hours, just till the end of the shift, then it's somebody else's problem. Some of the piping is so rusted out, you lean against it you fall through. Can't shut down production to replace it, too much loss of product. Complain about it and guess what, you're on the next chopper home. Then there's the storms. You ever been offshore in a tropical depression, Madison? A typhoon?"

Hunter was sweating and his mouth hung open. His eyes were focused somewhere on Marek's chest, as if thinking about where to hit him first.

"No? Didn't think so. Twenty-three years in the oil patch, playing their game, kissing their corporate asses, and what does it get me? If I don't get killed by a well blowout or a gas explosion or a helicopter crash, then I get laid off without pension 'cause the bean counters want to make an impression with the shareholders. Yeah, month on month off. It's fucking wonderful."

A motorcycle backfired in the street and everyone's heads spun toward the noise. Hunter's eyes darted around, and his body tensed as if he was getting ready to fight. There was another loud *bang* and then the motorcycle coughed and sped down the street.

The girl with Marek laughed nervously. Hunter said, "Well, shit." He looked around, confused, his train of thought derailed.

"Goddamn idiots could fuck up a Chinese fire drill." He raised his glass of whiskey and rolled it back and forth across his forehead.

Another girl came from the back to see what the noise was about. The two Thai women spoke to each other and then the second girl broke out a small wet towel from a cellophane wrapper and began dabbing at Hunter's face. "Take it easy, John," she said. "You gonna have heart attack."

"That's exactly what I'm gonna have, honey, but not quite yet." He smiled at the girl and eased back in his chair. The other girl refilled his drink.

The first girl finished scrubbing his face and began working on his hands, twisting the small cloth around each individual finger. "We were talking about offshore, right?" asked Hunter, his voice much softer now. "Let me tell you, my friend, every minute I'm out there I'm trying to figure some way to get off. I got big plans, Madison. Someday I'll tell you all about 'em."

No thanks, thought Marek, taking another drink of water. When the girl was finished cleaning Hunter, she wadded up the *phaa yen* and put it in the unused ashtray. "*Set laew*, John. Now you can sleep."

"Shit no. I ain't sleeping, I'm drinking. With my buddy Madison." Then he straightened in his chair and slapped his head. "Shit, I know what I forgot to do," he said, looking suddenly alarmed. "I forgot to eat! Goddamn if I didn't forget to eat. Jin!" he cried out in the direction of the back room. "Jinda, get your ass out here." He winked at Marek.

After a while Jinda came out from behind the curtain. She said nothing but glared out into the street, not looking at either of the men. She had put some makeup over the bruise under her eye.

"Jin, baby, make us some food. C'mon, me and my friend's hungry. Give us some of that good Thai food. Stir-fried vegetables with pork. Some shrimp maybe. And got any fried chicken? Maybe an omelet. And no goddamn innards," he said, poking at his stomach. "You know what I mean? No guts."

She stood motionless with her arms folded, looking solid and formidable, still staring into the street. Marek wondered if she had even heard what Hunter had said. Then she began moving around the bar tidying things – realigning some glasses behind the counter, moving a chair closer to a table – all the time carrying on a low monologue in Thai, which didn't seem to be aimed at anybody in particular. Her voice carried up and down the scale in a peculiar intonation – different from Marek's study tapes, which were in the Bangkok dialect – so that her voice seemed to carry some great and tumultuous emotions. She left the room and a few minutes later Marek heard the crushing tinfoil sound of frying oil.

"Me and Jin," said Hunter, grinning smugly, "we go back a long way." He took a long, fish-lipped slug of his drink, then smacked his lips. "Oh, we have our ups and downs, but she really loves me. I probably don't deserve her, I'm an asshole at times. Maybe it looks bad to you, but it ain't really. Promise you won't tell my wife."

"Wife?" asked Marek. "Here in Songkhla?"

"Nah, shit no. She's Singaporean. Well, technically speaking, it's ex-wife. Actually, wife number two. But anyway, she got married again and moved to London. She pretty much cleaned me out, but I still got the flat in Singapore. She couldn't touch it because of a technicality. The company gave it to me years ago when they were feeling more generous."

"So you live in Singapore? I mean, when you're off the rig."

"Don't work on a rig. A rig is where they drill. I work on the production platform. Yeah, sometimes I live in Singapore. Got a small place here in Songkhla. You oughta come by some time. And I travel a lot too. Has to do with what I mentioned before. My grand plans to get out of the oil business for good. I'll tell ya all about it someday."

The girl was now sitting behind Hunter and massaging his shoulders. Hunter, who had ignored her until now, suddenly took an interest in her. "What's your name, honey?" he asked.

She said it three times, and each time he repeated it his pronunciation was worse than before. Both girls giggled at his attempts. "It don't matter. Get yourself a drink. And your friend too. Madison, how you doing?"

"I'm OK," he said. But Hunter leaned over anyway and poured out another inch from his bottle.

Marek was about to protest when he was interrupted by the entrance of a group of young Thai men. Four local boys, dressed in torn jeans, T-shirts and flip-flops, entered the shophouse. One, the guy who acted like the leader, had long hair and an earring and was wearing sunglasses. They looked at Marek and Hunter and said something to each other and laughed. "Oh, fuck off." said Hunter, turning his back to them.

"Hey, you!" said the one in sunglasses.

Marek smiled and held up his glass to them. None of the boys looked much older than twenty, if that, and he was pretty sure they didn't understand any English beyond the two words the one kid had just said. They were all thin and wiry, as if they'd been doing hard physical labor but hadn't had much more than subsistence level meals. Marek imagined they had just gotten off a fishing boat after a few weeks at sea, working their hands to the bone on some Gulf trawler.

They settled at a table and ordered drinks. "Hey, you, farang!" repeated the kid in sunglasses. He held up a Mekhong bottle to them as if to offer them a drink. Marek refused, making gestures as if to say he'd had too much already. The Thai rattled on to the others and they laughed again. It probably meant nothing, but even to Marek's ears it sounded like they were being ridiculed.

Hunter smiled and turned to them. "You boys talking about us? Maybe you want to try saying something in English?" He kept a grin plastered on his face and the youths smiled back at him.

Everybody, including Marek and the two girls, were smiling through the uncomfortable charge in the air.

"You look worried, my friend," Hunter said to Marek, his smile bigger than ever. "You think there's gonna be trouble?"

"C'mon, man. They probably just got off a boat. Look at 'em. It'll probably take everything they earned in the last month just to pay for their drinks and women."

"I just don't like them in my face."

"They're just a bunch of kids trying to have a good time. Ignore them. They'll forget about us."

"These people, they're just always in your face. I really don't like it when someone gets in my face."

Just then the food arrived: two steaming plates of rice, a plate of fried mixed vegetables, some grilled shrimp, and an omelet that completely filled a plate. Hunter rubbed his hands together and then began piling vegetables, shrimp and pork on his rice and shoveling it into his mouth. "Help yourself, Madison," he said with his cheeks puffed out and his mouth full of food.

The girls were all in motion now. More had come from the back room to join the table of fishermen. Another had started making new selections at the jukebox. Two stood over Hunter and Marek's table, making sure they had everything they wanted. Hunter, meanwhile, had lost interest in everything except the food. He ate quickly and greedily, his silverware clanging against the china, completely self-absorbed. Marek ate only a little, partly because he wasn't very hungry, but also because he was wary of getting in Hunter's way.

When the last grain of rice had been swept off his plate, Hunter neatly set his fork and spoon on the plate and leaned back in his chair, his hands folded behind his head. He belched.

"That's more like it," he said. He picked at his teeth with a toothpick and stared contemplatively at the wall behind Marek. The fishermen, meanwhile, were having their own party with the girls. It looked like the time to make a move. Marek got up and stepped over Hunter's outstretched feet.

"Where you goin', man?"

"Take a leak."

He would take care of that and then walk out, calling out some excuse to Hunter like he had to get back to work.

In the narrow hallway to the left of the curtain, Jinda stood in the cramped kitchen. Her hair was pulled back and she was watching over a pan of sizzling oil. In her left hand she held a hand towel filled with ice against her cheek.

"*Hong nam?*" asked Marek. She nodded toward a door to his right. There was another room, Marek noticed, and through the partially opened door he could see the corner of a small bed, the sheets mussed up. A wardrobe lay on the floor, women's clothes spilling out. When he came out of the toilet Jinda asked, "You know him long time?"

"Just met him today."

She nodded. She was cracking an egg into the pan. The wall shuddered with the thumping bass of the jukebox. "He not bad man 'cept sometime drink too much." She was wearing a gold bracelet and a gold chain, and it occurred to him these were probably gifts from Hunter.

Back at the table Hunter was passed out, his large bullet head resting on his folded arms. The girl with the bangs was clearing the plates off the table.

"Happen all the time", she said. "You still want your Mekhong?"

"No, save it for next time." He gave her a 500-baht note. "Dinner and drinks are on me."

Each fisherman now had his own girl and they were all wearing bleary-eyed, happy-drunk faces and talking in loud, free voices, gleeful to be on dry land. Hunter was out cold, beyond the reach of their voices or the angry bass of the jukebox. Marek noticed the back of his shaven head had dents in it, concave dips that looked like they were made with a ball peen hammer.

Marek said goodbye to the girls and just as he was about to

turn and walk out the front, Hunter grunted, and with his head still down raised his right hand from the table.

"Yo Madison!" The voice was slow, coming from deep in his stupor. "Don't forget. We Yanks gotta stick together."

The air outside the bar still stank of seawater and fish, but Marek breathed it with the relief of a man freed from a dungeon. When he reached the pickup, he heard something like a chair toppling over and the quick scuffle of feet on the concrete floor. He got into his truck and sped away.

Eight

Marek and Philips were in the station pickup on the road to Hat Yai, heading for the Pink Lady massage parlor. "It's a tradition," Philips had said. "Jimmy and I used to do it at least once a month, usually the Saturday after the first payday, like today. I figured it was time you had a looksee at the joint. Southern Thailand's own little version of Sodom and Gomorrah. You'll love it."

They rolled down the windows of the Toyota pickup to catch the cooling night breeze. Marek, forced to raise his voice to be heard over the road noise, told Philips the story of his run-in with John Hunter.

"Can't say I know the guy," said Philips, tapping his front teeth as if it helped his recall. "Sounds like a well-balanced guy. Chip on both shoulders. You sure he smacked his old lady?"

"Definitely. She had a welt the size of a golf ball."

"Real ladies' man, eh?"

"Said Thailand was a shithole; for losers who couldn't get laid anywhere else."

Philips shrugged. "Sounds like a real wanker. Most of the guys I know who work in oil, man, they tell some real horror stories about places like Libya or Iran or Nigeria. They'd bribe somebody to get an assignment in Thailand."

"I thought he was gonna pick a fight with some locals."

"He's lucky he didn't. They would've all jumped him and he'd have ended up in the hospital with some serious knife wounds or worse."

The Pink Lady was a five-story "entertainment complex" in the middle of the crowded downtown of Had Yai. They entered the first floor from the car park side entrance and walked past a coffee shop and snooker room to the stairs that led to the second floor. At the foot of the stairs there was a display of soft focus photographs of dozens of massage girls. "I've never seen any of these girls here," said Philips.

They walked up the carpeted steps to what Philips called "the fishbowl". One half of the second floor was a reception area for customers, with a counter and cash register, hostesses, and vinyl chairs and sofas. The other half was a glass-partitioned enclosure where the girls, dressed in formal gowns and wearing numbered badges, sat on a terraced platform; some of them watching television, some working hard to make meaningful eye contact with potential customers; one, Marek noticed, was knitting.

A middle-aged woman wearing lots of gold and makeup greeted Philips by name and started conversing with him in Thai. Philips, apparently an established patron, chatted with the mamasan and intermittently mouthed greetings to the girls behind the glass. One of them blew him a kiss.

"The ones with the red numbers," he explained, "are the Tora Tora girls. You pay twelve hundred baht and that includes everything."

"Everything?"

"Yeah, everything. Bath, massage, all the extras. As much as you can fit in in ninety minutes."

The mamasan smiled at Marek and repeated, "Ev–a–ly–ting."

"The ones with the blue numbers go for an hour. And then you negotiate in the room for whatever else you want. I mean, besides the standard massage."

But Alex didn't even know what a standard massage was, nor did he ask, afraid Philips and the mamasan would see him as hopefully dense and inexperienced.

Around them was a swirl of motion. Customers, Asian and western men, were making their selections. A receptionist spoke a girl's number into the intercom and the girl would disappear out of the back of the glassed-in room. A few minutes later she'd reappear through a side door in the reception area, and the new couple would enter the elevator to be conveyed to the "massage room" upstairs.

Marek wondered how he could explain any of this to people back in Madison or Chicago. Even Rachel, who had a healthy appreciation of sex and enjoyed it every chance she got – and who also showed a curious fascination with the prostitutes on Rush Street – even she would have a hard time with this. Why? Was it that women were being used purely as objects of men's pleasure? Or was it the soulless calculations of a business transaction: money for pleasure? Shouldn't there be something more to it? Maybe the problem was him: his Midwest, Catholic upbringing, preventing him from enjoying something as natural as sex without guilt eating away at his conscience. There would have to be punishment later; or perhaps God would just strike him dead now.

At any rate, no one else in the room, not the other customers, nor the mamasan, nor the girls smiling and flirting behind the glass wall seemed to share his apprehensions. *Welcome to Toyland, the ugly man's paradise.*

And now, standing in front of a room full of virtually captive women, Marek couldn't help but feel a pang of self-consciousness. It was as if everybody in the room – the girls, the hostesses, even the other customers – could see right through him; through his clothes, his skin, his bones, and see a heart devoid of everything except a kind of languid lust; nudged awake by the urgings of his friend and the fact it was just after payday. There was no subtlety here. Everybody knew why he was here and what he was after. He could see the girls tittering and making side comments to each other and he began to feel that *he* was the one in the fishbowl.

Philips, of course, felt no such embarrassment. "If you're a tit man, you couldn't go wrong with number 243," he said. But Alex wasn't a tit man, nor an ass nor a leg man – not that he didn't like certain combinations of those various parts. But if he was anything, he was an *eyes* man; and feeling increasingly abashed as he stood in front of the team of overdressed hookers while the attendant receptionist bent forward ever so slightly to take his request, quickly chose a girl with friendly eyes. It was only after he'd picked her that Alex noticed she wore a red badge: she was an "ev-a-ly-ting" girl.

You paid before you went upstairs, and after the girl at the desk rang up your bill, she handed you a receipt, all very businesslike. Convenient, Alex thought, if you needed to itemize your expenses at the end of the month. *Let's see, total monthly fees for prostitution...*

"See you in the coffee shop downstairs after," said Philips, still pondering his selection, as Alex and his girl, who looked like she was dressed for the 1978 Senior High Prom, made their way to the elevator.

The room upstairs was Gomorrah slightly frayed at the edges. A light switch didn't work, the mirror behind the bed was tarnished, and there was a rust stain in the bathtub where the water dripped. While the girl filled the tub, Alex flipped through the channels of the in-house television: Thai soap operas and Japanese porn. When he turned around she was no longer in her dress but was wrapped tightly from armpit to mid-thigh in an oversized towel.

Her name was Ann, and she seemed much shorter now that she was out of her gown and heels. While they waited for the tub to fill, they sat on the edge of the bed, Alex feeling like he was on a blind date, not knowing where to start. They compared hands, his palms nearly twice the size of hers, then they compared feet and leg length, and with each measurement she giggled in awe and pounded her fist on his thigh as if she had never seen anything so funny. She had muscular legs and a splayed toe way of walking, and when Alex watched her cross the room to dim the lights he had an overpowering image of her in the middle of a rice field, her face shielded from the fierce sun by a wide-brimmed straw hat, stepping gingerly for fear of snakes, bending over to thumb the paddy into the soft mud.

She unwrapped her towel to join him in the overflowing tub, revealing a soft roll of baby fat around her tummy and a thin scar, a microshade darker than her skin color, going from her naval to her pubic hair. She had breasts like small birds and nipples the color of an apple bruise.

"How old?"

"Twenty-four."

He was going to ask about children but stopped himself.

Her eyebrows were thin penciled lines. She had a sprinkling of freckles across her nose and cheeks, and when she smiled small parenthesis-shaped dimples formed around the sides of her mouth.

"You from Chiang Rai?" he asked.

"No, Udorn, Isaan. You know Isaan?" She giggled. "Same same Lao."

Once the bathing started she became all business, frowning as she scrubbed his fingernails with a stiff brush, ordering him to turn so she could lather up his back. Alex felt as if he were watching himself from a distance, outside of the event, waiting to see what would happen next, waiting for the next experience to wash over him and lead him someplace else. He was curious in an objective, scientific way about how one thing led to another, how they got from here to the inevitable.

She had him sit in the tub again so she could wash his legs. She put his heel on her shoulder and with both hands soaped from his toes to as far up his leg as her arms could reach, which was not much past the knee, while he tried in vain to resist the tingling of his skin. She saw he was ticklish and became kittenish and playful, dropping the soap and letting her hands explore everywhere underneath him as she tried to find it; laughing at his absurd hypersensitivity to a stranger's touch.

She dried him off with a king-size towel and he discovered he had to urinate. When he came out from behind the curtained toilet, she frowned at him and made him wash himself off in the tub. She was again wrapped in the towel. She pointed to the king-size bed and once he was lying down continued to dry him. Her movements were practiced, professional, intending to arouse only in an offhand way – an accidental brush here, an excuse-me bump there.

He felt time moving. He began to think he would spend the entire hour and a half with nothing to tell Philips about except an exotic bath and a nearly fully clothed massage. The "ev-a-ly-ting" the hostess had promised surely meant more than that. His masseuse must have sensed what he was thinking.

"What you want?" she asked, her frank smile devoid of deceit or coyness, seemingly wanting nothing but the chance to please.

Everything, he thought, but said, "Ah ... massage?"

She laughed, and it was almost as if she were laughing at his inexperience.

"Massage, yes, I know." She knelt on the bed and removed her towel. Her small breasts, the soft turn of her shoulder, her slender arms, the puff of fat around her midsection; he marveled at her body. Touching her was an act of wonder and discovery as much as an act of desire. He could feel her breath on his face as he strummed her bony spine. Then, from a tiny handbag on the side table, she brought out a cylinder that looked like a tube of toothpaste or hand lotion. With both of her hands squeezing the tube she applied a layer of cool, ticklish gel up and down his body: across his chest, on his nipples, down each leg to his toes, around his waist and crisscrossing his genitalia. Then she screwed the top back on, laid the tube on the side table, and smiled at him so that the parenthesis dimples appeared.

The jelly was buzzing on his skin. It was part of the massage; she was going to rub it in, and it would make his skin and muscles feel all warm and tingly, like liniment you apply after a run, he thought.

So naturally he was utterly astounded when she smiled, gracefully bent over him, and began licking it off.

Nine

"What you think about that, Mr Aleck?"

"Huh? What did you say?"

Niwat's voice had been background noise to Marek's daydream, but he hadn't focused on a word the man had said. They were driving out to the deep-sea port to install a receiver and Marek, on this faultless morning, was imagining himself sitting on the floor of a thatch-roofed bungalow, a cool offshore breeze coming through the open door and Ann from the Pink Lady massaging his neck and teasing him about drinking too much beer, while the perfectly blue sea kissed the sparkling shore and the trees dropped coconuts full of sweet milk on their door step.

"I say, what you think about one man kill another man just for a Buddha statue?"

Marek sighed, reality invading his Gauguin fantasy. "The statue from the museum, you mean?" They were crossing the second Prem bridge and the view was dazzling: green forested hills on the island, the glistening waters of the inland sea beneath them, red and gold fishing boats heading out to open waters and, beyond the narrow strip of the peninsula, the deep blue of the Gulf of Thailand. He had to admit, even reality looked pretty good today.

"Yeah, from the museum. That guy who stole it hit the guard on the head hard, or knock him down, I dunno. But after one month in hospital that guard dead already. Just for some statue."

"*The Bangkok Post* said it was worth a lot of money. People kill for money all the time."

"Same same in America?"

"They kill you for a pack of cigarettes in America. Murder you for the change in your pocket."

Niwat laughed. "Crazy world, huh? But that man who steal from museum, he gonna have all kinds of shitty bad luck. Especially now that the guard die. I'm very glad I'm not him."

The security guard at the port gate inspected their passes and then went to the phone inside the booth.

"Security very strict here now," said Niwat. Government say people smuggling drugs or something."

The guard returned, unsmilingly handed the passes back and waved them through. They followed the directions to the berth number the captain had given them and parked the pickup between yellow lines adjacent to the access lane. The ship's name – *The Straits Victory* – was painted in white across the weather-beaten prow. It rocked in the water, seemingly vacant, but by the time they had gotten the equipment out of the back, a deck hand had appeared to help them.

The *Straits Victory* was a crew boat, used to carry supplies and men out to the rigs and platforms of EastAsia. Niwat explained that the men who rode the boat were usually Thais and other Asians – contractors, common laborers – too low in the pecking order to be given seats on the helicopter and having to settle instead for a gut-tossing eight-hour sea voyage. The boat had a long open deck for carrying cargo and, below, a bow-to-stern room furnished with benches and folding chairs lined up in front of a television, which sat atop a tall cabinet like a shrine.

The wheelhouse smelled of stale cigarette smoke, but Marek was impressed by its tidiness. Nothing – not a sheet of paper, not a ballpoint pen, not a paper clip – was out of place; and all surfaces were polished to a dull shine.

The captain was a burly, taciturn, Louisiana man named Beauchamps. He was working a crossword puzzle and chain-smoking Thai cigarettes, and after introducing them to the ship's electrician, he ignored them. The cheerful Filipino electrician was named Eddie. He knew much more about electronics than Marek and Niwat put together but was kind enough not to make it obvious. He was crazy about basketball and talked non-stop about Michael Jordan and the Chicago Bulls.

Marek was happy to let Eddie and Niwat do all the work. After it was finished and they had tested the signal, Eddie invited them down to the small mess where they drank coffee and spent twenty minutes discussing Chicago Bulls' basketball. After readily agreeing they were the best team in the NBA, Marek made his way back upstairs to find the captain and have him sign off the work.

"You're all set," said Marek, nodding toward the display. The big captain placed his cigarette in the polished glass ashtray – he must have cleaned it every time he finished another cigarette – and took Marek's clipboard. He tilted his head to see through the bifocal lenses and signed the top three sheets. His breathing was labored, as if he'd just walked up three flights of stairs.

"I dunno," he said in a gravelly bass voice. "It's a durn pretty machine and all, but y'know I made it all the way from Hawaii to Singapore using a hand-held Magellan I bought in Hong Kong." He said it without smiling.

Marek took the clipboard and shrugged. "Probably pretty soon we'll be wearing these things on our wrists."

* * *

Work began to pick up, and Marek saw little of Philips in the following weeks. There was another rig move, and then a pipeline inspection.

Sturges called one afternoon in mid-June and Marek could tell he was pleased about all the new work coming in, and only too happy to share good news with him.

"Ocean Drill were quite pleased with the report you did up for them. All the colors, the graphs, numbers of rig moves this quarter compared to last, et cetera, et cetera. I must say, it was impressive. Jimmy never did half anything like that."

"Blind 'em with science is my motto," said Marek. "Computers are good at that."

"Excellent. Keep up the good work. Oh, and there's more good news. The Thai Communications Authority has contracted a Belgian firm to lay fiber optic cable down the Gulf Coast, from Samut Prakan to Narithiwat. Our man in Europe is holed up with the Belgians and preliminaries look good. It'll mean a three-month contract for us, at least, if it comes through. Keep your fingers crossed."

"I will."

"Aye! And there's something else. But keep this one under your hat." Sturges was whispering now, and the quality of his voice changed, as if he were cupping his hand around the mouthpiece. "Rumor has it EastAsia's geomancers ..." it was Sturges' little joke, how he liked to refer to geophysicists, "... have indications of a big find north of their Ratchada field. *Very* big." Marek wondered why he was whispering, and who in the Singapore office he wouldn't want to know about it, since presumably everybody was on the same team. "Bigger even than the Ayuthaya field. Y'know what that means, laddie? Drilling, construction, wellhead platforms, production platforms, living quarters ... enough to keep us busy for years."

"That's great, Brian."

"But as I say, mum's the word. And if you hear anything around town, let me know."

With each new assignment Marek felt himself being drawn closer into the tightly knit club of Big Oil. He had no power, made no decisions, and his income would have been laughed at by the men who were in anything like an important position, but he nonetheless felt a little thrill that they would let him join. If he could keep them happy with his steady, reliable, continuous triangulated signal – and throw pretty charts at them now and then – then maybe they would let him stay for a while.

They moved their rigs whenever they had to and drilled their wells when they could. It meant that Marek would sometimes have to stay up all night monitoring the equipment. He passed long hours leafing through one of the hard-edged detective tales or absurd science fiction sagas he'd found in the cardboard box in the closet, part of him tuned in to the sounds of the radio, ready to jump at the slightest hint of trouble with the signal. Sometimes he slept all day; sometimes he had to set the alarm for three o'clock in the morning; and once he was awakened at 4:30 a.m. by a phone call from a panicky South Korean barge captain who couldn't raise a signal. The city power was out – had apparently been out for hours – and the UPS units were drained. Marek, with the help of the night guard and a flashlight, had to manually start up the generator in the shed.

He felt no regret at the loss of a normal working day. Instead, he relished his odd hours and the edgy sense of spontaneity and unexpectedness of the job. You worked when you had to and took your fun where you could get it.

It was nearly July now and sometimes, when he'd lie in bed waiting for sleep to overtake him, he'd think about last year's Fourth of July celebration in Chicago, the one he and Rachel had gone to. It was their first real date. They'd known each other only a week or so, and he had hardly even touched her. It was the city's celebration on the lakeshore. They were eating bratwursts slathered with horseradish mustard and drinking draft beer from plastic cups. A sudden cloudburst caught everyone by surprise and with no shelter to run to, they ended up getting soaked to the skin. They went to his apartment because it was closest. He gave her a big beach towel and one of his T-shirts and went to make coffee in the kitchen. He was grinding the coffee beans when she came out of the bedroom, dropped her towel and wrapped herself around him. Her hair was still wet, her skin smelled delicious.

He'd read that there were holy men in India who through

the power of meditation could reverse the action of the cilia in their intestines. He, on the other hand, could not even distract himself long enough to stop this one image from seeping into consciousness and overwhelming him: the aroma of ground coffee engulfing them; her slippery, goosebumpy flesh; Rachel lifting one wet naked thigh to wrap her leg around him.

If he had an afternoon free, he'd drive into town, check for mail at the post office, pick up the newspapers, and buy groceries and any supplies he needed. One day, stooping to get the mail out of his post office box, he glimpsed a tall blond man out of the corner of his eye. The man's hair was so light and short that for a moment he appeared to be bald. It startled him; his mind flashed on the drunken, belligerent John Hunter. In this case the blond man wasn't anybody he knew, but after that he found himself wary every time he went into to town. He'd scan the heads of the crowd in the market before crossing the street, or pause at the entrance to the supermarket, looking as far into the aisles as he could for any other westerners or shift his gaze from side to side as he slowly drove through the congested inner sois. He counted back the days to when he'd met Hunter in Jinda's. Didn't he say he was on a month on, month off rotation? Or was it twenty-eight, twenty-eight? Wouldn't he be back offshore by about now? And anyway, didn't he say he spent his field break in Singapore? Or was it sometimes in Singapore, sometimes in Songkhla?

If he went into town at night, he avoided Jinda's. He had no desire to replay that scene with the unpredictable, loutish Hunter. Instead he stuck to the usual expat places, the southern and northern sectors, where he was fairly certain that even if Hunter did show up, he would be easier to avoid.

Sometimes he went out with Philips, but due to Marek's unpredictable schedule, he was more often alone. He usually went to the quieter places where he could share a drink with a girl and practice his Thai (by now he had worked his way through the complete set of tapes from the *Conversational Thai* course). He began to see that rumors about work offshore were the conversational lubricant of the Songkhla bar scene, and second in popularity only to the more private who-was-sleeping-with-whom gossip.

"Y'heard about the new find by EastAsia?" The speaker was a Scot who worked on one of the ships that laid detonation cables for exploration teams. He was a short man in a dirty T-shirt and loose shorts, barely coming up to Marek's eye level, even though he was standing and Marek was sitting on a stool.

Marek, not wanting to betray Sturges' confidence, shook his head.

"Aye! A major, major find. Natural gas. No one knows about it yet. Lots of drilling and construction work coming up, they say." His fingers twisted a strand of long, oily hair. "This town'll be jumping very soon, I reckon. Welcome to Boomtown." He rubbed his hands together and grinned, showing Marek a set of yellowish teeth.

"I heard it ain't gas, it's crude," said someone else. "But it's loaded with H_2S. It'll cost a pretty penny to get that out safely, and they don't know if they want to spend it."

"That's a load of shit," said a third man, inexplicably wearing a hard hat. "It's the same fault line as the Ratchada field. How could it be oil? It's got to be gas."

"Anyway, the market's down. They don't want to make the investment just yet."

"The market's not down, it's up! Or it will be soon. That's why they're gonna go for it."

"I heard from the chief engineer ..."

"... I saw the fax myself ..."

"... I know a guy in the head office, and he says ..."

And so on. Marek followed as closely as he could but decided in the end he'd have nothing concrete to report to Sturges the next time he called.

The one bar – besides Jinda's – Marek hadn't gone to lately was the Time Out. It wasn't that he was avoiding Maew; he really *did* want to see her again and would have relished another night on the town with the fun-loving little bombshell. He had put off going back to see her because, even though she'd said she didn't want anything from him, he felt like he still owed her money and he couldn't think of a delicate way of giving it to her. How would one do it? Slip a folded 500-baht note into her palm when you shook hands? Sneak it into her jeans' pocket when she gave you a welcoming hug? And what would happen if she were too prideful to accept it? He could imagine a big, uncomfortable scene.

But in the end – no matter what he tried to tell himself about his noble intentions – it was lust that got the better of him. He wanted another chance with her, and this time he'd do it right – none of this getting too drunk to perform. Anyway, he had promised her he'd come back and see her, hadn't he? That was over a month ago. He would quickly figure out what to do (and whether to pay her anything or not) when he saw her and talked to her.

But she wasn't there. At least she wasn't up front, tending bar. He sat nursing a Heineken while two big guys at the end of the bar threw dice from a padded cup. Kenny Rodgers sang quietly in the background. The two men played dice without saying a word; the only sound between them was the muffled noise of the dice being shaken and the crack against the wooden bar as the cup slammed against it.

Marek finished his first beer and ordered another, hoping that Maew would come strutting through the back door at any minute, throwing back her long hair with a toss of her head, apologizing for being late, and then showing surprise and pleasure when she saw him. But halfway through the second beer she still hadn't appeared.

"Yaa-oo-laa!" cried out one of the fat men as he banged the cup against the bar.

The mirror behind the bar was covered with stickers from scores of oil services companies. There were logos from drilling contractors, pipeline construction outfits, helicopter services, logging companies, and even navigation aids services (Marek eventually spotted the blue and white Southern Cross insignia). "*When it's time to make hole, it's time to call GulfDrill*", said one. "*Let us swab out your hole today*", said another.

The barmaid sat leafing idly through a newspaper. She was in her forties maybe, with her hair pulled back into a bun, and looked like she had put up with about as much shit as she ever wanted to with customers in bars. Marek caught her eye and smiled, but she didn't smile back.

"Maew here today?" he asked hopefully.

She looked at him as if she were deciding whether or not he deserved an answer, then said, "Maew not here."

"Not here now? She coming in later?"

The barmaid looked around to the two men playing dice.

"She ain't comin' in later, no," piped up the bigger of the two guys. "She done run off and got married and left me short of staff," he said without taking his eyes from the dice game.

"Married?"

"Yup. Some guy came in and swept her off her feet. Or at least threw a lot of money in her general direction, but I guess that's the same thing." He looked at Marek with a deadpan expression of irony, a round head on a big round body, a horseshoe of silver hair, rheumy eyes above yellowish-dark pouches. "Where was that guy from anyway? Austria? Germany? Belgium? One a them places. Far as I know Maew's at this moment walkin' around in wooden clogs and puttin' her finger in a dike someplace. No pun intended."

"That'd be Holland," said the other dice player.

"Hanh?"

"That's Holland where they got them dikes and shit. Don't you know nothin'?"

"Whatever. Alls I know is she used to bring in more customers than a bitch in heat and then she ups and leaves. There oughta be a law. C'mon Noah, judgment day. Let 'em roll."

The dice crashed against the bar; end of conversation. Marek paid his bill and left.

Driving back to the station, he couldn't help but think about Maew, the Too-Hot-for-Songkhla little Miss Cat with her prosthetic nose and probably breasts too; and of course, her fun-loving, free-spending streak – at least if it were someone else's money. He tried to picture her on the streets of Oostende or Dusseldorf, heads spinning as she causally sauntered through the Wednesday market, picking out apples and turning her nose up at the smelly cheeses, her jeans as tight as a second skin.

Who could blame her? It was what anybody did, given the right circumstances. You threw your lot in with the first person that came along and offered you a better deal. It wasn't so different from what he'd done with Mr Brian Sturges in a bar in Singapore. Everything else took a back seat when desperation – or maybe in Maew's case, survival – got behind the wheel.

He sent a silent goodwill wish to Miss Cat, wherever she was, a benevolent thought-prayer only slightly tinged with regret; and then he turned on to the beach road and made his way home through the moonless night.

Ten

Yellow ink from a highlighter pen traced the coast from Surat Thani to Pattani, a buttery, unbroken measurement of Hunter's futility, drawn to scale. The map had been folded and unfolded so many times the creases were beginning to tear, just like the last thin membranes of his worn out hope. The months of searching, the days of library research, the frenetic travelling; all were beginning to seem utterly pointless.

Of course he was nuts. Fucking insane. How else could you explain this obsession with an ancient temple that maybe did, but probably did not exist? All those years offshore had finally gotten to him. The monotony, the danger, the helicopter rides, the storms, the toxic fumes, the electromagnetic waves … He had worked on those platforms for so long, and was so desperate to find a way off, that he was fantasizing the existence of something that was merely a tall tale from a travelling tenth century Buddhist monk. Or maybe this Temple of the Glorious Dawn really *did* exist, but it wasn't in Thailand at all. Maybe it was in what was now Malaysia, or perhaps some part of the Sumatran coast, or even some other mountainous coast a thousand miles away in the long dead, far-flung littoral empire of Sri Jiraya.

He lit a cigarette and paced the room. It was always like this when it was time to go back offshore, the world closing in on him. He could feel the pressure building in his ears and behind his eyes; soon the headaches would start, the unexplained flutters behind his rib cage occurring more frequently. Sometimes he would wake up in the middle of the night with his heart racing. Then he thought he was going to die, just like his father, the wall of the heart chamber exploding in his chest.

During the last week he had drunk more than ever, and the hangovers began piling up one against another so that his nerves became so raw and exposed he could barely concentrate on a comic strip. He had to rein in his frustration, or he would start clamoring like a madman at every motorcyclist or damn fool who jumped the queue at the bank. And all because in a few short days he'd be sealed inside the fuselage of the Sikorsky 61, silently screaming to get out, and carried out to the Ratchada Alpha platform like a piece of rusting, obsolete equipment.

He looked out to the crowded market below his window and something about the movement down there made him feel suddenly exhausted, as if every last ounce of energy had been sucked out of him. He had awoken at 4:30 that morning in Singapore and was unable to sleep another minute, though he was too tired to raise himself from the bed. He had flown to Had Yai on the midday flight, the shakes so severe he couldn't hold his cup out to the flight attendant, afraid he'd slosh boiling coffee all over his neighbor. And though he had left Singapore with the exhilarating rush from a suddenly burgeoning bank account – a result of Jack's pay-off for the statue stolen from the museum – as soon as he touched down in Thailand, that feeling was replaced by the depressing inevitability of the ticking clock.

Now it was dusk and the sun was easing behind the old Portuguese fort on Khaw Daeng. Even the ugly, trashed-out market was filled with a soft golden-orange light. Beyond the market, the whitewashed walls of the Songkhla museum stood in silence. It had been closed since the robbery. Hunter looked at it and felt the anger stirring in his gut. Somehow he had once again been betrayed by circumstances. He had planned it all so well, thought out every step, and yet it was like the gods at the last moment had pulled out the rug from under him. He had somehow managed to drop his flashlight. And then that stupid, bumbling guard Poncho got in his way. It made his blood simmer: a perfect crime nearly ruined by an idiot. He was sure that somewhere God or Satan, or probably both, were laughing at him.

But there was only rage and no regret, and if he thought about it long enough something else: relief. *Better you than me, Poncho.* And anyway, taking out Poncho had brought one very positive result – it had proved to Jack just how serious Hunter was. He now had his respect; he could hear it in the way Jack talked to him. Of course, that was the whole reason for the thievery to begin with; Poncho's demise had just added an extra layer of gravity.

He jabbed out his cigarette and turned back to the map. It was time to get serious again, to concentrate on the one flimsy lifeline he had to get him out of this life forever.

Maybe it was here, below the sweeping cape of Pattani, where the hills nudged close to the sea, where someone with a bit of imagination in an approaching ship could see, or imagine they saw, the white rump of an elephant high above the forested hills.

Still three days before he had to report to the hangar. He had time for one more reconnaissance before he went offshore, but where should he look? He stared hard at the map, as if he could force it to give up its secrets. But maybe he was trying too hard. There were times when you could see things better if you didn't look directly at them, like certain stars in the night sky. And sometimes, when you weren't looking for something at all, it came up and slapped you in the face.

That was how it had been with this thing from the beginning, whispering at him from a book he had never intended to read. Six months ago, with three hours to kill before he had to get to Kennedy, Hunter had found himself killing time in the New York public library. A title in the Southeast Asia section caught his eye: *Lost Civilizations of Ancient Siam*. He had little interest in the subject matter; he was only looking for something, some trivial fact or bit of esoteric information, that he could use to shut up Samuel Jenks, the angular, pipe-smoking maintenance foreman who, at every evening meal during the twenty-eight day shift, pontificated over the mess hall dinner table. He always tried to impress everyone within earshot with his deep and multi-faceted knowledge of Thailand. He was such a bloated asshole; Hunter would have gladly paid good money for one tidbit of information that would upstage him in front of the whole crew.

He didn't find any ammunition in the library book, but what he found was something else. It was a description by a tenth-century Chinese monk named I-Chi'ang; words that since that first day in the library he had read perhaps a hundred times and knew almost by heart.

After a week's journey from Palembang we approached the shore at dawn, on calm seas. The temple glowed in the morning rays with a golden, heavenly light. It is situated at the base of a towering limestone cliff, near the top of a mountain that the local monks call 'White Elephant', due to the fact that the shape and coloring of the limestone make it appear to be the rear legs and rump of an elephant. The temple itself is not visible from shore, as at that point you are too close to the base of the mountain and the thick forest prevents you from seeing it. It can only be seen when one is some way out at sea and the angle of sight is more favorable.

We were guided by local priests on a half-day's strenuous climb to reach the temple. This temple, and the village around it, have become the home to many pilgrims, and the artisans and craftsmen who live there have perfected their art and produce some of the most remarkable bronze statuary in the whole empire.

It is with good reason that they call the temple, in their local language, The Temple of the Glorious Dawn.

The author of the book, a professor of Asian Studies at Cornell, wrote that I-Chi'ang was describing a temple of the Sri Jiraya dynasty, which had spread across what is now Indonesia, Malaysia and southern Thailand, and controlled the shipping lanes of the Sunda Straits and the Straits of Malacca. It had extensive political, religious and commercial contacts, trading with India, China and Persia. Professor Nichols went on to say that little was known about the Sri Jiraya Empire – there was even hot debate about where its capital was located – though it ruled the area from 650 AD to 1290 AD, before finally being subordinated by the kingdoms of China and northern Thailand. Eventually, virtually all traces of the dynasty disappeared when Indonesia, Malaysia and southern Thailand were converted to Islam in the thirteenth century. Sri Jiraya was an empire, wrote Nichols, that, though it lasted longer than the Roman Empire, still remained shrouded in mystery.

Professor Nichols noted, almost as an afterthought, that the Temple of the Glorious Dawn was thought by some to be in modern day southern Thailand, though it had never been located, and had never been mentioned by any contemporaries of I-Chi'ang. Many scholars thought that the temple was a fabrication. But if so, Nichols wrote, it would have been quite out of character for I-Chi'ang. Everything else he'd written about had been confirmed by later scholars, and his credibility was thought to be unassailable.

Hunter found a free carrel and sat down with the book clutched between his hands. The more he read, the more intrigued he became. Just to think of it: an undiscovered ancient temple right in his own backyard, maybe within a hundred miles of where he got on and off the chopper every month. One brick from such a place would probably be equal to half a month's salary. One broken Buddha stone statue, a small bronze piece, a few religious tablets, would bring him a wealth most people could only dream about. Three or four bronze pieces could buy him a freedom only the wealthiest could afford.

He read I-Chi'ang's description again and again. It captivated him. It was wild, insane to think the temple and all its works were something real, still there in some overgrown mountain forest, just waiting for someone to discover them and bring all that wealth into the modern world. And why shouldn't it be him? After all, amateurs made discoveries like that all the time. All you really needed was a general idea of where it was and the time to look for it. And time was something he had, every other month when he was onshore, twenty-eight days of field break to use as he pleased. He ripped the relevant pages out of the book and folded them into his pocket, leaving the New York library with the sense that maybe, for once, he had gotten lucky.

Now he tapped a pencil on the unmarked coastline below Pattani. *If it's anywhere ...*

In the six months since that day in the library, he had spent nearly all his free time chasing down this forgotten temple. He had visited museums and libraries from London to Jakarta, bought, borrowed and stolen books that had anything to do with ancient Southeast Asian history; collected photographs of Sri Jayan temples and artifacts (that was how he was able to identify the most valuable piece in the Songkhla museum); and trudged and boated through miles of shoreline from Surat Thani to Songkhla.

He had researched the name of every ancient town and river mentioned by I-Chi'ang and had been able to trace some of them to modern-day cities in Thailand and Malaysia. He had even written to Professor Nichols in the guise of a researching educator from Bangkok's Chulalongkorn University; but the professor had never deigned to answer him.

In time, Hunter would let Jack in on his plans. He would need him eventually, and now that he had his attention because of the museum theft, it would make it all much easier. There were others too, from whom he would need help. But first he had to find the site.

He looked at the map, and then he saw it, as clear to him as the street lights now burning outside his window. Below Songkhla, sixty miles or so down the coast, there was a tan spot on the map near the coast. The area around it was green. The brownish area meant the elevation was at least 300 meters. It was labeled "Jewel Mountain". He rapped the map with his knuckles. That was where he would go tomorrow to look for the limestone elephant on the seaward side of *Khaw Kaew*.

* * *

It was a hard climb and there was no trail, but then Hunter wasn't expecting one. Spindly vines snagged his feet, thorns the size of sewing needles scratched his hands and threatened his eyes. He slashed his way through the thick underbrush with a parang, thankful he had put on his army surplus fatigues and a long-sleeved work shirt.

He stopped and rested against a towering tree. The only sound he could hear was his own labored breathing. Sweat poured off his brow and stung his eyes. He had started the climb at seven, and most of the last two hours he'd spent making slow progress, fighting the jungle like it was his worst enemy. The sun was high overhead now; he could make it out through the tops of the trees.

Here it was shaded, and the air was heavy and smelled of rotting leaves.

He removed his water bottle from the pocket of his backpack and took a long drink. He wiped his face and tried to dry his hands as much as possible so that the parang wouldn't fly from his grip. Then, when his breathing was back to normal, he started again.

He wanted to be sure he'd have enough time to reach the top, explore, and make it back down to his truck before sunset. The trail down should be easy and quick, as long as he didn't stray from the path he'd cut coming up; but he wanted to play it safe. The last thing he wanted was to be caught in this jungle after dark.

He worked hard for another twenty minutes. Then he lifted his eyes and knew he was near the summit, because he could see blue sky through the slender trees ahead of him. Rubbery, whip-like branches slapped at his face and torso; they were so supple the blade couldn't cut through them. He battled through a thicket of prickly brambles until he reached a large gray rock. The rock jutted out from the hill, forming a ledge, so he hoisted himself up on it and carefully stepped out to see where he was.

Below was the sea, as blue and calm as it always appeared from a distance. Behind him the hill rose slightly to his left, and there was nothing to see except the solid green of the forest; no sign of a limestone cliff or anything that could have been man-made, even something man-made a thousand years ago.

He sighed and sat down cross-legged on the rock. His cotton shirt was soaked with sweat. He shrugged off his backpack and opened his shirt to catch the offshore breeze on his bare chest.

It wasn't here, and he knew it because he couldn't feel anything. When he got close to it, he knew, he would feel a *zing*, a little shiver of electricity up his spine. It would happen like that; he was sure of it. Here he felt nothing; the only thing to show for his climb was the weave of scratches on the backs of his hands and the dead feeling in his legs and arms.

He was physically drained but relaxed, the way arduous exercise always made him feel. The Jewel Mountain, despite her promising name, had been just one more false hope. Maybe tonight, when the feelings of frustration and thwarted hopes mixed with the Golden Cat, he'd turn angry and spiteful. But right now, sitting in the fresh breeze with the calming sea far below his rocky perch, his muscles slack and supple from the hard work, he felt no anger, no frustration, only an unfamiliar sense of tranquility. If not this time, then next time. If not next time, well then, the time after that. He had eliminated one more point on the map, he could extend the yellow line another quarter inch or so. Surely, he was narrowing it down, and if the temple existed at all, he would find it eventually. Crazy or not, he would find it.

In the small inner pocket of his backpack he found the plastic soap case that kept the weed dry. He took out a joint, lit it, and sucked the smoke deep into his lungs.

He gazed out at the sea and watched the patterns of the waves form and recede. A few small, brightly colored birds flitted in and out of the underbrush. There was not a soul to be seen anywhere; no evidence at all that man had touched the planet. What would that be like, he wondered? Nobody around to get on your case about some silly bullshit. Of course, you'd need the women and the Golden Cat and the ganja, but all the rest of this life ...

Then he saw it, the glint of the metal fuselage in the sun, and a few seconds later the sound reached his ears, the rotors thrumming through the sky. His dreamy reverie was shattered. It was EastAsia's last flight of the day from Songkhla, cutting across his vision toward the Ratchada field. Tiny claws of desperation scratched at his insides. Maybe he felt all serene and mellow here, but *out there* his time was running out. He was sure of it. You could only beat the odds for so long before they eventually caught up with you, and Hunter had been beating them for too many years. He had a sudden perverse glimpse of his future – a painful, terrifying death from fire or water or scalding oil. He took several quick tokes and watched the Sikorsky slip across the cloudless sky.

Soon enough it would be his turn; he'd be hauled out to the platform, a prisoner without chains or handcuffs, self-sentenced to another twenty-eight days.

And then came the image. He didn't know where it came from; it just appeared all of a sudden on the screen of his mind. He saw the face of I Chi'ang, the itinerate Chinese monk, the only man to have recorded the existence of the Temple of the Glorious Dawn. He had never seen a drawing or picture of him, but Hunter could see him quite clearly now. He was an old man with a wispy gray Fu Manchu that grew down to his Adam's apple, but his face was smooth and youthful. He wore a silk robe of black and red and a matching skullcap. Hunter imagined Chi'ang making the hard climb to the temple, sometimes leaning against a wooden staff, worn smooth from years of use. From time to time he'd touch the Buddhist amulet he wore around his neck, not very different, perhaps, than the one Hunter himself wore. And he'd be smiling, always smiling, as he faced his ancient world full of wonder and astonishment.

Hunter nipped off the burning end of the joint with his fingernails and then threw the roach in his mouth and swallowed it. After he climbed down from this hill, he would get drunk and sleep with Jinda and forget about it. Forget about all of it until he had to face it again. Maybe he would see that guy again, what was his name? The American guy, from the Midwest somewhere. The one who worked for the GPS station ...

... And hadn't he said something about how part of his work was having to go out to the jetty to deliver the receivers? That meant he must have a pass for the deep-sea port. Free access to the port and any ship in it, no questions asked.

Madison, that's where he was from. Madison, Wisconsin. This was a guy he would have to get to know a lot better.

Eleven

When there was no work, Marek stayed at the station until half past three, just to be sure he'd be there if Sturges called. By then it was 4:30 Singapore time, and he could be fairly certain Brian had left the office and was perched on his bar stool at the Hard Rock, impressing some tourist with his tales of expeditionary drilling in the Empty Quarter.

He checked his email and the fax machine one more time then spoke to the maid on the way out.

"Back in an hour," he said.

He picked up the mail at the post office and bought a newspaper, then drove out to the Songkhla Bay Garden Hotel on the cape and parked in the gravel parking lot. There, a brick pathway led through a topiary garden to the grand, open-air reception area. From the reception desk there was a view of the casuarinas along the sandy beach and back towards the sculpted elephants and giraffes in the garden. Here and there stood a few dusty pieces of old-fashioned furniture, and a steady sea breeze stirred the potted plants on the marble floor. The guestrooms upstairs had teak floors, beds with tall posts for mosquito netting, and floor-to-ceiling panels which opened onto spacious balconies.

But time had passed the old girl by. None of the rooms had

air conditioning, the plumbing was ancient, and there was no swimming pool. Tourists seldom stayed there, preferring the newer hotel in the town center or the one close by the station; but Marek loved its tropical, gone-to-seed charm. It was rumored the hotel would be demolished and replaced with a concrete rectangle from one of the famous hotel chains. The view of the Gulf, they said, was just too good to pass up.

Except for a few bored-looking staff, the breezy reception area was empty. Marek walked through it to the veranda coffee shop on the Gulf side. The restaurant was popular with the expat crowd for Sunday breakfasts because of the blueberry pancakes, and on those mornings the tables, covered with grease-spotted white linen and mismatched flatware, were nearly all full. But when Marek came in the afternoons, he was usually alone. One wall had a large aquarium that was full of greenish water but empty of fish. Another had a mural poster of the Swiss Alps, but the sea air had compromised the adhesive and the corners had peeled away.

Marek ordered his usual iced coffee and spread his newspaper out on the rickety table. A rusty ceiling fan began to groan above his head, turned on by one of the waitresses. A cockroach scurried between the table legs. Someone once said they had seen a rat run out of the kitchen (even it didn't like the food, was the joke), but it was quiet, nobody bothered him, and he could sit here for as long as he liked.

He leaned across the table with his forearms on the paper to keep the pages from fluttering in the draft of the ceiling fan. He sipped his sweet iced coffee through a straw and read through the

Bangkok Post desultorily until he got to the editorial page, where a headline snagged his attention: "Songkhla's Loss a Tragedy for All".

A priceless piece of Thailand's heritage disappeared on May 3rd of this year and no one seems to care. That was the night the Ranod Bodhisattva, a tenth century bronze masterpiece of the Sri Jayan era, was stolen from the Songkhla museum. During the theft the museum guard was attacked by one or more of the perpetrators – or so police believe - when he attempted to stop their escape. The watchman was found unconscious and died a few weeks later, leaving a widow and two children. And though it has been two months since the burglary and violent death, investigators have yet to produce a single tangible lead.

The commentary went on to blame police incompetence, even hinting that the lack of any substantial clues suggested it was an inside job. "The icon is surely well out of the country by now, gracing the mantelpiece of some rich, unscrupulous collector in London or New York, while their cohorts in this country wallow in their ill-gained profits."

But the writer did not aim her arrows at only the officials; she also had some left for the general population. The fact that the ancient work could vanish with so little fuss was:

... symptomatic of a society that values instant profits in

business and commerce rather than anything of cultural
or artistic merit. The theft of this precious piece, not to
mention the ensuing death of the museum guard, has
produced nothing but lip service amongst the politicians
and yawns amongst the general public.

Thai people were turning away from the Buddhist principles that had guided the country for thousands of years, the writer lamented, and in doing so risked taking Thailand down a road which led to disillusionment and tragedy.

The essay ended with a plea to the Chief of Police, the Songkhla Governor, and even the Prime Minister to find the perpetrators, "...so that, if nothing else, the widow and fatherless children of the guard can feel that justice has been served."

It was impossible to live in the country and not hear many stories of corruption on all levels, from both Thais and expats, and Marek had heard his share: the payoffs to get equipment through customs, the kickbacks when big contracts were awarded. He had even seen it himself on a much smaller scale: Niwat's well-oiled movements through the local bureaucracy. And it was true no one seemed to care, or at least they accepted it as a natural, inevitable thing.

"One more?" The waitress had picked up his empty glass and was holding it tentatively. Just then he heard female voices and scurrying footsteps echoing through the reception hall.

Marek looked up to see three young women – two of them dressed in the local university uniform of white shirt and navy-blue skirt, the third, slightly older, in blue jeans and a Jurassic

Park T-shirt. Marek suddenly felt as if all the air had been sucked out of the room, and it would be a while before he'd be able to breathe normally again. The woman wearing the T-shirt smiled at him, then seemed to herd the two students toward him as if she were chaperoning them to a dance.

He couldn't take his eyes from her. She was tall and poised and smiled at him in such an engaging way that he wondered if maybe she had mistaken him for somebody else. They stopped in front of the table and all three women politely waied. The older one prodded one of the students to speak. "Excuse me, sir," she said. "Good morning ... Eh! ... Good afternoon."

The two students reacted to the mistake with a fit of giggles and jabbed each other to get serious. "We are from ..." and here she said the long, multi-syllabic name of a local university. "We are English majors. Our assignment is to interview farang ... ah, foreigners, for our class. Do you mind?"

He had to concentrate hard on what she said and hold himself back from gaping at the Jurassic Park woman. She wasn't dressed like a student. Who was she? Teacher? Elder sister?

"No, no, of course not. Please sit down." He stood and offered them seats. The pretty one sat across from him. She folded into the chair with feline suppleness.

"English majors, yes? And where do you study?" They looked surprised and then laughed, and he realized with embarrassment they had already told him.

"Oh yes, sorry. Ah ... what do you want to interview me about?"

They looked at each other and the pretty one, obviously much more confident in her English than the others, said, "Go ahead, Apple."

"It is for our conversation course. Do you mind?" asked Apple.

The other student brought out a Walkman tape player, plugged a microphone into it, then held it to within inches of his mouth. Apple unfolded a piece of notebook paper and began reading a list of questions: *What was his name? Where did he come from? How long had he lived in Thailand? Was he a tourist or did he work here? What was his job?* One question rapidly followed another, hardly leaving him time to answer before she was asking the next. She never lifted her eyes from the paper, apparently wanting to get through the ordeal while making as little personal contact with him as possible.

The student to his right held the microphone to his face and nodded encouragement at each of his answers. Across from him, the Jurassic Park woman had a hint of a smile on her lips, seemingly amused by it all.

After he had answered all of Apple's questions, the student looked up from her paper for the first time, smiled, and said "Thank you". She folded her paper away and giggled in relief, her part in the team assignment apparently over.

He turned to the second student, the one holding the microphone. "And you? What is your name? Will you ask me some questions like Apple?" The girl, a little stunned that she might have to speak English, looked at the Jurassic Park woman for guidance.

"Go ahead," she said.

"Ah … My name is Jum. Are … ah … you like Thai food?"

"Very good question! Yes, I like Thai food very much. But some is very hot." He said, fanning his hand in front of his mouth and blowing, the universal sign for spicy food. The women laughed.

"What kind of Thai food you like?"

"Umm … *kay yang, khaw niew*." Grilled chicken and sticky rice. He really did like it, but whenever he mentioned it, he always got a laugh, probably because it came originally from the Northeast and was thought to be rather countrified, like grits and cornbread.

"And do you know papaya *bok bok?*" Jum held the microphone as if it were a pestle and pounded it into an imaginary mortar. It was the Thai joke-name for *somtam*, papaya salad, another Isaan dish, and a phrase all Thais seemed to think was gut-wrenchingly funny. Even the two eavesdropping waitresses began to laugh.

"Oi," he said, "very, very hot. *Phet maak*." He gripped his stomach and made a tortured face. Their laughter erupted and filled the empty restaurant. It swelled like something organic, and the waitresses, infected by it, laughed louder as well.

Marek began to ham it up, waving both hands in front of his mouth, opening his eyes wide as if his tongue were burning. They roared and slapped each other; they couldn't stop. It amazed him. They laughed at his bonehead Thai and stupid jokes and pulled faces. It was too easy. He had never before in his life made any woman laugh as much as this, much less three at once (five if you count the waitresses); much less one as good-looking as the one seated across from him.

She shook her hair and threw her head back so he could see her throat. She modestly cupped her hand in front of her mouth, and as her laughter diminished her eyes lingered on him. But he couldn't fathom what her look meant. Probably she just thought he was a buffoon.

The laughter receded like a wave. "I think if you stay in Thailand long time, you can eat *somtam*," said Apple. "You will ... ah, how do you say ... get used to it."

"Well, I think, Apple and Jum, you both get an A for English. But you haven't asked me anything yet," he said, looking directly at the woman opposite.

She laughed. "No, I am not a student. I am just helping them because they are shy around foreigners."

"You are their teacher?"

"No, not really. But I sometimes tutor students in English. Part-time job. I graduated a few years ago in marketing but it's difficult to find work doing that. So I have a small tutoring business. Mostly I help students prepare for the university entrance exams, but I help students at the University sometimes too."

She spoke with an overly precise enunciation, as if she'd learned from tapes and videos and not by conversing with native speakers. In the oblique afternoon light, her black hair falling over her shoulders held a glint of copper. She had smooth honey-caramel skin; her cheeks and forehead were as smooth and fresh as a baby's.

But it was her eyes that held him. They were large and deep, and in the shape of them there was something different, something that seemed foreign to Thailand. Perhaps she was Thai-Malay maybe, or maybe Thai-Indian. Their shape was so exquisite, he had to resist the urge to trace the lines with his fingertips.

"Actually, my dream is to study for a master's degree abroad," she said. "America or England would be wonderful, but quite expensive. So I think maybe Singapore, but I have to improve my English too. Anyway, thank you very much for your interview today."

The students began to collect their notebooks and put away the Walkman. They stood. Was this it? Were they leaving already?

"Thank you, sir," they said, almost in chorus.

"Are you finished? Are you leaving?"

"Yes, sir. Thank you very much for the interview."

The gorgeous one spoke. "I'm afraid they have two find two more foreigners to interview. They have to hand in their assignment tomorrow. Thank you again for your help."

"No, wait. I mean ... what about me? Don't I get to interview you?" He could hear a hint of entreaty in his voice, but he couldn't let her just walk away from him.

The students looked at each other. Apple said, "Excuse me, sir. Can you say again please, slowly."

"I should interview you. I ... it will be good practice for you. It will only take a minute, I promise."

Jurassic Park woman let her eyes rest on him, then she smiled and said, "OK, but we shouldn't stay too long."

"Good. Please, sit down. Would you like something to drink? Some tea or Coca-Cola?" He called the waitress over. The women looked at each other and sat back down.

"What would you like to ask us?"

He made a big show of taking out his pen and unfolding his newspaper as if to use it for note taking. Then he held out his hand as if holding an imaginary microphone.

He alternated between the two students, asking them the same type of routine questions about food, hobbies and favorite sports that they'd asked him. He forgot their answers as quickly as they'd said them.

"Very good, Apple and Jum, you now get A plus! But I should interview you too, ajarn. So first, what is your name?" He had used the formal word for teacher, trying to impress her.

She laughed. "I'm not really an ajarn. But anyway, my name Saranya."

He made her spell it and wrote it in the margin of his newspaper, next to the editorial: *Saranya*.

"And where do you come from?"

"Songkhla."

"Where do you live?"

"Ruam Chang Road."

"I see. And what do you do in your free time?"

"Listening to music. I like reading English novels. Also sleeping." She laughed, and the others joined in.

"Do you like sports?"

"Yes."

"What sports do you play?"

"Mmm ... basketball." She put her elbows on the table and rested her chin on her intertwined fingers. She seemed to be enjoying this, as if she delighted in the challenge of talking to a real live farang. "But tennis is also enjoy." The students tittered along with her. "I mean, I like tennis too. My English is not so good."

She gazed at him, a curious mixture of coyness and boldness, waiting for him to say something. But he was running out of questions.

"Ah ... and what subject did you major in at the University?"

"Marketing, as I already told you." The students laughed a little louder this time. She grinned playfully at him, and he was beginning to wonder if she were having him on. Her English was miles better than the other two girls'; and more than that, she had much more confidence. She seemed to enjoy the interaction as a game and wasn't overly worried about making a few grammatical mistakes. She waited for the next question, looking at him steadily, and it made him feel as if he were being scrutinized; as if she were trying to determine if he had the mettle to match wits with her.

"Mmm, yes, very well. And what kind of food do you like?" His voice sounded phony and pedantic.

"Thai food ... because I am Thai, you see." All three of them laughed, and he felt there was nothing left to say or do except laugh along with them.

He gave her the thumbs-up sign. "You pass the interview. Your English is very good."

"No, I don't think so. I would like to improve but I have no chance. I have no chance to speak to farang."

"Well, there is me," he said. "I am a farang. You can talk to me." She nodded her head slightly but gave away no emotion.

"Can you repeat again please?" she asked.

He repeated his proposal. He went on to explain more about his job, about how sometimes he could be very busy, but how he also had lots of free time. He also told her he was trying to learn Thai. The solution was obvious: he would teach her English, and she could teach him Thai.

She discussed it with the others. He realized he'd made a mistake by not including them in the invitation. It was rude, and anyway, a young Thai woman – a student, a *good* girl – would never meet a farang male on her own. It simply was not done, at least not down here in the provinces.

"Yes," she smiled. "We would like you to help us with English conversation. And we can help you with Thai language. I think it will be very interesting. We can meet here in the coffee shop. Is Friday convenient for you? Four o'clock again?"

"Yes, of course. Very convenient. I will see you here on Friday at four o'clock."

Then they were standing, clutching their books against their chests. He stood to say goodbye and looked down on her faintly coppery hair, rich and lush, and caught a sweet, delicious scent rising from her. He wanted badly to offer his hand and feel hers in his, but he didn't. Respectable Thai women didn't touch men unless they were family. He just stood there with his arms bolted to his sides while they chirped their thank yous and bye-byes.

"See you next Friday," was the best he could utter as they turned to walk out of the room.

When they were gone the waitress asked him if he wanted another iced coffee, but it was time to get back to the office, so he asked for his bill instead. He began to think of the wonderful, witty things he should have said to her. He would have to wait three days for that now. At the very least he should have offered them a ride, though more than likely they would have declined.

He was nearly at his pickup when he realized he'd forgotten his newspaper. He rushed back to the coffee shop just in time to rescue it from the waitress, who was about to relegate it to the trash bin. She smiled at him, embarrassed, thinking she'd made a serious mistake. He took only one section. "And, sir?" she said, puzzled, as she offered him the rest of the newspaper. But he shook his head. He had the most important part. He found the page in the editorial section and read her name aloud: "Saranya".

Twelve

Marek spent the next few days searching the Songkhla bookstores for English language textbooks, not because he thought he'd actually be giving lessons from a book, but because he hoped to impress Saranya with his keenness to help her improve. He certainly did not have in mind some kind of formal tutoring. Rather, he pictured them passing time in casual conversation, floating from one topic to another on that easy laughter that came as naturally from her as a morning song from a robin.

The bookstores were no help. The only thing he could find was an ancient English-Thai phrasebook that dated back to when Bangkok was an R and R stopover for GIs in Vietnam. It translated sentences like "Take me to the Officers' Club" and "Boy, call me a trishaw". He bought it anyway. Then he drove the twenty-six miles to Had Yai and scoured the stores there. One shop near the train station had nearly an aisle full of English language textbooks, but there were so many genres and varieties it took him an hour to decide what to buy. He finally settled on a book that claimed to teach "conversation". It had various topic areas – sports, the weather, traveling – that he thought might work as jumping off points if he ever got stuck for something to talk about.

It was the idea of dead silence that worried him: long nervous lapses of speech that sullied his little pipe dream of easy-going chat sessions that would lead eventually to ... well, what exactly? He didn't know, and it was far too early to even guess.

What if he could think of nothing clever to say? What if his jokes fell flat and even his clownish speech and expressions didn't amuse her? He dreaded the thought of her being bored, leafing absently through a book or gazing silently out to sea. Or worse yet, lapsing into Thai (most of which he would not be able to understand, of course) for long discussions with her friends, ignoring him completely, and maybe even discussing some attributes she found lacking in him. Or (and was this better or worse?) simply staring at him with that half-smile, at once both remote and engaging, waiting for him to say something witty.

On Friday they arrived late. Marek had been waiting for over half an hour when they finally got there. They waied in greeting and apology.

"Sorry for being late. We were waiting for Jum but she cannot come today. She has a bad stomach."

Saranya looked even more beautiful than he remembered. The scent of her hair rose up to him and brought back a flood of memories from their first meeting: how the afternoon light had made her hair russet, how her laughter had risen so easily from her throat. She sat down and her skirt rose up her thigh. She flashed that brilliant, off-kilter smile and said, almost teasingly, "Teacher, what will you teach us today?"

Marek began by working through the ritual questions.

"How are you, today?"

"Fine. And you?"

"Fine, thank you."

"And what did you do today, Apple?"

"I study at school."

"And you, Saranya?"

"I helped my mother with the homework."

"Your mother is a student?"

"Oh, no, I mean housework." The women laughed.

It went on for a few minutes, a parody of conversation, accompanied on the their part with a lot of hesitation and laughter.

Then Marek spent a full five minutes having Saranya and Apple practice his name. He really didn't care if the bargirls couldn't say it correctly; but he needed to make sure these students – especially Saranya – could say it right. But since the Thai language doesn't have an "x" sound, their difficultly in saying it was monumental.

"Listen. Say it like this … Alex."

"A-lek."

"No, Al–lexs. Lexsss."

"Ah–lek–kus."

"No, not 'lek–kus'. Put it together. Lex! Al–lex!"

Both women were laughing so hard they were nearly in tears. And then Saranya said it: "Al-lexss".

"Yes!" he shouted, so loudly that it turned the heads of a couple of Malaysian tourists, the only other people in the coffee shop. Marek and Apple applauded and Saranya blushed beautifully with pride.

He opened the conversation book he'd bought and started leafing to one of the topics he'd marked as having potential.

Saranya stopped him with a question.

"Excuse me please, Khun Alek." He gave her a stern look.

"Ah, Alexsss. Excuse me, sir, what do you think about Thailand?"

He was surprised by the seriousness of her tone and answered non-committally. "I think it's a wonderful country. Very beautiful beaches and mountains. Food is delicious. People are nice."

This was followed by more questions. What did he think about Thai politics? What were his opinions about the current government in Thailand? Did he think Thailand was truly a democracy? What was democracy like in America? Were there poor people in America? What did the government do for them? What did he think the government should do for the poor in Thailand?

He was taken back by her questions. He didn't know how truthfully he could answer without being thought rude or insulting, or guilty of something far worse, like sedition. Anyway, he didn't know enough about Thai politics to have much of an opinion, though he wouldn't admit this to her. Her questions had the stiff, formal tone of someone who had learned language from a book rather than natural conversation. It made him feel unsure about his answers because, once again, he could not fathom how serious she really was. Was this some kind of a test? Maybe, for whatever reason, she was trying to find out if he had anti-government sentiments. Or, just as likely, she was gauging his willingness to be frank. Or then again, maybe it was nothing more than curiosity about foreigners.

Whatever the case, he felt he was quickly losing ground

in her estimation. He was tossing out bland comments like "interesting", "very nice" and sidestepping her charges like a matador. She prefaced her questions with, "And can you tell me, please ..." When he answered he translated for Apple, who said almost nothing but nodded her head like an obedient little sister. Sometimes Saranya would pause between questions, her lips slightly parted, her head tilted, looking up towards the ceiling as if evaluating his answers. Then she would blink hard for a few seconds and slowly nod her head before firing off another one.

"And can you tell me please, what is your impression of Thai people?"

"Oh, very nice, very lovely."

"Why do you say that?"

"Well, the people I've met have been very kind to me. I think they're very easy-going. Very tolerant." He realized he sounded like a tourist brochure, but he couldn't help himself. And anyway, he believed it.

"I don't think so," she said. Her brow wrinkled and lines deepened around her mouth. "That is maybe the good people. But there are many bad people, too. You must be careful. Some man maybe he smiles at you, but he only wants your money. You know? Some man maybe even Godfather. In the south of Thailand many, many Godfathers."

Marek laughed, picturing a Thai fisherman in a three-piece Italian suit and a fedora. "Well, I will definitely stay away from them. Why are you asking so many serious questions anyway?"

"I am interested in farang ... ah ... foreigner. I told you I would like to study abroad. But I have to learn more about the culture, how people think and feel. Many Thai people, they only want to hear the good things, the polite thing. But I would like to hear the truth. I want to know the people's real feelings. Do you understand?"

"Yes, I understand."

"And there are many things about your country I want to know about." She paused and took a sip of her orange juice. "Are people kind in America?"

"Some are, some are not. Like everywhere in the world."

"And American people are very rich, yes?"

"Some are. There are poor people, too. Most people are not rich."

He could tell she didn't believe him.

"And are there many Negro people?"

"In some places."

She shivered. "I am very afraid of the Negro."

How could you be, he thought, since you've likely never met one in your life? But he said nothing.

"And also this I am very interested in. The snow. I would like to know about the snow."

"The snow?"

"Yes, snow. Can you tell me please, is it delicious?"

Thirteen

"The way she looks at me sometimes ..." Marek's voice trailed off. Philips was sucking crabmeat from a pink claw. "I mean ... there's just something about her."

"There always is, mate."

It was Friday evening and they were eating crab at Nai Harn's seafood restaurant. The place was noisy and bright, filled with chattering groups of government workers, students and families. Before a frenzied waitress could set down a steaming plate of shrimp or crab on one table, another order would be shouted out at her from across the room. There was a roof above them, but the sides of the building were open to the evening air. The restaurant was illuminated with overly bright fluorescent lights, and outside the last dying rays of the sun painted the sky pink and purple.

"The snow, is it delicious? Where the heck did that come from?"

Philips shrugged. He tossed the shell onto a plate already loaded with others, then tore off some toilet paper from the roll between them and wiped his fingers.

"Y'know, there's a long, honorable history of teachers marrying their students in this country. Almost as long and honorable as bosses marrying their secretaries, or guys their maids."

"Who said anything about marrying?"

"You had that faraway look in your eyes."

"I don't know what to do. I'm hopeless as an English teacher. I couldn't tell a participle from a toenail."

"Don't worry about it, mate. They get grammar out the ying yang in school. Their Thai teachers give it to them all day long. That's about the only thing they can teach them, seeing as they're pretty much useless at actually speaking the language. They're just happy to hear real authentic English – even if it is your inferior Yank-type version."

"She's got eyes that seem to be lit from inside. I don't know how to explain it. Her eyes have their own luminescence. You ever see that in a girl?"

"Not when sober."

"Where will this all lead to, that's what I wonder."

"Where do you want it to lead to?"

Marek sighed. "I don't know that either."

"Well, just go with the flow then." He filled their mugs up with more beer and took a long swig. "I really cannot fathom what in the world you're all bothered about, anyway. Got a standing date every week with a lovely young thing and you act like it's root canal."

"Yeah, I know. But, you see, there's something else. There's this girl back home ..."

"Hang on!" Philips leaned across the table and grabbed Marek's forearm. "You're in Thailand now, mate. There is no 'girl back home'. Not anymore. That's over. End of story."

"Yeah, OK Drew." He was right, but for a different reason. She wasn't there anymore because she had decided that. But if he had a chance again with Rachel …?

Philips leaned back in the molded plastic chair and rested his hands on his belly. "Look, y'know how the Thais always say 'Don't think too much'? Personally, I think it's a load of crap and what they could do with is slightly more brain work. Still, sometimes it's apt. Like now, man. Don't over-analyze the situation. Enjoy it while you can. Whatever happens, you'll handle it. OK, you're a Yank, so you'll probably screw it all up first. But I'm sure in the end it'll turn out OK."

Marek wadded up a square of toilet paper and bounced it off Philips's forehead. "Thanks, Drew. You're a great help."

* * *

Marek and Saranya began meeting twice a week, at Saranya's suggestion. She also said they should they move their sessions from the hotel coffee shop to outside, under the casuarina trees that lined the beach. There was a grassy strip between the hotel wall and the sand with a few stone benches and tables scattered around. Vendors parked their carts along the curb to one side, where the paved road ended in a roundabout at the beach. It was better than the hotel, Saranya said, because the breeze was cool there. Also, Marek's iced coffee would be cheaper if he bought it from the vendors.

Sometimes all three friends came, sometimes only Saranya

and another. Other students from the college would occasionally join them, but most merely sat on their hands, hardly venturing a word in English, thinking perhaps that they could absorb the language by listening to Marek and Saranya converse. They always wore their college uniforms: the navy-blue skirt and the bleached white shirt with the University pin near the left collar. Sometimes one or two of them, as if to signal rebelliousness against the regimentation of the uniform, or maybe just because it was cooler, wore their long shirt tails outside the skirt.

Saranya was fastidious about her appearance. Her blue jeans were neat and pressed, her blouse was cinched neatly around her trim waist. Her skin always had a scrubbed, fresh aspect and her hair always looked newly brushed, without a knot or a snag or a split end anywhere along its flowing length. The other girls wore quiet jewelry or none at all, but every time he saw her Saranya had something different. Sometimes it was a hill tribe bracelet of hammered silver. Sometimes a band of threads was tied around one wrist. Her watch seemed to change as well. One day she wore a single topaz ring on her right ring finger, the next, every finger on her left hand had a ring, but none on her right.

She always arrived with an iced coffee for him. It came in a plastic bag tied up with a rubber band and he had to sip it with a straw. He tried to pay for it every time, but she would never accept a baht. So he paid her back by buying orange juice and fruit from the curbside vendors.

While they chatted about the day's events, they sipped their drinks and nibbled their snacks. The fruit – guava, watermelon, pineapple, papaya – came sliced in plastic bags along with various seasonings in stiff folded paper containers. The makeshift packages held salt, some kind of syrupy paste, and ground chili pepper mixed with sugar. The girls speared the fruit with wooden skewers and dipped it in the condiment of their choice.

"Chili powder! Yuck!" said Marek. "Salt on pineapple is bad enough but chili powder?"

"*Aroy!*" they said. "Delicious. You try it."

"Never!"

One day Saranya didn't come. The two students haltingly explained that she had stayed home to take care of her father, who was sick. The lesson was drudgery. Saranya's younger friends didn't have much English but worse, from Marek's point of view, they didn't have the nerve to even try. They were so shy and afraid of making a mistake that they nearly cowered anytime he asked them a question. He bit his tongue and kept smiling. They smiled back. The hour seemed like a day.

The next week Saranya was back again, and he was so happy to see her he felt like singing.

"How is your father, Saranya?"

She shrugged. "He is old," she said, and then changed the subject.

He sometimes stopped the conversations to correct the students' grammar. He'd make them say sentences over and over again, thinking he could burn the correct words and tenses into their brains. Jum was usually too shy or too weak in English to take part in free conversation, but she relished this task of repetition; it must have made her feel as if she were learning something. And it made Marek feel as if he were teaching. Occasionally he drilled them in pronunciation, forcing them to mimic his sounds, exaggerating his tongue and lips more for comic effect than for accuracy. Saranya had difficulty with words that had both r and l, and would furrow her brow as Marek tortured her with words like "problem" and "really".

One afternoon the students brought assignments from their classes, book reports of literary novels they had read. Marek had only a vague idea of the texts themselves but worked at repairing their clumsy syntax. Saranya would look over the girls' shoulders and ask Marek why he had made some change in the wording. Sometimes he could give no explanation except, "It just sounds better." The students would nod as if this really were an acceptable answer. Saranya would look doubtful but remain quiet.

Marek returned their papers, his pen marks like bird tracks across the handwritten sheets. They thanked him and stared seriously at their papers for a few moments. He wondered vaguely if all his little marks were doing more harm than good. He sighed.

"Take it easy," said Saranya, laughing. "Here, have some guava." She pronounced it "gwa – wah"

"OK, but not with chili sauce."

"You have before with chili sauce?"

"No, never."

"Then you must try. How can you know if it is good or not? You cannot know unless you try first." The playfulness in her eyes was like a challenge to him.

"No!"

"*Nii! Aw!*" She stabbed at a piece of green and white guava, dipped it in the hot sauce and then aimed it at his mouth. "*Kin si*! Eat!"

He had no choice. He bit it off the stick, looking at her face. She never raised her eyes but looked only at the morsel of guava as it went into his mouth. He felt the others' eyes on him. The fruit was crunchy and slightly bitter, and then the hot sauce hit him. He gasped. He reached for something to drink but his iced coffee was finished.

"What is wrong?" she asked, feigning surprise. Her friends gave a whoop of laughter. One of the vendors cackled. Marek couldn't spit it out, it was a gift from her. He chewed it quickly and swallowed. It burned all the way down his throat and made him cough. He rolled his eyes in exaggeration. "Too hot!" he bellowed.

The women laughed. "*Aroy*! Delicious!" insisted Saranya. Then she speared a piece of papaya and jabbed it towards his lips. "This will help to cool you off," she said.

It was embarrassing to have her feeding him like a child, but what could he do? Refuse it? He reached for the slab of orange-yellow fruit with his tongue. She met his eyes and giggled as he took it into his mouth. The fruit was fleshy and sweet, with a faintly smoky taste. He rolled it round his mouth then pressed it up against the roof to relieve the burning. Finally, he used his tongue to break its creamy surface.

She laughed again. Did she think he was ridiculous? He hoped not. Maybe she just kept her delight and happiness so close to the surface, she couldn't keep it from erupting.

* * *

It was OK for Philips to say go with the flow. But the fact was, Marek felt like he was adrift in the ocean, spinning in a vortex. What did Saranya really think of him? It was a question always in the back of his mind. At night in the bungalow, he'd choose one of the dusty paperbacks from the cardboard box of books, take it into his bedroom and read by the light of the desk lamp on his bedside table. The only sounds in the world were the humming of the air conditioner and the occasional chirping of a gecko. His eyes would cover paragraphs, sometimes complete pages, before he realized he hadn't processed a word because he was thinking of her. He pictured her leaning on her elbows on the stone table, listening to him with her lips slightly parted, or laughing and weaving her fingers through her curtain of hair. He'd think about something she'd said – over and over again, trying to recall her precise words – and wonder what she'd meant by it. And was her English really good enough to mean what he thought she meant?

It was all so confusing.

They had been meeting for over a month now, only missing one day when there was a rig move. Over the weeks she had learned much about him, yet he knew almost nothing about her, hardly anything more than after that first day. She talked a little about her family – her sick father, her mother, her brother – but almost nothing about the rest of her life. What did she do on days other than Tuesdays and Fridays, or on weekends? Did she go out on Saturday nights? Did she have a boyfriend?

She never tired of asking him questions and his normal reticence disappeared when he was around her. It was easy to be open with her because it wasn't her language and he was outside her culture. She wouldn't pre-judge him.

Sometimes he dared to flatter himself that she liked him. After all, it was her idea to meet twice a week. And she brought him coffee every time they met, didn't she? She hand fed him fruit, for God's sake, and in plain sight of everybody else. She wouldn't do that to someone if she didn't like him. But there were other times … sometimes that laughter seemed to break off any connection with him, to lift her above him. Other times he felt the laughter was like a wall, something to hide her true emotions.

He put down the book and turned off the light. He took off his shorts and let them drop to the floor. He closed his eyes and tried to recall her face. He saw her deep eyes and the wisps of her hair, almost like sideburns, that fell in front of her ears when she pulled her hair back. Her lacquered fingernails. He thought of the skin between the open folds of her white shirt. Then, alone in bed, with geckos clicking from the ceiling, despite the fact he knew it was unseemly, that it was somehow violating her spirit, he masturbated while burying his head in the pillow, picturing the burnished teak of her skin.

Fourteen

There was a woman on board, an engineer from the head office in Bangkok, and that screwed up everything. She got the VIP room, with the private shower and toilet and her own TV, which meant the OIM had to move out and share a room with somebody else like a mere mortal, and that always made him pissed off for the duration. But a woman upset more than living arrangements. There were procedural changes as well. "Like for instance," said Jenks, "you can't piss off the side of the platform."

His shift nearly over, Hunter gathered up his hot work permits and walked up the steel steps to the superintendent's office. He doubted if he would even see this female, since he'd given up eating in the mess hall with the rest of the crew and spent most of the off-shift time in his room. Guys sometimes went a little weird when there was a woman offshore, like they had to tiptoe around and be extra careful or she might see them for what they really were. Or did they think they actually had some kind of chance of getting laid and had to put on this act? It didn't matter to Hunter. It was just another day offshore, another piece of shit to get through. It wouldn't be his problem to deal with her in an emergency. The Safety Officer could show her where the life jackets were kept and politely explain that if she heard the abandon platform alarm, she'd better get her skinny ass into the lifeboat *chop chop* or she could kiss it goodbye.

Then again, she might be totally calm and self-assured, while the guys who'd been out here for ten years would be shitting themselves. You never knew. You could never guess how anyone would act in an emergency until the time was upon you, and then it was too late to do anything about it.

He guessed it would be a madhouse of panic and fear, screams and cries drowned out by the roar of flames. There wouldn't be much time to do anything anyway; it would be like Piper Alpha – a horrendous explosion in the middle of the night, half of the LQ falling away in the blink of an eye – and all the firefighting courses and emergency drills would do you about as much good as a life jacket in a plane crash.

He walked into the supe's office and thought about Garrett, as he always did, whenever Piper Alpha arose in his mind. Maybe, if you didn't know somebody who was actually on her when she exploded, you could work out here and keep that messy stuff from invading your head. But not Hunter. Because before he had gone to the North Sea, Garrett and he had worked together in Indonesia – Garret's instrumentation shop just across from Hunter's mechanical shop – and Hunter could still see him sitting at his desk, shit-eating grin on his face, aiming his nonstop banter at whoever walked in. "Hey, Hunter, they pay you for this crap work you do? How do you look at yourself in the mirror?"

But Garrett was long dead, in the wrong place at the wrong time. Hunter told himself it was quick, over in the flash of a fireball, and that Garrett had never felt a thing. But he feared in his gut that was just a pretty lie.

Garrett was the only one who understood it was all bullshit; that you played the game by their rules just long enough so you could live by your own. "You got your two buckets," he used to say. "One is for money and the other's for shit. When either one of them fills up, it's time to get out."

But nobody had ever considered the third option: it killed you before either bucket was full.

Hunter signed off the work orders and handed them across the desk to the dog-faced supervisor, who took them without raising his eyes. They had hardly spoken a word to each other in the six months since the maintenance shutdown when Hunter, who had to spend two hours reworking a turbine one of the Thai mechanics was supposed to have finished, told Jenks there wasn't a single Thai mechanic offshore fit to carry his toolbox. He should have known better. Word got around, probably embellished ten-fold by the time it reached the supe's ears. (The way gossip flew around an offshore installation made a beauty parlor look like a monastery where everyone had taken a vow of silence.) He had been one of the first Thais promoted to management and was very sensitive about his qualifications, especially in light of the snide chatter going on behind his back. Hunter was sure that ever since then he had been looking for a way to run him off.

Well, if everything breaks right, I'll take myself out of the rotation and that will be one less worry for you, Mr Dogface.

Hunter returned to his desk in the mechanical shop to write

up his logbook, always the last act of his twelve-hour shift. Behind him was a window, sealed like a porthole, through which he could see the sun setting in a blaze of orange and gold. The sea sparkled in slanting columns of light which pierced through purple clouds. Red sky at night, sailor's delight. Maybe the storm season would hold off for a few more weeks; just long enough for him to get his feet back on dry land; then it would be someone else's problem.

"Save some for tomorrow, John", said Jenks, rinsing out his coffee mug. "Time to put on the feed bag." He took a half-dozen paper towels from the dispenser and swabbed out his mug.

Hunter watched his quick little rat-like movements. He knew what was coming next. Jenks would put the cup upside down on the rack with the handle pointed outward at a precise 90-degree angle. Then he'd put his specs under the tap and use another four or five towels to clean them off. He'd walk back to his desk and say, "That's another one knocked on the 'ead", in a phony Cockney accent and toss Hunter the marker. It was the same every day, and Hunter loathed every predictable minute of it.

"How many trees have to die for you to dry your stuff, Jenks?"

He put his glasses on and blinked. "Since when did you become a tree-hugger, Hunt? You're in the oil business. That's an anathema."

Jenks was always using two-bit words Hunter suspected he didn't know the meaning of. One day he'd call him out on that.

Surachai from the night crew shuffled in, chewing on a

toothpick. "That's another one knocked on the 'ead." Jenks went to his desk and tossed Hunter the magic marker. "I know how you love to do this, John."

Hunter closed the logbook and turned to cross out another day on the big Mekhong whiskey wall calendar. He drew a thick black X on the date. Twenty-six down and another two to go; but who was counting? His eyes slid over the picture of the naked, big-breasted girl. It was nearly August now and they had all stopped speculating about her long ago.

"Hey, cheer up, Hunt. Maybe you'll get lucky tonight. Maybe that engineer's itching for a bounce. Y'know, all these male hormones out here got her hopped up."

"She's an engineer so she's probably ugly," said Surachai.

"No such thing as an ugly girl offshore, son," said Jenks.

In his room Hunter changed out of his coveralls and into shorts, T-shirt and running shoes. In the tiny gym below the helideck he did his bench presses and flies, his curls and presses, his rows and pull downs. Then he ran up and down the outside stairway for forty minutes. He paced along the edge of the helideck and let the stiff breeze cool his skin and dry his shirt as the long tropical sunset ended and dusk turned to night.

His body felt taut and strong, with just the right level of weariness; but he knew it wouldn't help him to sleep. He hardly slept more than three or four hours a night when he was offshore. The outside of his right knee ached, but that was always there, and there was nothing he could do about it.

How long had it been? Twenty-five years? Thinking of the time that had passed since the injury sent a shock wave through him. But even twenty years from now, even on his deathbed, he'd be able to remember it as if it'd all happened yesterday.

The maples beyond the end zone had been red and orange and the sky was a perfect China blue. He remembered the scent of the guy across from him and thinking, *funny how niggers smell different*. He was at tight end, and the coach had called his number. The quarterback rolled to the opposite side. He held his block for a second, then squirmed through the line and cut left across the field. It was crowded in there but then he slipped into the open. He could see the quarterback's eyes, big as saucers, and the ball floating out of his hands. Just before the ball touched Hunter's outstretched palms, somebody dove at his knees and the cartilage cracked like kindling.

He was screaming in agony as they carried him off on a stretcher. The cast came off after eight weeks and the doctor pronounced him completely healed, but he knew it wasn't the same. He did the physical therapy, all the strengthening exercises; but on the field he was a half-step slower, and sometimes when he'd cut to his right the knee would give and he would collapse onto the grass like an old man. The coaches said nothing but there was a hint of pity in their eyes. And that was maybe the worse thing about it, that goddamn look of pity.

He learned later there was not even a flag thrown on the play, though the guy had hit him early. Everybody said that.

And so ended his career, despite what the local sportswriter had said about him being the next great tight end. There'd be no letters of intent from UCLA or Alabama or Ohio State, and definitely no career in the NFL. His father hardly said a word about it and Hunter knew why. He could read it in his bitter look and hear it between the lines of his drunken rages: "*Did you really think you were better than the rest of us. That you had a chance to make it? If you did, you're a goddamn fool and you deserve what you got.*"

It didn't take long to track the guy down. One night he waited for him in the parking lot of a Shakey's pizza. The guy was with a couple of friends and Hunter held the baseball bat behind his thigh as he went up to him. He smiled – *remember me?* – then crashed the bat into the guy's knees. He felt that white anger rise from just behind his sternum and gave in to it. Hunter beat him on the kidneys with the bat and kicked him in the ribs and hip and thighs. He waved the bat around to keep his two buddies away, but they were too scared to do anything anyway. The guy was on his knees and trying to catch his breath to beg Hunter to stop, holding his arms against his body to protect his ribs, when Hunter kicked him one last time in the face.

Twenty-five years. And the pain in his knee would never go away.

He stood a long time at the edge of the helideck and watched the navigation lights blinking on the remote platform. The lonely structures scattered in the distance looked as if they came from a child's erector set; the enormous black sea could swallow them in an instant.

He finally saw the woman when he walked through the mess to get some fruit. Surachai was right: she was ugly. She was sitting alone with a book open in front of her. She had short cropped hair and was dressed in coveralls, as if trying to fit in.

He took two oranges, put them in the pockets of his shorts and climbed the stairs to the radio room. In one corner of the room across from the dispatcher's desk was a phone booth and the only phone, besides the one in the OIM's office, where you could make a call to somewhere outside of the company system. Hunter lifted a square plastic number from the hook and looked at the board; there were three people in front of him. It would take a while. Even though a sign in big black letters on the door of the booth, in English and Thai, said to limit your call to ten minutes, the Thais seldom did. He wondered what they jabbered on about for so long. After all, their shift was only fourteen days, over in the blink of an eye.

He peeled an orange and walked out into the games room. It was one of only two places on the platform you could smoke, and a pale gauze cloud hung in the air. A few guys were playing at the pool table; in a corner high against the wall a TV blared a Thai news program annoyingly loud.

A few of the men nodded at him and Hunter nodded back. He mouthed "hello" with his mouth stuffed with orange segments. These were the guys he worked with; they'd have to depend on each other if there was an emergency, and what did he know about them, about their lives off the platform, their dreams for the future? He knew only the names of a handful of mechanics in the shop – and of course the OIM and the Superintendents and Safety Officer. The others were just guys who worked in the same place as him, thrown together by circumstance, and there was no reason to pretend they were friends. You tolerated each other,

Hunter thought; you did what you had to do to get through your tour.

But he knew this: scratch beneath the surface, behind the smiles and the deferential nods, and you would find nothing but seething resentment. He was sure of it; he could feel it. They begrudged him his high salary, feeling he was overpaid and underworked, and they should get a larger slice of the pie. But hell, they ran to him for help whenever they met the smallest glitch. What would they do if he wasn't here? Shut down the train for three days while they figured it out? Call in a consultant from Singapore? Any rational person would say he was needed here. But it was not a logical matter; it had to do with their pride, their self-respect, their 'face'.

His number finally came up and he closed the phone booth door, creating a cocoon of silence. It was nearly five in the afternoon in Paris, a little later than he'd said he would call. He tapped in the long set of numbers and waited, listening to the clicks and buzzes on the line.

When Kambiz answered the phone, there was a hint of fading laughter in his voice, as if he'd just been pulled away from some scintillating and amusing conversation.

"Ah, Mr Hunter! Thank you so much for your fax."

It was the first time they had spoken, though they had exchanged faxes several times. After a few minutes of pleasantries, they got down to business.

"And you are interested in one of our properties in the Aegean?"

"That's right. But that's as far as it goes right now, Mr

Kambiz, just interested. Can you tell me something about access to the island? What's the nearest port?"

"Yes, of course." Hunter could hear the whisper of shuffling papers. "Let me fill you in on some of the details that may not have appeared in the brochure we sent you. The island is off the Turkish coast; the nearest port is called Bodrum. Quite a charming little place. The Karanda Marina there is more than adequate. You can easily make your own arrangements there without any hassle. The Aegean is an excellent choice, Mr Hunter. You know, so much American money these days is going into the Caribbean that properties there have become really overpriced. The eastern Mediterranean gives far more value for money. By the way, have you thought about Croatia? We are expecting great potential there once things settle down politically."

"Right now I'm thinking about the Aegean, Greece or Turkey."

"Yes, of course. I don't blame you. Do you know what they call the Turkish coast? The turquoise coast."

"Is there fresh water on the island?"

"Let's see … the island is 34 acres, a sandy beach on the western side, perfect for barbecues at sunset, I might add. And yes, there is a well and even a small bungalow, though it's been abandoned for some time."

Kambiz, the consummate salesman, of unstated Middle Eastern origin, probably Iranian. Over the phone he came across much smoother than in his letters, just the right blend of familiarity and respectful distance.

"What kind of price are we talking about, Mr Kambiz?"

"Let me see. This property is listed at three point two. But I believe the owner is open to negotiations."

Three million two hundred thousand American dollars.

"May I ask you sir, what line of business you are in?"

"Import export." There was no need for him to know anything.

"Excellent. The reason I ask, Mr Hunter, is because if you are free to travel, I would like to invite you to see the property first-hand. It is the only way you can really judge the magnificence of the place. We could meet someplace. Say Athens? Istanbul?"

In two days he'd be back onshore and could easily book a flight from Bangkok or Singapore to Istanbul. But he wasn't ready for that. There was the small matter of coming up with the money first.

"Well, Mr Kambiz, I do intend to fly out there soon to see the property and to meet with you in person. At the moment, however, I'm tied up with my business and won't be able to travel for a few months."

"That is a shame, sir. You know a property like this won't stay on the market for very long. I'm sure you appreciate that, sir."

"Yes, Mr Kambiz, I do. Thank you for all your help. I will send you a fax soon. By the way, what is the name of the island?"

"Let's see. The locals call it Abritus. But I guess, Mr Hunter, once it's yours, you may call it whatever you like."

Hunter thanked the radio operator as he left the room, feeling suddenly generous and happy. No man is an island; isn't that what they said? But if you had a three million or so you could own one. And that would be good enough for him.

Fifteen

"Hello?"

"Alex?"

"Yeah?" His voice sounded like a croak. Like a frog about to croak.

"Alex, is that you?"

He recognized his sister's voice immediately, from the very first word, but there was a confusing delay and echo on the line and they both began talking at once.

"Elly ..."

"Alex ..."

There was also foam rubber in his brain and his throat was stuffed with cotton. And a girl in his bed.

He looked over his shoulder to the bedroom and watched her sit up and toss her mane of black hair over her shoulders. She came out of the bedroom naked and glanced accusingly at him, as if it were his fault the phone had woken her up. She went into the bathroom and closed the door hard, locking it loudly.

"Elly, gosh, what a surprise." A knife of panic stabbed him. Why was she calling at such an ungodly hour? Something must be wrong. "Is everything OK back there?"

"Everything's fine. The kids are still on break, Joe's in

Washington for a week. How are you? We haven't heard from you in weeks."

"I'm fine, El. Ah … what time is it?"

"Six thirty. I thought Saturday would be a good time to call. I mean, I know the time's different there but …"

"Never mind, El." Saturday night in Detroit equaled Sunday morning in Songkhla. 6:30 Sunday morning. "This is a pretty good time to catch me at home," he said weakly.

"You haven't written or called in a while. We were worried about you."

"I'm great. Couldn't be better." Well, maybe if he had a handful of paracetamol and a bucket of ice water to stick his head into … Where had they finished up last night? And why had he broken one of his cardinal rules and brought a bargirl back to the bungalow? Philips was supposed to stop him from making that kind of blunder.

"And how's your job?"

"It's terrific. Just great. Very interesting. And every day's different. It never gets boring." Gin's Place. That's where he'd finished. The two French engineers Sturges had asked him to look after had long since gone back to the hotel. Even Philips had left by then. That was why he hadn't been around to talk Marek out of bringing this girl back to the bungalow.

"And what's the food like over there? I have this vision of you all thin and gaunt. Like one of those guys who's been lost at sea for three months."

"The food's great. If anything, I'm getting fat." He couldn't blame Philips for leaving early though. It wouldn't have made any difference. The girl was gorgeous. Dark skin and eyes set wide apart like an Egyptian princess, a slender waist and muscular thighs, lips of deep purple. She was also spoiled and horribly vain, but after five or six drinks that hadn't seemed to matter much.

"Your health OK? Joe says there's a lot of hepatitis over there, malaria, that sort of stuff. Are there any doctors there?"

Christ, where did she think he was living? "Yes, El, they do have doctors in Thailand. Anyway, I'm healthy as a pig." The toilet flushed and the girl came out with a towel wrapped around her. She went straight into the bedroom and buried herself under the blankets without even so much as a glance in his direction.

"Ah, the maid's here now," he said, pre-empting any of his sister's questions about the background noise. "I told you about all my servants, right? They wait on me hand and foot."

"You know, Alex, you've been over there for four or five months now. Your contract's nearly half over. You'll be back here before you know it."

Five months! Had it really gone that fast? He'd have to call Sturges and find out about a contract extension; right after he called Philips and cleared up some details about last night.

"Have you thought about lining something up back home?"

"Well ... ah ... tell you the truth, I hadn't thought about it too much."

There wasn't a chair within reach so he sat on the floor. This was going to be worse than he'd thought. He should have known this was coming. To Elly this was all just a lark, one last little fling before the wayward brother came back to the bosom of his home and family, found a wife and job and settled down. How

could he tell his sister he was having the time of his life and had no intention of trading it in for icy winters, outrageous taxes, and women who wouldn't glance at him twice?

"Joe and I were talking the other day. Y'know he's got a lot of contacts. Not just in Detroit, all over the country. Guys with your background – software and hardware – they're begging for guys like you. He could help you get a really good job."

"Really?" Marek tried to sound enthusiastic.

"Sure. I mean, why just yesterday he was saying that at St Francis Hospital they were so short-handed in the IT section they were desperate. You could walk in tomorrow and get a real plum of a job."

"Well, gee, El. That sounds really great." What a coward he was! Surely she could see right through his feigned, lukewarm interest. Why couldn't he just tell her that working nine to five in some office, changing hard drives, installing the latest Windows upgrade to fifty desktop PCs a day – it would be a kind of living hell?

"And it's not just at St Francis. It's everywhere."

"That's great, Elly. Really, great. The thing is, I do have the rest of my contract here and … well … It's a good job and I'm learning a lot … making a lot of contacts here too." He sounded ridiculous. Making contacts with whom? Slender brown women? "I mean in the oil business. It's really kind of a fascinating area. All kinds of things could open up."

He needed water and a pain reliever. He needed to shut up and get off the phone.

"But isn't it dangerous? We hear a lot about Thailand in the news here. There's all that stuff about drugs and AIDS ..."

"All that stuff's blown out of proportion there, Elly. I mean, after all, you live in Detroit. Aren't there drugs and AIDS there?"

"It's different."

"Different? Why?" Different because that was all down in the ghetto and not in safe, walled-in white suburbia? Even if that were true – which of course it wasn't – how could that make anybody feel better? "I mean really, El. It's a lot safer here than it is in Detroit. Really. I know that's hard for people to accept back there, but it's true." He was getting defensive now; there was an edge to his voice he couldn't restrain.

"It's different, Alex. It's different because we're here together, we're a family here. That's what makes it different."

They were both silent. He let his exasperation course silently along the line.

"We're just worried about you is all." Her voice was subdued. She sounded hurt.

"Elly, remember what you told me just before I left? You said I had a right to be happy. Well, maybe this is it. I mean, happiness is not something I ever think much about one way or the other. I always figured it happened or it didn't happen, whatever, you just went about your business anyway. But you know, Elly, maybe I'm really happy here."

"Well, I guess that's good then. If you're really happy. That's great." She sounded doubtful.

"Look, Elly, I don't know how much longer I'll stay. I don't know when my contract will end. But I'll try to get back home for at least a visit in six months, OK? Believe me, I'm fine here and it's not dangerous at all, probably less so than Detroit."

Marek knew she'd never believe that, but she nonetheless acted as if she did. She put the girls on, one by one, and they each said hi to their uncle and told him about the summer camp they'd attended in the Upper Peninsula.

"Don't worry about me, El," he said as he rang off, but knew she would anyway. And it made him a little sad that she might soon begin to see him as a lost cause: immature, irresponsible, perhaps even slightly irrational.

He went to the refrigerator, grabbed one of the liter bottles of water the maid had put in and downed it completely. He looked into the bedroom, and to his surprise, the girl was awake and dressed, combing her hair in front of the wardrobe mirror.

Then suddenly it hit him, like a fist to the solar plexus. It was Sunday. He had a date with Saranya. He was supposed to be meeting her and her friends at the hotel. They were taking him to the famous temple cave in Yala. He was to meet them at eight and here it was – he searched desperately for his watch and finally found it on the kitchen table – nearly 7:30.

He stuffed some bills into the girl's handbag as she watched him in the mirror.

"*Thawray?*" she asked.

"Five hundred." She frowned but said nothing. He waved down a motorcycle taxi heading toward the hotel, gave him fifty baht and put her on the back. They sped off and she never looked back.

He took a shower, making it as hot as he could stand, hoping he could somehow burn the alcohol out of his pores. He brushed his teeth a long time, also scrubbing his tongue hard.

He would be a little late but no matter, so would they, probably: Thai time. He called Philips.

"Do you know what the bloody time is?"

"I ended up with the one from Gin's Place. You know, the hot one? Brought her back here. You're supposed to stop me from doing stupid things like that, remember? You always told me, 'Keep work and play separate'. Or was it 'Don't shit in your own nest'?"

"Stop you? You were like a bloody train wreck. An avalanche. A tsunami. How was I supposed to stop that?"

"I'm meeting Saranya and her friends for a trip to Yala."

He laughed. "Serves you bloody right."

"And my sister called this morning. Six thirty."

"Yeah? And she wanted to know when you're going to give up all this foolishness and come home and get a life, eh?"

"How'd you guess? Christ, all I want to do is go back to bed and sleep for ten hours."

"Nonsense, you'll sleep when you're dead."

Marek got into the pickup thinking Saranya would see right through him, know he was a sex-crazed drunk, and wipe her hands of him forever.

He drove to the Bay Garden Hotel, parked his car in the gravel lot and walked to the front of the hotel where he was to meet them. They couldn't take his pickup because there wouldn't be enough room for everybody. He didn't like leaving the station without wheels – what if there was an emergency offshore? – but

Saranya's friends had promised him that if he needed to get back, they would drive him home immediately.

The sky was cloudless and the sea silvery blue, the morning quiet broken only by the chattering of mynahs and the clicking of the gardener's shears on the hotel hedges.

Eventually a white Mazda pulled up in the roundabout. The windows were tinted so he couldn't see inside, but the front passenger side door opened without anybody getting out. There was a chorus of "Good morning, teacher" (surely they were joking, thought Marek) as he approached the car.

"You can sit in the front," said Saranya. "It is more comfortable for you."

She was sitting directly behind him, wearing her hair in a long braid that tumbled down the front of her T-shirt. Unlike the others, he noticed immediately, she was also wearing lipstick and eye makeup.

"Have you eaten breakfast?" she asked.

"I never eat breakfast."

She rummaged through a bag and brought out a bell-shaped pale-green fruit. *Chumpoo*, she called it. "What do you call it in English?" He didn't know; he'd never seen it before. "I think it is rose apple," she said. It was pulpy and had almost no taste, but instantly freshened his mouth.

They were five: Marek, Jum, Apple, Saranya and the driver, Jum's cousin, a secretary at a canning factory. The girls radiated youth and good health and smelled of bath soap and fresh laundry. Almost absurd, thought Marek, to seem so healthy and fresh so early on a Sunday morning. Their cleanliness coupled with the pearly blue morning made him feel slightly giddy, as if he'd swallowed some drug ten minutes ago and it was just starting to hit him.

They began offering him food: curry-filled buns, sweet glutinous rice wrapped in banana leaves, and Ziploc bags of sticky strips of preserved mango. Someone had brought a loaf of bread, perhaps thinking that this was what farangs liked to eat for breakfast, but it was like no bread Marek had ever seen before. Each slice had a swirl of pink that tasted of artificial strawberry. It was so sickly sweet he could barely get down one piece and had to beg off offers of more.

They were soon out of the city and on the road to Yala, driving past rubber plantations and shimmering rice fields. Because of the food and the beautiful morning, but especially because of the company, he was beginning to feel as if he'd joined the living again. He loosened his seat belt and turned to face the others in the back.

"Now, today we are going to speak English all day, all the time, right?"

"Yes," they answered in chorus.

"That's what you said you wanted to do on this trip, practice English."

"Yes!"

"Can you speak English?" he asked the driver.

"Little bit," she answered, giggling.

He had them take turns. He told them to talk about anything: what they saw on TV last night, what their favorite food was, what they thought about the current government. Only the driver was unable to manage at least a few sentences, and only Saranya could talk at any level of fluency. After a while she began to dominate the conversation, just as she did during their sessions in front of the hotel, and he became concerned that it would turn into a two-way conversation, though no one else really seemed to care.

"Tell me about your father. What does he do?"

"He's a government worker. He works in the Saboi Ya district. He is not too high and not too low."

"And he was born in Songkhla?"

"No, he is from Ratchaburi. But he was sent here to work with the government, and he met my mother here. She was born in Songkhla."

"And what about your grandparents? Where are they from?"

"Tokyo," said Apple, and the other girls laughed. Saranya said nothing but seemed caught off guard.

"Tokyo?"

"Yes," said Apple, suddenly talkative. "That is why she is so beautiful. Her grandfather is from Japan." Again, the other two girls, Jum and the driver, laughed.

"Really? Japan?" Maybe it was a joke of some kind. Saranya smiled and then turned toward the window, suddenly reticent. He felt like he shouldn't pursue it – Saranya obviously didn't want to – so he dropped it.

"OK, OK, *paw laew*, enough English. You can rest now."

"But you said we must speak all day."

"My ears are tired."

"OK," said Saranya brightening. "Now it is your turn. Now

you must speak Thai." She said this with just the slightest bit of cheek and the others cheered.

He had worked his way through the three books and tapes from Dr Choonthan's course and regularly conversed with the bargirls (though in rather limited subject areas); still, he knew he couldn't really converse in the language with any depth. As a joke, he began to stutter through some of the sentences he had memorized from his taped lessons: "Uncle sells eggs in the market". "The bull is larger than the cow." "Bangkok is very hot this month." They were like random sentences generated by a machine, Dr Choonthan's theory of learning apparently being that it was better to practice the vocabulary and pronunciation in these disjointed sentences rather than simulate any actual, human conversation.

They encouraged him like kindergarten teachers, but teachers who could barely rein in their laughter. "Mother Ploi buys rice in the market." "Please take me to the American Embassy." "How much is the fried rice?" The students taught him a Thai tongue twister, and all four women howled at his mangled attempt to repeat it. He began to feel a little chagrined, but they made him continue. "*Phoot si! Phoot!*" they cried, "Speak!"; almost, thought Marek, like one trained a dog to bark. But he swallowed his pride and continued.

Saranya, who was sitting directly behind him, pointed out that when he said a word with a high tone he raised his head, when he pronounced a low tone he lowered it, and when the word demanded a rising tone he swung his head in a great upward arc. The overall effect, she said, was that when he spoke, he "shook his head like an Indian". This reduced Saranya and her friends nearly to tears.

"It's the only way I can remember the tones," he said a little sheepishly. Then he exaggerated the head movements as he spoke, and the others turned into squealing rag dolls.

The road was good, and the secretary drove fast, fearlessly overtaking busses and trucks despite the heavy traffic. A few times she made it back into their proper lane a little too close to the oncoming car for Marek's comfort. He tried to look at the scenery. Every so often he noticed on the shoulder of the road piles of shattered glass, like gems sparkling in the sunlight. Were these the splintered windshields of accident victims, swept neatly to the side of the road and out of everybody's way? What else could they be? But it seemed there was a pile every several hundred meters. It was mind-boggling to think how many crushed vehicles – and perhaps bodies – they represented.

The car filled with a citrus smell as Saranya offered him a section of tangerine, her elegant hand and long thin fingers appearing in the space between the two front seats. She wore three gold bracelets and her fingernails were lacquered a soft pink. He turned to thank her, meeting her eyes for the first time that day.

"Mai pen rai, khaa," she answered, adding the last politeness word – unnecessary between them as friends, he thought – and made it sound like a soft word one would whisper during lovemaking. He rolled the swollen tangerine section in his mouth, anticipating the juicy sweetness he'd find when he bit into it.

They drove for over an hour before they reached Yala town. It was still morning but as they got out of the air-conditioned

174

car the heat closed in around them as if they'd stepped into a steel foundry. They were parked in the city center near the train station, and the girls were looking for a favorite restaurant. All the shops had their awnings pulled out, but there were so many obstacles under them that you couldn't walk in the slight shade they provided. There were baskets of fruit, coolers holding plastic bottles of water, soft drinks, and tumblers of a strange yellowish liquid. The pavements were blocked with cardboard boxes full of plastic toys, woven throw rugs, garden tools, bicycle parts or just men sitting on stools fanning themselves with newspapers. For Marek the awnings were too low, and rather than negotiate through the impediments with a stooped head, he chose to walk in the sun. It was a brutal, crushing heat that made his head hurt. By the time they had found the restaurant, his shirt was stuck to him in several places.

This was a Muslim city, and though the shopkeepers looked distinctively Chinese, the men walking on the street or loitering at the corners wore skullcaps, beards and long Malay-type skirts. The women wore long colorful dresses and scarves. A few wore full Middle East-type abayas that revealed only their eyes.

The women had chosen a Muslim restaurant; they ordered chicken with saffron rice and a beef soup with leeks and tomatoes. Some of the people in the restaurant stared at them, but they didn't seem to mind. After lunch they found a small supermarket and stocked up on essentials: a roll of tissue, bottles of spring water, and a few canisters of Pringle's Sour Cream and Onion potato chips.

Wat Naa Tham was another eight kilometers from the city.

It was a very holy site, Saranya said, one of the holiest sites in all of Southern Thailand. Marek followed the others to the foot of the stairs which led to the mouth of the cave, then detoured when he saw what looked like a museum exhibit to the right. It had pictures of old Buddha images, the features smoothed by the erosion of time. There were bracelets and pottery, but he could find no English signs or explanations anywhere. He left the exhibit and climbed the stone stairs to the cave entrance.

There were many pilgrims and tourists and the crowd of people moved slowly up the narrow flight of stairs to the entrance. He saw a few other farangs ahead of him and heard snatches of Dutch or German. A trio of overweight Chinese girls, from Malaysia or Singapore or Taipei, chugged up the stairs in front of him, wearing dark glasses, sun dresses and floppy hats.

He had lost the others now; they were inside the temple. At the entrance at the top of the stairs, shoes overflowed the wooden racks and were strewn about the rock floor. Marek leaned against the stone barrier so he could untie his Nikes and remove his socks. Barefoot now, he stepped into the dusky twilight of the cave. The place was redolent with the pungent aroma of burning joss sticks. Thick strands of smoke interwove in the lateral shafts of light coming from crevices in the walls of the cave. The space was the size of a tennis court and dominated by a huge golden reclining Buddha. The air was hushed, the murmur of prayers and the soft tinkling of bells all that could be heard. As Marek's eyes adjusted to the light, he could make out smaller shrines and statues placed along the walls of the cave. He heard squeaking and looked up to see a dozen or so bats hanging between the stalactites twenty feet above him. Occasionally the drone of prayers was interrupted by the sonorous clang of an unseen brass bell.

Marek walked around the cavern looking for Saranya. The floor of the cave was cool rock, smoothed by the feet of hundreds of years of visiting worshippers. This place was ancient, so much older than any place of worship he'd ever been in before, and yet the Thais seemed hardly impressed by that aspect. They didn't walk around in a stunned sense of awe, and they were not like church visitors. The people seemed not so much to be worshipping as to be simply visiting, like tourists at the Louvre.

He finally saw the others near an altar in front of the large reclining Buddha. Saranya was kneeling on a mat, her hands held together in prayer. Between her fingers were two sticks of burning joss. Marek was fascinated by the sight of her piety; he moved closer to watch her. Her eyes were closed and her lips were moving, evidently mouthing some prayer. Her face was softly lit from the candles and joss and she looked truly beautiful and serene – but also something more; innocent and reverent. He couldn't take his eyes off her. This calm and worshipping face was completely devoid of any of the irony or brashness which often surfaced.

He watched her possessively. She placed the joss sticks in a vase of sand, then from her kneeling position dipped her head three times to the mat, then backed away from the Buddha on her knees, all the while pressed her hands together in a wai, before rising. She turned around and he caught her eye. She smiled at him: a beautiful, sharing, radiant smile. It was meant, it seemed, only for him.

He called Niwat from a public phone in a restaurant. Things were quiet at the station; there was no need for him to hurry back.

The restaurant was open-air, with a cement floor and molded plastic chairs. The others were off someplace, souvenir shopping or exploring some of the lesser caves. He and Saranya were drinking iced coffee.

"Saranya, what did they mean? About your grandfather being Japanese?" Her face showed nothing, neither surprise nor annoyance. She sipped on her straw and searched his eyes as if trying to discover what his motive for asking such a question could be.

"Yes, it's true. My grandfather was Japanese." She looked away as if to say that was all she was going to say about it. But Marek's curiosity was not so easily satisfied.

"Well, what about your grandmother?"

"She was Thai."

"Did she live in Japan?"

"No. Alex, it was a long time ago, during the war. World War II. My grandfather was an officer in the Japanese army. They came to Songkhla, I mean, the Japanese did. Many of them went on to Singapore. But my grandfather stayed in Songkhla until the end of the war."

"And after the war?"

"He did not stay. He went back to Japan. Or maybe the police, the army police? Maybe they captured him. Nobody knows." She was quiet then, absently stirring her drink.

"I'm sorry, Saranya. Really, it's none of my business."

"No, it's OK. Of course, we can know nothing of what it

was like then. It was so very long ago. It is not something we talk about in my family very much."

He was used to this now: her face composed, her eyes quiet and inward-looking, her lips slightly parted; but what kind of maelstrom of emotions was going on inside?

"You see, it was war. The Japanese came to Songkhla. My grandmother was a young woman. She used to help her mother who had a small restaurant. Somehow this Japanese officer and she came together. Maybe he used to see her in the market or in the restaurant. I don't know. But they came together and they fell in love. She always said that he was very gentle and very kind.

"But it was a war. And war is very bad. Then the war ended, and he was gone. And soon after my father was born."

Saranya was quiet for a while, as if gathering her strength before continuing.

"It was difficult. Many people, they looked down on my grandmother, on our family. Even today, some people look down on us. They cannot understand. For my grandmother it was very bad then. She was alone with her baby, my father, and no man, no husband. But still she was lucky. She married again a few years later. A very kind man who could accept her even though she already had a child from another man. He was much older and had lost his first wife somehow, I think to disease. He took care of my grandmother very well. That's what she said. But they never had any children, and the man died only a few years after they were married. And so her good luck quickly turned to bad, as if she was cursed, and she was alone again with her baby, my father.

"My grandmother took good care of my father, and her

brothers helped her. The family helped her even though many people in Songkhla thought she was a bad woman, or cursed. My father did very good in school. And then, when he finished school, he got a job with the government. He was very lucky. You see, a job with the government means security, and it was very good to have that job. The people now, they could not look down on my family."

They heard a snatch of Japanese from some tourists at a nearby table. They looked at each other and laughed, the tension broken.

"When I was small," said Saranya, "when my grandmother was still alive, she used to tell me about my grandfather. She used to talk about how kind and how handsome he was. I think she loved him very much, even until the day she died, many, many years after the last time she'd seen him. But it was very sad, too. I think she always believed he would come back."

"Come back to Thailand?"

"Yes. I think he told her that before he left. He would come back to Thailand. He would not leave her. He would help her some way. Somehow, he would return to take care of her.

"You see, she died thinking this, that he would not leave her, that someday he would return." There was a hint of hope in her eyes as well, not that she thought her Japanese grandfather would ever return, but rather that she had shared this intimate story with Marek, with the hope that she could trust him with it, trust him with the pain and shame it had caused her family. "But of course, he never did." She sighed. "Anyway, it is all such a long time ago. Better to just forget it."

The others returned, carrying their newly bought trinkets, and they ordered more drinks. The sun was high and hot, and during the drive back to Songkhla, Marek dozed off. They dropped him at the hotel, promising they'd be on time for their next English lesson. Saranya smiled joyfully at him as she said goodbye, a young girl full of happiness, with not a worldly concern or disappointment to pass a shadow across her heart.

Sixteen

Someone in the Time Out bar had told Marek about it: a section of the market, tucked back in the claustrophobic alleyways, where there were tables filled with canned and packaged goods smuggled in from the west via Singapore and Malaysia, things you couldn't find anywhere else in Songkhla, a mecca of snacks and treats from back home.

Marek found the entrance to the market between a hardware store and a fabric shop. At first it seemed like any other dry goods market in Thailand: lots of T-shirts, jeans, luggage, watches, toys, Walkmans, belts, umbrellas, sunglasses, clocks, miniature TVs... so much of so many of the same things that you wondered how any single vendor ever made a profit. Just as Marek was about to turn back, thinking he was in the wrong area, he saw one stall with a table full of canned and packaged foods. There were raisins and pistachios from California, canned Bartlett pears and peach halves in heavy syrup, jars of sweet dill pickles and olives stuffed with pimentos, bags of Oreo cookies and Fig Newtons, all the stuff from back home that he'd never seen in any shop in Songkhla.

All of it had been smuggled over the border from Malaysia, the story went, brought in under cover of night to avoid the heavy excise tax on foreign foods. Marek was dumbfounded when he did the conversion from baht to dollars: $3.20 for a jar of olives. A bag of Oreo cookies for $2.40. He held a can of peaches in his hand and wondered if it was worth nearly five dollars. Just this once, he told himself, I'll buy one item. A one-time treat. But it's got to be something really special. Then he saw the red and white can of Campbell's Pork and Beans with Real Bacon Bits. He paid the woman the equivalent of over three dollars and swore he would never admit to anybody in his life that he had paid that much for a can of beans.

The vendor smiled at him and raised her arm above her table of goods. "What else, sir?" she asked, a happy, confident fisherman with a big one on the hook, easily reeled in. He picked up the plastic jar of California pistachios and did the calculation in his head. Seven dollars. Well, maybe just this once. He forked over the money and wondered why the vendor wasn't wearing a bandit's mask. He received his change then zipped his goods into his backpack and made his way out through the cramped aisles.

It was three o'clock. In the closeness of the market the heat clung to everything. The old women selling fruit lazily waved the flies away from their apples and grapes. He squeezed between tables laden with prawns and pink fish and made his way to the wider access lane that ran along the old city wall. Here was a chaos of motorcycles, pushcarts, impromptu food stalls, and vendors carrying cloth bundles nearly half their own size. Some boys were unloading a ten-wheel truck, heaving big cardboard boxes on to their shoulders and carrying them into the market. From behind, he heard somebody call out "Hey!" and, for some reason, even amid the noise and confusion of the market, he knew it was meant for him. Then he heard the same voice again and turned to see John Hunter towering over everyone, dark sunglasses and shaved head, waving at him.

There was a samlor moving between them and many people walking and pushing in both directions, and Marek thought for a moment he could pretend he hadn't seen him, just slip into the stream of people and walk away. But it was too late. Hunter had sliced through the crowd, his big body moving easily and gracefully, and was upon him, gripping his forearm. He was grinning ear-to-ear as if this was one of the happiest coincidences of his life.

"Well, I'll be damned! Madison, Wisconsin in the Songkhla market. C'mon, I'll buy you a beer."

"Sorry, I can't, I've got to …"

"Oh c'mon. Hell, I know you paid for all that food and drink last time. At least let me buy you a beer. Make up for it."

Hunter drew him into a noodle shop with a bare concrete floor and tiled walls. He led him to a table in the back under the ceiling fan where it was dim and cool. They sat down on wooden stools and Hunter signaled the waitress.

"This is where I hang out to get away from it all," laughed Hunter. He was wearing a T-shirt and jeans, and when he sat down and put his elbows on the table the sleeves of his shirt rolled up his taut, oversized arms. "Carl-berg *bia nung*," he ordered, in a horrendous imitation of Thai. "Oh and chai rawn. Tea for me. I'm on the wagon, for a few days anyway."

Marek sat with his back to the wall, squeezed into the

corner of the shop, with barely enough room for his legs under the table. From somewhere behind him came the sound of a TV and something frying. Somebody coughed and the biting scent of chili peppers reached his nose. The girl brought their drinks and Marek took a quick swig from the bottle.

Hunter lounged against the wall and talked about something he'd seen in the newspaper, a new pub in Bangkok that was decorated in a Nazi theme, complete with swastikas and Third Reich flags. He found it hilarious.

"Imagine on the one hand that the Thais are either completely ignorant about, or just don't give a shit about, something we in the West are taught to believe is one of the greatest tragedies in history, y'know, like we're supposed to cry a fucking bucket every time the Holocaust is mentioned; yet on the other hand, it's so goddamn refreshing. No fucking political correctness here."

He was happy, upbeat, almost giddy, and Marek wondered if he were on amphetamines. There was no hint of the Hunter from Jinda's, the out of control drunk looking for a fight. Marek thought about Jinda and her bruised cheek and the way the other girls acted as if nothing had happened. He remembered the dull hate in Hunter's eyes when the young fishermen tried to talk to him.

Hunter took off his sunglasses and folded them next to the teapot. Marek had forgotten the striking blue of his eyes, almost transparent, and the fishhook scar across his nose. He was laughing about something else in the newspaper; a deputy minister caught stealing funds meant for highway improvement.

"Let's see, what does it say here?" He twisted on his stool and folded the pages until he found it. "Ah, yeah. For his crime he will be transferred to 'an inactive post'. That's what it says. I guess that means he gets his salary but doesn't have to do anything. Not a bad punishment for misappropriation of state funds, huh?" His eyes were bright, his grin had none of that predatory irony he'd had in the bar. "Fucking Thailand! Never boring, is it? Crazy, frustrating, infuriating ... but never boring."

Hunter nodded toward Marek's backpack. "Been shopping, huh? Me, I walk through the wet market every once in a while, just to remind myself never to eat any meat in the local restaurants. The smell, the rats, the blood. So what did you get anyway?"

Marek showed him the pistachios. Hunter squeezed the bag and looked at them critically.

"Food of the gods, eh? How much, if you don't mind?"

"One fifty, about."

"Cheap at twice the price."

"I was afraid they might be a little old, you know? There's no consume-by date."

"Don't matter," said Hunter. "They'll be OK. The California nuts are good but not as good as the ones from the Middle East. Best pistachios are from Dubai, best dates in Saudi Arabia. Best whiskey is Irish single malt, not Scottish as many people think, but Jack Daniels comes very close, though as a recreational drink nothing beats the old Thai Golden Cat. Best beef is Kobe steak from Japan. They feed the cows beer and massage their stomachs every day. Let's see, what else ..." He turned in his stool and caught sight of a pair of young girls walking hand-in-hand past the shop.

"Oh yeah ... best pussy. Where do you figure that is, Madison?"

He was grinning again, half challenge, half taunt.

"Everywhere? Anywhere?"

"Sumatra. Those young village girls had unbelievable muscle development. Don't know how they did it. Must have been trained from a young age; something handed down over the generations. They'd squeeze your prick like it was in a velvet vice. I was on a start-up crew down there and we spent so much time in the bars and whore houses we financed a goddamn housing boom."

Hunter refilled his cup from the porcelain pot on the table. The tea was tinged with a hint of copper and steamed the top of his glass.

"There are some advantages to being oil trash," he said, "besides all the shit. Digging sand out of my ass in Saudi one year and freezing my balls off in the Arctic the next." He leaned against the tiled wall and looked out to the street.

"But I tell you what man, this is it for me. This is the last fucking stop on the highway. The last of the one-night stands." He leaned over the table as if letting Marek in on some secret. "I'm getting out of this shit once and for all."

Marek remembered this as a theme that had played out in their first encounter. Maybe like Sturges he'd trade the field work for an office job. But somehow Marek couldn't picture Hunter in shirt and tie, playing desk jockey all day.

"Retiring or ...?" he asked.

"Oh, I've got some irons in the fire," said Hunter, vaguely, suddenly reticent. He rubbed his hand over his shaved head and fiddled with his sunglasses. Both men were silent; and then Hunter nodded, seemingly coming to a conclusion about something and began speaking again.

"I've tried a couple of things, you know, like gem trading. You buy them here, mostly rubies and sapphires, for a fraction of what you can get them for in the States – that is, if you know what you're doing and can trust the dealer. Then you sell them in the States for a tidy little profit. And then when I had a wife in Singapore, before we broke up, her cousin and her had a little shop, and I used to bring back lots of handicrafts from Thailand. Silk and whatnot. Amazing how much people'd pay for that shit down there.

"And another time I had these fake Rolex watches. Connection of mine here in town was trying to sell them. I took a bag of them offshore and got rid of all of them in two days. I mean, the guys knew they were fake. I wasn't rippin' 'em off or anything. But the folks back home would think they were real and be mighty impressed.

"Anyway, that's all small-time shit. The real money is in antiques, but that's a little trickier."

"Trickier?"

"As in illegal. But in this country illegal is only a temporary setback, you know, like the minister who gets caught with his hand in the till.

"I mean, you go to Bangkok and see these antique shops up and down Sukhumvit Road and in all the big hotels. Now, how can they sell the stuff, since the exportation of Thai antiquities, especially Buddha images, is strictly illegal?"

"Maybe it's fake," said Marek.

"Some of it is, for sure. But it can't all be. The big hotels, for instance. They have reputations to protect. They can't be selling imitation shit to their globetrotting business clients. No, they're breaking the law and getting away with it. Big time." Hunter lifted Marek's empty bottle of beer and signaled the waitress.

"No, thanks," said Marek. "I should get moving."

"What's the rush? Just one more. See, they're making huge profits. And sometimes I think ..." he leaned forward and lowered his voice to a whisper, "... why the hell can't I get in on this shit? I mean, how hard can it be?"

The waiter brought the beer and Hunter leaned back against the wall. Marek figured he was pulling his leg but said nothing. If taking him seriously would get him out of here quicker, that's what he'd do.

"Shit, the world is your oyster, right man?" said Hunter.

"Yeah, the problem is, oysters give me the shits," said Marek. Hunter laughed loud enough to make heads turn.

"I like you Madison. Y'know, you and me should become business partners. After all we're the only Yanks around here. We gotta stick together. Can't trust no one else, right?"

"I dunno," said Marek. "Don't think I'd make much of a businessman."

"Bullshit. All you gotta do is come up with one good idea or steal one from someone."

A scrawny black and white cat was weaving between his legs. A woman's voice from the street, haggling over something, cut through the din.

"So how's your job? Out there at the GPS station on the beach road, right? Near the new hotel? The Serene whatever?"

Marek shrugged. "OK, I guess. Work's kind of inconsistent."

"That's life in Big Earl." Marek thought he meant a place, then realized he was saying "oil" with a fake Texas accent.

"You get out to the deep-sea port much?"

"Yeah, sometimes. Just last week had to replace a defective receiver."

"I guess you got a pass and everything?"

"Yeah, you gotta have a pass to get through security. They're pretty strict about it."

"You hungry, Madison?" asked Hunter. "They got a decent pork and rice here. Set you right up."

"Pork straight from the market, huh?"

Hunter laughed. "Yeah, they had to wrestle it from a couple of huge rats. You're OK, Madison." He reached over and clasped Marek's shoulder, his strong fingers digging into Marek's shoulder blade. "No shit, man, we should be partners." He brought out his wallet and handed over his card; Marek felt compelled to do the same.

"Well, shit, I'll have to come over and visit you sometime."

Marek finished off the beer. "I really gotta go. I got to check the faxes from Singapore and see if there's any work."

"I like this place because of the wall," said Hunter, ignoring Marek's attempt to escape. They both looked out to the lane. The flow of people and vehicles had diminished, but it was still a mass of disarray and muted noise; like a background in a great movie extravaganza, with the red brick wall as a perfect backdrop, adding color and atmosphere.

"You interested much in history?" asked Hunter.

"Actually, it was my major," said Marek, signaling the waitress.

"You'd think this town was just a two-bit shithole, full of oil trash and stinking of fish, right? But it's got a long and fascinating history. There were people here trading with Persia, India and China before the first Europeans ever arrived. The Portuguese occupied it and built a fort on the hill across the lake. And World War II? We all know about Pearl Harbor, right? But did you know that on the same day the Nips were bombing Hawaii they were landing here, right on Songkhla beach? They went from here right down the peninsula to Singapore."

"Yeah, I heard Japanese soldiers were here during World War II. And they stayed throughout the war?"

"Some of them did. Most of them went down to Singapore. Know how they did it? They came off the boats, right here on Samila beach. The commander's name was Tsuji. Had this crazy idea. Was gonna dress all his men in Thai military uniforms, hijack about forty busses and load them up with his men and all the girls they could find in the local tea houses and then drive down to the border. Had this idea that this party convoy was gonna get waved right on through the Malaysian border. Didn't quite happen that way. The Japs got shot at before they could even get to the Songkhla bars. I shit you not. You can look it up."

The bill came and Hunter grabbed it. He took a few notes out of his billfold and gave them to the girl, ignoring Marek's protests. Then he rose.

"I'll be out of town a lot this leave," said Hunter. "but I'll drop by to see you. Out at your station. Maybe next shore leave. I've got a business deal you might be interested in."

"I kinda doubt it. Like I said, I'm not much of a businessman."

"Just hear me out. Won't cost you a dime. What have you got to lose?"

"OK," said Marek, ready at that point to say anything to escape, "but I'm not always there."

"Don't worry," said Hunter. "I'll find you."

Seventeen

The others had begun to treat them as a couple. If Saranya was late to the lessons, they left a place for her on the marble bench next to him. If he drove them anywhere, it was always Saranya who sat in the front seat of the pickup. Once the group was walking along the surf line when Marek stopped to take off his shoes. He removed his sunglasses and gave them to whoever was nearest so he could untie the laces. The others continued to walk while he shed his shoes, tied the strings together and flung them over his shoulders. When he caught up with them, it was Saranya who had his glasses, almost as if she, by rights, was the one who should carry them.

One day they were at the beach under the cedars in the waning afternoon light. The sun was behind the mountain and the clouds were shot with pink and rose. Light and shadow played on the sea, making it look now blue, now silver, now purple. Three children played along the surf, too far away to be heard, silhouettes against the sky and the golden sand. The whole world was still and at peace, and Marek thought he had never seen the beach look so pretty. Even the fruit vendors were silent, as if they too were captured by the spell of light.

"*Suay,*" said Marek.

"*Suay,*" echoed the others. "Very beautiful." But Saranya said nothing.

He could feel it when she stopped paying attention. Her distraction and boredom were something tangible to him by now, and she made no attempt to hide it. She bent her head to look at his fingers, and then started rummaging through her purse. She pulled out a nail clipper, and then she held his hand and began cutting his nails.

"Hey!" he said, feigning fear and surprise. The others laughed.

"Too dirty, too long," said Saranya. "You must have a ... what do you call?"

"A manicure?" asked Marek. His voice was squeaky. He felt his face redden in embarrassment. It was not just that she had pointed out his dirty fingernails; it was also that she was holding his hand, a sign of intimacy for all the world to see. You didn't touch someone of the opposite sex in public; all of Thailand would think she was a prostitute. Or that's what the books said. And yet, no one here on the beach in Songkhla seemed to care one bit.

The other girls showed no surprise at all. But maybe they were used to this; it was just Saranya breaking the rules again. Or maybe it was OK because they considered Saranya and him a couple.

But were they?

She clipped and filed his nails, frowning down at his fingers, while the others chatted in Thai, ignoring them. Saranya picked at the last bits of dirt beneath his nails, and then put his hand down on the table with a flourish.

"*Set laew*." She looked at him for the first time since starting the task and smiled. He could still feel the light touch of her moist fingers on his palm.

* * *

He invited Philips to join them on a trip to a waterfall just outside of Hat Yai. The others liked him from the start. With his easy-going sense of fun, he outshone Marek and thwarted any of his attempts at making the students practice English. His Thai was far better than Marek's, and he regaled the girls with stories and jokes, much beyond Marek's ability to understand. Marek, in fact, became slightly jealous. Saranya peppered Philips with questions, and he began to think she was maybe flirting with him.

They started along the path to the top of the waterfall and eventually, as if by design, the others fell away and he and Saranya were alone.

"Your friend is very funny. His Thai is excellent."

They climbed to the top of the trail, the seventh level. The water frothed over black granite and into a shallow, clear pool. They dipped their feet in, and small silvery fish nipped at their toes. Their feet touched under the surface and they both laughed. *I'm thirty years old*, he thought, *playing footsie with my girlfriend whom I've never kissed.*

"She's far too good for you, mate," said Philips later that evening when they were having a beer in the Time Out.

"No, really, what do you think is going on?"

"Think about what she does, not about what she says or doesn't say. It's all a bit subtler than we're used to. The other girls, they act as kind of chaperones, 'cause it's not really good for a single Thai girl to be alone with a man. Especially a farang man, since everyone knows we're all sex-crazed maniacs."

"But they *did* leave us alone."

"Yeah, I was kind of curious as to what would happen, so I told the others I was too tired to climb all the way up, and we just hung out at the second level and let you go ahead. Meanwhile, while you were up there enjoying a little privacy, I told them what a hell of a guy you were. Lied my socks off for you. Told 'em you weren't just handsome and strong, but also kind, generous and had a heart as big as Texas. Also, you've got nothing but respect for Thais and their institutions and traditions. You didn't ravish her up there, did you?"

It seemed all too easy coming from Philips. Maybe he was right; maybe Marek just *thought* too much about things. But wasn't he supposed to be able to understand more as time went by, not less? Yet he had felt even more at sea since they had somehow, without crossing any line that Marek could identify, become a "couple". Everything was so unfixed, so free-floating. It made him feel totally inept and helpless, like there was something he should know, some way he should feel, some way he should act that everybody else knew except him. It was like they were all waiting, especially Saranya, for him to do something, but he didn't have a clue what it was. Sometimes, when the girls were half-joking, half-serious, talking about literature or life or love, they would ask him questions and he would feel as if it were a test and that he was failing miserably. And then something would shift, someone would tell a joke, and they would all be laughing again.

Over the weeks he and Saranya spent more time together, and often went out alone without the others. They had dinner together or went to Hat Yai for shopping.

And then there was the basket of fruit. That was the first time Saranya came to the station. He answered the knock and found her on the porch, grinning, her motorcycle parked at the stairs. She was holding a wicker basket of mangoes.

"From my friend's farm," she said. "Too much for me and my family." He took the basket from her and invited her in. She helped him put the fruit away and had a cup of tea. It was perfectly normal, he thought, except good Thai girls didn't do this kind of thing. That's what the books said.

One Saturday in October they spent all day together. In the morning he drove them into Hat Yai where they saw the latest Schwarzenegger movie, sitting in the glass-fronted "sound room" where the English soundtrack was piped in, rather than in the main part of the theater where Arnold and all the rest of the actors spoke perfect colloquial Thai. Every so often she'd unwrap another chewy sweet and, holding it with thumb and forefinger, aim it delicately toward his mouth.

Afterwards they browsed around the big department stores, and she picked out an Arrow dress shirt and a pair of black Levis for him. They shared pizza and ice cream at a new mall. They leafed through magazines at the big bookstore near the train station, Saranya agonizing for nearly fifteen minutes about whether to spend 250 baht on a collection of American short stories, before Marek finally lifted it from her hands and took it to the cashier, paying for it himself.

It was raining when they returned to the bungalow, and they had to run from the truck to the porch. She found a pineapple in the refrigerator and got to work slicing it. Then she made some tea while Marek watched the CNN news. She walked into the room carrying the tray and smiled at him, the way she always did, a smile so unselfconscious and natural and so *personal,* like it was a gift for him alone. It was as if they were a domesticated couple, his woman bringing him his tea in front of the TV.

She sat down next to him on the couch, folding her legs underneath her. A bomb had exploded in an airport somewhere and the television newsreaders were stammering with excitement: this was CNN and they would get the facts first, even if they were wrong. Occasionally she would stab at a wedge of pineapple, balanced precariously on his thigh, and without turning her head from the paper hold it up to his mouth. He guided her hand and brought the piece to his lips; only then would she take one for herself. She quietly hummed as she turned the pages. He discovered he was gnawing on an ice cube. He wanted to touch her, to put his arm around her, but something held him back. He was afraid she would run away. Anyway, once the rain stopped, she'd get on her scooter and ride home.

"I have to check the email," he said.

There was no new email, no faxes. He walked out to the porch. It had stopped raining and sheet lightening burst over the sea.

The instant he saw her on the couch again he knew something was wrong. The newspaper was in her lap and she was bent over it with her head in her hands. Her long hair hid her face. It was her back that gave her away: though she tried to hide it, she was quietly sobbing.

"Saranya, what's wrong?"

Ashamed of her tears she turned away from him.

He reached for her hand. "Saranya, tell me."

She spoke in a voice so quiet he had to lean close to her lips. "How long do we know each other?"

"Five, nearly six months. Why?"

"It is a long time in your country? It is a long time for a man and woman?"

"A long time? What do you mean?"

"I don't want to be a Thai woman anymore," she said fiercely.

"What?"

"I say I don't want to be a Thai woman anymore."

She raised her head and he saw her red eyes. A tear fell wet on the newspaper.

"Saranya, what in the world is wrong?"

"I want to follow my heart. I want to do what my heart tells me. But I cannot, because I am a Thai woman." She stopped for a while, her shoulders heaving with her sobs. "If I follow my heart, people will call me a bad woman."

"Saranya, please. You're not a bad woman. What are you talking about?" But he knew. He knew exactly what she was talking about.

She looked up again, tears streaking her face. Then she fell against his chest. He put his arms around her and patted her on the back, feeling imbecilic because he could think of nothing better to say than, "It's OK, it's all right". He held her like that until the sobbing stopped. Then he lifted her head and kissed her. First on the forehead, then the cheeks, then on the lips.

An honest-to-God virgin who had never been kissed before. She neither resisted nor yielded. He moved his lips against hers for a long time until she learned the movement. He parted her lips. He instantly had a very hard erection. He pulled away from her. "Is this good? Is this good? Is this good?" he heard himself say.

What was he doing? Her face was distorted from the crying and the closeness. Her skin was feverish. Her dark eyes searched his, as if trying to pierce his mind to his true intentions. He felt her body in his arms, somehow both taut and relaxed, as if ready to give him everything or nothing.

"Why do say that?"

"Is this right? What we are doing?"

What had happened to the audacious, adventurous young student, the one who always took the dares, the one who was afraid of no one, not even farang? The woman he held in his arms now was a trembling, fearful child. This was no Philips-type adventure, no one-more-notch-on-the-belt conquest. This was no Dark Side, short-time, hotel love fest. Saranya buried her head in his shoulder while his thoughts raced.

"I must know," she said finally, looking up at him. "You must tell me the answer to one question. Do you love me?"

He felt as if he were about to plunge from a precipice without a parachute.

"Please, Alex. Please answer me. Do you love me?"

"Yes, Saranya," he said, feeling himself going over. "I love you. I love you very much."

It was dusk and he could hear the rain falling again on the roof. Her breasts and abdomen tasted of salt. As he penetrated her she cried out, and it was as if she wanted him deeper and yet at the same time was pushing him away, holding him back. She kept her eyes open and breathlessly whispered, "*Siew, siew.*" With his hands he turned her pelvis up and she gave another exclamation of pain and pleasure as he drove deeper into her.

After, when he rose from the bed in the fading light, he saw the dark stain on the sheets. There was blood on his penis and his pubic area, smeared across her abdomen. He washed off and when he came out of the bathroom, she was sitting on the floor next to the bed rubbing the blood out of the sheets with a wet towel. Her face was expressionless; she was just doing a common, everyday cleaning task, and his heart filled with tenderness for her.

He was worried about her, so he held her and asked, "Are you OK? Are you hurting?"

She folded the towel away and stood up. "No, not hurting." She smiled and tapped him on the heart. "It's OK," she said, "because you love me."

Eighteen

There was one boy in the village, perhaps twelve years old, who could speak a little English. Yes, he said to Hunter, his uncle could take him in his boat down the coast to look at the beaches. Could he just wait a few minutes while they found some petrol? Was he travelling alone? Why did he want to go to that beach? There was nothing there and no one went there. Many farang went to the beach in Songkhla, and some near Narithiwat. But no one ever came to that area.

Hunter went back to wait in the rented car. He unfolded the map and smoothed it down on the seat next to him. He lit a cigarette and tossed his lighter on the dash and blew smoke against the windshield.

He was parked in the shade of a big tree on a dirt road that ran along the beach. The kids from the village had begun to gather around him. They were all Muslims here, the boys dressed in long jackets and turbans, the girls with shawls around their heads. They watched him closely with huge black eyes, and from time to time one of them would say something and the others would laugh.

And why not? Because it *was* funny, really. And he could laugh along with them; laugh at their stupid clothing and their crude, retarded village life. And even laugh at himself and his foolhardy quest. He was just another crazy fucking farang whose time in the Dreamworld had nearly run out, yet again.

He tossed his cigarette out the open window. Smoke from charcoal fires drifted through the village. He wondered how people could live like this: the heat and the bare wooden shacks they called home, the stomach-turning stench of drying fish, their front yards littered with oily plastic bags and fish bones.

He looked past the village kids to the long sweep of beach and the open sea. A few of the villagers' long-tailed boats were already out in the water, their engines putt-putting like lawn mowers, but they were heading north to spread their nets between the village and the city of Pattani. Hunter would have his boatman take him south, around the rocky headland, and see how far they could make in a morning. He had all his gear with him, the tent and sleeping bag, the parang to cut through the undergrowth, even the Polaroid.

"Where's the boat?" Hunter asked, impatient.

The boy who could speak a little English grinned at him, then looked past him. "Coming soon."

Hunter thought about the man he called Madison, the one with the gate pass and the truck, and the background that would fit so perfectly with his plans. He'd looked for him secretly in Songkhla. He didn't want to be too obvious; he didn't want to just drive out to the GPS station, knock on the door and say, "Howdy, I'm gonna steal some ancient artifacts and I need your port pass to get them on to a boat." Anyway, he didn't know *what* he had yet. In fact, he didn't have anything. He was just doing the groundwork, bit by bit, so that it would all fall into place when it was time.

So he had watched him, spied on him, you might say. Parked down the road closer to the hotel, Hunter had watched Marek for a few days, not knowing what he was looking for. He watched him out of curiosity and because he was bored with everything else in Songkhla. He had seen him near the hotel with the young college girl – and what a fine piece of melt-in-your-mouth pussy she was – and thought *maybe this guy's not as dull as he looks*. And he had followed him into town one afternoon, losing him after he'd parked his car, and then finally catching up to him on foot in the market and making it seem like one big coincidence.

And Madison would do it, he was sure. It would be irresistible to someone like him. Greed filled in the bottom of the heart of every man, no matter how much they denied it. And Madison would love the adventure of it, the romance. That would be the final enticement.

"He comes now," said the boy, and Hunter twisted in his seat to see a wiry old man carrying a plastic jerry can and a funnel.

To find what I-Cha'ing saw you'd have to search with his eyes. Not from a car, not from the air, not even on foot from the road. You had to see it from the sea, approaching by boat.

Hunter wiped the sweat from his forehead with the back of his hand as the prow of the long-tailed boat sliced through the choppy water. The sun was nearly directly above them now. He sat low in the front of the narrow boat, his knees nearly up to his chin, his hands braced against the sides, the bill of his baseball cap pulled low to shade his face. Behind him, the old fisherman with leathery skin the same texture as the boat's weathered bench planks kept one hand on the long aluminum rod which served as both engine mount and tiller. With the other hand he continually wound and unwound his headpiece, occasionally using the cloth to wipe his face and head. He muttered something beneath his breath and then draped the cloth over his head to protect his face from the sun.

"Yes, I know it's fucking hot," said Hunter, knowing the man couldn't understand a word of English. They had been out in the boat for nearly an hour, and the old man was probably wondering when they would turn back to the village, and when he would get paid.

Hunter looked at his map. It was hard to say exactly where they were, but they'd have to turn back sometime soon, or they'd run out of fuel before they got back to the village. Without turning, he lifted one arm and motioned forward. He wanted the old man to take the boat around the next headland.

The boat's engine cut through the afternoon tranquility like an insult. As they rounded the rocky promontory, a pair of white-winged shore birds was roused to flight. They circled high and screeched down at the two men in the boat, their cries cutting through the din of the engine.

On the other side of the rocks, a small, curving white beach slowly revealed itself. Behind and above was the thickly forested mountain. The sound of the boat echoed within the small bay. Hunter began to reach for the field glasses in his pack and then stopped. He gestured so that the fisherman would turn the boat towards the beach in order to approach it head on. He signaled to the old man to cut the engine.

He felt a shudder down his spine, just as he'd known he would. Except for the two squalling gulls still circling above, there was no sign of life anywhere. They drifted soundlessly. He didn't need the binoculars because it was obvious to anyone with the eyes to look for it, towering above the forest. A huge dirty-white limestone cliff, in stark contrast to the deep green of the forest, which, if you had an ounce of imagination, looked much like the back end of an elephant lumbering across the top of the mountain, as if on its way to some elephant heaven in the skies. It must have looked exactly the same when I-Chi'ang first saw it a thousand years ago.

"*Khaw ruup chang*," said the boatman, wiping his face.

"*Chang*," repeated Hunter. "Elephant." Then he signaled for the old man to start the engine and take him onto the shore.

Hunter paid the old fisherman, then took off his boots and lifted the rucksack on to his back and waded onto shore. He had already made arrangements for the man to pick him up in two-days. If the old man had the slightest curiosity about what Hunter was doing here, he didn't show it; he just folded the money into his pocket, wrapped his pakama tighter around his head, and turned the boat around and sailed off.

From the foot of the mountain, Hunter could see only forest with a few patches of white limestone. There was no way to make out the shape of an elephant. He thought for a moment, almost afraid to take a step, and then walked along the beach.

He was like Friday, leaving the first set of footprints in

the sand. At the edge of the beach, twenty feet from the water, the underbrush was thick, and he had to use the parang to cut through it. He worked hard up and down the beach, hacking his way toward the base of the mountain, hoping for a faint hint of a trail. When he got to the base of the mountain, he worked along the edge of it, looking for an easy way up. It took him an hour or more, but he found it. The underbrush was not as thick here and the rock was easier to climb. He paused at the gap in the growth and looked at the way the rocky path went up, rising so easily and uniformly it could have been a stairway carved into the mountain.

Nineteen

Hunter stirred the ice in his glass of Golden Cat and gazed out the window of his guesthouse room. It was Sunday and the flower and fruit market below was crowded, as it was every week, despite the fact that it was noon and the sun was ferocious.

He drank and let the warmth of the whiskey wash over him. It would be too early to be drinking on most days, but not on the day before you had to go back offshore, not on your last day in the Dreamworld. And not when you had a surprise to spring on someone the way he had.

He didn't have to wait long. Before his second drink was finished, the gunmetal silver-blue Mercedes Benz rounded a corner and slipped into the street market. It knifed through the midday crowd, caution lights flashing, its occupants invisible behind the tinted windows, and parked in front of a cart of freshly cut orchids. Hunter grabbed his heavy backpack and hurried down the outside stairway and through the garden to the gate. He trotted to the end of the street and then back one block to get to the part of the market opposite his window. There he slowed to a walk and joined the others in the crowd sliding, shoving and pushing his way through. He reached the Mercedes, opened the back door and slid into the icy cool, cream leather interior.

The Thai man next to him, the one who liked to be called Jack, was wearing dark glasses and smiling at him. Marek saw the blue-black scorpion on the back of the driver's hand as it rested on the steering wheel.

"John, you're always so mysterious. Wanting to meet in the market like this. From where were you spying on me?"

Jack was wearing large sunglasses and his face seemed to be all jowls and double chin. The car smelled like air freshener and expensive leather.

"I'm just being discrete, Jack. Good business practice."

"You are so clever. You are wasting your time offshore. Now, how do we get out of this mess? I suppose if Toi ran over a few of them, the rest would get out of the way." He said a few words to the driver and the car reversed, forcing a few pedestrians to scurry out of the way, then backed around the corner to get on to the main street.

"Lunch at the Pavilion fine with you?"

"Whatever you say, Jack."

It was a toss-up as to what Hunter loathed most about Jack: his oiliness or his ostentation. The latter you saw in his gold-rimmed Ray-Bans, his Genève watch, and the pager on his belt. He wore his affectations without self-consciousness, as comfortably as he wore his tailored shirts. Even now, as the driver eased his way through the crowded market towards the Pavilion hotel, he chatted about some Burmese gems he'd purchased, and then went on to some land deal he'd just made, relating it all with a world-weary boredom.

Hunter hardly listened anymore; he just let Jack carry on,

hoping he'd realize how silly his monologue sounded. Sometimes Hunter wanted to laugh openly at him, mock his grasping insecurity, fling sarcastic barbs towards his Hong Kong suits or his engraved Cross pens. But of course he never did, because Jack really was powerful, he was what the newspapers called "a dark influence". He was involved in business and politics and had deep contacts in the police and the military. And his pride and rapacity did not allow for mockery. It was all about face, and if you trifled with that, you did so at your own peril. Despite Jack's British style of distancing his speech from himself, Hunter knew there were some things that were off limits.

At the hotel Jack told the driver to ignore the underground parking lot and instead turn into a space nearest the main entrance. The young attendant came over to say something, to tell him perhaps that the space was reserved, but when he saw Jack get out of the Mercedes, he merely smiled deferentially and waied. He didn't know Jack, Hunter guessed, but his car, clothes, even his physical stature spoke directly to the boy in a way that didn't require words. They said, *be careful with me, I'm powerful. Just let me do what I want and hope I don't get angry at you.*

Jack spoke rapidly at the boy and used every nuance of his body language to tell him he was nothing more than a flunky. Hunter was embarrassed, even a little disgusted, but he told himself this was Asia. That was how things worked here, and that was who Jack was.

In the restaurant Jack chose a table in the corner next to the large window. It was just the two of them; the driver with the scorpion tattoo had slid off somewhere. Hunter slipped into the booth opposite Jack and rested the weighty backpack on the floor near his feet. When the waiter came Jack ordered a half-dozen dishes and a bottle of Johnny Walker.

Jack removed his sunglasses and slouched against the back of the booth bench as if his body were made of some thick gel.

"It's so good to see you again, John. Of course, doing business with you is always a pleasure. But seeing you again like this, two friends having a quiet Sunday dinner and a few drinks, is really special, isn't it?"

"I know you're busy, Jack. I appreciate you coming out to see me on such short notice."

Hunter noticed for the first time that Jack was wearing a Western string tie, like you might see in Albuquerque or Sante Fe. Hunter had never seen anyone in Thailand wear such a thing before. It was preposterous, and so of course he complimented Jack on it.

"It's all the rage in Bangkok," Jack laughed. "Like bell bottom jeans last year. I've started making them in Had Yai. I'm shipping lorry loads to Bangkok every week. They cost six and a half baht to make, and I sell them for twenty. Strike while the iron is hot, eh John? In six months the fad will die. Then I suppose I'll have to market them in China somehow."

Hunter knew Jack was married and had children, but he had such a feminine, almost matronly, air about him that Hunter figured he was gay. He was tall and had a large head which he sometimes waved around, nose in the air, like a wealthy hostess holding court at a tea party. He was big-boned for a Thai, and his features looked pure Chinese, but Jack always insisted he was

Thai. "My father yes, he is Chinese, but my mother is pure Thai. And so of course I am Thai," he had said when Hunter had asked him once.

He kept his background vague. Any questions about his education, where he had learned his clipped European English, or what he actually did with his days, were dismissed with a few pat answers. If you asked him his occupation, he would answer in one simple word which, when he said it, seemed to encompass a whole world of possibilities: businessman.

But Hunter never asked. The only thing that concerned him was that Jack didn't cheat him. Everything else was irrelevant.

The food came and the waiter poured their drinks. They toasted each other and Jack, beginning to relax, slid out of his sports coat. There was far too much food for two people. Jack had ordered a huge roasted pork leg, a whole sea bass swimming in a broth with coriander and lemon grass, fried vegetables and a shrimp curry. While they ate they spoke desultorily of Bangkok, Singapore and life offshore. After they were finished eating, Jack ordered glasses of Remy Martin.

"I'll have this last little drink and then that's it," said Jack. "I have to give a presentation to the Rotary Club in Hat Yai tonight and it wouldn't do well at all to show up smashed."

He clinked glasses with Hunter and brought out a cigarette case and gold lighter. He offered a cigarette to Hunter and then bent over to light it for him. Jack had eaten very little; most of the pork leg still lay on the plate like something obscene, and the fish had barely a few dents in it. He blew smoke into the air and smiled at no one in particular.

"I'm so glad you called me, John. It's so rare I get to see you."

Hunter took it as a signal to begin the business talk. "Very soon I'll have some more pieces for you, Jack. You know, like the last one."

"That was very risky, John. That was not a wise business decision."

"Sometimes you have to take risks in business, Jack. You know that better than anyone."

"I handled that one as a favor to you, John, because you've helped me in the past. Especially helping me to get rid of all those Rolexes to your oil worker friends. And I will admit I was impressed with your fortitude – no, let me say your balls – in pulling it off. However, I am not interested in dealing with any more museum pieces. They are all documented and too easy to trace. And they attract too much publicity."

"These aren't in the museum. They're in the jungle."

"Jungle? Where?"

"I can't say."

Jack lifted his big head and laughed. "No, of course you can't. Is it an archeological dig?"

"No, at least not yet."

Jack looked amused. "So, let's see then … You've come across an archeological dig, and you're going to sit in the background while these hardworking young students, toiling to preserve our culture, do all the work and bring it all up. And then you're going to steal all the good pieces from under their noses. You're absolutely ruthless, John."

"I doubt if it will ever be a dig. No one even knows about it."

"Aha! Are you telling me you're a swashbuckling Indiana Jones? Discovered it all by yourself? Have you sold your story to Hollywood yet?"

Hunter felt a heat in his chest but smiled and took a drag on his cigarette. He really was as queer as a three-dollar bill, this guy, with his faggy head tilt and lilting laughter. But he came with the socially required wife and children. Par for the course, a whole nation of frauds. Three kids. He wondered how he'd done it. He must have found the act disgusting, or maybe they'd used artificial insemination.

"Probably worth a lot of money," said Hunter. "Difficult even to estimate their worth."

"You've seen these items?"

"Let's say, for the sake of argument, I have."

Jack sighed and cupped his hands behind his head. His mobile phone buzzed. He quickly answered it, then spoke a few curt sentences and rang off. He turned the power off then put it in the pocket of his sports coat.

He fixed his face into a friendly smile, his large teeth gleaming, and began speaking very slowly, as if talking to a child. "John, you must learn to be more open, more trusting. There is no need to be so mysterious. This all sounds so much like Boys Own Adventure. You can understand why I'm a bit dubious.

"And if, for the sake of argument, you have some valuable pieces, and I do not doubt for one moment that you are resourceful enough to obtain them, I have no desire to steal them from you. I'm only trying to assess my risk in terms of business. I assume that's why you called me. To talk business."

Hunter nodded.

"Well, then. You will simply have to open up and provide a few details."

Hunter took a sip of his Remy Martin. He couldn't ignore that nagging feeling that every time he included someone in his secret, even mentioned it in public, it had a better chance of slipping out of his hands. But Jack was a businessman and not a fool, and Hunter had known from the very beginning that he would have to be told some details or he'd simply walk away, laughing that faggy laugh.

"Ever heard of the Sri Jiraya Empire, Jack?"

"Hmm, I believe so. Something to do with history? Like Ayuthya."

"That's right. It was an Empire that dominated this area, well before Ayuthya. It lasted eight hundred years and produced some magnificent art, especially bronze and stonework. Some say it was based in Indonesia, others that it was not a state at all, just a number of cities loosely connected by trade. But some say it was actually centered here in Thailand, perhaps in Chaiya in Surat Thani province. After all, the names are similar enough."

"You'll have to excuse me, John. History was not my strong suit in school. In fact, I was rather bored by it all."

"You won't be bored, Jack, if you think about how much money can be made on this."

"Go ahead, John, I'm listening."

"There is an undiscovered ancient Srijaya temple, maybe the biggest one ever in the Southern peninsula, near Songkhla. I won't say exactly where Jack, but believe me, it's there. Lots of artifacts.

Statues, prayer tablets, pottery. Very rich."

"Does anybody else know about this?"

"Nobody except you, so far, but I've got a partner in mind. We will have to go and dig them out. It's a remote area and it will take some work. One man certainly couldn't do it alone. Maybe two men could, but it would be slow work. We may have to bring in more, probably Toi and some of your boys. We'll have to work fast, and we'll probably be dealing with some large objects."

"I see, but isn't it early to be contacting me? I mean, why not wait until you have the pieces in hand and then shop them around? You certainly don't need me to provide workers. You can get them anywhere."

"Yes, but who could I trust? Anyway, this has to all be set up before time, because we'll have to work fast. The site is remote, but we won't be able to keep it a secret for very long once we start removing pieces. Word will get out, and then we'll be faced with all kinds of problems. We'll have people stealing from us, or looting the site, or demanding all kinds of bakshish to keep quiet. If the newspapers found out, all hell would break loose and the Thai government would take over all the pieces. And we would get nothing. Probably end up in jail."

"That would be unfortunate."

"Everything has to be in place before we remove the goods. We'll need to get them off the mountain and into Songkhla, then into one of your factories, have them boxed up in your shipping crates. We want to put them right on a ship to Hong Kong or Singapore without fucking around. We don't want to sit on them in Songkhla or the whole thing could collapse. You're the only one who's got the manpower and equipment and logistics to get it done fast."

"I much prefer Manila. I mean as a place to deal with contraband."

"Whatever. Can you find buyers for a large shipment like this?"

"That is not difficult, John, if the quality is as good as the last piece you sold me. But that's a big *if*, isn't it? I must admit I'm somewhat concerned that no one, not even you, has seen any of the pieces. We don't really know if they exist."

"I never said I hadn't seen them," said Hunter.

Jack blew out a cloud of cigarette smoke and squinted at Hunter as if he were appraising him.

"I see all kinds of problems here, John. Let us say that there are some real quality items, and let us say that I can get buyers. And I can receive these pieces and package them as ordinary cargo. There is the not so minor problem of getting it through the deep-sea port. The port authorities have become incredibly greedy lately. I guess it's all part of the country's rising expectations. They will demand quite a lot, probably thousands of dollars."

"The authorities won't be a problem. My partner – ah, this guy – he has a port pass. He has total access at all times. He can drive right through and board any ship without question."

"I've still had to pay bribes, even with a pass."

"He won't have to. He works for a powerful company and he's very clean. Everybody knows him by face. They wave him through anytime he drives up, whether it's high noon on a Sunday or 3 a.m. They'll never suspect anything, and they'll never look at his cargo."

Jack smiled. He was beginning to get interested. "I'll say it again, John. You're much too clever to be turning screws on some offshore platform."

"I know, Jack. This is going to get me off it forever."

Jack looked into his Remy and pursed his lips. "There is still the not inconsiderable problem of verification. I mean, what if I arrange everything, make all these promises to my business associates and buyers, and then nothing materializes?"

Hunter lifted the backpack from the floor – it took both hands – then laid it on the curved part of the booth seat between them. He unzipped it and opened the flaps wide, reached in with both hands and pulled out the stone Buddha head.

He held it low between them so no one else in the room could see. Bits of mud and grass still clung to the gray sandstone features. At first Jack sat absolutely still, then he reached out and touched the face, ran his hand along the brow and the nose and the sleepy looking eyes.

"And this is ...?"

"It's real Jack. Just as I said. I just got back yesterday." He slipped it back into the rucksack and zipped it up. Then he lifted the bag over the table and gave it to Jack.

"It's yours," he said. "A little gift. From one businessman to another."

Jack grunted as he lowered the bag to the bench. "I think I'd better order another Remy," he said. "For both of us. And you John, tell me the whole plan, from the very beginning, and what you need me to do."

Twenty

This time when Philips called to invite him to the Pink Lady, Marek said no.

"Boss is coming from Singapore today. Semi-yearly audit. Except I have a feeling it's going to be more of an inspection of the Dark Side than a look at the office accounts."

"Bring him along to Hat Yai. He can check out the massage rooms. You know, make sure they've got the proper quality soap, that kind of thing."

"He's got an old girlfriend in one of the bars here. Forget which one. Her name's Nit or Noi or Nok. Claims he's dying to see her."

"Pity. Ah well, maybe next time. As for me, I'm due for a rub and a scrub. Y'see I get one every month whether I need it or not. You have fun with your boss, Mr A-lick."

A soft rain tapped at the windows and aluminum awning, and Marek wondered if it was raining in Surat, where Saranya had gone to visit her father in the hospital. He thought about her in one of those speeding minibuses in the rain, bald tires, some maniacal bug-eyed *yaa baa* addict at the wheel ... but no, she'd be all right; she had traveled yesterday.

Surprisingly, he'd felt some relief when he told Philips he

couldn't go. It was not something he could explain to him. The women in a glass cage, the room with the peeling paint and the dim light bulbs, racking his brain to think of something amusing to say while the tub filled with water, seeing himself in the mirrors whichever way he looked, and the girl next to him on the bed, still in her prom dress, looking so much smaller. And the vaccination scars on her arms, the shiny welts on her belly where the knife had opened her for the Caesarean. One more product of rural poverty and destitute parents; the stories of a cruel and wayward husband, and the children left behind with grandparents in the village; stories which could be all true or a complete fabrication. And he couldn't say which would depress him more.

But no, that wasn't right either. They didn't need his sympathy, nor would they understand his melancholy about their fate. He was just one of those farang who "thinks too much". And Philips would agree with them.

It was just that now, it would have felt different, odd; not morally wrong exactly, just wasteful, mistaken. Now there was a new chapter, a new book; to stay in the old one would be to atrophy.

He remembered as a boy on a family trip with his parents and sister, driving through Pennsylvania at sunset. The road coiled through a series of low hills, but these hills were nothing like the ones in Wisconsin or anywhere he'd seen in the Midwest. It was like being at sea. Each time they crested another long hill he saw in front of him mounds of deep green drenched in the golden light from the setting sun. Then they'd dip into the shadows and make the long, slow climb over the next hill and see it all again:

miles of verdant green stretching into the yellow-red blaze of the sun. "Hey Jude" was playing on the radio, the perfect song at the perfect time. No one in the car said a word; they were all struck mute with the serene, heavenly beauty of it.

That's what it felt like now: as if he'd somehow worked his way out of a shadow to the top of the hill, and what he saw in front of him was a splendid future of green and gold.

What was he thinking? He'd spent one night with her, one night of her life. Who knows what she really thought about him? She might come back from Surat and be completely changed.

Brian Sturges stood on the porch grinning, briefcase in one hand and cigarette in the other. Niwat was to his right and slightly behind, shaking out an umbrella. He wore a crisp, clean light blue shirt and tan slacks; and though slightly damp from the rain, his smile was firmly in place.

"Here he is then, our man in Songkhla."

"Hello, Brian."

They shook hands, Sturges freeing his by putting his cigarette in his mouth. He was heavier than when Marek had last seen him seven months ago, the desk job in Singapore evidently not doing much good for his physique.

"Come in and sit down." Sturges entered the room slowly, his head moving from side to side, taking in the room from wall to wall and ceiling to floor.

"I must say, it's a hell of a lot tidier than when Jimmy was here. Yes, indeed." He was wearing shorts, sandals, and a loud Hawaiian shirt with the top buttons open. It was the way all the head honchos seemed to dress whenever they came to Songkhla. Rain or shine, business or pleasure, they all outfitted themselves as if they were on a holiday at the beach.

"It's the maid, Brian. She does all the work. And of course, Niwat supervises. Here, have a seat."

Sturges sat down on the sofa with its lumpy cushions and uttered a soft grunt. Niwat disappeared into the kitchen and quickly re-emerged with a chipped plastic ashtray which he set down on the coffee table in front of Sturges. The maid followed with a tray of coffee, tea and ice water.

"Good, good. So the household staff is treating you well?"

"Great. Niwat takes care of everything."

Niwat smiled and deflected the compliment with a wave of his hand.

"Yes, I can see that." Sturges tapped his cigarette into the ashtray, his pale blue eyes twinkling at Marek as if they shared some inside joke.

"And the social life?" His wooly eyebrows jumped as he blew a stream of smoke out the side of his mouth. By "social life", Marek guessed he meant sex, and suddenly Marek wondered if he knew about Saranya. Maybe that's what the silly grin and the bouncing eyebrows were about. But no, how could he?

"Well, you know, it is Thailand after all," said Marek.

"Yes, indeed it is. And I for one can't wait to experience it first-hand again. But that will have to wait 'til later. Work before pleasure and all that, eh?" He lifted his briefcase to his lap and balanced it gingerly on his knees – not an easy thing to do with his oversized paunch.

"Came directly from the airport, Niwat and I. My bags are still in the car. I'm staying in town but I thought, hell, let's get the work out of the way and then we'll have the rest of the time to enjoy ourselves. Fancy a bit of golf this afternoon?"

"I don't play, Brian."

"Really?" Sturges looked at him with wide-eyed surprise. "Pity. I brought my clubs up. Hope to get a game in before it gets dark. And I've set up one for tomorrow morning with the base manager and the Schlumberger and Haliburton chiefs. You had some clubs, you could join us. Good for business, you know. Golf, I mean."

While Sturges talked about golfing in Singapore, Niwat slipped out the sliding screen door to the back where the storage and generator shacks were.

"The golf is all right there but it's bloody expensive, as is everything else. Cost of living's outrageous. Beer five dollars a glass. That's US, not Singapore. And there's fuck all to do. Government's bloody petrified somebody might have a good time. Oh, it's clean and green, as they say. I would call it antiseptic. Like living in fucking Disney World without the rides."

He leaned across the closed briefcase and punched his cigarette out in the ashtray. "Now here's a perfect illustration of what Singapore is like. Years ago it was a bit wilder. I'm not talking Patpong Road exactly but, y'know, a bit freer. People used to hang out on Bougas Street and watch the transvestites parade up and down. You could have a beer and grilled shrimp at an outside table. Bloody entertaining, especially watching some guy who didn't know they were blokes take a fancy to one of them.

"Well, that was all a little too wild for our family-oriented government, so they cleaned it all up. Sent the ladyboys on their way, didn't they? Know what happened? Tourists complained! Said they came to see the action on Bougas Street, like what they'd read about or their mates'd told them. Get there and it's a fucking shopping mall, no different than Houston or Manchester. Pissed off 'cause they're being cheated out of the real Asian experience, y'know? Raised bloody hell about it, didn't they?

"So what does the government do? After years of deliberation, they decide they're going to bring back Bougas Street as a tourist attraction. Just read it last week in the paper. There's even some talk about bringing back the transvestites, though I don't see how they can do that and still keep the city's reputation. It could lead to something nastier, like prostitution. Which, just between you and me lad, would be a bloody improvement."

He unfolded a pair of reading glasses from his shirt pocket and perched them on his nose. Then he shook out a packet of sugar, tore it open and poured it into his coffee.

"Course, we don't have that problem in Thailand, do we?" he asked. He lifted the plastic cup to his lips and took a sip, his eyebrows raised in expectation.

"What, transvestites?"

"No, lad, *pros-tee-tyu-tion*. Illegal in Thailand, isn't it? So not a problem, right? Heh, heh. Don't you just love this country?"

He flipped open his briefcase, shuffled around inside for a moment, then pulled out a flimsy pink sheet before snapping it shut again. "The point is, lad, y'got paradise here in Songkhla. Stick with it as long as you can. Now then, how's the equipment?

Any problems?"

"No, no problems. Just routine stuff. The city power supply, you know what that's like. That note I sent you a few weeks ago about upgrading the PC?"

Sturges peered at the paper and grunted, but whether it was because of something on the sheet or to acknowledge what Marek had said wasn't clear.

"We could use something a little faster. Maybe a Pentium 400," Marek continued, not sure if Sturges were listening to him or not. "Graphics take forever."

Sturges looked over his glasses and frowned. "But do we need it, really? OK, you've got your reports – and a fine job you're doing on those, I might add – spreadsheets, word processing, emails. That's about it, right?"

"Well, yes but ..."

Sturges sighed and crossed his arms on his chest. "I know what you're going to say, Alex, the graphics are an important part of the reports. And I wholeheartedly agree. But they look fine now. In fact, they look bloody great. You've really impressed the clients with them, did I mention that? I think we can get by on what we've got, don't you? Maybe in six months' time ..." he shrugged and let his voice trail off.

"But y'know, I'm glad you brought it up. There's a lot of talk in the company about upgrading. Perth wants to improve our stations in Indonesia, seeing as there's a lot more business there these days. It means of course, that there'll be less money to spend in other places, at least temporarily." Sturges's eyes had returned to the inside of his briefcase.

"Like here, you mean?"

Sturges cleared his throat. "We may have to tighten our belts a bit, just temporarily, y'know until we get some more clients. Ah, here it is." This time Sturges pulled a thicker document from the case and waved it at him. It looked like it was about twenty pages long.

"This here is a copy of the report from Perth. I just received it two days ago. I'll leave it with you, and you can peruse it when you get a chance. It's all in here. It's Southern Cross's new and revised plan for the first half of 1996. It's all spelled out very clearly."

"They planning to cut back on us, Brian? What does that mean, exactly?"

Sturges gave a dismissive chuckle. "Now lad, it's nothing serious. We just need to find a way to cut expenses a bit. Maybe the household budget? We'll talk numbers later."

Sturges could see Marek was not happy with his answer. He frowned and closed his briefcase. He put it to one side and took his glasses off. "It's just part of the bloody business, Alex. It's part of the goddamn cycle we're always going through. Oil prices up, let's throw a party, spend like there's no tomorrow; prices down, the shareholders get nervous. I've seen it a dozen times. You make it through, don't worry."

Make it through? Out of nowhere a black thought came to Marek, a feeling that he might not have a job in Songkhla much longer. But that couldn't happen. Not now.

"I didn't even know we were in a down cycle," he managed to say.

"Well, we're not, not exactly. Not yet anyway. Look, Alex, it's not all doom and gloom. Actually, the corporate strategy – yeah, I know, corporate strategy, but you know how these fucking guys talk – the plan, let's say, is to *expand* in Thailand. And they would like us to find a way to do it."

"Us?"

"Yes, you and me. Though mostly you, since you actually live here and have got your finger on things. Perth would like you to keep your eye open for other opportunities. Talk to people. Ask questions. Find out about what they do and see if we can help them. Y'know, sell Southern Cross a little bit."

"I thought we had an agent who did that kind of thing?"

"Perth wants you to get more involved on that side, seeing as you're already here. Y'know, kind of kill two birds with one stone."

"I thought you said we had lots of work coming up. What about the fiber optic cable they're going to lay along the coast?"

Sturges winced. "Oh that. I'm afraid that fell through."

"And EastAsia's new field? The one that's supposed to be bigger than the Ratchada field."

Sturges shrugged. "Apparently the development is being delayed. We don't know for how long. Months, maybe. Look, Alex, I'm not saying we have to go into panic mode. We've got enough work for the time being. We can cut corners a little if we need to. It's five, six months down the road we have to plan for. That's why we need you to be … ah … what's that fucking word they're always throwing about? Proactive! That's it! We'd like to see you try to dig up some work for us here. Be *proactive*. In the very best sense of the word."

"Proactive," echoed Marek. The word sounded hollow and phony in his mouth. "But I don't see how I can do that, Brian. People either need our service or they don't. I can't exactly hawk our GPS receivers to the local tuk-tuk drivers."

Sturges laughed, a little too heartily. "Oh, I like that Alex. Can you see one of these guys in one of those little trucks? The floor half rusted away but there's a GPS receiver stuck where the radio should be. That's good, Alex." He laughed again.

"But seriously, I should think there would be some opportunities. Some people need our service and don't even know it. Like I hear there's a new supply boat company in the area, Malaysian. The word is they don't feel they require any navigation aids. Just go back and forth to the rigs and the platforms every day. Got radar and a compass, having a GPS receiver seems redundant to them. You could sniff around, make them see how important it could be, like if there was an emergency or they got caught in a typhoon."

Sturges must have seen the doubt in Marek's eyes and quickly continued. "The company's offering incentives. A nice percentage of any new contract. It's a great opportunity for you."

A great opportunity. He was reminded of his sister. It wasn't that Marek thought such opportunities were bad in themselves; they just felt so foreign to him, like wearing a tuxedo, something he could never pretend to be comfortable in.

But he decided he wasn't going to let it upset him, not today. After all, this was the new Alex, coming over the ridge into the golden blast of sunlight.

"OK, Brian," he said, "I'll nose around, see what I can do. But I've got to tell you, I'm not much of a salesman."

"Nonsense, you'll do fine. Look, you're doing a great job here and I want you to stay here in Songkhla for as long as possible. We've just got to play the game a little bit, get Perth on our side, and you'll be all set. And you know, don't laugh, but golf can really help you make the right kind of connections."

They heard the back screen door slide open and then Niwat said, "Brian, can you come out here for a second? Need you to see something."

Niwat led them from the back door to the generator shed, holding one hand above his head to keep off the drizzling rain. "I talk to the guard," he said.

The shed's two large wooden foldout doors were open, as usual. Inside the guard was on his haunches, shuffling through some cardboard boxes and lifting coils of cable, searching for something. When he saw Sturges he stood and waied.

"What is it?" asked Sturges.

"The toolbox is gone," said Niwat.

The guard smiled ruefully at them, then took off his baseball cap with the Southern Cross symbol on it and scratched his head.

"Gone?"

"He says he can't find it."

"Well, what happened to it?"

"He says he don't know what happened. He says it was here not so long ago. He says some tools are around here. He used them the other day to fix the back door. But the box and most of the tools all gone now."

"Well, what does he think happened to them?"

Niwat spoke quickly to the man in Thai, and the man replied. "He doesn't know."

"Oh, for fuck's sake," said Sturges. "The fucking guard doesn't know what happened to the fucking stuff he was supposed to be guarding?"

The guard made another half-hearted attempt to look through the stuff as he stammered a few sentences in Thai.

"He says there were some kids out here the other day. They hanging around all afternoon. He think maybe they sneak back sometime when he not around. Like maybe he in the toilet or go down the road to get some noodles."

The guard was chagrined, grinning and nodding his head. Niwat looked at Sturges as if begging him not to explode.

"That toolbox was nearly brand new. We ordered it from the States, something like seven hundred fucking dollars. It wasn't some cheap crap you pick up in the Songkhla Sunday market."

"I know, Brian," said Niwat.

"Well, can't he find those kids or call the fucking cops or something?"

Niwat shrugged. Everyone knew they'd never see the toolbox again.

"For fuck's sake," muttered Sturges, and then he turned and stomped back toward the house.

They drove to the hotel, where Sturges checked in, and then they had lunch in the air-conditioned restaurant. The view of the beach through the large windows was streaked with rain. Sturges' mood was foul throughout the meal, and nobody said much of anything.

After lunch, they went back to the bungalow and spent the afternoon going over their expenses for the last six months. Marek, meticulous as ever when it came to office paperwork, had all the receipts ordered and categorized: here were the ones for electricity, cooking gas, diesel for the generators, salary for the maid and guard. He also had the receipts for various equipment he or Niwat had purchased. They estimated what their expenses would be for the next six months. Sturges was pleased that everything was in order and all the numbers balanced neatly, and his mood begin to lighten – especially when the rain stopped, and the sun peeked out. At one point he looked out of the window and clapped his hands. "May just be able to get a game in after all," he said.

At 3:30, with all of Marek's receipts replaced in the orderly file cabinets, Sturges announced that he and Niwat would be off to see a couple of clients. He glanced at his watch and smiled. "Don't worry, I'll keep these meetings short. Should be teeing off by five. Plenty of time for nine holes at least." Now he was rubbing his hands. "And you, lad. We'll pick you up about seven, get a bite to eat on the island, and then we're off to the Dark Side for a bit of rest and relaxation."

* * *

It was the first time he'd ever seen Niwat drunk. The Thai man leaned over the bar, supporting himself on his elbows, and put his face close to Marek's. "The Super Bowl is fixed," he said.

"Mafia. There's too much money gambled on it." The words were slurred, and his eyes were nearly closed. He wrapped his fingers on Marek's forearm. "Believe me, everybody knows this. Otherwise, how can the Cowboys lose to the Rams in the playoffs?"

"The playoffs are fixed too?"

"Sure! All fixed! Too much money involved."

They were in the Offshore Bar. Sturges was at the other end of the room in the middle of a group of drillers, loud beefy guys who were half-deaf from their years on the drilling floor and who were all missing bits of fingers.

Sturges was buying rounds and swapping stories about godforsaken corners of the earth which had no reason at all for anyone to go to, except they had oil.

"Well, somebody ought to do something about that," said Marek, realizing just then that he was getting a bit thick-tongued himself. "Or at least fix it so that Green Bay wins once in a while."

It was the fourth – or maybe the fifth – place they'd been to. After a sumptuous dinner on the island, featuring huge grilled prawns and a sea bass brought up wriggling from a bamboo cage at the end of the wooden pier, Sturges had driven directly to the Dark Side.

"The trick is," said Sturges as they clambered out of the truck, "to start at one end and work your way down, never losing site of your ultimate goal."

"Which is what, exactly?" asked Marek.

"Why, to reach the other end, lad, of course. Oh, and don't forget to keep an eye out for little Miss Nit, love of my life."

They never found Nit, not at the Number One Bar or any of

the other places, but it didn't stop Sturges from having a good time. At every joint they went to, he bought drinks for three or four of the girls, who crowded around him like he was their long lost knight in shining armor. They stroked his arms and the gray hairs of his chest and patted his belly and told him in so many words they wanted nothing more out of life than to spend one lusty night with him.

"It's all expense account," shrugged Sturges. "Entertaining the troops."

Marek thought about how just a few hours earlier Sturges was advising him to find ways to cut down on expenses, and now here he was spending what would likely turn out to be hundreds of dollars on drinks for bargirls. If there was irony there, Sturges didn't appear to be bothered by it.

Sturges led Niwat and Marek from place to place, working his way down the row of shophouse bars, full of frenetic energy, work and business long forgotten.

At Gin's Place he went behind the bar to pick out the cassette tapes and open bottles of beer for the customers. "This is paradise here, lad," he said, while carrying fistfuls of bottles out of the cooler. "Don't forget it."

Now Sturges left the drillers and put his arms around Niwat and Marek. "C'mon, laddies, let's not lose sight of our mission."

They walked out like that, Sturges with his arms around them, and it was awkward getting through the narrow door. They were at the end of the row with only one bar left, and Marek was thankful for that. But Sturges seemed to have an endless supply of energy, and Marek thought he just might decide to work his way back to the first bar: round two.

The bar was dead, end-of-the-street dead, end-of-the-night dead, the three of them the only customers. The stereo was off, and the two girls in the place were watching a soap opera on TV. Sturges made them turn the sound off and put on some music, but it didn't help. Even buying the two girls drinks didn't seem to liven up the place very much.

They stared at the muted TV, watching everyone's idea of rich Thais play out their domestic melodramas.

Sturges looked at his watch. "Well, there is golf tomorrow morning," he said, slightly deflated, then rose to go to the toilet.

Niwat had not touched his drink, and he looked like he might just put his head down on the bar and pass out, but then he spoke.

"He fired him," he said.

"What?"

Niwat sighed heavily, as if it was all too much effort.

"Brian fired the guard. Because of the toolbox gone. Or I should say, he told me to fire him. Which is what I gotta do tomorrow."

"Fired him? When?"

"At dinner. You were in the toilet. He just told me to get rid of him asap and find another."

"Why didn't he tell me? I'm supposed to be the manager of the site."

Niwat shrugged. "I dunno. Here he comes."

Sturges was striding down the empty room, his arms thrown wide as he serenaded the empty bar: "*Plenny a room at the Hotel California …*" He slapped Marek on the back and said, "Ah lad, things have changed in Songkhla. Used to be, you walk into the loo and some bird'd follow you in and have her lips around your todger before the door was half-closed."

"Niwat told me you fired the guard."

"Eh …? Oh yes, that. Well, had to, didn't I? Can't have a guard that robs us blind, can we?"

"He says the kids took it."

Sturges made a face. "Yes, and I'm bloody Hans Christian Anderson. C'mon, lad! He took it, or he let his mates take it. And even if he didn't, if what he said was true, well, it's a dereliction of duty, isn't it? You can't bloody well have a guard that's not guarding, can you? So he's gone, and good riddance."

"But his sister works for me too. How's that going to play out?"

Sturges shrugged. "Don't see it as a problem. She can keep on working for you if you want."

"I thought … I mean … I'm supposed to be the manager here, Brian. Don't I have any say in this?" Marek realized they were both drunk, and this was a foolish time to be trying to talk seriously, but somehow once he'd started, he couldn't stop. It was like he'd had a balloon inflating in his chest, something ugly swelling within him since he'd first heard Brian say the word "proactive". And now it felt like Brian had him in a headlock.

"I mean, I'm supposed to be the fucking manager, right? So don't I get some say on whether or not my staff gets fired?"

Sturges was smiling as if amused by his sudden anger, which only made Marek more incensed.

"Look, I've made it easier for you. Niwat will tell him it was my decision, and you're clear of it. No one will blame you for it. After all, you have to live here. I understand that."

"You could have discussed it with me first. What's the point of being a manager if I don't even know what's going on? And what about him? How's he supposed to survive, support a family now?"

"Now, now, son, don't be going all teary-eyed on me. He had a job to do and he didn't do it. End of story. If we'd kept him on, what would have disappeared next? A generator? The truck?"

"All I'm saying is, I'm the manager, right? I should ..."

"Let it go, lad. No point in it. It's for the best, believe me. Now let's head back next door. I'm determined to find love someplace tonight."

"Yeah, but ..."

"Alex, just leave it." Sturges suddenly stopped smiling and his jaw jutted out. His face was flushed, and his shirt was stretched taut against his belly. His eyes narrowed onto Marek and his words came slowly, his voice barely above a whisper.

"Look, this is the oil business. We all leave our ego at the door, understood? Because nobody really gives a rat's arse, and everybody is replaceable, OK? The sooner you realize that, the easier it will be for everybody. Believe me, I did you a big favor by having Niwat do the dirty work. He'll take care of it, Thai style, first thing tomorrow, and then we'll move on. Understood?"

Marek blinked, taken aback by his boss's sudden intensity. "OK, Brian."

"Fine. Now let's wake up our fine Thai friend and head back next door and do what we were doing twenty minutes ago, i.e.

having a fucking good time."

Back in the Offshore Sturges again became his old fun-loving self, treating the girls to another round. The drillers were gone, and Niwat found an empty table to pass out on. Marek stood at the bar, the opposite end from Sturges, and carried on a loud conversation in Thai with a serving girl, a childish attempt to demonstrate he was superior to Sturges because he could speak Thai.

But no matter how sullen he acted, Sturges was having none of it. "Well, lad, I've made the choice. She's not the looker Nit was but then you don't really notice after fifteen drinks, do you? What about you then?"

"No, not tonight, Brian."

"Well, you live here. You can get it any night. As for me, I don't think I could get up to play golf tomorrow unless I had someone to help me burn off the alcohol tonight. Know what I mean?"

Sturges drove as if he'd been on nothing stronger then mint tea. He dropped Niwat off at his place in town, then sped up the beach road to let Marek out at the station.

When Marek climbed out of the truck, Sturges' girlfriend looked at him with bright eyes, as if she thought she was supposed to get out with him. "Just remember, take one of every vitamin you can find in the house and drink a liter of water." Sturges snapped his fingers. "No hangover."

It was raining again. As the truck pulled away and Marek fumbled for his keys in the dark, the guard – who would be out of work tomorrow – came around and locked the gate behind him.

"This here is paradise," Marek said, finding it difficult to form coherent words. "Didja know that? Fucking paradise."

But the guard, not understanding a word, just smiled.

Twenty-one

The day after Sturges went back to Singapore the guard was gone. Niwat said it might take a week to replace him. Then the maid stopped coming. "Because she is shy," explained Niwat. But it was a matter of face: her brother had been accused of theft, the family had been disgraced, and there was no way she could continue working at the bungalow.

He told the story to Saranya as they had dinner at the Serene Bay Hotel.

"No problem," she said. "I can wash your clothes."

"Don't be silly. I'll just take them into town to one of the laundries."

"You think I cannot do such things? Washing clothes and cleaning?" She wasn't smiling, but her eyes were twinkling. "Maybe you think I'm a spoiled child? Good for nothing?"

"Absolutely! Good for nothing, that's you. I don't know why I even bother to try and teach you English."

She stuck out her tongue and jabbed him in the forearm.

"No joke. I can help if you want."

"You have better things to do with your time. I'll just take my laundry into town when I get the mail." She said she wanted wine, and he understood. It was a kind of celebration.

Marek asked her about her family. Saranya shrugged and looked at the rice on her plate. "My father is old. And he is sick. At least now he is out of the hospital and in my uncle's house."

"Why doesn't he come back to your house in Songkhla? He can see a doctor at one of the hospitals here."

She shook her head. "He will not. He says the doctor in the hospital in Surat is the best. He trusts him. So he will stay at my uncle's house. For now." She sighed. "Anyway, this is life. But let's not be serious. Not tonight."

They walked along the beach in the cool night air and held hands like old lovers. Before, the litter on the beach, the plastic bags and bottles, the polystyrene containers and broken beer bottles, had irritated him. Now he decided he could ignore it because he was with her. Maybe he was becoming Thai: happiness was a matter of choice; it was what you chose to think or not to think.

She was not an experienced drinker, and though she hadn't finished her second glass she was slightly tipsy and held tight to him as they walked up the three steps to the bungalow. She put her hands around his neck and pulled him down to her.

"I missed you so much," she whispered.

Her lovemaking that night was so urgent, so demanding, it startled him.

He woke up in the night and watched her sleep, untouched by worry or doubt. He went out to the porch and looked at the sea. He had read the report Sturges had left him, the one from headquarters in Perth. They wanted each station to cut its budget by ten per cent. Marek wanted to tell them: *fine, cut my salary, just don't make me leave.*

But he knew it wasn't that easy. They had other alternatives. For one, they could close the station all together if there wasn't enough business, though as long as EastAsia was still operating here that didn't seem likely.

No, there was something else, something Sturges had never even hinted at.

"In the third quarter of 1995 we began a trial run of maintaining an unmanned station at Prachuap Khiri Khan, Thailand," the report had read. "One local technician was hired part-time to perform daily checks and routine maintenance. This would effectively eliminate full time salaries for a Station Manager and any auxiliary staff such as a housekeeper, guard, cook, driver, etc. If successful, this would save the company a considerable amount of expense. The trial period will last for three months, after which further decisions will be made."

Marek had to grudgingly admit that it made perfect sense. After all, as long as the power was running and the signal was clear, there was really no need to keep somebody at the station full-time. Just have someone come around every once in a while to make sure the generators were topped up, check the cables, and so on. It was something Niwat could easily do.

The fact that Sturges had never mentioned a word about an unmanned station made Marek fear it was the most likely possibility. He tried to recall every word Sturges had said, what had been outwardly stated and what implied. If he had to kiss a dozen bosses' asses to stay, Marek would, and he wouldn't think twice about it. And if, despite that, they cut him loose, he'd have to be ready for that. Have something lined up or have enough money to get by for a while without work.

Because there was no way he was leaving now. At least, not without Saranya.

* * *

He wanted her to move in with him; to hear her laughter at any time of the day and lie with her at night, skin to skin, her breathing as much a part of him as his own. He hinted at it, joking that since she was willing to wash his clothes, she could make his coffee and cook his breakfast as well.

But they both knew it was impossible. In a town where so many people knew her and her family, it would create a scandal of immense proportions. She would instantly be condemned as a whore; and the town's scorn would not just be aimed at her, it would fly all the way to Surat and disgrace her family as well.

"We have to accept it," she said in the morning as she was leaving him. "For now."

So outwardly their relationship didn't change; and nothing seemed more fatuous than their weekly charade under the casuarinas at the beach, with Saranya's friends, where they carried on their English lessons. And most nights she stayed at her family home in Songkhla with her younger brother.

Since there was seldom any work, Marek began calling in on some of the other service companies, the ones who did the logging, and perforating, and all the other downhole jobs Marek had scant knowledge of. They sometimes used his services and

Marek told himself it wouldn't hurt to show his face, have a little friendly banter, let them know you were just one of the guys.

And from time to time, if they had a problem with a computer, he would look at it for them. It was usually not difficult to put right, and he refused to accept any payment, except maybe the promise of a beer at some later, unspecified date.

One morning he was driving past the golf course, and, almost before he realized what he was doing, he turned into the car park. He asked if they rented out clubs, but they said no. They were only a small, nine-hole municipal course. The clubhouse itself was nothing more than a bare, one-room shack with a couple of counters, a cooler and a small kitchen.

He left wondering how much a decent set of clubs would cost. He really had no idea. It could be 100 dollars or 1,000 as far as he knew. He would have to ask Niwat.

"You want new or second-hand, Mr Alex? Used set naturally cheaper. I think second-hand good for beginner. You buy new, spend too much money. Maybe get bored with the game. You lose out a lotta money."

"Yeah, used I guess. I'm not really planning on buying just now. Maybe in a couple of weeks."

"Second-hand set probably cost you about five to eight thousand baht. I think it good if you play, Mr Alex. You practice a lot, and next time, when Brian comes, you can kick his ass. He's one shitty player, specially when hung over. Ha!"

With no maid at the bungalow, Marek had to drop off his clothes at a laundry in town every few days when he picked up the mail. And since there was no guard, Niwat offered to camp out there at nights; but Marek would have none of it.

"You belong at home with your family at night. We'll cover for each other during the day, until you can find another guard."

They installed a floodlight at the back and kept the shed locked with a heavy-duty padlock. Marek wasn't worried about any more thefts. He decided that whoever stole the toolbox were probably opportunists rather than big time thieves, and weren't likely to make a bold move for anything larger than they could easily carry.

Twice the city power supply cut off in the middle of the night when Marek was asleep. He awoke to the chugging of the generators kicking in. The first time it was 12:30, the second closer to 2 a.m.

"That'd be the knocking shop up the beach road," said Sturges, when Marek called him the morning after the second power cut. "Police closed it down for a while, but apparently they're up and running again. Must've made the right payoffs."

"The what?"

"Knocking shop. About three kilometers up the road. It's a combination karaoke bar, snooker hall and short-time hotel. You get the girl out of the bar and just have to walk twenty feet to the room. No muss, no fuss. Trouble is, when the lads decide to finally leave, they're pissed out of their minds. So they get in their cars, tear arse up the road, and fail to notice the sharp curve a couple hundred meters on. Naturally, they smash into the pole and bring down the power lines, thereby putting us on UPS for the term. Just make sure the generators are topped up and the UPS's are working. You'll be fine."

Within a week Niwat had found a new maid and guard. This time they were a married couple, distant relatives of his wife from Nakhorn Sri Thammarat who, Niwat explained, would be staying with him for the duration. They were standoffish around Marek but began to loosen up when he spoke Thai to them. It would take a little time before they saw he was not the boorish ogre they typically envisioned when they thought of farang.

He supposed he should have been happy that he wouldn't have to drag his dirty laundry into town and tidy up the place himself anymore. But it meant that Saranya would be spending less time at the bungalow. She would come for brief periods in the morning or afternoon, but if there was a chance someone else would see her, even a lowly guard, she could not spend the night.

"You understand, yes? It's so difficult in Songkhla," she said. "So many people know me, because of my father. He is karatchakarn, you know? Government worker."

"Yes, civil servant."

"Yes, and he knows so many people. When I see them I don't know them. Have no idea who they are. But they know me."

"I understand."

"It would be so bad for my family. The people could say so many mean things."

There were a couple of rig moves and it was good to have the work, but it kept him tied to the station. They talked on the phone every day, and Saranya came out every few days to bring him fruit and groceries, but she never stayed more than an hour or so. She chatted easily with the maid, and Marek noticed that after the first time, the maid waied her respectfully whenever she came over.

He had to stay up all night while the rig moved to its new coordinates, keeping his fingers crossed that there wasn't an incident at the "knocking shop". When the move was finished, it was nearly dawn. He went out to the porch and looked at the sky beginning to lighten over the sea. The world was calm and benevolent at this hour and his thoughts clear, despite the fact that he had been awake all night.

They could get married and stop all this silly tiptoeing around. All he needed was a little more money, just enough so that her father could get the best medical care and her brother could go to university. He could probably pull it off on his salary now, except he didn't know how much longer he'd have any income.

He'd find a new job. Maybe Sturges or Philips could help him. Niwat had all kinds of connections – he could help him for sure. He'd start asking around in the bars – there were good guys there and someone would help him out.

Somehow, it would all work out. It would have to.

Twenty-two

Information Release No. 1
September 11, 1995
0800 hrs.
Tropical Storm Watch

*Tropical storm "OWS07N92" has developed NW of
Palawan Island near position 12.3N 117.3E just within
the EastAsia weather watch area. Max winds near the
center estimated to be 40 kts. It is expected to remain
within the area for the next 36-48 hours as it moves
to the WNW-NW, then leave the area and continue
tracking towards the Gulf of Tonkin. It is not expected
to be a threat to EastAsia's operations in the Gulf of
Thailand.*

*We will closely monitor and update the storm
movement.*

Narong S.
Incident Commander

Marek received the fax on a Friday morning and immediately called Sturges.

"Nothing to worry about. It's just at the edge of the area they monitor. Nowhere near the fields at all and doesn't sound like it's moving toward the Gulf. Probably land in Vietnam. The southern part of Vietnam gets nailed pretty hard during the typhoon season."

"I'm sure I should probably know this, Brian, but when exactly is the typhoon season?"

"Well, now actually. September through December. Don't worry, lad. There's never been a typhoon in the Gulf of Thailand. Not since they've been keeping track of such things. Otherwise, how's it going?"

"Quiet."

"Let's hope they find something soon. We could use the work. You read the report I left? From headquarters?"

"Yes, I meant to ask you about that, Brian. When you were here you never mentioned anything about headquarters' plans for unmanned stations."

"What? Oh that. They're doing a trial run up in Prachuap, or something."

"Yeah, seems like they see it as the way of the future."

"Nah, never happen. Can't run a station without someone being there. The place would be gutted in one night. You saw what happened with our toolbox when we actually had a guard there. Imagine what it would be like with no one there."

"So the trial run is not going well?"

"Oh, I don't know. They haven't told me anything. Can't

imagine it would work, though. Look lad, don't worry about it. It's just a half-arsed plan some senior manager had – someone who probably knows fuck-all about the business. Look, you just keep doing what you're doing, and if you can drum up a little business, well, all the better."

The next day, tapping out the rig report in his office, Marek heard tires on the gravel and three quick, impatient blasts of a car horn. Hunter was sitting in a black Toyota pickup, engine idling, a confederate flag bandana tied around his head and dark shades hiding his eyes. He was tapping cigarette ash out the window and wearing his supercilious grin – the guy who had one over on everybody.

"Hey, Madison. Hop in."

Marek wondered how he knew where he lived, but then realized he had told him, as he told everybody he met, exactly where he worked.

"Can't. Working."

"It can wait. Got something important to show you."

"Really, just finished a rig move. Gotta get the report out today."

"This won't take long. Look man, I just got in from Singapore. Think I'd be wasting precious drinking time coming all the way out here if it wasn't about something important? I'll get you back in plenty of time. You'll finish your report by nightfall. Promise."

In the end Marek decided it would be easier to humor him for an hour or so than stay on the porch arguing. And he had to admit, he was curious. What exactly did this half-sloshed oilman think was so important, and why did he feel compelled to share it with him?

"I gotta get back by five," he said, climbing into the cab.

"Hey, no sweat."

Hunter handed him a frigid can of Singha. He sped down the beach road, talking sarcastically about some absurd political goings-on in the country, taking long pulls from the can of beer he kept between his legs.

"This country is run by complete idiots," he said, and with a flourish, flung the beer can out the window. "But still, ain't it great to be out of anal obsessive America and be able to trash a place just like the locals do?"

Marek thought for a moment they were going back to the teashop near the old wall, but then Hunter pulled into a compound with an old large house, a backpackers' guesthouse.

"Home sweet home," said Hunter. "C'mon."

The Mermaid Guesthouse was a two-story, wooden frame house, fronted by a lawn with a couple of mango trees. A towering banyan tree sent a network of roots to the ground, and a young blond couple smoked in the shade of its canopy. As they walked past the open air reception area, Marek could see two men inside watching TV. One had a completely shaved head, the other had hair to his shoulders.

Hunter led the way up an outside wooden stairway to a door on the second floor. He unlocked the door and held it open, waiting for Marek to kick off his shoes and go in. Inside the air was cooled, the air conditioner humming. The room smelled of cigarettes and toilet disinfectant. *Just like an oil worker*, thought Marek, *leave the a/c running even when no one's around and damn the expense, just to avoid ten minutes of discomfort when you get back.*

It was a large, one-room apartment with windows on three sides and was full of the afternoon light. To Marek's right there was a small kitchen area with a stainless steel sink, a thigh-high pastel blue refrigerator, and a bare counter running along the wall; to the left a wardrobe, a table with two chairs, and a rattan bookshelf. There was no bed frame, just a mattress on the floor. In the opposite corner, a couple of Persian rugs and a half dozen cushions of various sizes and shapes formed a snug sitting area.

"Kind of basic, huh?" laughed Hunter. "I got rid of all the furniture. It was all crap anyway. And I sleep on the floor when I can. Better for your back, y'know? And also, you can't fall off the bed when you're drunk. Go ahead, take a load off. You'll find sitting on the floor with those cushions to be more comfortable than most Thai furniture. That's a set up I learned in Iran."

"Iran? They let Americans in there?"

"They did when the Shah was in power. Shit, there were tens of thousands of Americans there then. The rugs are Isfahani. 'Bout the only thing here that belongs to me, 'cept for my clothes and shit."

There were no pictures or hangings on the walls, but there were neat piles of magazines and newspapers stacked in the sitting area. At the foot of the mattress were a large, almost new television and VCR, and on the floor in front of them, a tidy stack of seven or eight videotapes.

"I worked out a deal with Khun Suchart, the owner," explained Hunter, cracking an ice tray against the sink. "I fixed this room up myself, painted it, even did a little of the wiring. All the furniture here, what little there is, I bought myself. He keeps the rent down 'cause he knows I'm only here a couple of nights a month. It works out OK for both of us. He gets money for nothin' and I don't have to stay at the King Hotel with all those other oil freaks."

Hunter brought over two tumblers, half a bottle of Golden Cat and an ice bucket and set them on the rug in front of Marek. Then he sat down cross-legged across from him and made the drinks.

"Welcome to my humble abode, Madison," he said, handing Alex his drink. They clinked glasses.

Hunter had kept his bandana on but taken off his sunglasses. His face was newly sunburned. There was a weariness around his eyes but also a kind of excitability, and Marek wondered again if he was on speed. Hunter, grinning to himself, settled into his sitting position, his back straight, his arms across his thighs and his hands cradling his drink. Marek had never seen a man Hunter's size look so comfortable and natural in that position.

"Know how you can tell when the rainy season's really here? When it starts raining in the morning. Not just those afternoon showers like we get all the time, but when it rains in the morning, like it did a couple of times last week. Then you know the hard weather's just around the corner."

"There was a storm warning yesterday. Got a fax on it. They said it was just at the edge of EastAsia's weather watch area."

"No shit? They didn't bother to tell us. Just goes to show you."

But what exactly it showed, Hunter didn't say. He fell silent, looking into his drink, and seemed in no hurry to show Marek what he thought was so important. Marek was about to mention his report again when finally, Hunter spoke.

"So tell me Madison, what do you see yourself doing five years from now."

The question caught him off guard. He shrugged. "I dunno, working, I guess. I'd like to be doing what I'm doing now, but I don't think that's going to happen."

"Why?"

"They're talking about making cuts. Maybe unmanned stations."

"The technology's gonna pass you by anyway," said Hunter. "Ten years from now we'll be wearing GPS receivers on our wrists. You gotta be ready for that, my friend. Anyway, that's not really you, is it? Sitting in an office all day. Looking at a computer screen."

"What do you mean?"

"You love to travel, right? Told me about how you bummed around Europe and Asia before you landed in Bangkok."

Marek shrugged. "Yeah, I guess. But can't make much money doing that."

"Maybe not. So what you do is make your money in other ways. Ways that will give you plenty of time to do your traveling or whatever else you like to do. And make sure you have plenty of money to do it right. Working for someone else, that's really a chump's game, wouldn't you say? I mean, look what they're doing to you now. You've worked there for how long ... six, eight months?"

"Yeah, about."

"Right. You were there when they needed somebody, had all the qualifications, saved their asses by being in the right place, right time. And yet ... and yet, as soon as they can get rid of you, they will. Just to cut a few decimal points off their fucking measly budget.

"Don't get me wrong. I'm not rattling your cage, 'cause it's no different for me. Hell, it's no different for any of us. They'll wring every last ounce of blood out of us, and then, when it's time to cut their losses, they'll let us float with the breeze.

"And you know what really gets me? They're always talking about company loyalty. But that loyalty only goes one way, because if you mention loyalty when they're about to run you off the platform they'll look at you like you just stepped out of a loony bin."

It was like chapter two of his tirade at Jinda's, the oil worker as blue-collar victim. But Marek didn't buy a word of it, not with the salaries they made, not with their work schedule. He couldn't work up much sympathy for a guy who worked six months a year and got paid for twelve, a guy who made upwards of seventy thousand dollars per annum and paid no taxes.

"Case in point. A few years ago, EastAsia had this campaign to save money. They called it "Cost Breakers". They formed committees and organized meetings and put these Cost Breaker stickers up everywhere. Well, I knew one of the guys who got put on the offshore Cost Breaker committee. Had to go into meetings with all the suits once a month in Bangkok and present ideas on how they could save the company money. What they were really looking for was ways to cut the workforce but not cut production, only they wanted the fucking workforce to come up with the suggestions. Then it wouldn't look like they were being the greedy corporate men. Clever, huh?

"Well, anyway, what this friend of mine suggested was that everyone in management take a four per cent pay cut. That way, they'd cut the budget to where they wanted, and no one would have to be fired."

"What did they say to that?"

Hunter snorted. "What do you think? Thank you very much and don't let the fucking door hit your ass on the way out. They dropped the guy from the committee within the week. Point is, Madison, they don't give a rat's ass about me or you."

I'll finish the drink, thought Marek, *and then I'm out of here.*

Hunter rose from the floor, unwinding his long body with surprising grace, and went to get his cigarettes and an ashtray.

"I guess that's the nature of the beast," said Marek. "It's the reality we live with."

"It's their reality, their rules, a mug's game. That's why the only way you can beat them is if you play outside of the rules."

Hunter sat down again with the cigarette between his lips, squinting against the smoke as if he suspected Marek didn't believe him.

"Outside the rules? I wouldn't know how to do that. Wouldn't know where to begin."

"Sure you would. You're halfway there already. I mean, you're not the type to have a house in the suburbs and a two-car garage. You're already outside those particular rules. Right?"

It seemed now as if Hunter were sitting closer and Marek again had the feeling, as he had at Jinda's and at the teahouse, of being cramped and hemmed in by Hunter's massive size. Hunter took the glass out of his hand and mixed him another drink.

"Well, am I right or am I right?"

Marek shrugged and took his whiskey. His thoughts of leaving had vaporized. The only way out, as always, was on Hunter's terms.

"Let me show you something." Hunter put his cigarette in the oversized ashtray, went to the wardrobe and brought out a worn canvas rucksack. Whatever it held was heavy; Hunter's biceps bulged as he carried it back and placed it on the rug between them. He worked the big zipper open and with both hands reached in and brought out a gray stone Buddha head and placed it on top of the rucksack. Then he straightened up and rested his chin in his hands as if waiting for the head to speak.

Marek wondered what he was supposed to do. Touch it? Pick it up? It was smooth stone, and the face was perfectly shaped, with a large nose and ears. It had tight ringlets of hair, and inside them were flecks of black earth. He ran his hand along the cheek; the stone was rough but surprisingly cool to the touch.

"Congratulations, Madison. You're the second person to touch that head in the last thousand years."

"It's an antique, right? That's what you said before, in the teahouse. You deal in antiques?"

"Not exactly. Not yet, anyway. Now I'm just finding them. How much you think something like this would go for?"

"No idea."

"I'd say six figures, minimum. Talking US dollars. There are eleven more up there, too."

"Up where?"

Hunter stood up, as if what he had to say was so important he couldn't contain himself in a sitting posture.

"Can I trust you, Madison. I mean one American to another?"

Marek shrugged. "I guess so. I can keep secrets, if that's what you're wondering."

"The deal is this: there's an ancient temple up in the hills in Pattani. Very secluded. I learned about it … well, it doesn't matter how. But I've been looking for it for nearly two years, and I finally found it." Hunter was pacing the room, tapping his fist into his palm as if it helped him concentrate.

"I'm letting you in on the deal. We go up there … you, me, a couple of other partners … say two, three days. We tear it apart, bring down everything we can. And then we walk away rich men."

Marek laughed; he couldn't help himself. It was an absurd joke; a crude oilman's elaborate scheme to make him look like a fool; leg-pulling on a grand scale, the working-class guy getting one over on the college-educated egghead.

"You don't believe me." Hunter sounded hurt. "What the hell you think that head is, plaster of Paris?"

Then he brought out the Polaroids.

There was a stack of ten or twelve. They showed an overgrown stone and brick structure, tree roots and weeds clinging to the sides. Far shots showed it as a mound of dirt covered with weeds and small trees, with parts of the red and gray structure barely visible. There were shots of Buddha statues large and small – and it was only then that Marek realized that Hunter had actually removed the head in front of him from one of the torsos; had actually taken what? – an ax, a chainsaw? – to an ancient work of art and destroyed it so he could bring the head down here.

He felt a shiver down his back. This guy was serious and probably crazy.

"This head comes from there?"

Hunter shrugged. "I didn't rip it off from a museum, if that's what you're thinking."

"This is 1995. People don't find lost temples anymore."

"I did."

"How come nobody's found this before?"

Hunter unfolded a well-used map and laid it out on the floor between them. He tapped a nail on a brownish smudge in Pattani province. "It's here," he said. "See this area in here? No roads, no villages? This is all part of Khao Ruem Fon National Forest and Wildlife Refuge. Access restricted. Impossible to get up the hill from the south or west. See this road here along the beach, on the east side of the hill? It's dirt. Know when it was built? Less than six months ago. Nobody's found it because nobody's bothered to look. Too much trouble. Too remote, too hard to get too.

"Besides, nobody cares. The average Thai couldn't give a flying fuck about ancient history. Especially this stuff. This is part of the Sri Jaraya Empire, which Thais consider to be foreign, Indian or Indonesian. Oh sure, there are a couple of university professors who would get all wet about it, one or two high society twits. But hey, we'll be doing them a favor. We'll make sure it's all preserved and taken care of."

"By looting it?"

Hunter spoke slowly and deliberately. "Madison, nobody gives a fuck."

"Yeah, but it's still illegal."

Hunter shrugged. "This is Thailand. Legal, illegal ... those terms are defined by who you are, who you know, how much money you have."

Marek shuffled through the Polaroids again, feeling Hunter's eyes on him all the time. His knees and back were beginning to ache from sitting on the floor. Surely it was all a preposterous joke. The pictures were probably fake. But then why had Hunter brought him here?

"So why are you telling me all of this?"

"If I could do it on my own I would, but that's impossible. It's too big. There's heavy work involved. But I trust you Madison, 'cause you're an American and 'cause you're straight. Probably to a fault, but you're an honest guy. I could tell from the beginning. Plus, this is made for you, man. You like your bit of adventure, right? Well, how does this sound? Fucking adventure of a lifetime. And the money, man. Just think about the money and how much freedom that could buy you."

"You're gonna go up there and hack off the heads of these statues and bring them down and what ... sell them at the Sunday market in Songkhla?'

"Hey Madison, how about taking me serious for five fucking minutes?" Hunter's eyes were hot, despite the hard-edged smile. It was as if for a split second his mask had dropped. Then his voice lightened, and he was back in control. "Don't worry. All it takes to move contraband in this country is the right connections. And I got the right connections."

It was insane. Marek should stand up and walk out the door. He should get the hell away from this madman and avoid him for the rest of his life. But instead he heard himself asking, "So how would you do it exactly?"

"There would be five of us: you, me and three of my partner's men to help with the work. We're up there for two, maybe three nights at the most. We tear it down and take whatever we can carry, the best pieces for sure. Bring it back down to Songkhla and transfer to my partner. He takes care of all the rest. He sets up the buyers and transports the goods. We sit back and wait for the money to come in." He spread his arms as if appealing to Marek to see the obvious. "Clean and simple."

Another partner. Marek was curious about him but reluctant to ask. He didn't want to show too much interest in the deal. It was all too absurd anyway.

"So what do I get out of it?" he asked. "I mean, just for the hell of it."

"Two hundred thousand dollars."

"What?"

"It sounds good in dollars but even better in baht. Your cut will be a cool five million. That's for three days' work."

Hunter folded up the map and stood. He was looking down at Marek and waiting for an answer.

"I dunno," said Marek. "Sounds crazy to me."

"It is crazy. The good kind of crazy. The kind of crazy no one else ever thinks about and exactly the kind of crazy that works and makes people rich."

"Look," said Marek, his knees cracking as he stood. "I gotta get back to that report."

"Sure, no problem. You don't have to say 'yes' right now. But don't say 'no'. Think about it. Sleep on it."

"Yeah, sure."

"Good. Only thing is, we can't wait forever. I'm going offshore tomorrow. I have to know whether you're in or out before I get back next month on the eighteenth." He found an old receipt on the table and wrote some numbers on the back of it. "Call me offshore. If I don't hear from you before my shift is over, well, I guess I'll see you around. But I hope I hear from you. I need you to make this work right. We could be a great team, Madison."

He held out his hand. It was a strange gesture. Most expats who lived in Thailand gave up handshaking because the locals so rarely did it. Hunter's grip was powerful, and he beamed at Marek as if they were as close as brothers, as if to say, *it doesn't matter if you let me down, you'll always be my buddy.*

"Oh, and I'm sure I don't have to tell you to keep this our little secret, right?"

Hunter held the door open, and as Marek walked into the lifeless air of the afternoon, he felt the first few drops of the afternoon rain.

Twenty-Three

Marek woke to the rattling of windows and rain like steel pellets pounding the roof. The bedroom strobed in blue-white light and then nearly instantaneously an angry burst of thunder crescendoed across his roof and exploded, shattering the air into millions of tiny pieces.

In the morning the lawn was littered with twigs and palm fronds, and the wind was brisk off the sea. By the time Marek had poured his second cup of coffee, the maid had already collected three or four fallen coconuts and was sitting on the ground near the generator shed, hacking their tops off with a cleaver.

Niwat came early and before even entering the bungalow had climbed the superstructure of the antennae. He stood on the narrow steel rungs at the top, two stories above the ground, and Marek could see his white gloved hands working at the wires and cables.

Marek ran a function test on the Cray and the displays remained steady. "Wind can be a big problem," said Niwat, pulling off his cloth gloves in the kitchen. "Wind can loosen the cables."

In the afternoon Marek went to the post office as usual, but instead of heading back to the bungalow after he'd picked up the mail, he walked to the museum across from the old town wall.

Inside it was dark and quiet. He paid his entrance fee to a sleepy receptionist. The hallway floors were cement, uncarpeted, and his footsteps echoed throughout the building as he wandered among the dark rooms, thankful at least to be out of the midday sun. The displays had almost no English explanations; the museum itself seemed like nothing more than a storeroom of ancient cooking implements, large Chinese water jars, and long eroded religious tablets. Then he found it: a small room midway between the front entrance and the courtyard, labeled Srijaya.

It was dominated by a bronze statue of a sitting Buddha with a phalanx of cobras coiled protectively around his head. The display cases held smaller stone images, reclining or standing Buddhas, each pose described by a tongue-twisting Sanskrit word which meant nothing to Marek. According to what he could make out from the spotty English descriptions, all the pieces had been found in the southeast of Thailand, along the coast, from Nakorn Sri Thammarat in the north to Pattani in the south, with several pieces found just north of Songkhla at Khaw Daeng. Nearly all the pieces were over a thousand years old, and all were displayed in cheap wooden and glass cabinets like the ones in which his grandmother might store her linens.

In one case there was a small cardboard label which read: *Ranod Bodhisattva, tenth century AD.*

But there was no figure next to the label, and Marek knew why. Nine months ago, the day after he had arrived in Songkhla, the Ranod Bodhisattva had been stolen. A guard who had tried to stop the thief had been knocked unconscious and later died.

Didn't someone say the thief was a large man, possibly a farang?

That's what had brought him to the museum. There was no proof that Hunter had done it, no proof even that it was a farang. But what if it was? Marek needed to see for himself, to feel first-hand the audacity of a man who would walk into this room in the middle of the night and rip off a 1,000-year-old bronze statue. Anyone who would do that would have no problem plundering an ancient temple in the middle of nowhere.

"It *is* crazy," Hunter had said. "The good kind of crazy."

Marek stood in the silent dark room with its priceless pieces of art and thought about a stolen artifact, a dead museum guard, and a brooding, violent American oilman who sometimes sold antiques.

* * *

There was no work and Marek kept himself busy by filing and re-filing old paperwork. Saranya's father had returned to the hospital and she had moved back to Surat Thani to be near him. Marek was spending more time on the Dark Side, sometimes with Philips and sometimes alone. He was drinking too much and felt heavy and dull, which he tried to alleviate by going for long morning swims.

"I'll probably lose my job," he told Philips one night after too many beers. "Maybe sooner than later."

He wanted to tell him about Hunter, whom he now suspected was not just an antisocial misfit, but also a violent criminal. He wanted to tell Philips – or anybody – about Hunter's mad scheme to raid an ancient temple, because he wanted someone to assure him that it couldn't possibly be true, that it was all a hoax, that Hunter was nothing more than a blustery lout with alcoholic fantasies.

But was he? He had stolen the Ranod Bodhisattva – or had he?

But of course, Marek couldn't say anything to anybody. It would surely find its way back to Hunter in this tiny village of expats. Hunter knew where he lived, could track him down in a few minutes.

"This is Emile LaCroix from Mercier. I'm on the *Asian Tiger*. We've lost the GPS signal."

It was three o'clock in the morning, no power in the bungalow, and the streetlights along the beach road were all out. Another "knocking shop" incident maybe, but the generators should have taken care of that.

"Are you sure it's not the receiver?"

It was the usual poor ship-to-shore telephone reception. The *Asian Tiger* was pulling a pipe-laying barge for Mercier. LaCroix was the company man on board. He could barely be heard, but he was likely yelling into the phone at the top of his lungs.

"Our tech says there's nothing wrong with it. We get no signal at all. We expected to tie-in to the Echo platform at 06:00. We're already behind schedule and this is going to fuck us up royally."

As the fog of sleep began to lift from Marek's head, he realized something was drastically wrong. It was the dead silence of the night. The generators hadn't kicked in.

"We've got a power outage here," he said. "I'll check my generators and call you back immediately."

"Yes, and please hurry. Because meanwhile we are paying this fucking ROV and the fucking ROV technician five hundred US dollars a fucking minute for doing nothing."

Marek put on shorts and a T-shirt and clambered down the back steps and headed to the generator shed. The door was ajar; the lock had been cut with bolt cutters and lay dismembered on the ground. The guard was nowhere to be seen. The generators inside were cold. Marek fiddled with the connections and tried to start them manually, but they wouldn't work. Then he saw that the generators were dry. He looked around for the four plastic jerry cans of fuel. They had disappeared.

He called Niwat.

"There is an all-night petrol station on the road to Hat Yai", said Niwat. "It will take me thirty, forty minutes to go there and get back to you. Meanwhile you better call Mercier."

"The company man is going to have a heart attack. Please hurry."

Again, reception was terrible, but Marek didn't mind. It gave him something to hide behind, a reason to sign off as quickly as possible. "The signal is down due to a power outage."

"Don't you have backup?"

"We have some problems with the backup right now, but we should be up and running in about thirty minutes."

"I goddamn hope so. You know how much money this is costing us?"

"Hey, it's not my fault there's so many fucking thieves around

266

here," he said to the empty room after he'd hung up. But no fuel for the backup – that was his fault. That was one of the few real responsibilities he had at the station: make sure the power was always on.

He wondered who the little weasel was that had ripped off the petrol. Was it the kids who had stolen the tools? Maybe it was the guard who'd been fired, his little act of revenge.

It was nearly four hours until they got the generators running. The gas station had been closed, and Niwat had to drive nearly to Nakorn to find one open. Marek called the *Asian Tiger* to confirm they were getting a reading.

"Yes," said LaCroix, "and about fucking time."

Fuck you too, thought Marek, hanging up the phone. The sun was up now and there was no way he was going back to bed.

"We'll have to get another guard. Soon. Someone reliable," said Marek. "But look, Niwat. No need to tell Brian. I mean, he'll probably find out anyway. But if he doesn't, well, what harm is there?"

Niwat looked at him strangely for a second and then nodded.

Two days later Sturges called, and Marek was sure it would be about the four-hour episode of lost signal. But it was a completely different topic.

"I've set everything up. You'll meet him next Thursday in his Bangkok office."

"Who is this guy again?"

"Logistics Manager, Asian Sun Resources. They're brand new in the area. Starting exploration in the next few months. They bought Exalt's old fields and word is they're convinced there's something there."

"And explain again, what am I supposed to do?"

"Just do the old glad handing, you know. We're in the middle of negotiations. But this is a sure thing. They're going to do some exploratory wells."

"Doesn't our agent do this kind of thing?"

"He's in Jakarta. We need somebody up there now. You're perfect. You're the man in the field. You know more about what we actually do than any agent. Look I've talked you up big, faxed him some examples of your reports. He's willing to meet and talk about it."

"OK Brian, whatever."

"C'mon, you'll have a great time! I'll forward the air ticket to you today. You're staying at the Dusit Thani, right across from Patpong, you lucky bastard."

"OK, Brian," said Marek, laughing, relieved that Sturges had apparently not heard about the incident with Mercier. "Maybe I could use a change of scenery."

"That's the spirit, lad."

The next day he heard a motorcycle in the driveway and ran to the door to see Saranya coming up the steps. Their eyes met and she smiled at him, a brief fleeting smile that flitted across her face and then disappeared. She smiled – because that was what Thais did, no matter how they felt inside.

Then she was pressed against his chest, clinging to him, her body racked with horrible sobs. She held him for a long time without speaking. Then she looked up at him, her tear-stained face distorted in pain, and said, "My father is dead."

Twenty-four

The Bangkok taxi driver dropped him at the address on the business card and Marek, unaccustomed to the rush and blare of the city, blinked at the harsh morning light and the stark gleaming glass tower that rose above him. In the mirror of the elevator he straightened his tie and noticed despondently that he had missed a spot on his chin when he'd shaved that morning.

The offices of Asian Sun were on the twenty-seventh floor, and the reception area had two huge tanks with models of a wellhead and production platform, and goldfish swimming through the risers.

The logistics manager came out to meet him, arms outstretched for a double gripped handshake, and they walked back to his office making small talk about Bangkok's traffic. On the walls of the office were photographs of drill ships and land-based rigs, softly lit as if they were portraits of famous people. The window behind the manager's over-sized hardwood desk allowed a view of Bangkok's sprawling high rises and a flock of construction cranes.

Marek felt like a pretender to this world. His tie pinched at his neck and he had to stop himself from tugging at it.

The manager's name was DeVros and he was from South Africa. He had a droopy mustache which he continually plucked at. He was telling a long-winded story about how it had once taken him two hours to drive to his apartment after work because of flooded streets. Marek waited for him to finish, quietly tapping his fingers on the imitation leather of his briefcase, purchased the day before to make him appear more businesslike. The manager laughed at his own story, a bit too loudly, then waited for Marek to begin.

"We understand you're starting exploration soon. Exalt's old fields?"

The man shrugged. Everything in this business was a big secret. Once you acknowledged you had something in the pipeline you had to watch out for anybody who might try to take it from you.

"Maybe. We're in the process of analyzing the seismic data we purchased from Exalt. We haven't formalized any drilling plan yet. The thing of it is, if we drill, we'll likely start small, maybe just one rig. Probably just rely on the on-board GPS."

"Well, as you know, that's not so accurate. You need the corrections for real accuracy. We can guarantee accuracy to within a meter." Marek the salesman, phony as a three-dollar bill. He could hardly convince himself. "We'd hate to see Sun Asian miss the next big Gulf pay dirt because you were off by a meter and a half." Marek laughed, but it sounded forced.

"Umm, yes, that would be a shame. But you see the problem is all these bloody cutbacks. We are all of us trying to shave off as much fat as possible. We just cannot open any new contracts right now. It's this bloody price of oil. It's so low now it's hardly worth drilling for. If we decide to drill, we'll really have to cut corners."

If they decided? Sturges had made it sound like it was a done deal.

"We can write a contract for any length of time. Maybe a three-month contract would be right for you. By then you'd have a pretty good idea of what you've got. I mean, Exalt Oil was happy with our service."

"Yes, I'm sure they were. But ..." There was a lengthy pause. DeVros looked at the ceiling as if he were contemplating whether he should go on.

"Was there a problem?"

"Not with Exalt, as far as I know. But ... I just heard something this morning." He shuffled through some papers on his desk. "Mercier? Loss of signal or something when they were tying in?" He let his intonation rise slightly as if to say it was something no one could be certain of, as if to say maybe it didn't really happen, just another oil field rumor, and Marek could clarify the whole thing right here. Then he leaned back in his reclining chair, knitted his hands behind his head and waited.

Marek felt sweat break out on the back of his neck. He felt like his tie was choking him. He understood the implication and he could hear a tremor in his voice.

"There was a power outage. Our backup was ... well, it was down for a few hours. It was unavoidable. We explained it all to Mercier."

DeVros shrugged and pulled at his mustache. "Of course. Shit happens." He shook his head sympathetically. "This is the oil business. Nobody knows what the fuck is going on from one day to the next. Anyway, why don't you leave me your card and

I'll get back to you."

The manager stood and Marek, feeling an undertow pulling him out of the door, fished a card out of his briefcase. They shook hands again.

"Ah, Songkhla," said the manager. He tossed the card on his desk with barely a glance at it. "They have the best crab at that restaurant on the beach, what's it called? You know, the one by the mermaid."

"Nai Waan."

"I really must get down there again soon."

The manager walked him back to the reception area and signed him out, the whole painful process taking less than twenty minutes.

In the elevator Marek had to fight down the feelings of anger and inadequacy threatening to overwhelm him. Word was spreading; they were going to blame Southern Cross – him! – for the interruption of the signal which had probably cost Mercier tens of thousands of dollars.

But almost as bad was his pathetic attempt at being a salesman. He'd never cut it, that was the brutal truth.

In the cab he unknotted his tie and told the driver to take him to the American University Alumni Association. They rode on an elevated expressway and then exited to streets choked with traffic. The sky was cloudless and the midday sun so ferocious the wheezing air conditioning could barely keep up with it. The taxi spent long minutes inching through clogged intersections as motorcycles swarmed around them and construction equipment toiled frighteningly close around and above them. The driver wiped his brow with a handkerchief and sighed, "Bangkok too hot."

They passed a glittering temple and Marek thought of Saranya. He had seen her yesterday at Wat Saket in Songkhla, where her father's body was laid out for four days before the cremation. Philips had told him what to expect, but he had still found it unnerving.

The reception area inside the temple grounds was awash in garish fluorescent light. The open casket was near the altar in the center aisle, one arm extended from the box in a way that struck Marek absurdly as an appeal: *Help! Pull me out of here!*

Mourners in black sat passively in rows of folding chairs. Some chatted quietly. He saw Saranya across the room, sitting with two old ladies. He assumed one of them was her mother. She smiled and nodded at him. A teenage boy, her brother probably, stood on her other side. Apple and Jum, still dressed in their university uniforms, approached Marek and gestured for him to come towards the casket.

It seemed as if all heads in the place had turned toward him, the only farang in the room. He heard someone whisper, "ajarn". They were calling him "teacher", even though he wasn't one.

In front of the casket was a large bunch of flowers and a framed photograph of a much younger and healthier version of the man inside, hair jet black, cheeks pink as if daubed with rouge.

One of the girls handed Marek a small metal cup. On a stool next to the casket was a bowl of water, scented with jasmine buds. Feeling dozens of eyes upon him, he dipped the cup into the bowl and let it fill with water.

He didn't look inside the casket, focusing instead on the old man's hand. The palm was wet, smooth and pale brown like old polished wood. Marek tipped his cup over the palm and watched the water flow across it and into the receptacle below.

"Symbolic cleansing of the dead body," Philips had explained. "You ask forgiveness for any wrongs you've committed against the dead, and the act of washing provides absolution for you. A bit strange for us, eh? But it's over before you can sneeze, and it makes them feel good when you partake in stuff like that."

Saranya had made it known she wanted him to come and do this, though he had never met the man. What possible acts of transgression could he have committed? Unless of course, you counted the fact that he had taken his daughter's virginity. Probably most of these black-clad women, watching him now with a mixture of curiosity and amusement, would consider that reason enough for him to be begging forgiveness from the dead.

Later he sat outside in the temple courtyard on a marble bench. Some kids were kicking a takraw ball around in an open part of the temple grounds. A mangy dog nosed around for something to eat. Saranya brought him a plastic cup of Coke and ice and a bowl of noodles.

"I'm sorry," he said.

She sighed. "Thank you for coming."

A group of mourners passed by on their way out of the temple and Saranya stood and walked out with them, chatting as if they had met by chance at the market.

She came back to him and apologized. She couldn't talk with him because she had to take care of the guests. Marek understood.

It was a way to deal with grief: stay busy and focus on other people.

He wanted to embrace her, to reassure her, but he couldn't, not in front of all these people, not in the temple grounds.

"Saranya, don't worry. I will help you. You and your family. I promise."

She lifted her eyes for a moment and said, "I must go."

* * *

The taxi driver pulled into the parking lot of the American Cultural Center. Marek got out of the cab and walked to the building, feeling the sun on the back of his neck. The place had the look and feel of a United States government building of the seventies, built back in the middle of the cold war, when America was opening libraries and cultural centers to win the hearts of minds of South East Asia.

He had heard that they had back copies of the Bangkok Post here, going back for years. He found the library on the second floor. Inside it was cool and subdued, with a few people in easy chairs and students camped out at the long tables with their books spread around them. He had to fill out a form, and a few minutes later the librarian brought him spools of microfilm that held copies of the Bangkok Post from nine months ago, as he had requested. The machine was in a small room behind the counter, and after showing him how to use it, the librarian left him alone.

It took Marek twenty minutes to find it, but when he did, the story leapt off the screen.

Relic Stolen from Songkhla Museum

A tenth century bronze icon was stolen from the National Museum in Songkhla after a daring pre-dawn break-in. Museum guard Sombat Wongwein was injured during the theft and is now unconscious in Songkhla Provincial hospital. However, Chit Mongkol, a samlor driver who always parked his bicycle near the museum at night and was awakened by the alarm, told police he saw a large man wearing a ski mask running away from the museum. "He was big, maybe a foreigner," said Chit.

The relic was known as the Ranod Bodhisattva, a thirty-centimeter tall statue in the Srijaya style. It was discovered in 1963 in an ancient temple site in the Ranod district of Songkhla province. Museum director Prachit Songserm said, "This is a great loss for the museum and for Thai culture". He said its value on the international art market was "inestimable." Songkhla police are continuing their investigation.

Marek read the story twice, then switched the viewer light off and sat in the dark, listening to the muffled sounds from the main library. Either Hunter had incredible balls or he was completely out of his fucking mind.

Maybe, Marek thought, he should go home. Forget Thailand, forget Saranya. Go back to Wisconsin as a thirty-year-old failure without a job or career, a sad case in the eyes of his sister, a complete loser in the eyes of his surgeon brother-in-law. He could slouch, tail between his legs, back to his old boss and see if he could get his job back; that is, if the technology hadn't passed him by.

No, he wasn't going to leave Saranya. But he would very likely be out of work soon. Would she marry someone who didn't have a job? This was not some inscrutable mystery he was dealing with. Her father was dead. She needed security, a chance for a life without having to worry every waking moment about where the money was coming from.

He had to be realistic about it, look at it from all angles. 200,000 dollars was a lot of money for a few days' work. And it could be used to help so many people. After all, it wasn't as if he would be selling heroin; he wouldn't be hurting anybody. What had Hunter said? The Thais didn't care about this stuff anyway, didn't even feel it was part of their culture or history. They'd sell it themselves if they knew where it was and how to get it. And what about Hunter's partner? He was Thai, wasn't he? And he was only too glad to do business with them.

They'd be taking things that only a few people really valued and using them to help others. Of course, there was the not so minor problem of it being illegal. He could end up in a Thai prison somewhere, and from what he'd heard, that wasn't a trip to the beach. But Hunter had that covered, didn't he? He had the connections to protect them.

Marek walked back to his hotel room rather than taking a taxi, almost as if he were trying to delay the inevitable. He was drenched with sweat by the time he reached his room, but the first thing he did was take out his wallet and find the receipt with the phone number scratched on the back. It seemed to take forever, but eventually the connection went through to the offshore operator and Marek, after a moment's hesitation, asked for John Hunter.

Twenty-five

A wave slaps Hunter hard in the face and fills his mouth and nostrils with seawater warm as blood. He coughs and vomits brine and tries to squeeze the burning water from his eyes with the heels of his hands. His life vest has vanished, and he is fighting the weight of his waterlogged coveralls. A length of nylon rope or hose is caught up in his legs, dragging him downward despite his furious kicking. His face goes under and he sees a stiff corpse spiraling gracefully down until it disappears in the cloudy water. With superhuman effort, he fights against the tow and bursts through the surface of the water. He sucks air deep into his lungs. Far away, he sees a narrow strip of bright orange: a life raft. There are men on the raft; Filipinos chattering gleefully, one of them laughing in a high feminine pitch.

Now the raft is close, and Hunter can see there is a man looking at him. It is Garrett, and his eyes are holding a grave secret; a secret he and Hunter once shared but that Hunter has forgotten. Hunter can feel its weight, but it remains inchoate, inexpressible. Then Garrett's face turns into Hunter's father's alcoholic visage, world weary and full of self-pity. He looks at Hunter as if he is embarrassed that they would find themselves together here.

Hunter yells, but no sound comes from his throat. The Filipinos refuse to take the situation seriously; they are singing and roasting chicken on a brazier in the middle of the rubber raft. His father, pretending to be preoccupied, ignores him. He turns to the outboard and rip-starts it. Hunter shouts again, but he is drowned out by the snarling motor. He tries to yell louder, and water fills his mouth and throat. He is swallowing seawater, choking, trying to clear his lungs …

Hunter woke in the dark room clenching the sweat-soaked sheets, a scream trapped in his throat. He lay in bed breathing hard and then got up and raised the blinds on the window. The sea was black, and the platform was bathed in stark yellow light from the halogen floodlights. The flare from the production platform cast an eerie orange glow on the quiet waters of the Gulf of Thailand.

It was 4:40 a.m.; no point in going back to sleep with the alarm about to go off in twenty minutes. He sat at the edge of the bed and twisted his head from side to side to wrench the stiffness out of his neck.

The dream was always the same. Being swallowed by the sea; Garrett on the brink of letting him in on something momentous and then metamorphosing into his father. Both of them rising from the grave to tell him … what? His father dead for twenty years now, his heart exploding as he was rutting away on top of a whore in Montreal. And the garrulous Garret. Calling Hunter from the North Sea to tell him he was going to marry a girl from Aberdeen during his next field break; then dead in his bunk three days later, when his North Sea platform exploded in an oil and gas inferno so fierce it boiled the seawater and twisted the steel girders like they were sticks made of molding clay.

Hunter went to his locker and found his shower kit. There, buried beneath the shaving cream and toothpaste and washcloth, were his two little soldiers waiting patiently for him: the miniature bottles of Smirnoff he had cadged from a flight attendant on Singapore Air and smuggled offshore in the toes of his running shoes. He needed them now; not only to wash away the tattered remnants of his nightmare, but also to celebrate his last day on the platform.

He twisted the cap free and took a swig from the tiny bottle, swallowing its contents in a single gulp. Vodka because it was harder to detect, or so they said. They'd run him off in an instant if they knew he had alcohol out here, probably even send him back to shore on a crew boat in the middle of the night rather than let him wait for the first chopper, if for no other reason than just to prove they could. But they'd never know. Today was a travel day, and Hunter had no responsibilities except to board the first flight at dawn. And then it wouldn't matter how much alcohol he had in his system, because they never breathalyzed men who were *leaving* the platform.

He lay on the bed and felt the vodka spike his brain and blast the tension from his neck. He was thinking of the look on the supervisor's face when he realized Hunter wouldn't be coming back to work. He'd be shitting his pants when he discovered he didn't have a farang maintenance specialist at his beck and call anymore. He might actually have to get his own hands dirty.

He put the empty bottle back in his shower kit, then broke off the top of the next one, wishing he'd brought more. After all, how much of a celebration could you have with two shots of vodka?

Once again, he brought out his calculator and note pad. It wasn't enough. The rough estimates that Jack had given him, the limited number of pieces they'd be able to bring down, the payoffs and expenses … it would leave him short of the purchase price for Mr Kambiz's personal Eden on the Turquoise Coast. There had to be a way to get more.

The building began to stir. Hunter heard some movement in the room next door and then water running in the shared toilet. The day shift was waking up. Heavy footfalls on the steel stairway and then the first announcement of the day crackled from the loudspeakers: "*Passengers to remote platforms Charlie, Delta, Foxtrot; boat leaving in seven minutes, LQ boat landing.*"

In a few minutes he'd go downstairs and have a leisurely breakfast, then take a last walk around the LQ to find some lonely corner to toss the two bottles into the sea. Maybe, if he had time, he'd put on his hardhat and safety glasses and cross the bridge to the production platform to say a quiet farewell to every last fucking little piece of rotating equipment that had ever given him a hard time. But there would be no teary farewells or heartfelt handshakes with the crew. As far as anyone else knew, Hunter was going on field break and would be back as usual in twenty-eight days. They would all get a nice surprise when he didn't show at the hangar, and by the time they realized he'd done a runner, he'd be far away and the offshore life, the hyper-real starkness of it, would be something that existed only in his memory.

He sucked the last drops out of the bottle then ran his tongue along the miniature rim. This was goodbye to the place he'd called home every other month for the past three years. No more sleeping in these claustrophobic, sterile rooms, hoping the roar outside was only a high-pressure blip through the flare line and not a separator exploding. No more punching through swells big enough to pitch you overboard, heading to some rusty remote platform while black clouds coalesced overhead. No more flying on helicopters wondering if today it would be *your* turn to experience hydraulic problems. No more sitting in the mess with guys you loathed, under stark fluorescent lights that highlighted every blackhead and busted nose capillary.

He tried the calculator again. Those nagging, reproachful numbers. There had to be a way to get more. He *deserved* it. And he was taking all the risks. He suddenly thought of the fat Chinaman, the one with the specialist shop in the bowels of the warehouse district near the jetty. It was Jack who had introduced them, and hadn't Jack said he was the best? It would be risky, for sure. But it was the only way ...

Twenty-six

Marek peeled away the soil and clinging grass and saw a face: the Buddha's face, smooth features eroded by dirt and rain, and hair sculpted in tight curls like cornrows. It was made of gray stone and he'd thought it would be light, like pumice, but it was as heavy as a bowling ball. The rough bottom of the head was still hot from the chainsaw. He wiped away some dirt and saw a smile, heavy-lidded, tight-lipped, serene. A smile so typically Thai it could have been carved yesterday.

Hunter was on the first tier of the massive temple, ten feet above, holding the chainsaw aloft in one hand as he cleared away vines and crumbled brick from an alcove. The temple was covered in grass and weeds; strangler figs grew out of the dirt, their roots intertwined with the brick. In places the walls of the temple had collapsed, revealing empty chambers.

Hunter was convinced the temple had been looted before, perhaps hundreds of years ago, and any bronze or gold items were long gone. "It's a shame, but these heads will still go for close to six figures. And there's other stuff."

All around them on the clearing floor lay shards of pottery and brick. *An archeologist's dream*, thought Marek. *And we're the nightmare.*

Hunter, balanced on the ledge, took careful aim just above the shoulder of the figure in the alcove, then pulled the starter rope on the saw. The obscene scream of the blade ripping into the stone echoed off the limestone cliff and the forest around them. Marek was sure it could be heard for miles, maybe even down to the village at the foot of the mountain. The head fell away, and Hunter lobbed it onto the soft grass next to Marek. "Lucky number seven."

They had started from Songkhla the previous day, well before dawn. There were five of them: Hunter, Marek, the tall Thai with the scorpion tattoo on his hand, an older Thai man Hunter called 'Skull', and a young man barely out of his teens whom Marek assumed was Skull's son.

It was a long, tough trek up the mountain, made no easier with all the gear and provisions they were carrying. In places there was only the hint of a trail, and they had to hack through the bush with parangs and knives. They scrambled over wet stones along a stream bed, and over the rock steps of a cascade, and shinnied over fallen logs and tree roots as thick as a man's thigh. Then, around midday, they climbed the last ridge and there it was, dominating the meadow in front of a huge limestone cliff, partially collapsed but still majestic in its breadth, the ancient temple of the Sri Jiraya dynasty. Marek almost laughed aloud. It was absurd – an ancient lost temple half a day's travel from Songkhla, all but forgotten by the world, and Hunter had found it.

They'd walked through the knee-high grass in silence, almost in awe. As they got closer Marek could see the structure was made of russet brown bricks. Hunter tore at the soil with his bare hands, pulling away vines and tufts of grass. Then he wrenched off a clod of black earth, snapped it in half and handed a piece to Marek. Beneath the layer of dirt was a shard of rust-colored clay that crumbled in Marek's hands like brown sugar.

"Welcome to the Temple of the Glorious Dawn."

Now, on the second day, Hunter had sent Scorpion and the boy out at first light to work on the trail or find a smoother way down. Meanwhile the three remaining men had formed a kind of production line. Skull, wiry and agile despite his age, scampered along the edge of the tier, cleaning out the roots and dirt from the alcoves so that Hunter could get in with his saw. Marek cleaned the heads and carried them to where they had set up the tents.

When the rain came, they took cover in Hunter's big tent. Hunter lit a joint and passed it around along with the whiskey bottle, while the rain hammered the tarpaulin. Marek, every muscle in his body aching from the long climb and handling the heavy stone heads, sat cross-legged and looked through the opening to the desecrated mound of brick and dirt, marveling at how much damage they had done in one short day.

"Knew a guy in Saudi, a driller from New Mexico," said Hunter, exhaling a long stream of smoke. "When he was on home leave, he'd find these old Indian sites and go in with a goddamn backhoe and rip up everything. Take whatever pottery and whatnot survived and sell it for a fortune. Shit you not. Pre-Columbian shit. High society bitches in Manhattan were soaking their panties over this stuff. He had photo albums he used to pass around in camp. Buy the stuff directly from him, no middleman. Had it made, man. Didn't have to go at it with an axe and a chainsaw, let me tell ya. Just rent an excavator for a week." He took a long drink from his water bottle and then sighed. "Then the Indians – I'm sorry, my bad, I mean the *native Americans* – started getting all hot and bothered and put pressure on the federal government to stop the supposed rape of their culture. They pushed all the right political buttons. There's no worse animal than a self-righteous politician, is there? Especially around election time. Well, they put an end to it. Last I heard my friend the driller might be facing time."

He said it matter-of-factly, as if going to prison was an interesting piece of trivia about an acquaintance, not something that could be applied to him in an identical situation.

Hunter chuckled, sensing Marek's discomfort. "Don't worry, Madison. I told you. I got connections. No one can touch us."

The afternoon work was hard. The air was steamy and the soil muddy and heavy. Heat rose from the ground as much as it came from the sun; it was hard to breathe and hard to move. Marek's tee shirt and shorts were soaked through; he wanted nothing more than to lie down in the stream that ran along the forest edge and stay there for hours. But Hunter continued with an obsessive intensity, even as the light faded and the night insects began to bite.

Night fell quickly once the sun went behind the mountain. Hunter clambered down and put away the chainsaw then marched the circumference of the temple, shining his flashlight into the collapsed recesses, hoping there might be something – some pottery or small bronze piece – the ancient thieves had missed.

"Bastards beat us to it by a couple hundred years, at least,"

Hunter said as he strode past to clean off in the stream behind the campsite.

Marek was the first to see the two beams of light approaching from the trailhead. Scorpion and the boy were walking so quietly that if they hadn't had their flashlights on, Marek never would have known they were approaching. They walked directly to Hunter at the edge of the stream. They talked in low tones for several minutes while Skull and Marek prepared dinner: boiled rice and sardines from a can.

"Slight problem," said Hunter, clearly agitated about something. "Toi and the kid, they worked their way down the trail to the bottom. Cleared it out so it'll be easier going down. Then they decided they'd take a look at the pickup, you know, in the rubber at the head of the trail where we parked it yesterday. Make sure everything was copacetic.

"Only when they got to the truck, they found some guy looking it over. Turns out he was the village headman's brother, or at least that's what he claimed. Very nosy about the truck. Asked them what they were doing. Toi told him some story about how they'd heard there was land for sale, that they were maybe thinking of investing in a rubber plantation. This guy was no dummy though. He spotted the J.C. Oil Tools sticker on the back window and asked if they were working for a foreigner or a foreign company. Believe me, nothing gives these guys a hard-on like the possibility of foreign cash, especially if it's got something to do with oil. All of a sudden, anything you're looking to buy, well, they just happen to be selling it; whether it's land or a couple of their daughters.

"Toi naturally denied there were any foreigners involved, but he's not sure the guy believed him. He said the guy kept looking at the J.C. sticker, running his finger over it without saying anything. Says you could just about hear the wheels turning in his head.

"Finally the guy says there might be some land for sale and did Toi want to meet the owner? Toi backed off and said they weren't ready for that yet. They were just having a look around. At that point they couldn't just turn around and head back up the trail. So they got into the truck and drove off. They came back in an hour and parked in another spot a couple of hundred yards away."

"Think the locals know about this temple?" asked Marek.

"I doubt it. But the thing is, if the headman suspects there's big foreign money sniffing around his village, he's gonna feel like he deserves some of it. I doubt if he's gonna fall for the rubber plantation BS if he thinks there's an oil company involved. I remember when EastAsia was looking for some land to build a new warehouse on a few years ago. Everybody in the damn province knew about it. In the end they couldn't find any plot, even a piece of swampland, that cost them less than five times its real value."

The Thais squatted at the edge of the fire, silently and single-mindedly devouring their food, as if nothing else in the world mattered. The last pink strips of sky in the west had vanished, but a solitary bird whistle still echoed off the limestone cliff. The night chorus of insects, toads, and night birds was beginning to warm up.

Hunter sat on a rock and smoked, too distracted by his

thoughts to eat. "Nobody in that village knows about this temple, I'm pretty sure of that, for the simple reason it hasn't been looted before, at least not in the last five hundred years or so," he said. "But somebody down there has probably figured out you can get to the wildlife refuge from this side. Maybe they think we're poaching, illegal wildlife trade. Gibbons or hornbills or something. Tiger penis. Doesn't matter what they think we're doing, if they smell money, they're going to come looking.

"Toi says the trail would be fairly obvious to anyone who came looking for it, now that it's been cleared. Lead them right into our laps just in time for lunch tomorrow, less than a half-day's climb from the village."

The Thais had begun to clean up after dinner and there was a clattering of tin pans and utensils. None of them seemed to be as disturbed as Hunter was about being found out. You could hear one of the men quietly singing in Thai as he washed off the utensils in the stream. Skull was monopolizing the Thai conversation, talking loudly, his voice cracking with excitement, presumably relating the day's events to his two friends.

"OK, here's what we'll do," said Hunter, standing up. "All five of us will work on the temple tomorrow. We'll get a few more heads and see if we can't get down two or three full statues. Get as much as the five of us can possibly carry or drag down the mountainside. Whatever happens, by this time tomorrow we're gonna be packed and ready to go. Day after tomorrow, we're going down." Hunter called over Toi, scorpion hand, and told him the plan.

"Who's on guard duty tonight?" Hunter asked.

"I go first; Sammy take the next shift." Sammy, Marek guessed, was Skull.

Hunter went into the tent and came back with a small caliber pistol and handed it to Scorpion.

"You take care of this," Hunter said to the Thai. I don't want that goofball Sammy handling it. You tell him if he sees or hears anything, he wakes you up."

"You don't really think they're going to be coming up here tonight, do you?" asked Marek.

Hunter shrugged. "I doubt it. They're spooked by the jungle at night. But daylight, that's different. Never underestimate the power of greed." He stood up and grinned down at Marek. "After all, look where it got us. Look where it got you." Hunter walked away, and Marek could still hear the laughter in his voice when he spoke again to the Thai.

Marek lay in his sleeping bag under the mosquito netting, his hand around the amulet Saranya had given him. She had said it was very special, very powerful, from a much-venerated monk from Ranod. She knew nothing about this adventure, of course; he'd told her he had to go back to Bangkok for business. But perhaps he'd given something away in his tone of voice or in his eyes, because she reached into her handbag and brought out the amulet and gave it to him, squeezing his hands in hers.

She had come to the bungalow in the morning. She sat stiffly at the edge of the sofa, as if she were a stranger, as if this were the first time she'd ever been in the room.

Her father had been cremated. Her mother, brother and sister were moving permanently to Surat Thani. They were going to sell the family house in Songkhla. It was old, though, and Thai people didn't like moving into old houses, so they would tear it down and build a new one. The insurance money would pay for part of it, and she could get a loan from her uncle. It would cost money, but in the end, they could make a bigger profit selling the land with a new house on it.

She spoke in an emotionless monotone, as if she were speaking about someone else. Once the house had been sold, she too would move to Surat Thani to be with her family. And to find work. There were lots of jobs in the tourist industry there because it was close to Samui Island. Her English was good; she could easily get a job in a hotel on the island or as a tourist guide.

She has come to say goodbye, thought Marek.

"But what about continuing your studies? You said you wanted to study for a Master's."

She shrugged and looked at him blankly. Wasn't it obvious to him?

He had a horrible vision of her behind the reception desk of a two-star hotel, placating pushy Hong Kong Chinese, fending off drunken Brits.

He got up from the chair and sat beside her. She wouldn't look at him. She reached for her tea.

"Remember what you said? You said it was OK because I loved you. Remember? Even if everything else in the world has changed, that hasn't. Do you understand? You are not going to work on Samui Island. You are going to go to graduate school and study for a Master's degree."

She shook her head violently. "There is no money. I have to work so that my brother can continue to study. Chaiwat is going to be a doctor."

"Saranya, I can help. I have some money coming soon ... from America. I want to help you and your family."

She looked at him for the first time. She was searching his eyes, he thought, as if unsure whether she could believe or trust him.

She was quiet for a long time, looking at the floor. Then she spoke. "Do you know what Thai people call it, Alex? 'Rent A Wife'. From when the American GIs were in Vietnam." There was a bitterness in her voice, a tone he had never heard before. "When there were army bases in Thailand, the American soldiers all had Thai women living with them. For taking care of them, for sex. But then the war was over, and the GIs left. And the women, their girlfriends, their rent-a-wives, stayed in Thailand."

"Do you think that's what you are to me?"

"No. Yes, maybe." She had begun to sob. "I don't know."

"I am not leaving you. I will take care of you. And your family. I promise."

"It is so difficult," she sobbed. "We have no money. So very difficult. You ... you should find another girl. Someone who does not have so many problems. You can have an easier life."

He held her to his chest, as if holding her tighter would make her stop talking this nonsense.

"Do you love me?" he asked, his voice barely a whisper.

She nodded into his sternum. "Yes. *Rak maak*."

"All right, then. So it will be OK." He held her for a long time, letting her sob in his arms.

Twenty-seven

Dawn was filled with the cries of solitary birds and the mournful call of a gibbon deep in the forest. Skull, the night watchman, sat near the extinguished campfire on a tiny foldout canvas stool that looked like it could barely support a healthy twelve-year-old. He sat with his legs folded on the seat, leaning against a tree trunk, his mouth agape, fast asleep.

They worked hard in the early morning, before it got too hot. Hunter and Scorpion hacked and muscled their way up the ancient stone staircase, ripping down the saplings growing from the brickwork and tearing up bricks and stones and flinging them to the bottom.

"Let the archeologists deal with that shit," said Hunter. "They ought to thank us. Putting this thing back together will keep them busy for years."

Marek, Skull and the boy worked their way up to the second tier of niches. These held standing Buddha images made of sandstone like those on the other levels, but smaller and lighter. They were thin figures with one arm raised in what Hunter had called the "How" pose because he said it reminded him of the Indian in old Hollywood western movies. Hunter had said to keep them intact, that they'd try to bring them down whole, so they tore away the centuries of roots, weeds and dirt and, after using the ax and saw to cut away the base, carefully lifted them out; all the while standing on the ledge of the second tier, thirty feet off the ground. They improvised a sling out of burlap and rope so one of them could ease the figures down to ground level, bumping them along the soft earth of the temple to the other man waiting below. The statues were heavy enough to make it hard work, and after they'd finished with the second one, they took a break in the shade of a tree.

Hunter appeared next to them, pouring water over his face. He was gazing toward the trailhead as if expecting the villagers to arrive at any minute. Marek could clearly see the pistol tucked into his belt.

Hunter went back to work and Marek sat on the grass and tried to block out thoughts of being in a Thai prison. A cloud of tiny insects formed around him. He unscrewed the top of the bottle and poured water over his head, then washed over his face, chest and armpits. His shoulders and forehead were already stinging from sunburn. He felt an unfamiliar tightness in his arms and back. He pushed away the unpleasant images of internment by thinking how good it felt that his body was getting stronger. Two days of this work and he could feel he was already building muscle. He wondered if Saranya would notice and what lies he would have to tell her about his three-day "business trip" to Bangkok.

Then Skull screamed.

"Ngu! Ngu!" he cried. "Snake!"

Skull leapt to his feet like he'd been blown backwards out of a cannon. His eyes were as big as golf balls and he was pointing behind Marek, who turned to see a shadowy movement between himself and the tree trunk, a link of dull coppery S-curves in the grass.

Marek began to stand and the snake, panicking, trapped between him and the big tree, reflexively stopped and sprang up to strike. The cobra fanned its hood out to full width, its body as thick as the big end of a baseball bat, flicking its tongue as its head waved back and forth. Marek was frozen to the spot in a half-standing, half-stooping position, afraid to move because it might provoke an attack. He was within easy striking distance of the creature's fangs, thinking: *this is not really happening.* The creature had tiny black eyes and a milky yellow underside. In the dappled sunlight under the tree you could see the fine detail of diamond-like shapes on the inside of its flared hood. Time had stopped, and there was an eerie quietness as Marek waited for the snake to attack, knowing he would be far too slow to avoid it.

Suddenly, out of nowhere, Scorpion appeared. Waving one outstretched hand in front of the cobra to distract it, he moved in slowly. Then, hands as swift as a prize fighter's, he grabbed the cobra's tail just as it made a vain leap for Marek's thigh. He held the tail in the air with his right hand and quickly planted a foot on the snake just behind its head, pinning it to the grass.

The snake was a good five feet long. Its muscular golden body flexed and twisted furiously; it was trying to turn its head around to see what had it.

"That's a big mother," said Hunter, just behind him, his voice full of awe. Scorpion bent over and in one quick move grabbed the snake below the head and lifted his foot. Fearlessly, he lifted the heavy snake up and showed them the open mouth and the fangs as he squeezed its neck. Then he put it back on the ground and again pinned it beneath his foot. He took a long knife out of a holder on his belt and with one quick motion sliced off the head.

"Now we're really in deep shit," laughed Hunter. "Goddamn king cobra is an endangered species in Thailand. We'll have the tree huggers after our asses now."

He came up close behind Marek, who could hear his heart pounding in his head, and said: "OK friend, you can go wash out your shorts now." Hunter picked up a tree limb and poked at the head of the cobra.

"Nice thing about cobras is, they always warn you before they attack. Now, your Malaysian pit viper, that's different. They just hang out in the tall grass and wait for their prey to saunter on by. Toxin's three times more powerful than a cobra's. Affects the muscles. You lose all motor control, and in twenty minutes your heart just stops."

"Don't tell me. They're everywhere around here," said Marek, surprised at how winded he sounded.

"Shit yes," Hunter laughed. "More common than cobras, that's for sure. But they're not on the goddamned endangered species list yet, so feel free to go ahead and kill it if you see one. Oh, and be careful of this head. There's still venom in these fangs. People have been known to be bitten by dead snakes. Reflex action."

Marek had no intention of going anywhere near the cobra's head, whether it was dead or alive.

"What's he gonna do with it?" asked Marek, as Scorpion held out the snake's body for Skull and the boy to admire.

"Probably put it in tonight's curry. Cobra meat, man. Eat that shit and you can fuck ten times a night."

"How many of those stone heads you think you could carry down?" asked Hunter.

"I don't know. Two? Maybe three."

"Try three. We'll leave everything else up here. Tents, tools, cooking stuff. We're going down with only the goods. The boys will each take two heads and one of the small statues. I'll carry two of the statues."

"How?"

"I'll strap them to my back. I'll be fine. I'd almost be willing to start down right now if there was enough daylight left."

Hunter took Polaroid shots of the nine heads and five complete statues, then went to the temple and took some shots of the ruins.

"Before and after," he said. "My clients will be quite impressed."

"Aren't those awfully incriminating photographs?" asked Marek, but Hunter just laughed.

Marek put three of the wrapped heads into his rucksack and tried walking with it. It was unbalanced and heavy, but it wouldn't be impossible. They would be going down after all; it would surely be easier than the path up.

During dinner the Thais were more animated and talkative than usual. Maybe it was the fact that in the morning they'd be going back down, or maybe it was the cobra. Toi had ground it up and mixed it with tomatoes and chili peppers and ladled it over rice. "Our victory dinner," said Hunter. "We beat the cobra. And we got the loot."

It looked like ground hamburger. All Marek could taste was the peppers.

"Hey Sammy," yelled Hunter. "You eat snake, go back Songkhla. You *boom-boom* all night." He entwined his fingers and clapped his palms together, making a coarse sound. The Thais roared.

Later, after it was dark, the Thais walked over to the temple. Marek and Hunter watched them from outside the tents. Across the meadow they could see the sticks of incense being lit and waved back and forth. Then they were stationary points of light, like yellow stars on the horizon, as the Thais wedged them between the temple bricks. Marek caught a whiff of the perfumed joss as it floated across the meadow.

"They were talking about the cobra," said Hunter. "They said it was a manifestation of the temple spirit, that it came out to protect the temple from evil intruders. They think the temple spirit might be looking for revenge somewhere along the way."

"They really believe that stuff? It's the twentieth century."

Hunter shrugged. "The thing is, to their minds, nothing happens by accident. No such thing as coincidence. So there must have been some reason the cobra appeared when it did, where it did. It's all too obvious to them."

He was smoking a joint and taking sips of whiskey straight from the bottle. "Now as for me, I'm much more worried about humans than spirits. Like the guy Toi ran into yesterday. Who knows what crazy ideas are being hatched in the village now he's told everybody what he found."

Hunter squinted as he took a long drag off the joint. "Village gossip, man. Everything gets exaggerated and distorted. I'm sure their curiosity's all fired up. If they find the trail head, I'd expect them to be coming up here very soon for a look-see. Hopefully we'll be back in Songkhla before they do. And if eventually they make their way up here and find the temple, well shit, they're welcome to whatever they want. We'll still have all this." He waved the joint in the direction of the carved out heads and statues. "No reason to get greedy."

"How much is all this worth?"

Hunter didn't answer. He took another long pull on the joint and lay back on the mat with his hands behind his head, in his own world. A few minutes later Marek went into the tent and got under the mosquito netting. He was thinking about how good it would be to use the money to help Saranya and her family. It assuaged his nagging sense of guilt for helping to destroy an ancient temple.

Hunter came and rummaged through his pack for his flashlight then went back outside, zipping up the tent. Marek could hear him speaking his own brand of pidgin English to the Thais.

"I take watch tonight. All night. At five we start get ready to go down. I wake you up then, and we start taking down tent to hide away. Everybody happy, huh? Tomorrow we go home."

Twenty-eight

"I told you these guys were good," said Hunter. He had to shout over the din of the tumbling stream.

He meant Scorpion. In his day of trail clearing, Scorpion had found a way around the steepest drops along the stream. Marek had dreaded it all morning: weighed down by three sandstone Buddha heads, losing his footing on the slippery boulders and plunging to the bottom, breaking a bone or two in the process, Hunter furious because the heads had been smashed to bits, leaving him there to be devoured by red ants. But the Thais had cut a trail twenty yards into the thin growth above the cataract and then down a series of step-like tree roots. The new trail had a rich earthy smell, and the slashed tree limbs emitted an odor that reminded Marek of a library. They joined the stream below the waterfall where it once again descended gently, and they could walk along the edge of the water on the dry rocks.

Marek had awoken that morning with cramps in his stomach, and after a breakfast of sticky rice, it had gotten worse. He'd hoped he'd be able to cope with it until reaching a proper toilet somewhere below in civilization, but now there was an urgency he could no longer fight. He rummaged through the packs until he found the toilet paper, then went off to find a private place to release his watery bowels.

"Revenge of the cobra," said Hunter brightly, as he reappeared. He was grinning from behind his sunglasses and Marek felt the urge, not for the first time, to take a swing at that supercilious grin. He wouldn't allow Marek even this one private moment of embarrassment. He had to shout it out to the world like it was one more thing he could lord over him.

As they resumed the trek, Hunter said something to the Thais, patting his belly and nodding toward Marek. They all grinned in his direction. Ha ha. Big joke. Pussy white man has the shits. Can't handle his cobra. Marek fell in behind them, the three heads feeling much heavier than when he'd taken off the pack five minutes ago.

They descended quickly and easily down the cleared path. The skyscraper trees thinned out, the canopy became sparse and sunlight stippled the trail. They reached a ridge and walked along it for a while, the hot electric buzz of the cicadas assaulting their ears. Then, through a gap in the bush, they saw the blue waters of the Gulf of Thailand. The sea looked peaceful and unreal, like a movie backdrop.

"Home again, home again, lickety split," said Hunter.

He reeked of sour sweat and in the sunlight his three-day growth was speckled with gray. His eyes were hidden by the plum-colored lenses but Marek knew what they'd look like: the slightly bruised appearance, the yellowish sclera. Because Hunter, the genius of this operation, had been up all night pulling guard duty and entertaining himself with whiskey and ganja. But here he was, standing as tall as ever, without a hint of fatigue in spite of hauling forty pounds of awkwardly arranged Buddha statues on his back, his denim shirt straining over his shoulders and biceps, wearing his shit-eating grin as if the world had just declared him king.

They could see a narrow strip of beach, deserted except for a solitary fishing boat. "Looks quiet," said Marek. He imagined he could hear the waves breaking on the beach, but they were too far away for that.

"Yeah, well, looks can be deceiving."

"But no hordes of villagers rushing up the mountain to see what the farang are up to."

Hunter grunted. "Shit, it's just past midday. They haven't worked up the energy yet. Come on, let's get off this fucking mountain."

They were in the secondary growth now, thorny and scratchy, the part the Thais hadn't cleared since they didn't want to make the trail too obvious from below. Marek heard the cough of a pickup truck like a rude intrusion into their private world: civilization. They punched through the secondary growth and were at the top ridge of the rubber plantation. There was nothing left but an easy walk down the terraced slope, through the forest of dappled rubber trees and their porcelain cups of creamy latex to the dirt road at the bottom.

It took them another twenty minutes to walk to where Scorpion had moved the car after the first day. Hunter's rented pickup was parked on a dirt two-track near a dilapidated wooden shack. The shack was on short stilts and had a sheet of thick translucent plastic for a door. Outside it stood an old rubber press, a few scattered plastic pails, and a pile of empty brown bottles.

"Somebody was here last night," said Hunter. He kicked at a pile of gray ash and coals, a few still yellow-orange with heat. "Why you park the truck here, Toi? So close to this house?" The man with the scorpion tattoo shrugged. He and the other Thais had already unloaded their packs in the bed of the truck. They were beginning to tie things down and cover them with the canvas tarpaulin.

"Nobody here," said Toi. "They see this truck, they think maybe the owner come here. The owner of this land, you know, some guy they never see before. Some guy who live in Had Yai or Nakorn. They don't know this his truck or not. They stay away."

Before Hunter could respond two motorcycles came up the dirt road and turned into the two-track, stopping a few feet away from the back of the pickup. The two young drivers were dressed in dirty T-shirts and jeans torn at the knees. One of them had a pakama wrapped turban-like around his head. They turned off their motorcycles, and for a full minute their black eyes took in the scene: the three Thai men, the pickup truck with something covered in the back, the two foreigners. The one with the turban finally rested his eyes on Marek, staring at him openly and aggressively, then unsmilingly said, "You. Money."

Scorpion went to talk to them. Marek turned away and gave his rucksack to Skull to be loaded into the pickup.

"Fucking small-time punks," muttered Hunter, and Marek could almost hear the blood simmering in his veins. It was like the time he'd seen Hunter in Jinda's, focusing all his rage and spite on the Thai fishermen. The only difference was that Marek felt it now too. Anger, a violation; that these two boys thought he would be so stupid or intimidated to just hand over his money. Something he would have laughed off before, back then. He wondered what had changed in him and how it had happened. He walked to the front of the pickup and sat on the bumper until the two Thai boys had left and their Honda two-strokes were buzzing like angry hornets on the main road.

"They from the village," said Scorpion as they tied down the tarp. "They think we working for the oil company. They want to know if we gonna hire some men. Say they need some work."

"What did you tell them?"

"I tell him we not work for oil company, we working for the army. Doing a survey in the hills. Cannot say too much. Top secret, you know? Ha ha. One guy, he want to know why two farangs working with the Thai army. I tell him you experts from America. Maybe he believe you with army, some kinda old colonel or something, but I don't think he believe about him," he said, pointing toward Marek. "Anyway, I give him a lot of names of important people, generals and like that. He don't know them, maybe he think I bullshit, but he don't know for sure so he gotta be careful."

They saw them again where the dirt road met the highway at the edge of the village. The two boys on motorcycles were talking with a group of four or five men. As Hunter turned onto the main road, the group stopped talking and followed the pickup with their eyes, their faces expressionless. The one who had asked Marek for money was smoking a cigarette and gave them a look of pure insolence.

"They're going up there today, aren't they?" asked Hunter.

"I don't know," said Scorpion. He was sitting in the front passenger seat, staring out the side window. He shrugged. "I try to make him think it dangerous. Army business. He should stay away. But I don't know if they believe. Anyway, we got what we want, right?"

"I won't feel good about this until it's all packed and on the boat, and we got our money."

Hunter drove back to Songkhla fast, his eyes never leaving the road, not saying a word until they were almost run off the road by a truck carrying pigs, and then he filled the dead air in the cabin with his curses.

Twenty-nine

"What's wrong with you, mate? You look like you're carrying the weight of the world on your shoulders."

Marek and Philips were drinking beer in a small beach café just outside Philips's college. It was late afternoon, three days after Marek had come down the mountain, and the longer he didn't hear from Hunter the less real the whole exploit seemed. Maybe Hunter had decided to cut him out completely. Or maybe the villagers had gone up the mountain after they'd left and discovered the depth of their crime. He could be arrested at any minute; right here in fact, as he shared grilled chicken and beer with Philips.

But he couldn't tell any of this to his friend.

"It's just that I can't get a hold of Saranya," he said. "Every time I call the number she gave me for her uncle's house in Surat, nobody seems to know her. And I can't seem to make myself understood."

"Maybe it's the wrong number."

"It's the number she gave me."

"This is Thailand, remember, so even if you dial the right number, you sometimes get the wrong phone."

"That doesn't make any sense."

"Here it does. Or maybe she's changed her plans and she's staying somewhere else. Maybe they can't understand your Thai."

"So why doesn't she call me?"

"Her father's just died what … less than a fortnight ago? Give her some time, mate."

"Yeah, OK. Then there's this other thing. Slight problem with being out of a job."

Sturges had reluctantly confirmed it over the phone. "It's just a trial period, maybe six months. Perth want to see if it's feasible to have an unmanned station. I'm sure it'll fail. Something will go wrong with the gear and the clients will complain. But in the meantime, I'm afraid we'll have to put your contract on hold, starting next month."

"On hold?"

"What I mean is, we'll have to suspend it for the six months they're doing the testing. Maybe after the six months, when Perth sees the error of their ways, we can rehire you. I mean, I can't guarantee anything, but …"

There was silence over the line as Sturges let the implications hang in the air.

"Tell you what," said Philips, bringing Marek back to the moment, "they need an English teacher here. At the Fisheries College. Two in fact. Why don't you apply?"

"I'm hardly qualified to teach English."

"You've got a degree, haven't you?"

"Yeah, in history."

Philips shrugged. "You're a native speaker and you've got a degree. You'll do. And, as luck would have it, my roomie's moving back to England next month, so there's a room free. I have to rent it out to somebody; might as well be you. It's all yours for the special price of 1,500 baht per month. Whaddaya say?"

"I dunno, I'll think about it."

"Nah, you don't want to do too much of that, mate. That'll keep ya from havin' any fun!"

Marek called Saranya again the next day. This time no one answered, and for hours he had the horrible sinking feeling that she was gone from his life. That's the way things seemed to happen in Thailand. Things just changed overnight; people left, they went to Bangkok or Phuket without any explanation and you never saw them again.

Six days after he'd descended from the mountain, at nine o'clock on a Wednesday night, Marek got the phone call. Hunter delivered the instructions slowly, as if speaking to a child. He wouldn't hang up until Marek repeated them word for word, twice.

"You have to get to the factory by midnight. Any later and they'll turn you away at the gate. Think you can do that?"

"I guess that depends how long they take at the first place."

"They won't be long. Everything's ready. They're just waiting for you. Just don't get lost or anything."

It had rained nearly all day, but now the night was cool and dry, and strong winds churned the waves on the Gulf and whipped the horsetail boughs of the casuarinas.

Marek drove through the labyrinth of streets behind the warehouses, one hand clutching the slip of paper with the directions scratched on it, Hunter's "or anything" like a dark threat in the back of his skull. He tried to quell the gnawing feeling that he was walking into a trap. He had a horrific vision of being stopped on the road between Songkhla and the deep-sea port with a truck bed full of stolen ancient artifacts. He imagined the worst and then tried to convince himself that Hunter had more to lose than he did, and that that meant it would be all right.

He found the shop next to the garish Chinese shrine and beeped once, as he'd been told to. Everything then unfolded exactly as Hunter had said it would: the doors opened, a boy came out with two small wooden ramps, and Marek backed the pickup into the barren shophouse. Before he had even turned off the ignition, a group of men began loading the truck with tightly bundled parcels. At least Hunter had picked a good place to hide the stuff. No one in the world would suspect this hole-in-the-wall in the midst of identical hole-in-the-walls, in this derelict part of the city near the old fishing port.

The men said nothing to him. It was almost as if they couldn't see him. It was only after they'd pulled the tarpaulin taut over the truck bed and tied it down that a fat man, who looked like a statue of the prosperous Buddha and who had supervised the loading without lifting a finger to help, said, "OK. Finish."

Within minutes Marek was on the road to Yala, looking for a fish-packing plant with an oversized image of a crab on the gate. It was where Hunter had said it would be, twenty kilometers out of Songkhla, surrounded by a forest of rubber plantations. A uniformed guard shone a flashlight into the cab and then another pushed back the gate.

The grounds were like an expensive housing estate:

perfectly trimmed lawns, flowering bushes and tall palm trees. Bright incandescent light flooded the area so that the outlines of the trees and the edges of the building stood out in sharp contrast to the plantation beyond the wall.

A man with a radio to his face waved the truck into the loading dock. Marek noticed the pistol strapped to his thigh. More men appeared and all of them seemed to be shouting into radios. Someone motioned for Marek to get out of the truck and pointed to a door up a short flight of cement stairs. There was a serious efficiency here that Marek had rarely seen in Thailand. Before he had even reached the door, they had untied the tarpaulin and were carrying off the wrapped parcels.

They had all they needed from him now, except for the port pass. And how difficult would it be to take that away from him? Marek felt a frisson of panic surge up his spine and he thought about running – back down the stairs, turn left around the building to the wall ... and then?

He pulled open the office door and was hit by a blast of refrigerated air.

"Mr Aleck. You come early. That good. Have a seat. You want coffee?" Scorpion beamed at him and held out his hands in greeting. The Thai had never used his name before; Marek was surprised he even knew it. He sat down on a vinyl sofa and watched Scorpion fill a mug from a large urn. The room was dominated by a big wooden desk, covered with ledgers and piles of loose papers. More hardbound ledgers crowded a single bookshelf. A television in the corner was tuned to a Thai game show. There were two windows opposite each other; one looked out to the loading dock, the other, Marek guessed, looked into the factory. Both had vertical blinds pulled across their width.

Scorpion handed him the coffee and then leaned on the edge of the desk, grinning down at him. He wasn't a big man, not overly muscular, but slender and sinewy, fit in a way that denoted discipline and asceticism rather than sports.

"Not take long time," he said. "You have pass, right?"

Marek sipped the coffee and nodded. He thought, *this is the man who saved me from a cobra. Why would he harm me now?*

Scorpion seemed to be in a good mood. He laughed. "That good. Cannot forget the pass, Mr Aleck."

It took them nearly two hours to crate the artifacts and repack the truck. Marek heard a forklift moving outside and men shouting directions, and though he was tempted to get up and peek out the window, he had the feeling Scorpion didn't want him to do anything except stay on the sofa. And that was what he did, leafing through a three-day-old Bangkok Post while Scorpion watched the game show, occasionally giggling at the antics of the contestants.

The phone on the desk rang. Scorpion lifted the receiver but said very little, just a few acknowledging "khrap"s. After he hung up, he grinned at Marek. "Almost finished," he said cheerfully.

After a few minutes he asked, "Mr Aleck, how long you know Mr John?"

"Five, six months. You?"

"My boss do business with him a coupla times. Think you can trust him?"

"I suppose, as much as anybody. Why?"

"My boss say he can trust him. You know why? He say Hunter scared of something. Hunter never say, but my boss think like that. He say maybe he scared of somebody working offshore, or maybe somebody got something on him somewhere, you know? Boss say that's good. Say you can trust a scared man to do the right thing. Too scared to try and fuck you over, you know? What you think?"

"Never thought Hunter was scared of anything."

"Boss say, sure. Can see it in his eyes. But for me, I don't know. I don't see that. I think better not to trust anybody too much, you know?"

Before Marek could say anything, a man opened the door and said they were finished. They had turned off the dock floodlights and the loading bay was deserted; the men with the radios and the handguns had disappeared. The truck stood in the shadow of the building as if abandoned. Beneath the green tarp you could make out the outlines of a half dozen wooden crates. Scorpion walked him out to the truck, holding his wrist in the fashion of Thai men. For a moment Marek thought he was going to get in the cab too, but he didn't. He held the driver's side door open for Marek and said, "Be careful, Mr Aleck. Watch out for those cobras, you know?" And then he laughed.

Thirty

It was raining again. The roads were dark, only an occasional house or small settlement to break the monotony of the dark forest of rubber on both sides of the road. Every time Marek saw a pair of headlights in the mirror, he had to fight down the thought that somebody was coming for him. A Kawasaki chopper overtook him. The man glanced at Marek as he passed, but he was wearing a helmet and a dark visor, and Marek couldn't make out a single feature of his face, or even if he was Thai or farang. He had to tell himself to calm down, that it was only his imagination working overtime.

After that there was only the rain, pelting the windshield and drumming on the roof, coming out of the dark like some phantom with a million fingers. As he crossed over the two bridges, he could barely make out the flickering lights of the city across the inland sea.

His anxiety lifted as he approached the gates of the deep-sea port. The causeway and the entrance to the docks were bathed in an unreal white fluorescence that killed shadows and revealed every grease spot and crack in the cement. It was too bright for anything bad to happen.

The guard was wearing a yellow rain slicker and had a plastic bag covering his cap. He stood under the shelter of his guardhouse while he checked Marek's pass.

"What ship?" he asked. He looked at the truck bed and put one hand on the tarp.

"*Pacific Star.*" Marek held out the clipboard with the fake bill of lading and export documents. He recognized the guard; he had waved Marek through many times before, and there was no reason why this time should be any different. The guard glanced at the clipboard, then handed Marek's pass back through the window and – as he had done so many times before – lifted the gate for Marek to pass.

He found berth twenty-seven and parked between the yellow lines of the loading zone. There were a couple of smaller offshore supply boats and one larger container ship docked at the long jetty. The big ship was lit by floodlights on the pier and on the ship itself. Cranes whirred and whinnied, lifting containers on board.

Marek's orders were to sit there, not get out of the truck, and wait for the men to come from the big ship and unload him. "Don't move from the pickup," said Hunter. "They'll be waiting for you."

It was nearly twenty minutes before the men approached. There were two: one was driving the forklift, and the other was sitting on a palette on the front. Their faces were obscured by their hooded raincoats. He could hear them talking – Southern Thai for sure – and could feel the pickup getting lighter as they removed the crates from the bed.

The forklift made three trips and then the truck bed was

empty. It was nearly 2 a.m. now and Marek was exhausted, more from the tension than from anything he'd done. But he still needed to get his forms signed off. They had to carry the act through all the way, Hunter had insisted on it. And there was always the chance the guard would check on the way out. But there didn't seem to be anyone around.

Then he saw someone walk out of the glare of the floodlights and into the dark shadows toward him. Marek rolled the window down, but instead of coming to the window the person in the raincoat, his face in shadow, walked around to the other side of the cab. Fine, he wanted to get out of the rain for a minute, no problem. Marek opened the door for him.

There was a smell of rain and diesel oil, and the man sat down and pulled his hood back. It was Scorpion. He was grinning. Rainwater slid off his poncho and onto the floor and dashboard.

"Hey, Mr Aleck, how are you?"

What was he doing here? And how did he get here this fast? But no, not really fast, he'd had plenty of time to get here from the factory; Marek had sat here for twenty minutes before the unloading even began. Then he remembered the guy on the Kawasaki; the guy whose face was hidden by the opaque visor.

Scorpion lit a cigarette. "Where's Mister John?"

"Hunter? I don't know."

"What I mean is, where do Mister John stay? You know, in Songkhla?"

"Some guesthouse. Near the old market. Why?"

"See, we got some problem. We need to talk to you and Mr John. See, those heads and those statues. They not the same.

318

They all fake." He was grinning at Marek, like it was a joke. But something in his tone of voice said he wasn't joking.

"Fake? That's crazy. How could they be? You were there. You brought them down from the mountain with us."

Scorpion blew cigarette smoke toward the windshield and shook his head. "Not the same. Look the same on the outside but different. We checked them at the factory. Drill a little hole in the back and check the stone deep inside. That stone maybe one, two month old. The heads all fake. Same with statues. You guys switch them on us."

"No, I just picked them up ... you saw me ... at the factory ... how could I ... why would I?"

He was stammering. He realized he could say nothing to defend himself. From Scorpion's point of view, he could have picked up the fakes anywhere. After all, they'd brought them down from the mountain six days ago. A full six days to make the switch.

"Hunter ... you said yourself ... Hunter was too scared to cheat you."

"No, I not say that. My boss think like that. I never believe Hunter afraid. Anyway, Maybe Hunter not do this. Maybe you do this, Mr Aleck. Maybe it your plan to cheat everybody and John don't know nothing about it. Maybe you eat that cobra, make you go a little crazy. Hah!" Scorpion's laughter filled the cab, ending in a high-pitched *heeheehee*.

"No, not me. I just picked them up. I followed Hunter's orders. It's Hunter. He set me up." He had to look away from Scorpion's grinning face. It was then that he realized that two men were standing outside his door, dark figures also in ponchos.

Scorpion reached over and took the keys from the ignition. "C'mon, Mr Aleck, let's go."

Marek started to protest; he had to get back to the station.

But Scorpion wasn't listening. He reached over and opened the door on Marek's side.

"Let's go," he repeated.

Later, Marek couldn't remember even stepping out of the truck. He only remembered walking toward the flood-lit ship, Scorpion gripping his elbow, the other two – one of them Skull, looking lost and childlike in a poncho three sizes too big for him - walking a step behind him.

Walking towards the ship, feeling powerless and numb, Scorpion's fingers pinching his skin down to the bone. He tried to explain the truth to them, that he was only involved so that he could help Saranya, but it was pointless.

He wanted to tell them to stop, to let him think this out; that there must be an explanation. Surely they understood he was not responsible for the fakes. He was a victim, like them. They were all being used by Hunter – Hunter was the one they should get!

No way to escape, walking toward the ship with its wheezing and groaning cranes and the clanging of chains and rigging. Super-lit like a stage where everyone was waiting for him to appear, the rain suddenly coming on very heavy.

Thirty-one

A room. Windowless, bare walls, three strides deep, two across. A thin, quilted mattress on the floor. The bucket in the corner. A storeroom maybe, with nothing stored, or a compartment stripped of its furniture. Not even a wardrobe or desk or bookshelf, nothing except the bare metallic walls. No, not walls. On a ship you called them bulkheads.

He found a light switch, but it was useless. There was no light. Not even a bare bulb. The only light came from the slit under the door. That slit was Marek's lifeline to the outside world. It brought him light, air, sounds and even scents. He could lie with his cheek against the floor and peer out of his prison room with one eye. But there was never anything to see. Only some grating and opposite his door, another bulkhead.

They brought him food, Skull and another one. He heard the key in the door and then light from the hallway poured into the room, blinding him. Skull put the metal bowl on the floor, wordlessly, and the other blocked the door behind him. Marek tried to blink the light out of his eyes to see if Skull's face held any hint of his future; but it was nothing but a dull mask.

It was a bowl of soupy boiled rice with pieces of pork. He

didn't think he could eat but he ended up gulping it all down and wanting more.

After that, he tried to sleep. He took off his jeans and rolled them up to use as a pillow. Maybe sleep could be the great escape and keep his worried thoughts from overwhelming him. He thought of Hunter and tried to recall every word he'd said, sifting through them like a paleontologist examining bones, looking for some hint that he would betray him. He thought of Saranya and had to bite back an immense welling of self-pity. No matter what happened, one thing was sure – he had blown any chance of happiness with her.

Miraculously, he fell sleep. For how long, he had no idea; they had taken away his watch and everything in his pockets. He woke to a gecko or a cockroach walking across his face and slapped wildly at it in the dark.

His jean pillow was sweat soaked; he crawled to his life support crack and breathed in the slightly fresher air. What, if anything, could the smells tell him? Metal and grease, a hint of boiled rice and garlic, a taste of the sea from time to time when a door opened somewhere and a draft blew in. And sounds? A faint bump from above deck once in a while. The whining of cranes. But no engines; he was sure that they had not left port.

Considering everything, he thought that was a good sign.

* * *

The older one was instructing the younger one, and the subject was the male body – in particular, Hunter's.

This younger one had a stud in her tongue, and it excited him no end as he drove his tongue as deep into her mouth as he could. He realized: they all taste the same; no matter what they look like, no matter what age, or the shape of their body, or the size of their pussies, they all taste the same. And the taste is garlic.

He paid them generously, and after they left, it was Hunter alone in his Hat Yai hotel room with his bottle of Black Cat, just the way he liked it. He had been in the hotel for a week, deserting the guesthouse in Songkhla without saying a word to the owner, but leaving an envelope of cash to settle up his account. Anything he didn't need he'd left in the room, free for the taking. He had called Marek from here yesterday to give him the directions and had no intention of ever contacting him again. There was no reason to. Even if he had gotten away with delivering the bogus relics to Jack, he would be getting no part of the down payment Jack had already paid Hunter, and certainly nothing of the sale of the genuine articles to the new buyer.

But he knew Jack, and he knew there was no way Jack wouldn't discover the switch. Too bad for Marek, in a way. But you could say too bad about everything and everyone, so what was the point? He had no malice toward Marek. He was a fool, of course, with his simplistic notions of adventure and true love, but whatever happened to Marek didn't make much difference in the long run. It wouldn't affect Hunter's plan one way or the other.

The plan. It was working so smoothly he felt like shouting. His Liechtenstein account had been freshly fattened with Jack's latest deposit, which Hunter had insisted he make as a down payment before the delivery. The nine heads and five torsos, the real ones, had already left the fat man's workshop, soon to be spirited out of the country by the owner of an antique shop in downtown Bangkok, heading toward a California buyer. The broker's cut was big, naturally, and so was the paycheck for the fat man, the man who, from a modest little shophouse near the fishing docks, operated one of the best antique sandstone forgery factories in all of Asia. And how ironic that it had been Jack himself who had introduced the forger to Hunter at one of the Muay Thai tournaments Jack sponsored! But good quality was never cheap, and Hunter had still got the better part of the buyer's 2.4 million dollars. Very sweet indeed.

He took some more ice from the minibar and fixed himself another drink. All his worldly belongings were here in the room with him, packed into two Samsonite suitcases and a nylon backpack. If anyone was looking for him, they'd never think to look for him in Hat Yai, and especially not in this hotel, a two-star dump a mile from the city center, patronized by cheap Charlies up from Malaysia for a weekend of whoring.

Anyway, he'd be gone tomorrow morning. The agent for the California buyer had arrived in Bangkok that day and had confirmed the statues' authenticity. The deal was sealed, and three hours ago, just before Hunter had called for the sister act, his banker from Liechtenstein had rung him and, with just the right touch of restrained goodwill, informed him that yes, the 1.8 million dollars had cleared and was now in his account.

He wondered if Jack had discovered the truth yet. At least he had one genuine head, one of the two Hunter had brought down from his first foray up the mountain. The other he'd given to the fat man to use as his prototype. He grinned to think of the look of utter shock on Jack's face when he realized Hunter had the cojones to actually rip him off. It was nothing personal against Jack – well, other than that the guy was a preening old queen. No, it was simply that once Hunter had discovered he could, he'd seen no reason not to. And anyway, he needed more money than Jack had been willing to pay. So Hunter had simply used Jack, his men, his connections, to get a better deal for himself. Hey, he was a businessman after all. Jack would understand that. And maybe, in the back of his mind, after that initial spell of spitting anger, he might even respect it.

Hunter had arranged for a taxi to pick him up at dawn the next day and take him to Phuket. He could blend in easily there with all the tourists, retired people, beach bums and tropical drunks. No one would take him for an oilman, much less a plunderer of ancient artifacts. Communications were good there too. Once he settled in, he'd call Kambiz to inform him that he was ready to take a look at some property on the Turquoise Coast.

* * *

Marek was lying on the mattress trying not to let black thoughts overwhelm him when he heard footsteps and voices in the hall. The key rattled in the door and he sprang up from the mattress, hoping they'd realized it was all a big mistake and were going to let him go. When the door swung open, he was again blinded by the light from the corridor. He could make out the figures of two men but couldn't see who they were. Then he heard Scorpion's voice.

"Mr Aleck, come with us please."

They took him up a flight of metal stairs, and as they walked out onto the catwalk on the open deck, they opened umbrellas. The wind was blowing hard and the rain came at an angle. With no sun, it was impossible to tell what time it was. There was no one else in sight and no cranes were moving. Marek could see a section of the dock to his left, two men in hard hats and yellow raincoats.

Inside the superstructure they climbed another flight of stairs. Scorpion knocked on a door and it instantly opened.

The air inside the room was blue with cigarette smoke. Two men stood by the door; another sat behind a desk facing Marek. The room was paneled in dark wood, perhaps the captain's quarters. There were lounge chairs and a large TV, a bookshelf full of videocassettes. All the curtains were closed and every light in the room burned.

The man at the desk was speaking loudly into a mobile phone in Chinese. He spoke in demanding tones and a high feminine voice that might have been comic in another situation. He looked nothing like a sea captain, or for that matter, any person who might work on a seagoing vessel. He wore a flowery, long-sleeved shirt with French cuffs and gold cufflinks. His skin was as smooth as pewter and every hair was perfectly in place.

Eventually he rang off and said a few curt words to the men. Scorpion shoved Marek toward the chair in front of the desk, and the men all filed out.

There was a long silence as the Thai man stared down at his hands. He wore large gold rings, so big that Marek wondered how he could manage simple everyday tasks like pouring coffee into a cup. But then, he didn't look like the kind of man who poured his own coffee.

"It's Marek, correct? Alexander Marek? Unusual name for an American, isn't it? Alexander." He spoke with the perfectly rounded vowels and inflection of an upper class British gentleman.

"Your men took my wallet and ID. You know who I am and where I work."

"Indeed. Yes, we do."

There was another long silence. The man's soft, feminine hands played with a plastic drinking straw, twisting it around one finger and then another.

"Do you have any idea, Mr Marek, what the penalty is for attempting to smuggle antiquities out of Thailand? It's quite severe, I can assure you. You see, in the last few years, many governments around the world, including yours, have been urging the Thai government to put a stop to the looting and illegal selling of national treasures. They've been quite insistent. And of course, the popular press in these countries make it sound as if these invaluable items – not just from Thailand, mind you, but from Angkor Wat as well – are for sale at every night market in the country. Surely, you've seen these kinds of stories in the papers, haven't you, Mr Marek?"

Marek said nothing.

"Well, perhaps you don't read much. Anyway, all of this has

put tremendous pressure on the Thai government to, in effect, do something. They would love to show the world that they have in fact caught somebody in the very act. *In flagrante delicto*. Especially if it's a farang. Then they could show the world that it's outsiders causing all this trouble. Rich Americans taking advantage of poor, innocent, trusting Thai people."

"You're Hunter's contact, right? The powerful connection."

The man put the straw down and plucked a cigarette from the Marlboro pack on the desktop. He brought a gold lighter out of his shirt pocket and looked at Marek as he lit it.

"What exactly did Toi tell you?"

"Toi? Oh … Scorpion. He said all the pieces were fake. You drilled a hole in the heads and inside it was the wrong kind of rock or something. But that can't be. Scorpion was with us on the mountain. He knows they're not fake."

"They were all excellent replicas, I will say that. The torsos, too. You delivered a truck load of fake goods to my factory. Perhaps you and Hunter enjoy the irony of it. I deal in fake Piaget watches, Nike footwear, and Christian Dior cosmetics, and you deliver me fake Buddhist antiquities."

"No, I didn't know …"

"I take it, Marek, you're a gambling man. You gambled that I would never check. Rather stupid of you, wouldn't you say?"

"I don't know anything about that. I followed Hunter's instructions. I picked up the things from a shophouse in the warehouse district. They must have made the switch there."

The man's expression never changed. His heavy eyelids were

like walnut shells, and his fat cheeks seemed to pull his jaw down so that when he wasn't talking he had an expression of complete vacuity. He sighed and took a long pull from his cigarette, letting the smoke drift from his nostrils.

"Where is Hunter now, Mr Marek?"

"I don't know. He lives in an old guesthouse near the market. You can check there."

"We did. He checked out a week ago. He thought it was a big secret, but we knew he lived there. He's a fool if he thinks he can hide for very long in Thailand. What arrangements did you make to meet, after you had dropped off the merchandise?"

"Nothing … I … He said he'd call me when it was over."

The man let out a sharp bark of a laugh that was so loud it startled Marek. "That was the arrangement? He would contact you, and you have no way to contact him? That's not very bright, is it? In fact, it's hardly believable."

He was right, of course. And as long as this man believed Hunter and he were partners, anything Marek said would sound like a lie.

"Obviously, you and Hunter have sold the nine heads and five statues to some other buyer, thereby effectively multiplying your profits."

"No. It's Hunter. He set me up. That must be obvious to you."

The man shrugged and stubbed out his cigarette.

"Do I look like a fool? What's obvious to me is that you and Hunter are in this together. After all, you're both Americans, right? I think this is all a very clever plot to make him look like the bad guy and you look completely innocent. So that I let you go and go chasing after him, and then you both get away. Am I right?"

"No, that's crazy."

"So tell me, Marek, where is your partner, Hunter?"

"He's not my partner. I hardly know him. The last time I saw him was when he dropped me off after we'd come down from the mountain. He called me on Tuesday to tell me to pick up the merchandise and deliver it to your factory. I assumed he called me from Songkhla, but I guess he could have called me from anywhere. Bangkok. Or Singapore. Anywhere. I'm telling you, he set me up."

"And what's your cut for this? I hope you demanded a huge sum."

This was going in the wrong direction. Marek had to try to turn things around, convince this man he was telling the truth.

"Look, I don't know where Hunter is but look ... if you want to recoup your losses, why don't you just do the obvious thing? You've got a buyer set up, right? Hunter said that's why we had to wait a week. So sell him what you've got and you get your money back. No damage done."

The man rose out of his chair and with surprising strength struck Marek hard in the face with his fist. For a moment Marek couldn't breathe and he thought his nose might be broken. Almost instantly blood began to drip into his hands, and he could feel a gash on the outside of his nose. *So that's what the rings are for,* he thought.

The door opened at the sound of the violence but quickly closed again when the man hissed a few words. Then he sat down again, rubbing his hand.

"My buyers are my personal friends. It has taken me years to cultivate these friendships. I have been invited into their homes, in Zurich, Malibu. I've had dinner with them and played with their children. And you think I should sell them some fake goods? You think I should cheat my friends, my business partners? You're bleeding all over the carpet. Here." He tossed Marek a box of tissues. "Stick a wad up your nostril and lean your head back, it will stop in a minute.

"The way these people trust me? That's how I trusted Hunter. You see, when my man Toi returned and gave me the list of merchandise you had brought down, I made a payment of seven hundred and fifty thousand dollars into Hunter's account in Liechtenstein. That was our agreement. Toi of course had helped bring the merchandise down. He knew the heads were real. And Hunter, well, as I said, I trusted him.

"But I'm not an idiot, Marek. What was it your President Reagan said? 'Trust but verify.' So I tested them, just to be sure, at the cannery. Did you know that if you drill through the outside layer on a fake piece, one that's been recently fabricated, the stone inside is as white as the snow on Everest? No matter how good someone is at making the outside of the stone look old, they can't change the inside in a month. Any amateur can tell it's not 1,200 years old."

Marek lifted his head from the back of the chair. The bleeding had stopped, but his left cheek was tender and he felt puffiness below his eye.

"So, Mr Marek, who will pay me my three-quarters of a

million dollars? You?"

"You know I can't," he answered, his voice sounding as if he'd been weeping.

"Of course, it's not just the money, is it?" He lit another cigarette and took a long drag, then blew the smoke out noisily as if to show nothing but disgust for everything the world held. "How long have you lived in Thailand, Mr Marek?"

"Nine months."

"Then surely, you have been here long enough to understand the Thai concept of "face"? You do understand that sometimes the loss of face is more important to Thais than any monetary value that might be involved, yes? Because without face, you have nothing, even if you're rich. And for a businessman like me, well, let us say that if the truth of this transaction, as it stands now, were to be known in Thailand, it would be a great loss of face for me. I simply couldn't allow it to happen.

"Yes, I know, you farang think this whole face business is stupid, childish. And I must confess it does seem even to me to be a waste of energy sometimes. But then, we're all part of our culture, aren't we? Some things we just cannot change. So, then … your partner. Where is he?"

"I swear, I'm not his partner."

"OK, you're not his partner, then. You're his errand boy."

"He offered me a job. I agreed to do it because I needed the money."

"Needed the money for what? You have a good job, don't you? They pay you well."

"Yes, but …"

"But what?"

"I … I just needed the money. That's all."

The man sighed.

"You know, it's like what I always told Hunter. You really must learn to open up if you want someone to trust you as a business partner." He barked out a command and the door burst open. Scorpion grabbed Marek by the shirt and jerked him out of the chair, and Marek realized that any kind of false friendship between them was over. Scorpion pushed him toward the open door and then the Thai man raised his hand.

"Notice, Mr Marek, I did say business partners. I'm sure we can find some mutual ground to meet on. It all depends on you answering my questions properly. Because they won't stop until you do. Oh, and did Hunter tell you about Toi here? Trained with the US Special Forces. Knows all kind of nasty little tricks normal, civilized people like us couldn't even begin to imagine. Goodbye, Mr Marek."

It was all a bluff, Marek thought, and he continued to tell himself that, even when they threw him against the wall of his cell. But then two of the men held him while Scorpion grabbed his left hand and – before Marek even had time to think – clutched the little finger of his right hand and in one deft, swift movement cracked it backwards. Marek screamed in pain and shock. The finger was at a grotesque angle. He tried to straighten it but when he grasped it and tried to pull it back into shape there was a jolt of pain that shot up to his shoulder. He collapsed onto his mattress, howling in pain.

Scorpion turned just before he went out the door.

"You have three more chances, Mr Aleck, to tell us where Hunter is."

Thirty-two

Sometime during the night thunder woke him, fracturing a dream about flying so low on a passenger jet he could see into people's houses. Hunter staggered to the window, his head in a fog. The rain was pelting the glass, falling so fast and hard he could barely make out the street below. For nearly an hour lightning and thunder traded off almost continuously. He fell asleep for what seemed like only minutes before his alarm woke him. The soi below his room was flooded and no cars were moving.

He quickly dressed and went downstairs to see if his driver had arrived. The lobby and coffee shop had two inches of water on the floor. Several housekeepers with push brooms were slushing the rainwater toward a drain, but it was a hopeless task.

It was raining steadily, and there was no sign of a taxi or driver. The front door of the hotel had a barricade of sandbags, and the street outside and the whole town as far as he could see were flooded.

"Nobody go to Phuket today," said the harried desk clerk. "Too much flooding. Outside too deep now. Car cannot get here. You gotta wait maybe coupla days."

Hunter grabbed an umbrella that was leaning against the reception desk and stepped past the sweeping maids. There had to be a way out of the city. Surely the flooding would be restricted to these back streets and sois; all of downtown Hat Yai couldn't be flooded. He needed to find someone, maybe at one of the bigger hotels near the shopping centers, who could drive him to Phuket today.

Once out of the sandbagged safety of the hotel the water was well up over his ankles. In the street it was deeper. It was difficult walking because the water snatched at his flip-flops with each step, nearly ripping them from his feet more than once. The water was an opaque grayish-brown and he couldn't see where the sidewalk ended and the street began, or where the potholes were. He had to walk slowly, gingerly testing each step before moving forward.

It didn't surprise him that most of the shops along the road were open. Hunter knew those Chinese shopkeepers would shit a brick if they missed even a 50-baht sale. Like the hotel the shop owners had built little sandbag forts; it obviously wasn't the first time flood waters had reached their store fronts, although now the water was threatening to go over the bags. In some shops whole families, including old women and little kids, were carrying their goods up the back stairs to higher ground. One man in a sleeveless undershirt and shorts seemed resigned to his fate, reading his newspaper at a marble-topped table while the water lapped at the lower shelves of his dry goods store.

The wind was gusting, and even with the umbrella Hunter was more wet than dry. He turned the corner and instantly his hopes to get to Phuket were blown away with the driving wind. The main road into the city center looked more like a wide canal than a street. Here the water seemed not just to be accumulating, but flowing, punctuated with wavelets pushed by the stiff breeze. Several cars were abandoned, and one small Honda looked like it had floated right into a street light.

Kids were splashing around in the water. Two were floating in a green plastic tub. A man was paddling a kayak, his face composed, even bored, as if this were something he did every day.

Hunter stood on the pavement, quickly despairing of any chance at getting close to the big hotels in the city center. He was standing on the banks of a fast running river that extended as far as he could see. Walking anywhere was out of the question; you'd have a better chance of swimming for a taxi. Plus, there were all the usual third-world dangers. It wasn't uncommon for people to be electrocuted while wading through floodwaters. The water brought out other things too, rats and snakes fleeing the inundated storm sewers.

It was hopeless. There was no way he could get to Phuket today. He would have to return to the hotel and wait it out. He turned and began slogging his way back.

"Hey Hunt!"

He turned to see a large flatbed truck plowing through the inundated street. In the back, holding on to the side railings, was a group of people huddled under a plastic sheet. Next to them was a tall man in a full-length raincoat: Jenks. His face was mostly obscured by the hood, but Hunter could make out the grayish goatee and the glint of his silver-framed glasses.

Jenks pounded on the top of the cab to get the driver to stop. "What the fuck you doing here?" he yelled.

Hunter's first thought was that he could hitch a ride on the truck to find a taxi near the train station. But his bags were back in the hotel, and a taxi would never be able to make it back out here. And anyway, he wanted as little to do with Jenks as possible.

"Wanted to see if I could make it into town. I'm supposed to get a taxi today."

"Shit," said Jenks. He pulled back his hood and Hunter could now plainly see the know-it-all look he was so used to offshore, the kind of expression that implied Hunter was a jackass for even entertaining such a thought for a second. "You ain't going nowhere. It's worse outside the city than it is here. Lot of the roads are cut off. The airport's closed until tomorrow, at least. I got the last flight in with my fellow travelers here and this is our luxury ride into town. Nice, eh? Someone said there's a trestle out, so even the trains ain't moving. When you go back to work?"

Never. "Still got a couple of weeks. You?"

"Simmon's totaled his Harley on Samui. He'll live, but he'll be in the hospital for a couple of weeks, so I'm taking his shift. They just called me in Bangkok yesterday. Cut short my field break by a week, but what the hell. The overtime'll be good. But seriously, seeing all this now, I doubt if I'll be able to get to Songkhla tomorrow. Maybe the choppers ain't even flying. What the hell you doin' here anyway? I though you lived in Singapore."

"Staying a little longer in Hat Yai this time."

"Really? Where?

"Ah … just around the corner."

"Didn't know there were any hotels up this way."

"It's a small place. Quiet. Out of the way."

"Quiet? Shit. I get enough quiet offshore. I want loud! Fucking rambunctious! Tell you what, get in the truck. We'll get a bottle, sit in the hotel room and watch TV and tell lies. Maybe hit the massage parlor, what d'ya say?"

"Don't think so, Jenks."

"Why the hell not?"

"Ah, well … there's this girl, you know?"

"Shoulda guessed it. Hunter's shacked up with some pussy in a dive in Hat Yai. Well, shit, what else you gonna do in this shithole? Hope you're not on the ground floor. Could get a little wet."

He wasn't sure he'd ever hated Jenks more than he did right now. Everybody in the street – and there seemed to be many more people wading by than there were just minutes ago – was looking at them. They were the center of attention. The few vehicles that could make it down the street slowed down to take in the oddity that was two farang caught in a flood.

"Well, then fuck ya. But if you change your mind, I'm in the Century Hotel. You may have to swim to get there. Otherwise, I'll see you offshore. Onward, James," he said, and pounded on the cab again to get the driver moving.

The truck lurched forward and the people under the sheet of plastic, all Thais, gave a cheer. Hunter waved. Jenks merrily flipped him the bird in response.

Thirty-three

Sometime later they brought Marek food and he forced himself to eat, despite the pain in his hand keeping him on the verge of vomiting. The knuckle of his little finger had swollen to twice its normal size, and his right hand was so tender he kept it cupped in his left for protection. It was so painful he no longer thought about his smashed nose and the swelling that was nearly closing his left eye.

He wondered how they would continue. Scorpion had said he had three more chances. Did that mean three more fingers? Would they break them on the right hand first before moving on to the left? Or alternate: right hand, left hand? Once they started on his left, he would never be able to fret a guitar again. Soon enough he would have a hard time even holding a pen. And if they continued as promised, he'd be lucky to be able to type a letter or even fish a few coins from his pocket.

And after the three more chances, then what?

"So where is Hunter, Alex?" Same routine. The Thai man, the boss, the one they called Mr Jack, dressed in a navy-blue blazer, an expensive-looking shirt and tie, an absurd outfit for the tropics but in this air-chilled stateroom he looked as comfortable as if he were in a boardroom in Hong Kong.

When they had brought him out to the deck it was still raining. Marek assumed it was twenty-four hours after his first interrogation, seemingly midday again, his second full day on the ship; but he had no way of knowing for sure.

"We were never partners," he said. "I told you. The only thing I know about Hunter is that he lived at the guest house in Songkhla. He drove a Toyota pickup to the mountain, probably rented or borrowed. Maybe stolen for all I know. You know all of this already."

"As you know, he left the guesthouse a week ago. Is he still in Thailand?"

"I don't know. He has – or had – a place in Singapore. Maybe he's offshore, working."

"He's not that stupid. A platform in the middle of the Gulf of Thailand might seem like a good place to hide for a while. But there's only one way back onshore, and that's through Songkhla. And I'd know when he came onshore. I have eyes everywhere in the town. He'd be trapped. So where is he?"

"I don't know." Marek raised his deformed left hand. "You think I'd be doing this for him?"

The man sighed, a deep regretful sigh. He opened a tin of breath mints and pushed it toward Marek. "Please," he said. Marek made no move for them.

"It's true, you know. I have a thousand eyes and ears in this town. More. Hat Yai, too. No one can elude me forever. It's only a matter of time. Perhaps I shouldn't tell you this, but we're beginning to get some leads. Hunter was never all that clever, you know. He can't cover his tracks completely. You might as well save yourself more discomfort and give him up now. Then you can go free."

"I don't know where he is."

"Maybe not exactly where he is at this moment, but you know more than you're telling."

Marek said nothing, and after a minute, Jack called his henchmen.

When they brought him back onto the deck it was still raining. He began shouting at the top of his lungs. There was no one near enough to hear him or care, but he continued crying out for help until Scorpion hit him hard in the abdomen, leaving him gasping for breath.

By the time they got him into the room, he had recovered enough to fight back. His right hand was useless, so he kicked, aiming for their testicles, and swung his left as hard as he could. He took them by surprise momentarily and caught Skull hard enough in the throat to make him sputter. Then one of them landed a shot to the side of his face which rattled his teeth and blurred his vision. All three of them were hitting him now, grunting and grinning, laughing as they pounded him. They pinned him against the wall and Scorpion grabbed the ring finger of his right hand and snapped it back like it was a dried twig.

He had passed out from the pain and the blows. When he came to, there was a bowl of soupy boiled rice with a few pieces of pork floating in it, still warm. He ripped off a rectangle of his shirt and held it in the soup for a minute, then wrapped it around his hand as a poultice, gently easing the two broken fingers as straight as possible.

He lay on the floor peering with one eye under the door, praying for some sign of hope. The ship was deathly quiet.

It was like a bad dream, and like a bad dream he felt it couldn't go on much longer. He'd wake up; somebody would stop it. They must know that he had no idea where Hunter was. Surely, they wouldn't think he'd lose the use of his fingers for Hunter.

But he was all they had, and that was why they were keeping him.

Maybe he could escape when they crossed the open deck; make a run for it and jump over the side. He was a good swimmer, and if the water didn't break his back, he could probably make it to land.

Or perhaps he could jump the guards when they delivered his next meal. Hit them with something. But what? His rice bowl wouldn't faze them. And anyway, there were always two of them, the biggest one blocking the doorway like a club bouncer.

His only chance was to get one of them alone. And he could think of only one way that would happen.

* * *

The storm had knocked out the power, or maybe the authorities had turned it off to prevent electrocutions. No air-conditioning, no TV, the ice in the minibar quickly melting. Hunter lay on his hotel bed, the sheets damp with sweat, with nothing but his quickly diminishing bottle of Black Cat. That and the ceaseless rain.

His body was vibrating like a tuning fork. He needed a joint badly, but he'd smoked up the last with the hookers from yesterday. Wasn't it always like this? Just when you thought things were going your way, somebody or something fucked it up. The flooding was bad enough, but then Jenks showing up ... that was really bad luck. Who knew who had seen him when he was standing out there in the middle of that street, like being in the middle of a fucking floodlit stage for the entire world to see.

He needed a Plan B for getting out of Hat Yai. Maybe tomorrow the airport would be open, and he could fly to Phuket. Or anywhere, just get out of this goddamn shithole. But flying was a last resort. Hat Yai airport was too small; there was no getting lost in the crowd there. If Jack's men were looking for him, they'd spot him in a second.

He got off the bed and walked to the window. He felt woozy when he stood up and he realized he'd been drinking for many hours. He leaned against the wall and waited for his head to clear. The window was slightly open – a vain attempt to get some air in the room – and above the sound of the rain, he could hear a truck plowing through the flooded soi, sending wavelets against the buildings.

He tried to convince himself that the rain had tapered off, that the sky far to the west was beginning to lighten. Maybe tomorrow he'd be able to get a taxi. He had this comforting image of himself in Phuket: just another tourist in a loud shirt, ratty shorts and forty-baht flip-flops, enjoying the sun, getting drunk in the outdoor 'bar beers', and chasing pussy.

Thirty-four

"It's true, you know. What I said about us being partners. Let bygones be bygones, eh?" Jack had a tittering nervous laugh, an irritating girlish staccato. "Once I get Hunter, and justice is seen to be done, then there's a world of opportunities open to each of us."

Jack rested his hands on the desk, his obscene, giant gold rings looking like costume jewelry. As usual, they were alone. Marek had been surprised when Scorpion hadn't been part of the escort team today. There were two new men, men he hadn't seen before.

"I think you know by now how this works. Just get me Hunter. Then you will have earned the reward I'm offering. I have mentioned that, right? No? Twenty thousand dollars for information leading to the apprehension of that foreign thief."

"If I knew where he was, don't you think I would have told you by now? He set me up."

Jack shrugged. "As I said yesterday, maybe it's all part of some ingenious plan you two have cooked up together."

"Yeah, great plan, huh? Here's me with two broken fingers, possible broken nose, no money and no 800-year-old artifacts. Oh yeah, and I'm your prisoner."

The Thai man's look was all innocence. "But Mr Marek,

you're all that I have. Until I find Hunter, I'm afraid you'll have to do."

"But you'll never get Hunter. He's long gone."

"Ahhh, that's where you're wrong. This storm that we're having – and by the way it has a name now, tropical storm Sara – has completely inundated all of southern Thailand and northern Malaysia. The airport's closed, the railway's washed out, all roads between here and Hat Yai are impassable. If Hunter was in Songkhla or anywhere around here when he called you to pick up the articles, then he very likely is still here. And that's what me and my men," he nodded towards the door, "are trying to learn.

"Hunter checked out of his guesthouse because he knew that's where we'd look first. But where did he go? We think he stayed in the area because he had to follow through on a deal to sell the real artifacts to someone else. So where is he? My only conclusion is that you, Mr Marek, must have some idea."

The Thai man held out his hands expectantly, but Marek said nothing. So Hunter was still around. That was a surprise. Locked in his soundproof and windowless storeroom, Marek had no idea the weather had been so bad. Would Hunter's being around make any difference to what he was about to attempt? He couldn't see how. When you were as desperate as he was, there was hardly any point in predicting what might happen if you actually succeeded.

"Alex? Where's Hunter?"

Marek was quiet for a long time. Then he leaned over the desk and whispered. "You're very clever, Mr Jack. You see right through us. In fact, there's no use in trying to fool you anymore. You're right. We do have a plan. Do you want to know what our plan really is?"

The Thai man smiled and bent forward. "I'm glad to see you've finally come to your senses."

With his good hand Marek grabbed the knot of Jack's thick silk tie and twisted and pulled hard. He held a finger to his lips, but the man couldn't talk. He could barely breathe.

"Hands on the desk," whispered Marek as he rose from his seat to get leverage. The Thai man was making a funny sound in his throat. His face was quickly turning purple and his eyes looked like they were going to pop out of his head.

"Really, don't you think neckties are a bit ostentatious in the tropics?" said Marek. "At least yours came in handy today," he added, twisting it tighter. "Gun?" The man looked terrified and his eyes involuntarily flitted toward the desk drawer.

"Thank you," said Marek. He tugged the man upright and came around the desk. With his thumb and functioning fingers, he opened the drawer. A small handgun in a leather holster was lying atop a white towel. Still holding on to Jack's tie with one hand, Marek managed to work the gun out of its holster. He didn't know if it was loaded, but from the look of terror on Jack's face, he assumed it was ready to fire. "You and I, Mr Jack, are going to walk out of here together. That's my fucking plan."

There was a noise in the hallway, a scuffling of feet, and in the instant Marek was distracted, the Thai man grabbed the heavy brass ashtray and slammed it onto his injured right hand. The gun went flying into a corner. Marek tried to stifle a scream. The Thai man yelled, and the door burst open and the two guards came rushing in. Marek threw Jack at the desk and then dove for the gun in the corner. It seemed like twenty people were all shouting at once. Marek had almost reached the gun when someone came crashing onto his back. There was high-pitched screaming and a lamp smashed to the floor. The guard was trying to get him in a headlock. He was very strong, but Marek was bigger. Marek reached the gun with his half-useless right hand then brought it over his left shoulder at the same time the Thai was trying to choke the life out of him. He knew he was fighting for his life. He fired blindly, an ear-shattering explosion that seemed to echo throughout the ship. There was more shrieking.

Suddenly Marek was twisted onto his back and was grappling with the guard for the gun. The guard was powerful but Marek, driven by fear, had so much adrenaline pumping through his veins he could no longer feel the pain in his hand. The grip on the pistol was all he had; if he let it go, he was a dead man.

Then something heavy came down on the guard's head and he fell lifelessly onto Marek. Marek thought the man had been shot, but then he realized he'd been hit with a truncheon. And that one – or perhaps both – of the two uniformed men now standing above him had done it.

Marek rolled the lifeless body off him and sat up. The room was full of men in khaki uniforms, moving quickly and deliberately. One man near the door was barking out orders. The unconscious guard was being dragged out by his heels.

Jack was yapping like an enraged chihuahua at everyone in uniform. They ignored him. Two of the soldiers marched Jack out of the room, and Marek could hear his voice fall away as it echoed down the ship's corridors.

He was too dazed to register what was happening, but relieved that everybody was completely ignoring him. He sat up on the floor and leaned against the bed, trying to catch his breath. Then he felt the warm liquid rolling down his face and into his eyes. He wiped the blood from his forehead with the back of his arm and wondered why he didn't feel any pain.

Then Niwat come into the room, and just behind him Philips. A shadow of concern crossed Philips's face – the first time Marek had seen anything like it – and then quickly disappeared.

"Right, then. So tell us, Alex," he said, out of breath, "since when do you computer nerd types decide to take on the Southern Thai mafia all by yourself?"

Thirty-five

"I thought I was dead," said Marek. "How did you ever find me?"

They were still in the stateroom of the ship, Marek sitting on a chair with a patched-up forehead, Philips leaning on the edge of the desk. Niwat had found the ship's first aid kit and now crouched on the floor wrapping surgical tape around Marek's two broken fingers and an improvised splint.

"I dropped by the bungalow a couple of times over the weekend, but there was no sign of you. Nobody knew where you were. Not Niwat, the maid, the guard, nobody. It was like you'd fallen off the face of the earth.

"So I thought, well, right. Sometimes a man's got to get away, do his own thing, whatever. So I didn't pursue it. Figured you'd come back when you were good and ready. But yesterday, as I was driving past the post office in Songkhla, I thought I saw your pickup parked across the street in the market. So I did a U-turn and sure enough, it was yours. Or the station's, I should say."

"My truck? They drove my truck into town?"

"Well, one guy did, anyway. Hey, nobody claims these are the smartest bunch of crooks around. Of course, I didn't know at the time that you weren't driving it. I decided to stick around and wait for you to come out, so's I could give you some stick about disappearing for two days. Slight problem, the guy who came out of the shop and got into your pickup wasn't you. Some Thai guy, right? He gets into the truck as if he doesn't give a flying fart who sees him."

Except for the three of them, the room was empty. The uniformed men, who turned out to be a security force from the local Navy base, had rounded up many of the Thais onboard and were, according to Niwat, now rummaging through the cargo.

"I thought now, hang on, that's a bit strange. Alex disappears and there's some Thai guy driving his pickup around town? So I follow him. Have to admit when he turned into the port here, I was a bit flummoxed. I couldn't get past the port gate, of course, but even from there I could see where he parked the pickup and what ship he boarded.

"Bugger me. I was confused at this point. So I wrote down the name of the ship, *Pacific Star*, went right back in to town and got a hold of our man Niwat here ..."

Niwat had finished wrapping the hand and was packing the first aid kit away. He said, "Drew ask me if we got a job out at the port. I say no, nothing going on now. He told me all about following the truck out here and tells me the name – *Pacific Star*. I ask around and I find out she supposed to load a shipment for Mr Jack. That makes me a bit nervous. Mr Jack is a powerful man in Songkhla. Famous businessman. Everybody say he's gonna be governor someday. But corrupt too." He shrugged as if apologizing for telling us something so obvious: famous businessman equals corruption. "I tell Drew I worried and we gotta check it out. So

I call my friend at the Navy base. I tell you before I got a lotta friends there, right?"

Marek laughed, despite the throbbing in his hand. "Yes, Niwat, and once again I am astounded by your web of connections."

"Actually, he's my brother-in-law. Lieutenant Colonel. He owe me a favor, you know? I tell him the story then he say he gonna send some boys to check it out. Actually, Navy and Jack don't get along too well. Goes back a long time, don't know why exactly. Think have to do with some casino on a boat Jack set up and cut the Navy out of. Now my brother-in-law say they think Jack smuggling some weapons or something. Maybe to separatists. That's the excuse they use anyway. He say he put a team together today, and I ask if Drew and I can come too. So here we are. Only wish we come earlier."

"No, you guys did great. Really great. Don't know where I'd be if you hadn't shown up."

"I dunno, mate. When we busted in here it looked like you were taking on all four of them yourself and doin' just fine."

"Only four?" said Marek with fake incredulity. "I thought there were more like seven or eight."

"Yeah, that'd be about right. Wait'll word gets out around town. It'll be up to one against ten soon. Alex Marek, aka Superman, fighting for truth, justice and the American way, takes on ten bad guys and lives to tell the tale."

"C'mon you guys," said Niwat. "We gotta go to a hospital and have a doctor take a look at your hand and head."

* * *

353

They kept him at the hospital overnight. Marek tried to fight it. He didn't have much time and he needed to find Hunter, needed to get his share of money from him and then find Saranya.

But the doctor, a serious man who looked younger than Marek, insisted he stay in the hospital. They put four stitches in his forehead and told Marek they'd have to operate on his hand. They pumped him with so many painkillers and sedatives he was blissfully unaware of anything that was happening to his body. Afterwards the doctor, who was not fluent in English, slowly and solemnly explained they'd had to break the little finger and reset it again.

"The ring finger should heal OK. That was a clean break. But the eh ... small one, that one not so good. So we have to reset it."

"Will I be able to use it again?"

He shrugged. "Maybe not full ... er ... mobile. Maybe not like before. But I think you can use OK." Then he smiled. "It will be good story to tell your girlfriend."

A good story ... he wondered how much the doctor – or anybody – knew about what happened. Neither Niwat nor Philips had asked a single question about how Marek had ended up battling for his life on the *Pacific Star*. If Niwat and Philips had any suspicion that Marek was somehow involved in some shady business with Jack, they kept it to themselves.

According to Niwat, the Navy patrol had detained many of the men on the ship, including Jack. They were accused of operating an illegal gambling den on board, or possibly running arms to the separatist group known as the Pattani Liberation Front. Or maybe both.

"But did they find any arms on board?" asked Marek.

Niwat shrugged. "Who knows? It's only rumors anyway."

There was never any mention of ancient artifacts, Buddhist sculptures or 1,200-year-old sandstone heads, relics of the long-forgotten Sri Jiraya dynasty. Genuine or not, Marek was sure they'd never surface again in Thailand.

In the morning they released him with two small plastic bags full of painkillers and instructions to return in a week to get the stitches removed from his head.

Philips drove out to pick him up. There were squalls at sea and one short cloudburst on the drive in, and in some places a few inches of water across the road.

"They told me it was flooded all over the south," said Marek.

"Yeah, courtesy of Tropical Storm Sara. They had to evacuate the rigs offshore. In Songklha the flooding's not too bad. Water drains off quickly, 'cause you've got the sea on one side and the lake on the other. But yeah, the roads between here and Hat Yai are wiped out. People stranded in places. Hat Yai airport's closed. Dunno if the trains are running now. Take another day or two, they say, before things can get moving again. That is, if we don't get more rain."

Before they reached the station, Marek told Philips the full story, leaving out nothing. Philips stayed silent, just drove with his eyes on the road. Finally, he spoke.

"I dunno, maybe there's something to what this Hunter guy said. Maybe, in a backwards way, you really were preserving those artifacts. Maybe they're better off with some western collector than here in Thailand, where they're likely to get plundered, or put into a museum and stolen from there, or smashed to bits before they even get halfway out of the ground."

"I didn't do it to save them. I did it for the money. I wanted to use it to help Saranya, to help out her family. To help us. Have you seen her? Heard from her?"

Philips shook his head. "She'll call, don't worry. Anyway, it took some balls to do what you did."

"No," said Marek. "It was just supposed to be up the mountain, down the mountain and drive over to the port. That's exactly the way Hunter explained it. An easy 200,000 dollars. Anybody would have done it."

"So where is this Hunter? Any ideas?"

"No one knows. Jack, the men on the ship – they seem to think he's still around."

"I guess he would be if he didn't get out before the storm. So what happens now?"

"I find him. Get the money he owes me."

"Look, mate, why don't you just quit while you're ahead? I mean, what are the odds of you finding him, much less getting any money from him?"

"I've got as good a chance as anybody of finding him. I'll tell him I'll give him up to Jack and his boys unless he comes through with the money. I won't get greedy. I just want the money he owes me. What he agreed to pay for the job I did. I know he's got the money. Jack gave him a down payment."

"You know, they won't keep that Jack character locked up for long, no matter what he's done. He's too powerful, even for the Navy."

"I suppose you think I should run?"

"He and his henchmen might already be free. What can they hold him for, really? If all the stuff you took to the ship was fake."

"They want Hunter, not me. Jack knows I'm no hero. I would've given him Hunter if I could."

"And what about Saranya?"

"That's why I'm doing this," Marek answered. "That's why I've got find Hunter."

Thirty-six

The station seemed cleaner, tidier than when he'd left it five days ago. He could see that the maid had been there, and that some things had already been packed up and carried away. The plan was to empty the station of everything not necessary for the basic running of the GPS. This was becoming an unmanned station now; no need for chairs, or sofas, or a kitchen, or even a toilet.

With two fingers taped to the long metal splint, Marek was pretty much useless for doing any packing or lifting. He spent his time clearing off the computer hard drives, making two sets of backup copies of everything that was important, one for Sturges and one for himself.

Later, after everyone had left for the day, the phone rang. It was her.

"Saranya, where are you? I've been trying to call." His voice echoed unnaturally in the cabin, now devoid of almost all furniture.

She spoke to him in Thai, something she had never done before over the phone. It was as if she were trying to define some new relationship with him. Her voice was neutral, no hint of gladness or relief, no sense that she had missed him. Except for the words she spoke he could have been conversing with a complete stranger, someone who was calling to ask about details of an item for sale.

"I'm sorry. I have been busy in Surat. My family ... and the storm, the floods. They say the road between here and Songkhla is open now. I can see you tomorrow. I will come to the bungalow. Are you free? If you're not free, perhaps we can meet another day."

He hated when she was like this, distant, completely non-committal, as if everything that had happened between them didn't matter. As if nothing had happened between them.

"No, of course I'm free. Please come. Please. What time will you be here?"

"Maybe three. I think I can get there by three."

"OK, I'll be here. I'll be waiting for you."

He got into the pickup and drove toward the city, his thoughts scattered in a thousand different directions. He couldn't keep any of it straight: Saranya, Jack, Hunter ... *And what will you do when you find him?*

He couldn't answer. He didn't know. But something in him had changed after that desperate attack on Jack and the winner-take-all fight with the guard on the floor of the stateroom. He was no longer afraid of Hunter, and he would not let him get away with it. Hunter had set Marek up. Played him like a puppet.

He pushed through the door of Hunter's guesthouse and saw a middle-aged man bent over the reception desk, holding a magnifying glass in his hand and peering at a sheet of lottery results. He glanced up at Marek momentarily and then returned his gaze to the sheet. On the counter next to the sheet were a half dozen green and red government lottery tickets, looking like cheap paper currency from a poor country.

"We all booked up," he said. "No room."

"I'm looking for John Hunter," Marek said in Thai. The man looked up at Mark without raising his head. Then he lowered his eyes to the glass.

"He's not here," he replied in English.

"Where is he? Do you know?"

This time the man lifted his head and put down the glass. "You his friend?"

"Yes. Do you know where he is?"

The man looked at Marek's hand, at the bandaged cut above his forehead. "I don't know where he is. But I don't think he is coming back. He left a note. Paid everything he owe me and gave me plenty extra to take care of the electricity and water."

"Did he leave a number? An address? Anything?" The man shook his head and went back to his long columns of minuscule numbers, the conversation apparently over. As Marek reached the door he called after him. "You see John Hunter, you tell him he can come back stay here anytime, OK? He's a good man."

* * *

Hunter allowed himself a second bottle of Black Cat because, after all, he'd be out of this shithouse soon. The power was back on, and things were slowly starting to return to normal. The rain had stopped, and the roads were slowly opening. They said the airport might be open tomorrow. He'd be on the road to Phuket in another day, two at most. Finally. That was something to celebrate.

The rainwater had drained from the hotel and the coffee shop was open again. His spirits were rising. He was rich. He'd gotten away with it. He'd even talked to Jinda. He was so happy and wished her good luck, and told her he'd be back, maybe in another year or so, when things had cooled down.

Yeah, the coffee shop. And tucked away in a corner next to the coffee shop was the hotel nightclub. Must be a karaoke place. On second thoughts, he wouldn't have the second bottle up here, he'd have it down there in the club. After all, he'd be gone tomorrow; and there was no way you could expect a man like him to stay cooped up in this fucking room with the walls closing in on him. There'd be drink down there, and food if he needed it, and girls. Why not celebrate right? Surely it was safe enough. Hell, he wouldn't even be leaving the hotel.

He showered. He ran the razor across his bare head and even shaved off his two-day growth of beard. He put on a freshly washed and ironed cotton shirt and a pair of jeans.

It was dark inside the bar. There was a small stage where a man played on keyboards with a computer and screen next to him. A television showed a video of women rolling across the grass, or standing on the seashore, or riding horses. The Thai lyrics scrolled across the bottom of the screen.

He sat down at a booth and ordered a whiskey Coke. He could hear the voices of Thai men and women from some other booth, but it was too dark to make out any faces. Soon enough the microphone was passed around and someone began singing.

The girl brought his set: the bottle, the ice bucket, the tumbler, the sliced limes. She used the ice tongs to fill the tumbler with ice, poured in two fingers of whiskey, dropped in the lime slice and stirred it for him. He thanked her. She gave a soft *khaa*, like the purr of a kitten, then placed the glass gently on the coaster before him.

He wondered what service would be like in Istanbul. He imagined it would be like anywhere else in the world – as long as you had money, you could get whatever you wanted, the best. And he wouldn't be restricted to Turkey. There was a big wide world to see. Just in his neighborhood, he'd have the Greek islands and the coast of Yugoslavia. Guys had told wild stories about adventures there. Nude beaches, girls hungry for money and cock.

And what was to stop him from coming back here once things cooled off? OK, maybe not Hat Yai or Songkhla, that might be a bit risky; but surely he could slip into Phuket or Pattaya, where no one would know him from Adam. Yeah, there were offshore guys who lived in those places, guys he knew and had worked with. He'd just make up some bullshit story about how he'd been offered a better job, shipped off to Sudan or some other godforsaken place, chasing the black gold like everybody else.

Hunter let the whiskey warm his stomach and his brain, embellishing his fantasy until a couple of girls asked to join him in the booth.

He bought them drinks and they laughed a lot, and with their laughter they made him feel generous and manly and important and happy and he thought, *this is how it will be from now on – I will just wait and people will come to me to make me happy.*

* * *

Marek drove through the narrow streets near the fishing dock, wondering if Jinda's was even open yet. It was. The New Year's greetings still hung on the wall, but the highchair was gone. One of the girls even remembered his name, though he hadn't been there since the time he'd first met Hunter there months ago.

"Where's Jinda?" he asked, ignoring the girls' pleas to sit down with them. One of them pointed to the back room. Jinda was in the narrow kitchen area, chopping garlic and chilies on a wooden cutting board.

"Jinda, I'm looking for Hunter. For John."

Like the owner of the guesthouse she looked at his hand and head but didn't say anything. She turned on the gas fire, put some oil in a wok, and threw the chilies and garlic in, everything exploding in a sizzling cloud that burned Marek's eyes and made him cough. She turned away from the fire and filled a plate with rice from the cooker.

"He do that to you?" she asked, pointing the rice spoon at his hand.

"I need to find him, Jinda. It's important."

"He hurt you, now you gonna hurt him back."

She turned her back to him to attend to her cooking. Her hair was pulled back in a bun and he noticed faint streaks of gray. She seemed older, or maybe just wearier, than the last time he'd seen her. The smile lines that had formed around her eyes now seemed like furrows of worry. She stirred the rice into the snapping oil of the wok and spoke without facing him.

"He hit me sometimes, you know that, right? People say he's not a good man. Do a lot of bad things. We Thai people believe if you do good, you get good; and if you do bad, you get bad. You believe that?"

"I don't know. Listen, Jinda, he owes me some money. All I want is my money."

"But the bad gonna come back to him. It's natural. If not you, somebody else, right? Nobody can change their fate."

"Where is he, Jinda? Do you have any way to contact him?"

She turned off the gas and spooned the fried rice onto a plate. She called one of the girls in to take it to a table. When the girl had left, she turned to him, wiping her hands on her apron.

"He called me. Last night. He very drunk, say he miss me, say he got to go away for a while. He say he lonely for me. Want me to come to his hotel."

"Where?"

"I told him impossible. The roads are closed. Nobody can get into Hat Yai because of the flood."

"He's in Hat Yai? Now? Where?"

She picked up a glass on the counter. Marek hadn't noticed the nearly empty flask of Mekong whiskey. She took a long drink, but her eyes never left him.

"You supposed to be his friend but you too late. I already told those soldiers."

"What soldiers?"

"Soldiers or special kind of police, I don't know. They had uniforms. And they talk like they very powerful. Came today, morning. Banging on the door until I wake up and open it. They didn't want any food or drink or anything, they wanted to know about John. I don't trust them, so I say I don't know.

"They said I had to help because John was a criminal. He had done a bad thing. Stolen a lot of old Buddhas and killed a guard at the museum last year. They say, didn't I know? Didn't I watch TV? Didn't I want to help Thailand?

"I thought about how John used to hit me. He treat me very bad sometimes and I think, yeah, he could do some bad things like that. But I don't know about these guys, so I still don't tell them nothing.

"Then they say they want to see my, my ... *tabian*."

"License? Registration?"

"Yeah, my paper. So I show them. They tell me it not real, it's fake. They say I'm in big trouble. They gonna close my shop. I say no, I do everything legal. They can check with the provincial office. They say they bigger than provincial office. They gonna shut my place down because it is illegal."

She paused to wipe the sweat off her face and take another drink. "What I gonna do if they close my shop? How can I make money? How I gonna live? What these girls gonna do?

"They say maybe they could help me if I tell them where John is. I say no, this got nothing to do with John. This my business. One guy, he has a tattoo ... *malaeng pong* ..."

"Scorpion."

"Yeah, here on his hand. He punch me so hard in my stomach. They say they take away my *tabian* and close my shop for good unless I help them. What can I do? Lose everything for John? Why?"

"What did you tell them?"

"The Paradise Hotel, in Hat Yai. That's what John told me last night. That's what I told the soldiers. No choice. If I lie to them, I know they come back and hurt me and close my shop. After they leave, I try to call the hotel to tell John, but they say nobody there by that name. I know John tell them to say that. He don't want no one calling him. But I know he's there because he told me to come there last night."

"But nobody can get in to Hat Yai. That's what you said. Because of the flooding."

She guffawed. Her expression turned bitter. "They very powerful. They can get in. Soldiers in this country can do anything." She finished off her whiskey and walked past him into the restaurant.

Marek ran to his pickup and sped off for Hat Yai. He made it as far as the Hat Yai–Koh Yoh intersection. The intersection was flooded, and police cars and barricades blocked the road. They weren't letting anybody through except a few big ten-wheel trucks loaded with food and other necessities. Marek begged the officer to let him try to get through and although he spoke Thai, the officer, barely lifting his eyes from a clipboard, answered in English: "Cannot. Cannot. Cannot go."

* * *

There was plenty of singing going on around Hunter's booth now. He wouldn't have guessed it, but this dive karaoke bar in a sleaze bag hotel seemed to be one of the most popular places in town.

Most of the men were Malays, singing horribly, but happily, off-key. And they all had girls to keep them company.

Hunter had his two. He bought them many drinks and a few rounds of the microphone, and finally they talked him into singing a song, and wouldn't you know it, there on page 42 was old Willie and "You Were Always On My Mind". So he said, what the hell and sang it – he was just drunk enough to do it. When he finished there was even a smattering of applause.

A man approached his booth still clapping after all the others had stopped and said, "Very nice, John. You sing so well."

He couldn't make out the man's features in the gloom, but he knew the voice, of course: the ex-Thai Special Forces and Muay Thai expert. The man Jack always sent to do his dirty work.

Another Thai man whom Hunter didn't recognize stood by the side of the booth. They were both wearing camouflage uniforms. The other man said something to the girls and they quickly fled the booth. Then he sat down next to Hunter, blocking his exit.

Scorpion was smiling at him. He sat down and placed a blue rucksack on the bench between them.

"Mr Jack always say you very good businessman, but we never know you such a good singer."

Hunter wondered what he had in the bag and wondered if he should try to make a run for it. The guy next to him was big, but not as big as Hunter. But the two of them were tough, and he had no doubt that they were both carrying weapons. And if he made a ruckus, called out for help, he knew exactly what would happen. The place would clear out, and those that stayed in the room would completely ignore him.

"Have a drink, Toi. You and your friend. On me."

Scorpion called the waitress over and ordered something. The three men sat in silence until she returned with two bottles of Singha.

"That storm very bad, huh?" said Toi. "You stay here the whole time?"

Hunter nodded. He had noticed a sign for a fire exit and thought if he could get out of the booth he might be able to make a run for it.

"Lotta roads still flooded, you know? Funny how we able to get here. Oil company say they need some big trucks. Need to get some help for all the people stranded in Hat Yai, bring them food, whatever. But need big trucks. You know, Mr Jack very good at that kind of thing. People need something in Songkhla, he can get it. He very happy to help people out, you know? So he get some big trucks to help the oil company, and Lek and me are the drivers! No problem getting through the water!" At this he laughed, a high squealing laughter that didn't signify mirth so much as a kind of superiority.

"How did you know I was here?" Hunter thought if he could just keep them talking, delay them until there was an opening ...

Scorpion shrugged. "It not so difficult to find you. Mr Jack got a lot of connections. You know he get arrested two days ago? You look surprised. No bullshit. Actually, it a funny story. They kept him for about four hours."

"Arrested?"

"Yeah, stupid Navy people. They think he selling guns or

something. But they don't find anything on the ship. Only some shitty fake Buddha statues. Nobody care about that."

The music seemed louder, the singing worse, the Malay drunks more boisterous. It all seemed to be pinning him back into the plastic covering of the booth. He was trying to build a plan, but his thoughts tumbled meaninglessly in his mind. Scorpion was speaking, but he could barely hear him.

"... and Mr Jack sent us here to give you something special."

Hunter said nothing.

"Yeah, he want to give you a bonus for the work you did. He like to give it you himself but he very busy these days. He got some political problem he need to straighten out. Maybe you see it on TV?"

"No, the power was off. And the TVs only have Thai stations, so I don't bother."

For the first time Scorpion made eye contact with the other Thai and the big man grunted. Hunter thought it was meant to be a laugh.

"You know Mr Jack going to be Governor of Songkhla some day. But there's a lot of people try to stop him. This is Thai politics, you know."

Hunter began to stand up and the big guy, quick as a boxer, clamped a hand on his forearm and pulled him back down.

"Hey, John, where you go?"

"My room. Too much whiskey. You tell Mr Jack I'd vote for him if I could." He got up again, but this time a pistol suddenly appeared in the big guy's hand.

"John, take it easy. We all gonna go in a minute. Go together.

Just hang on. I told you we got something to give you. A little bonus. Don't you want it?" He turned to the rucksack and unzipped the opening. "Mr Jack want to thank you for all the work you do for him. So here's your special bonus."

Scorpion upended the bag onto Hunter's lap and onto it rolled a head, a human head still purplish and bloody, a fat head with dull staring eyes and thick lips, blood and viscera still oozing from the throat. The karaoke music went silent for Hunter and was replaced by a screaming ocean of blood running through his ears. He could feel the vomit rising in his throat. He threw the head off his lap and vomited.

It was the head of the fat Chinese man, the Prosperous Buddha, the best manufacturer of fake sandstone artifacts in all of South East Asia.

Both Thai men were holding him now, as if afraid he would fall over.

"Mr Jack say, you give him one head, one real head. Now he return the favor to you."

Thirty-seven

It was well after four and he had nearly given up hope when he heard the motorcycle turn off the beach road and onto the gravel driveway. He had the door open before she'd even dismounted.

"*Sawatdii khrap*, Alex. How are you?"

Saranya walked into the bungalow without taking off her helmet and sunglasses, as if she'd only stopped by to drop off the two large papayas she carried.

"Saranya, sit down. Here, let's sit at the table."

"It looks so empty. Where is all the furniture?"

"They took it away. You know what I told you before? They're going to make it an unmanned station. I won't be working here anymore."

"And what will you do?"

"Sit down, Saranya."

She stood motionless for a minute and then, as if resolving some inner struggle, took off her helmet and sunglasses and shook out her long hair, filling the empty room with her scent.

"Alex what happened to you?" She gently touched the bandage on his head and his nose and splinted hand.

"I fell off Drew's motorbike. It's OK. Good as new in no time."

"You must be careful." She was quiet for a long time then sighed and said, "I think I cannot stay too long."

"Why not?"

"I have to go back to Surat Thani tonight, on the bus. Have you eaten yet?"

"I'm not hungry. Are you going to sit down?"

She didn't answer. Instead she picked up one of the papayas and took it into the kitchen, where she skinned and sliced it. She brought out the pieces on a plate with a single fork and placed it on the table in front of him. Then she sat down next to him. Marek felt as if he'd won some minor victory just to get her to sit down, but he knew she could just as easily bounce out of the chair and out of the door in the next second.

"How is your family?"

She sighed. "My uncle is very kind to help us now. My mother, well, of course she is … we all are … it's very difficult."

"When are you coming back to Songkhla?"

She sighed. "I don't know."

"What about graduate school?"

"Now we need more money. My brother must go to the university. He's going to be a doctor. The money is not enough."

"Maybe I can help."

Her look surprised him. She looked at him as if this were the last in a long list of lies she'd heard from him; that she was so used to his untruths they no longer fazed her.

"No, I can find another job."

"Where?"

"I told you, at the hotel on Koh Samui. They need lots of

people who can speak English. I can work there. The pay is good."

"But I don't want you to go to Koh Samui. I want you to stay in Songkhla."

"What we want is not important. What we need to do is important. You are farang, you are free, you can go wherever you like, do what you want. I am Thai, I have to take care of my family."

"You're angry with me."

She shook her head. "You don't understand."

"I'm trying to understand. Are you planning to come back to Songkhla at all?"

She shrugged. "Who can say about the future?"

Well, you can, he thought, suddenly tired of it all and more than a little angry. The cool aloofness, the reserved formalities and restrained body language, the unspoken signals. Of course, it was the Thai way of doing things, where nothing important was ever said and the social surface stayed as undisturbed as a secret forest pond.

This was the girl who'd given herself to him, who'd told him she loved him. What had happened since then? Was there some rule he'd broken? Was he being boorishly farang? Perhaps he was supposed to read her mind, and then apologize for all the sins he had no idea he'd committed.

He looked at the plate of papaya and the single fork. Maybe that's what bothered him the most. The one fork meant he was supposed to eat it alone because for some reason she just couldn't be bothered to share any more time with him.

"Why are you playing games, Saranya?"

"What?"

"I haven't seen you for two weeks. I try to call you, the number you gave me in Surat, but nobody ever answers, or if they do, they don't even seem to know you. Then you call me, out of the blue, and don't even want to talk. You just tell me you're coming at three. But you don't come until almost four thirty, and the first thing you tell me when you get here is that you can't stay. What's going on?"

For a moment her face showed no reaction. Then she reached for her helmet.

"No, Saranya."

"If you are angry at me, I can leave," she said, her voice choking with emotion. "Then you can be happy. When I am gone."

"No, you're not leaving."

"You cannot make me stay."

"Stop!" He shouted it much louder than he'd intended, and it reverberated in the empty bungalow. He stood and gripped her arms.

"Please, Saranya. I need you to be honest with me. To tell me what is happening."

She forced her eyes closed as if she couldn't bear to look at him. Or as if she didn't want him to see her cry.

"The last time I saw you, you told me you loved me. You gave me this." He reached inside his shirt and pulled out the amulet. "But now you seem so cold. I don't know what to think."

"Please let me go." He did and she sat down at the table and held her head in her hands. He thought she might be sobbing, but he left her alone until she was ready to speak.

"Do you think I lied to you, Alex?"

"I don't know. You tell me."

"It's so difficult. What we want and what we must do. They are never the same, are they?"

"Tell me about it, Saranya. Just talk to me."

"It's easy for you. You are farang. You have no family here. No obligations. But for me it is very different.

"Now my father is gone. I must be sure my brother goes to university. This is what is important. Not what I want."

"I told you before. I can help."

Again, she looked at him doubtfully.

"You don't trust me, do you?"

She shook her head. "How can you help? You don't even have a job anymore."

"I can get another job. I have some money saved up. The point is, don't give up so easily, Saranya. Don't just forget about us, just because things seem difficult now. It's like you're looking for an excuse to get rid of me. And you're acting like a martyr."

"A what?

"A martyr. Someone who likes to show everyone else how much they suffer."

She stood, her eyes blazing with anger. She was angrier than he'd ever seen her.

"Do you think I am acting? Like in a movie? I will go now."

"No. Wait. I'm sorry. Of course you're not acting."

"Do you know how difficult it is for me? I mean, to come and see you like I do. What other people may think or say? Many,

many people in Songkhla, they know my family and love to talk. Even today, I have to borrow my friend's motorcycle to come here. She asked where I was going, and I said I just want to go to the beach to be alone to think. I have to lie all the time to see you."

"OK, Saranya. I'm sorry. I know. We both do it. We do it because we love each other and that's why we should be together, even though right now it's hard to imagine what the future looks like."

She sat down again, and he held her hands. Her emotions were running over. She found some tissues in her bag and dabbed at her eyes. It was a long time before she attempted to speak again, and even then she spoke haltingly and wouldn't meet his eyes.

"My uncle knows a man, a businessman in Surat. He is very rich. My uncle says that he is a good man."

He had half expected it. It was the obvious reason for her strange, distant behavior. She had come to say goodbye.

"What are you saying?"

"He will take care of me; take care of my family. He will make sure my mother is comfortable in her old age and that my brother goes to medical school."

"And this man, do you love him?"

She raised her face to him. Her eyes were wet. "That's not the important thing."

"It is the important thing. What kind of marriage, what kind of life, can you have with him if you don't love him?"

She said nothing. She held his injured hand in hers and her shoulders rose and fell with her soft sobbing.

"Saranya, I lied to you. About my hand. I didn't crash a

motorbike."

"What? What happened?"

"I'll tell you the truth. I'll tell you everything. Listen carefully, because everything I did, even though it may seem wrong, even though it may seem very bad, I did it for us. For you and me, for your family. And when I'm finished, I want you to ask yourself if your uncle's rich friend would have done this for you."

And so he told her. When he was finished, he waited for her to speak – to chastise him or forgive him – but she said nothing.

"Saranya, I did something wrong. I made a mistake. I got involved with some bad people, and they tried to hurt me. But it's very important that you understand why I did it. I did it for us. He was supposed to pay me two hundred thousand dollars. That kind of money could set us free. You wouldn't have to worry anymore. Jit could go to university and become a doctor. You and I, we could start a life together. This was my dream. This was why I did it."

"And your friend Drew?"

"He knew nothing about it. I just told him about it yesterday."

"It was wrong," she said. "Very wrong. How could you do this to a Thai temple?"

"I'm sorry. Very sorry. I only thought about the money. I thought about how I could use the money to do good things. For you, for your family, for us."

"It's very bad to steal from a temple," she said evenly.

When he said nothing she said, "Are these men ... this Mr Jack ... will they come for you? Do they still want to hurt you?"

"No, I'm nothing to them. They want the other man, Hunter.

And also I have some powerful people, Navy people, on my side."

"And the real Buddhas, the ones you brought down from the mountain - where are they?"

"Nobody knows."

She held his amulet. "But you had this with you, all the time?"

"Yes."

She fell against his chest. "Alex, please hold me."

He put his arms around her and again marveled at how slender her body was. It seemed as if a shred of wind could blow her away.

"No, I don't love him. I mean my uncle's friend. He is not unkind, but he is fat and thinks about nothing except money. Life with him would be horrible." She looked up at him. "Alex, do you love me?"

"Yes, again. Yes, always."

She sighed and lowered her head back onto his chest. "And me, too. I could never stop. I was afraid to see you again after my father's death. Everyone said I should forget about you. That you were a farang and could never understand. That things would be hard if I continued with you. The time when I gave you the amulet, that was supposed to be our last time together. I was supposed to say goodbye, but I couldn't. I could never get myself to do it."

He kissed her brow.

"There is a lot we must do," she said. "You have to go to the temple in Surat and make an offering at the temple there and also to the monks. Alex, you have to ask for forgiveness. It was a very serious offense that you committed, but if your heart is in the right place and you are sincere, you will be forgiven."

"OK, that's fine. And when I go to Surat, I will visit your mother and your uncle and talk in a serious way to them."

She raised her eyes to his.

"Is that what you want to do?"

"Yes."

"Then yes. That will be good. It will be difficult, maybe, but it will be OK," she tapped him on the sternum with her knuckles, "because you love me."

Thirty-eight

It was the kind of day Marek liked because it made him think of days in Wisconsin. It wasn't cold – not by Wisconsin standards, anyway – but the sky and sea were matching shades of gray and mauve and the winds came strong off the Gulf and showers swept through the town. Saranya laughed at him for wanting to walk in weather like this; it was another sure sign that all farang were peculiar. She herself wouldn't dare to go out in it; for her to spend fifteen minutes in the chilly dampness would almost surely result in a cold. But for him it was a chance to relish a kind of nostalgia, not for anyplace he ever knew, but for light and color that was so much a part of his home country, but that he hardly ever saw in Thailand.

There was nobody along the beach this day; there almost never was on days like this. The sea was dotted with whitecaps. Storm clouds scuttled on the horizon above shrouds of slanting rain lines. Marek wanted to be close to the energy of the sea meeting the shore, so he left the brick sidewalk for the damp sand near the crashing waves.

He walked for a while, alone with his thoughts. Niwat had said the road to Hat Yai might be passable tomorrow, but Marek wouldn't be going. Instead he and Saranya would drive up the coast to Surat. They would go to the temple, and he would bring a basket of food for the monks and make a donation for them to perform a special prayer. "To make merit," Saranya had said, "and to ask for forgiveness. Anything can be forgiven if you are sincere in your heart."

Atonement. And then, if he was lucky, a new life.

As he walked near the shoreline he saw a group of a dozen or so people ahead. It was odd for Thais to be out in this type of weather. Maybe they were having a party and he should walk back on the sidewalk to avoid the inevitable sozzled attempts to engage him.

But as he got closer, he realized they weren't partying. Instead they stood stiffly in small groups of two or three, immobile. Nearing them, he saw they were smiling, stiff, frozen smiles stretched across their faces. But they weren't laughing or talking, just standing uneasily with their arms straight at their sides or gripped at the elbows. His heart suddenly sank; he had seen this before, at the scene of a car crash with two dead bodies on the pavement. The Thais had milled around with weird rigid grins on their faces while a policeman and ambulance attendant tried to deal with the corpses. It was what they did when faced with fear or pain or death – this mirthless grin, a warped version of the Thai smile promoted in the tourist brochure. You can cope if you can just somehow manage to smile.

And now they were doing it here, on the beach. Somebody's drowned, he thought, a child's been swept out in the undertow.

Two girls broke away from the group and ran toward him. He vaguely recognized them from one of the Dark Side bars. They were grinning but their eyes were wide with fear.

"It's a dead farang," one of them cried out excitedly. "Maybe you know who he is."

He walked closer and heads turned to look at him. He could see now that there was a young policeman in the crowd, and he was talking into a radio as he stood above the body. Marek took a few steps toward the corpse, in a kind of morbid fascination. He didn't want to look at it, but he did.

It was Hunter. The body was stiff, the legs bent in an odd fetal position, as if he was on his knees and one elbow. He was wearing jeans and a torn T-shirt. His skin was hairless and unnaturally white, except for blackened areas where the blood had pooled.

Marek turned away from the body and was faced by the two girls. Their faces were wet and they were smiling, smiling almost as if they were excited by this – death washing up on the beach. Marek realized he had forgotten about them.

"No," he said. "I don't know him."

Then he walked away from the beach and back toward the hotel and his truck.